Emily's Trials

Endorsements

Henry McLaughlin is as talented as he is thoughtful in his prose and observations of life and faith. His brilliant mechanisms for bringing all this together on the written page are sure to thrill any reader eager to escape into the beautiful and sometimes wild west.
—**Rene Gutteridge**, Head Writer @ The Skit Guys, Author of the "Boo" series

A woman chooses justice and fights for her life and the innocent. Historical novels don't get better than this.
—**DiAnn Mills**, Christy Award winner

Henry's prose is meticulously detailed and rich with memorable imagery. His characters experience an inspiring amount of growth over the course of his novels; the nuanced evolution of relationships new and old will keep readers riveted to the pages.
—**Book Life**

Emily's Trials

Henry McLaughlin

A Christian Company
ElkLakePublishingInc.com

Copyright Notice

Cover and Interior Design: Derinda Babcock, Deb Haggerty
Editor(s): Peggy Ellis, Cristel Phelps, Deb Haggerty

PUBLISHED BY: Elk Lake Publishing, Inc., 35 Dogwood Drive, Plymouth, MA 02360, 2023

LIBRARY CATALOGING DATA
Names: McLaughlin, Henry (Henry McLaughlin)
Emily's Trials / Henry McLaughlin

458 p. 23cm × 15cm (9in × 6 in.)

ISBN-13: 9798891340527 (paperback) | 9798891340534 (trade paperback) | 9798891340541 (e-book)
Key Words: Female attorney; murder; Kansas; romance; 1880s; historical; faith
Library of Congress Control Number: 2023947120 Fiction

Dedication

To my wife, Linda.
Without her love, encouragement, and support,
this book would not have made it to publication.
My first reader, Honey, you are always first in my heart.

To Jesus, my savior
who inspires and guides my stories and my writing
journey.
Thank you, Lord, and may I always write for you.

Acknowledgments

Writing is one of those rare things we do alone yet can't be successfully accomplished without a community that comes alongside us.

Emily's Trials is one of many examples of this.

The story began many years ago when I had an idea I sent to my agent at the time, Barbara Scott. I wrote, "What do you think of a female attorney in the 1880s in the American West?" She wrote back, "This is the best idea you've ever had. Send me a proposal for a three-book series." All I had was an idea for a female attorney in the 1880s. And I wondered how she knew all the other ideas I'd ever had.

Many people have been with me along this journey. I hesitate to name names because I know I'll forget someone. I thank all of you who critiqued, encouraged, challenged, and supported me through the process.

Thanks to Les Stobbe, Deb Haggerty, Peggy Ellis, and everyone at Elk Lake Publishing for sharing the vision of this story and guiding it to publication.

Chapter 1

Abilene, Kansas, 1885

"Miss Peyton, you gotta come quick. Your Pa's been hurt. Bad."

Startled, Emily gouged the legal document with her pen, ripping the paper on her desk in half.

"Deputy?" Matthew Quick's presence registered in her mind, his words in her heart. "Father's hurt? What happened?"

Cold, blustery wind and rain blew around the drenched figure in the office doorway. The papers on her desk tornadoed past her ears, scattering on the floor.

Quick snatched her shawl from the hat tree in the corner. "Don't rightly know, Miss." He stepped behind her and held the garment open. "Doc says for you to come. Now."

"All right. All right." Emily pressed her fingertips to her brow, squeezed her eyes tight, and inhaled. She drew the shawl close about her and tied her bonnet, pulling the brim low against the wind gusting through the still-open door. *Father, you have to be all right.*

She cast her eyes toward heaven. *Nope. No help there.*

Emily strode out into the dim early afternoon light. Quick followed, closing the door behind them.

The deputy hurried to match her pace, keeping between her and the street as she quick-stepped the boardwalk to Doc's office.

"What happened?" she asked.

"Like I said, Miss Emily, I don't rightly know. Jed Abbott found him where the road forks on the way to his place. Said it looked like some of the road washed out, and your father's carriage tipped over the edge into a gully."

Emily shook like an aspen in a hailstorm. She rubbed between her eyes. *This can't be happening. Father can't be hurt.*

The sound of running feet on the boardwalk behind them made Emily stop and turn, ready to scoot against the storefront to her right. Terrence McCarthy skidded to a stop on the slippery boards. "Emily, I just heard about your father. Do you know if he's all right?"

The warmth and compassion in Terrence's hazel eyes comforted her. "I don't know." She nodded at Deputy Quick. "We're on our way to Doc's now."

"Do you mind if I come along?"

A frown whiffed across Deputy Quick's face.

"Please," Emily said. "You know you're always welcome in our family."

They reached the end of the boardwalk. The side street in front of them was a morass of mud, rain, manure, and who knew what else. Terrence touched her elbow.

"Allow me." He scooped her into his arms. "Ready?"

He darted off the boardwalk and through the squishing muck and wind-driven downpour. Looking over Terrence's shoulder, she saw the deputy's coal-black eyes smolder. His cheeks reddened above his tangled, mousy brown beard as he followed them.

Terrence set her down under the overhang of the corner building.

He tipped his hat. "Forgive me for being so forward, but I couldn't allow you to walk in that slop."

On any other day, she would have laughed and teased. Today, his gesture touched her, easing the pain of the unknown. She touched his arm, the briefest brush on his leather coat. "Thank you, Terrence. That was noble of you."

Terrence on one side and Quick on the other matched her stride for stride.

"Doc told me to fetch ya," Quick said. "So, I'll come along to make sure you get there in one piece and dry as possible. Any carryin' of damsels oughta be done by one who's not courtin' another."

The deputy's eyes reminded her of a foal seeking a treat.

"Don't fret, Deputy," Terrence said. "Priscilla understands Emily and I are just friends."

"Deputy Quick, Terrence." Emily's voice flared. "We don't have time for this nonsense. My father may be dying." She marched off, leaving the two in her wake.

Doc Everett's office occupied the middle third of the block, with double doors opening into a waiting area. Inside, Jed Abbott stood at the window, a white mug in his hands.

"Is my father in there?" She headed toward a door to the left of the Franklin stove that struggled to cast the dampness out of the room. Sweat beaded on her forehead in the humid air.

Jed set down his coffee mug. "Yes, he is, Miss Emily. Doc asked me to have you wait out here 'til he sends for you."

Emily slowly turned a complete circle, unable to focus on anything in the room. Her hands twitched, seeming to have minds of their own, seeking something to latch onto. Nothing. Her rock lay on the other side of the wall. Inaccessible.

Fists clenched, she inhaled, and willed her heart to slow. Deputy Quick handed her one of Caroline Everett's delicate china cups filled to the brim with coffee. The warmth radiated into her cold palms and gave her hands something to do. When she lifted the cup to her lips, it rattled against her teeth. She lowered it without sipping. Terrence picked up an Afghan from one of the chairs and slipped it around her shoulders.

"Mr. Abbott, how did you find my father?"

Abbott shuffled toward her, his shoulders hunched, slate gray hair shaggy and curled. "I went lookin' for him when he didn't show up at my place first thing this mornin' like he promised. Thought somethin' might've happened to him in the rain."

He ran a large, gnarled hand across his mouth and gulped his coffee. "Found him just after the fork to my place. His rig was turned over, and he were under it." He swiped his eyes. "I thought he was dead, Miss. He twern't moving. Looked like my granddaughter's rag doll, legs pointin' funny. I knew they was broke. He had a big gash along the side of his head too." A shuddering breath rasped in the man's chest. "I got him in my wagon and brought 'im here as fast as I could."

Emily imagined her father splayed in the mud, limbs akimbo, rain soaking him. She rubbed her forehead.

The treatment room door drew her attention. "How long has he been in there?"

Abbott shrugged. "Doc and Miss Caroline's been working on him 'bout fifteen minutes, I reckon."

Emily closed her eyes and pinched the bridge of her nose. Father left after breakfast for the Abbott farm with papers for Jed. He wanted to get there and back before the clouds dumped their early spring rain. The clouds didn't cooperate. Rain started within an hour after he left and, at mid-afternoon, hadn't stopped.

A scream pierced the door separating her from her father. Emily's cup shattered on the floor and coffee splattered her tan dress. She bit her knuckles to keep her own scream silent.

Terrence's arm encircled her shoulder.

Deputy Quick slid a chair behind her and helped her sit. "Want me to fetch Pastor Dalton to come pray?"

Emily shook her head, biting back the retort simmering in her mind. Why bother? Praying didn't help when Mother left.

Another scream. This one faded into a moan before the silence returned.

Emily stared at the puddle of coffee on the carpet. The shards of the cup looked like icebergs in a muddy, green ocean. The deputy knelt on one knee and picked up the pieces, depositing them in a trash box next to the stove. He dabbed up the coffee with his handkerchief.

Emily closed her eyes, remembering her father's kiss on the top of her head when he left this morning—the reminder she was still his little girl. The one view she allowed him in her womanhood. Now, she wished she were a little girl again, curled in his lap, burying her head in his chest, inhaling the sweet aromas of his pipe and law books. Safe and secure.

She shuddered. Those days were gone. These were her days now.

What would the next days bring?

Chapter 2

Terrence refilled his coffee from the pot on the stove, grateful to give his hands something to hold on to, something to drive this feeling of helplessness away. His friend—no, his substitute father—lay on the other side of the door. George Peyton was many things to him. Chess partner, baseball supporter, and fellow debater on politics and business. Counselor and confidant. The man filled a void in his life, and now the abyss threatened to return.

He offered silent prayers for George's healing and Emily's strength. Emily placed no stock in prayer or God, but she respected the place the Creator held in his life.

Across the room, Emily sat rigid in the straight-back chair. At times, she massaged her forehead with two fingers or clasped her other hand in her lap, worrying a handkerchief. She alternated between staring out the window and locking her gaze on the dark wood door of the treatment room. Occasionally, a blink of her eye released a tear that would roll slowly down her cheek till she daubed it with her handkerchief.

Her chin—usually set so firm—seemed delicate as the shattered china cup. Her hands, slender and sensitive enough to play piano, and write elegant script on documents for the bank, were stiff and jerky in their movements.

So unlike her usual, confident self. Terrence saw for the first time a crack in her façade of independence—her love for her father.

A tear blurred his own vision. He scraped it away, grateful no one saw his emotion. Behind the door lay the man he had come to love. In the chair, the young woman he cherished as a sister. He stood now, useless as a busted baseball bat.

He paced, hands behind his back, fingers twitching. From the window, with the dreary storm distorting his view, to Doc's bookcases on the opposite wall, their mixture of medical and political tomes pebbling off his brain like hail on a tin roof.

The blanket had partially slipped from Emily's shoulder. With a soft tug, he adjusted it. She smiled and touched his hand as he shifted the blanket.

"Coffee?"

She nodded. "In something a little more substantial, I think."

He filled a mug from a side table and handed it to her, grateful to be useful, to be of some service. Her lips made a delicate O as she blew across the surface, almost childlike in its innocence.

"Don't you have to get back to the bank?" she said, voice huskier than normal, more tremulous.

He squatted next to her, eyes meeting. "You and your father are more important right now. Things at the bank can wait."

"You're a good friend, Terrence."

He ducked his head as a warmth seeped up his neck. "It's easy with people like you and George."

"Humph. Not everyone thinks so." Her eyes clouded, her face drooped, and she nibbled at her lower lip.

He wanted to embrace her, console her. She'd never allowed herself to be this vulnerable before. But it wasn't his place. It wasn't proper. He wasn't family and friendship had its limits.

He stared at the treatment room door, willing Caroline Everett to come through to give Emily the physical comfort she seemed to yearn for—even if she wouldn't admit it.

And with news of George.

This waiting brought back the aching memory of his father dying behind a closed door. A door he was not allowed through. No final hug, no final "love you, Da."

Lord, don't let this happen with George. I don't know if I could stand losing two fathers. Or seeing another sister go through the grief of losing her father.

He stretched his hand toward Emily, tugging the blanket a little tighter.

A half-smile flickered at the edge of her mouth, then disappeared like the flame of a snuffed candle. "Thank you." Her voice a whisper.

The front door opened, the wind gusting rain into the room. A thin figure in a leather duster entered, rain beading and running down the coat to drip on the floor. A derby hat crowned the lanky reddish hair of Micah Jenkins, a teller at the First Abilene Bank.

Jenkins removed his hat, rainwater running from the brim, dripping to the floor.

"Ah, Terrence, there you are." His eyes focused on Emily. "Miss Peyton, I am so sorry to hear about your father. How is he doing?"

Hands clasped in her lap, Emily sighed. "We don't know. Doc is still working on him."

"If there is anything you need from me or Mrs. Jenkins, or anything we can do, you be sure to let us know."

Emily bobbed her head. "I will, Mr. Jenkins. That's very kind of you."

"What brings you out in this muck, Micah?" Terrence said. It had to be important for Micah to risk his hypochondriacally delicate health in the chilled rain.

"Um ... Mr. Warner needs you at the bank right away to go over the accounts with him."

"Can't it wait? We should hear about Mr. Peyton's condition any minute."

"I understand, Terrence, but Mr. Warner insisted. He's meeting with Mr. Montgomery tomorrow morning and wants everything in order."

Abraham Montgomery. Priscilla's father, future father-in-law, if Terrence could sway him. Biggest rancher in the area and the bank's wealthiest customer. Yeah, Warner would want to be sure he was on top of that account. *Still, can't the man give me a couple more hours to be with the Peytons?*

Jenkins was not the one to argue his case. He would have to deal with this himself.

Taking his Stetson from the coat tree, he bent before Emily again. "I need to deal with this, Emily. I'm sorry. I'll be back as soon as I can."

Nodding, she brushed the corner of her eye. "I understand, Terrence." Eyes red, she sniffled. "Take care of your work." Her voice seemed to catch in her throat. "Hurry back. I know Father will want to see you."

As he walked to the bank, he ignored the rain and let Jenkins scurry ahead.

After crossing the street, he stopped in front of Casper's Mercantile and stared at Doc's office.

What if George didn't recover? A cold, black void swallowed his heart. Grief surged through his chest and into his throat. He swallowed the lump. Life without George, without his wisdom and counsel, his tenacity, his curmudgeonly humor, loomed as malevolent and gray as the storm drenching the town.

He closed his eyes, but no prayer would come. His mind blanked by the grief that tore at him like an unbroken horse.

What would he do without George?

Chapter 3

The gray sky glowered into dusk outside the waiting room. Emily rested her head against the window glass, the hard coolness somehow comforting. A swift-moving stream of runoff carved a miry canyon in the street, the soft sides crumbling in the torrent. The rain stopped. Branches hung limp. Large drops at the end of the leaves fell from their precarious perches into puddles on the ground.

The room where her father lay was quiet. Had been for a while.

In the waiting room, Jed Abbott slouched in one of the chairs, legs stretched out, arms crossed, eyes closed, breathing steady in the stillness. His lips moved silently, dispelling the illusion he dozed. The deputy had left earlier, promising to check back.

Terrence had been summoned to his duties at the bank shortly before, taking his comfort with him, and more of her foundation shifted. He'd come to Abilene, breaking away from his wealthy and stifling family in New York. Determined to make it on his own, he used his education and head for numbers to land a job with the bank. And became her friend over a baseball game. So supportive of her dream, defending her to people in town who thought she was reaching above her station.

Emily turned to the examining room door, willing it to open, and for her father to walk out and embrace her. It might as well have been granite.

The door to the street opened. Terrence? Emily's heart sank as Sarah Dalton, the pastor's wife, walked in, a basket on her arm. Sarah placed the basket on a small table near the stove. "Deputy Quick stopped by the parsonage and told us what happened."

Deputy Quick needs to learn to mind his own business. Emily cringed. *Did I say that out loud?*

Sarah approached Emily and placed a hand on her shoulder. "We're so sorry. Pastor is back at the parsonage praying."

Don't insult the woman.

Sarah turned to the basket. "As for me, I thought you might be feeling a little hungry, so I brought some ham and beans and sourdough bread."

Emily took the plate, but her hands felt like blocks of wood. Her fingers gripped the fork as if it were a foreign object. Her stomach reminded her she'd not eaten since breakfast. The meat lumped in her mouth, a morsel she could neither chew nor swallow. The sounds of Jed Abbott wolfing down his plateful and asking for seconds roiled her stomach.

She placed the plate on the table and gulped lukewarm coffee to get the one bite down her throat. "Thank you, Mrs. Dalton, but I don't seem able to eat anything right now."

Sarah wrapped her arm around Emily's shoulder and gave a gentle squeeze. "I understand, Miss Peyton." She pulled a napkin from the basket. "I'll cover the plate and leave it on the back of the stove to keep warm."

Tears brimmed against Emily's lashes. She brushed them away like mosquitoes.

A clap of thunder rattled the house, and rain beat against the windows. Watching raindrops splatter and run down the glass, she bit her lip to keep back emotions raw as scraped skin.

Sarah Dalton took Emily's hands. "Can I pray with you?"

Emily looked at the woman's hands, callused and worn, holding hers, then at Mrs. Dalton's face, creases around her mouth, and wrinkles at her eyes. Emily pulled her hands away. "If you think it will help you, go ahead."

"But—"

The inner door opened, and Caroline Everett motioned to Emily. "Emily, Doc says you can see your father now."

Emily melted into Caroline's arms, holding on to the woman who'd been her substitute mother, feeling once again like the little girl whose puppy had died. Caroline held her close, stroking her back. After several seconds, she whispered, "Are you ready?"

Emily nodded and stepped toward the door. Caroline greeted Sarah and spoke to Jed. "Jed, you still here?"

"Wanted to make sure George is all right."

"He's as well as can be expected. We think he's out of danger, but we need to keep an eye on him. You run along home. There isn't any more you can do here."

Emily turned to Jed, stood on tiptoe, and kissed his cheek. "Thank you, Jed, for bringing my father in."

The rancher, face turning crimson, ran his fingers through his hair. "'S least I could do, Miss Emily. George's a good friend—my best friend. Me and the missus'll be praying he's all right."

More prayers. Might as well throw stones at the moon.

She took his gnarled hand in both of hers. "Thanks again," she whispered to keep the tears from flowing.

He nodded, squared his shapeless, rain-soaked hat on his head, and shuffled out the door.

Caroline took Emily's hand, her voice soft. "Come, child."

Emily stopped in the doorway as if an invisible barrier prevented her from entering the room. Fingertips to her forehead, she studied the form stretched out on the examining table.

A white sheet covered her father from neck to feet, his legs unusually straight, splints outlined under the shroud. His left arm, splinted and thickly bandaged, lay across his body on top of the sheet. His right arm lay straight at his side, another bulky bandage extending from his hand to his elbow.

More bandages encircled his head, with a small red smudge over his right ear. His nose pointed slightly to the left, both eyes were blackened. Dark bruises covered his cheeks and jaw.

Doc Everett wiped his face with a cloth and, with a soft smile, gestured for her to step closer. Blood spattered Doc's white shirt. Sweat glistened on his baldpate and plastered his gray fringe. His dark brown eyes drooped like a hound dog's. Caroline stepped to her husband's side and clasped hands with him and Emily.

"He's going to make it." Fatigue graveled Doc's voice. "But it's going to be a long time before he's back to his old self." He rubbed his chin. "The only thing I don't know is how his brain is. He took a hard blow to the head when he fell out of the wagon and another when the rig landed on top of him. We'll just have to watch him."

Doc's words floated past her as she moved closer to her father. She touched the fingers of her father's left hand. His eyelids fluttered. He mumbled.

"He's half-asleep. His body needs to rest. If I let him wake up, there won't be any keeping him quiet, and he's bound to hurt himself."

Emily nodded, eyes on her father. She gingerly touched his cheek, flinching at her father's sharp intake of breath.

"He's in a lot of pain. Will be for a while." Doc touched her shoulder. "We'll leave you alone with him but don't expect too much right now. I gave him some medication to help him sleep and keep him quiet. It'll be two or three days before we'll really know how he is."

The door clicked softly behind her, and finally alone, Emily let one tear slide down her cheek. She stroked her father's thick brown hair above the bandage, leaned over, and kissed the one area on his cheek that wasn't bruised. Her father moaned.

"Sorry." Emily choked back more tears as she scanned his body. *Is there anything that doesn't hurt?*

She sat on a stool Doc left near the table and rested her hand on his bandaged arm. Despite Doc's hopeful words, dread engulfed her. *What if he doesn't make it? What will happen to our plans?* To her assuming a more prominent role in the practice? Father thought that in another year, people would acccpt her representing them in court. Now what? Some still scoffed when Father told them she wrote the wills, contracts, and deeds.

"Father, we still have so much to do. You have so much to teach me." She rested her head on her hands. "I don't know if you can hear me, but I love you."

She walked to a window. Full dark now, the night even blacker under the clouds. The rain poured again, splatting against the house like a parade of drummers. The void clenched her heart in its cold, wet cloak, heavy and suffocating.

A curse left her lips like a bullet and shattered against the glass.

Back at the table, fists tight, she looked at her father. "George Peyton, you will not die. I need you. We have too much to do."

The sob broke through, wracking her chest.

She let the tears flow.

Chapter 4

George Peyton opened his eyes and turned his head. Pain lanced up his spine so sharply it left him gasping for breath. His ribs gripped his lungs in a vise, preventing them from expanding. *Wonderful. Breathing hurts.* He cataloged his body and found the only places he didn't hurt were his right foot and left hand. Everything else throbbed or ached or felt like an epee pierced from his stomach to his backbone.

Try this again. Slow breath. Nope. Still hurts.

Shallow breaths, easy breaths.

Do the eyes work? Yeah. No pain as long as I don't turn my head. Can't see much, though. White ceiling with a crack like the Mississippi meandering across it and a water stain in one corner. Peripheral vision blurred—shapes along the wall vague.

Where am I? What is that smell? Chemicals? And cigars. Doc's office. Nothing else smells like it.

"Hello?" *Is that my voice?* Weak and trembly, no tone, none of his courtroom baritone. *Sound like an old man who drank rotgut and gargled glass.*

The door snicked open, and familiar-sounding footsteps approached. A face loomed over him. Emily. His sweet Emily. Her blonde hair hung limp around her oval face. Red rimmed her swollen light blue eyes, her forehead wrinkled, her nose red and puffy, lips pale and thin.

She smiled. He tried to return it. His facial muscles felt slow and unresponsive. Her lips were tender on his cheek.

"What—" Fire rose in his throat as he tried to force the word from his brain. *Happened.* Crystal clear in his mind, why couldn't he get it out his mouth?

Emily laid her hand on his shoulder. "Easy. Don't try to do too much. Three days ago, you were in a bad accident. Do you remember?"

He shook his head. Pain surged. He scrunched his eyes. Hot tears trickled.

"Doc, we need you," Emily yelled over her shoulder.

Ow. Now that's a courtroom voice.

Doc's square face loomed over him, his fringe of gray hair standing out as if electricity had arced through it. George watched his friend smooth it into place. Cigar jutting from the side of his mouth, Doc's cool, soft fingers touched and probed, held George's eyes open, and checked his pulse.

George winced under his friend's ministrations, each touch sending shards of agony.

"Everything hurt?" Doc's eyes fixed on George's.

"Ye—" George nodded, cringing.

"Well, you broke or bent almost everything, so you're going to hurt for a while."

"He seems to have trouble talking." Emily's voice quavered.

Doc nodded and lifted one of George's eyelids. "Like I said the first day, George, I don't know how much damage you've got inside. You have to be patient. Healing will be slow, might take months before you're back to normal." Doc clamped his cigar between his teeth. "Of course, normal for you is an entirely different animal than for the rest of us mere mortals. So, you may get there quicker."

Emily touched her father's cheek. Soft. Gentle. "You just focus on getting well and doing everything Doc tells you. I'll take care of the office."

George wanted to nod, smile, and embrace his daughter, but his body wouldn't respond. Tears welled again.

Chapter 5

Emily poked at the eggs growing colder on her plate. She laid down the fork and sipped now tepid coffee.

Mrs. Marcand leaned against the sink, her arms folded under her bosom. "Emmie darlin', you've got to eat. You ain't ate hardly anything since your Pa's accident. You had little enough meat on you to begin with. You gotta be strong if you're goin' to run the office."

Emily broke off a piece of biscuit and slid it between her lips. Dry as sawdust. She sipped her coffee.

Mrs. Marcand. The woman had been in her life for eighteen years, and Emily wasn't sure of the housekeeper's first name. Emily knew her as Mrs. Marcand or the Widow Marcand. The woman showed up at the front door within in a week of Mother running off when Emily was eight.

Thin as a fence post but with the strength of a plow horse, she declared Emily and her father needed her services if they were to survive. She cleaned house and cooked breakfast and supper, kept their clothes clean, and nagged them to go to church. Emily and her father never went, and Mrs. Marcand never stopped nagging.

From the way she pampered and stared at Father, it was clear she was in love with him. It was also clear Father wasn't interested. Emily knew from an early age, Father would never trust another woman with his heart.

Mrs. Marcand pushed away from the stove. "Well, if your Pa's coming home today, I best get his room ready for him." She strode out of the kitchen like a charging buffalo.

Emily poured a fresh cup of coffee, pushed her plate to one side. She rested her chin in her palm and studied the contract on the table. Gibberish. The words should make sense. The terms weren't complicated. A simple land transaction, similar to dozens she'd written over the past three years. Now the words stared at her like symbols of some incomprehensible language.

Seven days since her father's accident. Doc figured he could come home today or tomorrow, more because of the man's cantankerousness than his physical readiness. He rebelled at the doctor's confinement, at his immobility, and the sluggishness of his brain. Problems speaking plagued him as words wouldn't come or came out wrong. Even his usually precise handwriting now seemed more like a ninety-year-old than a man not yet fifty.

Reality hit again. Now, the practice was her responsibility. Something she long dreamed of loomed like the green-black clouds of a pending tornado. The umbrella of her father's protection would be gone. People would have to deal with her. And she would have to deal with them and their doubts about a woman's competence as a lawyer—her ability to function in a man's world.

Emily Louise Peyton could function in a man's world. She would prove it to them—if they gave her the chance.

The gong from the clock at the foot of the stairs jolted her out of her reverie. Eight o'clock. Time to go. She scraped the remains of her breakfast into the bucket next to the sink, piling the plate on top of others to be washed.

The contract went into the tan leather briefcase Father gave her when she passed the bar. She rested her fingers on the gold lettering embossed into the supple material: *Emily Louise Peyton, Attorney at Law.*

Yes, I am. And a darn good one too.

The warmth of the early spring sun affirmed winter's fading and the fullness of spring's promised arrival. Yellow crocuses popped through the damp earth under a warm blue sky full of the promise of summer.

Hope glimmered. Father lived, and together, they would continue.

"Good morning, Emily." Terrence McCarthy touched the brim of his hat, a slight tug with his thumb and forefinger as she turned the corner toward the office. His hazel eyes smiled, warm and inviting.

"Good morning, Terrence."

"How's your father?"

"He'll be coming home today or tomorrow."

"That's good news." His eyes held hers. "Or, is it? Seems there might be a challenge in managing the office and your father's care."

Terrence, more than anyone other than her father, respected her as a person and an attorney. Never a snide remark or disparaging comment.

"Caroline Everett has arranged for herself and Mrs. Dobbins to help Mrs. Marcand take care of him, fix meals, take care of the house. Mrs. Marcand has taken care of the house for years—Father hasn't been able to drive her away—but she'll need the extra help now."

Emily resumed walking.

Terrence matched her stride despite being six inches taller, all of it leg. "Well, that's a blessing."

A blessing? Blessing doesn't have anything to do with it. Just Caroline being Caroline.

They strolled in friendly silence. Emily enjoyed not having to make small talk, to simply walk with a friend. A friend? She glanced at Terrence out of the corner of her eye. Yes, a friend. A man not threatened by her, a man without romantic inclinations. They'd just get in the way.

When they reached her office, Terrence waited while she unlocked the door. "If there's anything I can do for you, Emily, please don't hesitate to let me know. Just get word to me at the bank, and I'll come right away."

Those hazel eyes, those green flecks. "Thank you, Terrence. I surely will."

Chapter 6

Emily surveyed the office she loved, the room she'd dreamed of working in since she learned to read and write. She luxuriated in the aroma of the leather couch and the cowhide bindings on the law books lining the shelves. The mahogany table and chairs in front of the shelves gleamed a rich, burnished brown, almost black, in the morning light.

Her father's oak rolltop desk snug against one wall, positioned near the south-facing window. Her desk stood centered in the room, an oil lamp with a rose-patterned globe on the left-hand side.

Her world.

Coffee. Emily set her case on her desk and hung her cloak and hat on the rack in the corner. She stirred the embers in the Franklin stove until the small mound glowed red then added kindling. After the wood caught, she added a few larger pieces. Soon the heat nudged away the early morning chill, and she set the coffee pot to brewing.

Mug of coffee close to hand, Emily slid the papers she'd been working on at home out of her case. She chewed on the end of her pen as she studied the document that now made perfect sense. Two minor changes later, she set it on the pile ready to go to the print shop.

The main door opened with a whoosh, and a large man stomped in, swinging the door so hard it slammed closed.

"Where's that lawyer feller?" He hovered tall and wide with a slight paunch. His face, weathered and creased, sat as a square lump on his shoulders. Dark eyes peered from under large, unruly, dirty-gray brows that matched the hair spilling over his ears and brushing his shoulders.

"How can I help you, sir?"

"I told ya—I need to see the lawyer." He pulled a folded paper from his pocket and shook it at her. "I just made an offer on two hundred acres of land on the other side of the Smoky Hill River, and I want the lawyer to look at this sales agreement—make sure I ain't getting cheated."

Emily stood and extended her hand to take the paper. "I'm a lawyer. Wh—"

He snatched the paper to his chest. "You?" The man blew air through flared nostrils like a steam locomotive. "No, missy, I need a real lawyer."

For a moment, she entertained the image of the man hanging by his ankles over an anthill. She inhaled slowly. *Here we go again.* "I am a real lawyer, sir." She nodded at the wall by her father's desk where their licenses hung.

"Well, if that don't beat all. A woman lawyer? Wonder what this world's coming to. Next thing ya know, women'll wanna vote and run for president." He spat on the floor. "Not in my lifetime, I'll tell you that."

Now that's a tempting thought. "Sir, if you let me see the document, I'm sure I can help you."

He clutched the paper and pointed at George's desk. "When's the other lawyer coming back?"

"Not for a while, Mr.?"

"Ford. Delbert Ford." He pulled on his ear. "I heard this Peyton feller's the best. Any other lawyers in town?"

Emily thought of the pistol in her desk. *Maybe I can tell the marshal he walked into the bullet.*

"There are several. But you're right. My father and I are the best."

The man scratched at his matted beard, gaze roaming the room. "Maybe I'll talk to the marshal."

"Suit yourself, sir."

Ford opened the door, hesitated, and looked back at her. "A woman lawyer? What kind of favors did you have to do to get that license?" He walked out, the door rattling closed behind him.

Emily's pen sailed through the air, hit the door, and clattered to the floor.

Chapter 7

Two hours later, Emily checked her notes and wrote the last paragraph of a will for Marshal Dobbins. She shook her head. The man didn't have much to show for giving fifteen years of his life to the town. She placed the document on the stack for the print shop.

The pen she had flung at the door lay on her desk, the nib bent at a right angle, the wooden shaft split. Another skirmish lost. *At least I kept a civil tongue in my head this time.*

Father's words echoed. "Patience, Emily. Patience. They will come around. They'll see there's no reason a woman can't be a lawyer. Give them time." He'd said those words three years ago, and the only people who accepted her in her chosen profession were Terrence McCarthy, Doc Everett, Caroline, and a reluctant Mrs. Marcand.

How much patience is it going to take? Pain in her hands told her to loosen her fists. Indentations from her nails creased her palms.

Emily exhaled, tension dissipating with the released air. Her stomach rumbled. Coffee was a poor substitute for food, especially six cups in a few hours. She slipped on her cloak and adjusted her hat, using the mirror next to the door to ensure the angle conveyed confidence and competence.

A stop at the printer's, and then to Doc Everett's for dinner and a report on her father's progress.

As she passed the bank, the door opened, and she stopped short, rising on her toes to avoid crashing into Terrence McCarthy.

"Emily." He grabbed her arm to steady her. "Please accept my apology. I didn't see you coming, and I just walked out like a horse seeking water. Are you all right?"

How can this man always make me smile? "Yes, I'm fine. I was too focused on my destination and not paying attention to the world around me."

He touched the brim of his hat, lips curved in a smile. *Did his eyes twinkle?* "Perhaps I should accompany you. To clear the way, so to speak?"

A chuckle bubbled from her lips. "I'm on my way to the printer's and Doc Everett's office. You're more than welcome to join me." *Emily, what are you doing? I'm going to enjoy the company of one of the few men who doesn't see me as a freak.*

"I can go with you as far as the printers, but then we must part ways, I'm afraid." He shrugged. "I'm meeting Priscilla at the Randolph House for dinner."

"That's nice." A chill flickered across Emily's heart. *Should I say something? No. Not my place.*

"Please tell your father that, as soon as he's able, I'll be over to resume our chess games."

Will his mind let him play again?

She smiled. "I'm sure he'll enjoy that."

They parted at the printer's shop. After leaving the work, Emily headed for Doc's. The people she passed were shadowy shapes of wispy gray on the edge of her consciousness. Thoughts of what lay ahead swirled. She wanted her father home and in the office. But he wouldn't be in the office. Doc's prognosis stung. Her father would need at least a month of physical healing.

Last night's whispered conversation played again. "Emily," Doc had said, "you need to understand. Your father may never be able to return to his practice. If his brain stays muddled and he can't communicate, I don't see how he'll ever come close to the man we used to know."

She bit back tears and the fear boiling in her stomach. *How can he not be the way he was? God, why did you let this happen?*

Caroline had wrapped her arm around Emily's shoulder, pulling her close, patting her arm. "Don't fret, darling girl. Mrs. Marcand, Mrs. Dobbins, and I will be there every day once he's home. We'll take care of him while we pray for God to continue to heal him."

Pray? For God to fix something he broke in the first place?

The silence of Doc's empty waiting room echoed in Emily's heart. The dark paneling and furniture gave the room a somber, almost funereal air, resisting the efforts of the bright sunshine to cheer it up. The white and blue Afghan draped over a chair further broke the solemnity.

The door to the examining room stood closed. She knocked with a lot more firmness than she felt. *Will he be able to come home today?*

"Come in." Her father's voice resonated on the other side, the baritone strong and vibrant.

Her father sat in a wheelchair, both splinted legs extending on boards, canons ready for battle. His left arm nestled in a sling across his chest while his right hand lay in his lap, not bandaged, but swollen and bruised. White cloth encircled his head, his thick brown hair splaying above it like an over-used paintbrush. The bruising on his face had faded to pale yellows and purplish greens. His once-straight nose still pointed to the left.

She kissed his cheek. "You're looking very good."

His smile still resembled a grimace. "I'm feeling good. Ready to go home, if only that—" His voice stopped, and he frowned, his right hand clenched and pounding his thigh. He looked at her, eyes pleading.

Emily stroked his cheek. "Give it time. The words will come."

He shook his head—a violent movement—as if to rattle the word out. "Quack." He rested his head against the back of the chair, expelling a long sigh. "If only that quack—say so."

"I heard that." Doc Everett walked in. "You can go home today. Tired of you taking up space and griping about the coffee." He turned to Emily. "If you're ready, he can go home. Otherwise, I'm about to park him in the outhouse."

"Be better than—stinking cigar—Don't know how—" George cussed, inhaled, frowned. "Caroline puts—smelling like a wet Billy goat."

Doc flashed a wink at Emily. "Because she appreciates all the fine things I bring to her life."

George's lips moved. His mouth twisted, and his right fist clenched as sweat beaded at the edge of his bandage. Emily placed her hand on his shoulder and squeezed it lightly, swallowing the lump in her throat. "Easy, Father. Easy. Don't try to do too much."

George closed his eyes, and his chin drooped to his chest.

Doc moved behind the chair. "Let's give you one last meal before we send you home." Emily held the door as Doc pushed her father into the kitchen and dining area.

Caroline stirred a pot on the stove. Emily drew in the aroma of venison and fresh-baked bread along with green beans. Four place settings framed the pitcher of yellow and purple prairie violets on the plain square table.

Caroline's embrace cocooned Emily, the aroma of lilac water and bread dough sweeping her to her little girl place, if only for a moment.

"It's good to see you," Caroline said. "Have a seat. This is ready."

"Let me help." Emily poured coffee as Caroline dished out the venison stew and placed a basket of sliced bread on the table.

Her mouth watered in anticipation of the first bite of butter-slathered bread. The slice stopped halfway to her mouth as she watched her father lift a spoonful of stew. His slow movement lacked its usual refined grace as he held the spoon in his fist rather than balanced in his fingers. He stuffed the food into his mouth before it could slosh out of the spoon. He chewed and smiled at her. "Is that—me?"

She passed it to him and prepared another slice for herself.

Caroline touched her arm. "He's doing very well, considering. His muscles aren't back to where they should be, but they will be. Let him do as much as he can for himself."

Doc harrumphed. "Let him do everything for himself. Don't pamper him."

George nodded. "Only way—get better."

"As if you'd ever let anybody do anything for you." Emily smirked. "Your stubborn pride may just do you some good this time."

Her father's crooked smile brought the lump back to her throat. The muscles of one side of his mouth wouldn't cooperate with the other. She missed his face-splitting grin that lit up her heart.

Doc wiped his mouth with his napkin and laid it beside his bowl. "Now, you two." He nodded at Emily and George. "George, I know you're going to do what you want, when you want. Just remember, you are not going to be as quick or as coordinated. You will need time to build that up again."

He turned to Emily. "You, young lady, keep him out of the office until I say he can go back." He pointed his finger in the air. "Even more important, don't take the office to the house. He needs all his energy to focus on his recovery. I don't want any extra pressure on him."

Emily frowned. "You mean I can't even discuss a case with him?"

"Yeah," George said. "Need—that."

Doc tugged at his ear, glanced at his wife. They shrugged at each other. "I mean there's a fine line I don't want to you to cross, George, until you're stronger. You can discuss cases, but, Emily, if he gets aggravated or if he wants to take over, close your mouth, pick up your papers, and leave the room." He sipped his coffee. "Try to keep the office talk to no more than an hour a day over the next couple of weeks. Then we'll see how you're doing."

A couple of weeks of that, and I'll be the one in the corner babbling nonsense.

Chapter 8

George tossed the papers on his dining room table, whipped his glasses from his face and flung them onto the documents.

Emily jumped. "What's the matter?"

"Get me some—" Arrgh. What's the word? He motioned with his right hand, indicating putting something under his arm, hunching his shoulders.

Emily frowned. He swung his arm back and forth.

Her eyes brightened. "You mean crutches?"

"Yes."

"How will you use them with one good arm and two broken legs? Why do you want them, anyway?"

"Going to the office."

Mouth agape, Emily stuttered, "No. You're not. Doc wants you to stay home for at least another three weeks."

He waved his hand. "Doc doesn't know what he's talking about." Gesturing at the table, he said, "Can't work—this. Have to see—" Mouth stopped working. Again. He could picture what he wanted to say, but the image hovered a hand's breadth from his lips. Blood pounded in his ears as the anger rose. He cussed.

"I wish you could forget how to cuss." Her eyes burned into him. "I know you're frustrated. Put that cussing energy into making your mind and mouth work properly."

George jabbed at the papers, picked them up and pointed at the name.

"You want to see Bill Jaspers?"

He nodded.

"Why?"

Waving his arms, he gestured around the room. "Need to talk." He waited, let the image form. "Face-to-face."

"You shouldn't come to the office. Too much pressure. You know what Doc said."

George shook his head. "You're as—exasp—erating as Doc." He wanted to pace. *I think better when I can walk.* He grabbed the arm of the wheelchair, his tiny, barely mobile prison. *Can't leave the first floor of my house. Can't even go out on my porch alone.* His caretakers feared he would push himself down the stairs.

Emily chewed on her lower lip. "How about if Bill came here?"

He nodded. "Would be—great. Need to—dis—talk. Can't do it all by paper. Have him—tomorrow." He made a sweeping gesture with his good arm. "Have all clients come here. Move the office." His face twisted as another thought struggled to come out. "Sooner."

She held up her hand. "Slow down a minute. You'll never get any rest if the clients know they can see you here. Let me talk with Doc before we do anything like that. Make sure it's all right."

George rolled his eyes. "Of course—it's all—right. I know how much—" He banged his fist on the table.

"Pressure?"

He nodded, blinking back the angry tears. Fear-driven nausea roiled. *What if I never speak correctly again?* He pushed the thought down, but it continued to bubble up. He watched the knuckles of his right hand turn white as he gripped the arm of his chair.

Emily leaned forward, her light blue eyes warm and concerned. Her hair, the color of sunshine and gold. The slight asymmetry in her nose that didn't show unless you knew to look for it. So like her mother. Pain and hurt welled, his heart pressing against his ribs.

She placed her hand on his. "Does it bother you when I fill in the word you're looking for?"

He shook his head, then nodded. "Stupid." He tapped his temple. "Can see the word—can't get it out." He paused. "—Court? Have to speak. Can't."

"I can do it."

"I know, but ..."

Emily leaned back in her chair and tapped her pencil against the tabletop. "I know. I know. Will a judge and jury think I can?"

George nodded. "Proud of you." The thought formed; the words took shape. He opened his mouth, and the words stumbled. "—right case—you'll show—'em."

Her eyes softened and a small smile twitched her lips. "Sometimes I wonder if the right case will ever come along."

He pointed to himself and then her. "You think— holding—you back?"

She shook her head, the emphatic gesture swirled her hair. Gathering the papers, Emily smiled. "I think we've done enough for one night. Tomorrow, I'll ask Doc about having the clients see you here."

He grabbed her wrist. "Just do it."

She frowned. "I can't. I won't endanger your health." She pried his fingers loose.

He sighed and pushed away from the table. "Can't see how I'm—" He slammed his fist into his leg. "Going to get well—stuck here—go crazy."

Emily kissed his cheek and hugged his neck. "Then we'll go crazy together. Good night. I'll talk to Doc tomorrow."

After her footsteps faded up the stairs, George wheeled his chair to his room, past the contraption Doc and Terrence rigged so he could get himself into bed. He rolled to the window that looked out over the rear of his property. The full moon cast bright light over the landscape stretching to the horizon. No color, but each tree and boulder stood as if drawn with a sharp-edged pen.

A half-mile out, a stream flowed. And a quarter mile to the right, the stream formed a bend. The bend formed a pool, deep and dark and cool, even in the summer heat. There he fished and forgot. Forgot the office for a time. Forgot the clients and the courts. Even forgot the betrayal that had plagued him for the last eighteen years, the betrayal that cast the pall of loneliness over his heart. The same betrayal made Emily hide her heart behind a wall, never to be hurt again. Now he couldn't get to his forgetting spot.

He tasted the salt of his tears.

Chapter 9

Terrence noticed Charlotte Taylor waiting outside the Randolph House, thick ebony hair tumbling over her shoulders, coat doing little to disguise her trim figure, dark blue eyes fixed on Tiny. Priscilla never looked at him like that, eyes sparkling at the simple sight of him.

He whispered to Tiny, "You are so blessed, my friend, to have a girl like her."

"I know."

Charlotte embraced her man and planted a kiss on his cheek. "I'm glad Mr. Montgomery let you off early. I missed you somethin' awful."

Tiny grinned and held her at arm's length. "You sure bless these tired eyes, darlin'."

Glancing at the sky, she said, "It's getting late. Let's eat quick so I can get to work."

Tiny frowned, his jaw worked as if trying to hold back words.

Charlotte placed a finger on his lips. "Shush. Only a little while more. Once we're hitched, we'll never look back."

His head drooped. Charlotte looked at Terrence.

"Want me to tell her?"

Tiny nodded.

Terrence inhaled. "Tiny feels like there's never going to be enough money to get the ranch or the stock."

Tiny wiped his nose with his sleeve. "That hundred acres north of town sold. That was the cheapest piece around." He scuffed his boot on the boardwalk. "Seems like every time I think I'm gettin' close, the price of the land goes up or the stock gets more expensive."

Brow furrowed, Charlotte lifted Tiny's chin with her finger. "Don't fret, sweetheart. How many times've we been over this? Maybe six months, definitely a year. With both of us saving, we should have enough."

Tiny shook his head, his shaggy, walnut-colored hair whirling below the brim of his hat. "Need to do it sooner." He stepped back and gestured at her coat. "Can't have you wearing them tight dresses and them cowboys pawing at you. Tears me up just thinking 'bout it."

Tiny's anguish burned into Terrence. Usually cheerful to a fault, his friend's outburst hit him like a hot blast of steam from a locomotive. Even Charlotte seemed embarrassed, her eyes darting to see if anyone heard. A few heads turned in their direction, but people kept walking.

Charlotte grasped Tiny's hands. "Tiny, hush. Don't talk like that. Not on the street."

Terrence touched his friend's elbow. Tiny covered his face with his hands, then dropped them to hang limp at his sides. "I'm sorry, darlin'. I jes want a place so bad for us, and it's just gettin' further away."

Looping her arm around Tiny's, Charlotte turned toward the restaurant. "No frettin' tonight. We'll put it aside and enjoy our meal and let the ranch take care of itself for now."

Tiny's mouth curved in a smile. "You're right, Charlotte. Forgive me for gettin' into such a state. I'm just so anxious for us to git hitched and settled."

She patted his arm. "It's all right, darlin'."

"Want to join us, Terrence?" Tiny said.

Charlotte's eyes narrowed, then quickly relaxed.

Terrence squeezed Tiny's shoulder. "No thanks. I'd only be in the way. You two enjoy yourselves." He touched the brim of his hat and turned away.

Chapter 10

The sound of her father's palm slapping the dining room table reverberated off the walls. Cups and saucers rattled like Spanish castanets. Emily jumped and placed her hand over her heart.

Her father's baritone rocketed a curse that seemed to spin around the room. Caroline blushed, and Doc started to rise out of his chair, clenched jaw threatening to bite his cigar in half.

When she'd questioned Doc earlier in the day about having clients visit the house, he suggested they all have supper together. Maybe this wasn't such a good idea.

Settling in his seat, Doc put his cigar in the ashtray at his elbow. His voice calm, he said to his friend and patient. "George, there's no call to talk like that in front of the ladies."

George glared at him then swept his eyes over Caroline and Emily. He bowed his head. "Sorry—Caroline, Emily, Mrs. M—forgive me." He fixed his gaze on Doc. "But if you—stubborn—"

Doc leaned back and rubbed his chin. "Because you talk like that, I can't let you have your clients come to the house. George, you turned so red, I thought you were going to pop your heart."

Emily's stomach dropped, and she extended her hand toward her father. He brushed her away with a wave and sank back into his chair, the wheels squeaking on the hardwood floor.

Doc sipped his coffee. He ran his finger around the rim of his cup. Not looking up, he said, "Emily's told me how frustrated you get when you can't find the words. Caroline and Mrs. Marcand have seen the same thing." Doc leaned forward, folding his arms on the table. "George, the burden will be too much on your brain and on your heart. Your body is demanding all your strength to heal itself. You interfere with that by seeing clients, and you'll delay your recovery."

He paused. George looked at him. "In fact, you'll probably never recover at all. You want to spend the rest of your days in that chair? Or worse?"

Her father looked at her, then out the window. "No."

Emily sighed. Maybe his stubbornness was wearing out. The struggle to keep her father in compliance with Doc's orders taxed her until her body collapsed into bed each night. She needed all her will power not to curse and fling a coffee mug at him. Her hope for relief teetered on the knife edge of her father's frustration.

She started to speak, to reinforce Doc's words, but thought better of it. Let him come to the decision by himself. He'll be more likely to stick to it.

The silence hung for almost a minute. George cleared his throat. "How long—" He waved his hand as his mouth struggled to speak "—like this?"

Emily covered her smile with her hand. Victory. A small victory, but she'd take any kind.

Doc shrugged. "At least four more weeks, maybe six. Then we'll take another look."

"Four weeks?" Veins on her father's neck and temples bulged.

"At least. We might be able to move it up some if Emily, Mrs. Marcand and Caroline tell me you're making progress sooner." He jabbed the air with his cigar. "Even after we get the casts off, your muscles will be very weak. Building up their strength will take longer."

Doc paused, eyes somber. "That's just your bones, George. Don't know when, if ever, this talking thing will heal."

Her father nodded, shoulders slumped. Emily studied him, looking for any sign he was agreeing on the outside but determined to disobey on the inside. He held her gaze and wagged his finger at her. "All right. You win—you're going to—work harder—No more—easy on you."

She laughed. "When were you ever easy on me?"

He cast his gaze to the table, his mouth curving down. Sadness stabbed her heart as memories flooded. Caroline's hand on hers comforted, but pain still burned, and heaviness weighed her heart like a boulder. "I'm sorry," Emily whispered.

George nodded and reached his right hand toward her. She took it and enjoyed his reassuring grip and the gentle smile in his eyes.

Chapter 11

Terrence left his boarding house, Mrs. Crenshaw's breakfast of ham, eggs and biscuits settling peaceably in his stomach. He whistled a jig as he looked forward to his first official day as head teller. Everyone in the bank knew he'd been doing the job for three months. Still, having his worked recognized and rewarded warmed him. His chest puffed out a little.

And tonight. He stopped himself from dancing to his tune. Dinner with Priscilla and her family. Maybe his promotion would make him look a little better in her father's eyes. More suitable for his daughter.

Priscilla.

Six months since she'd allowed him to come courting, defying her father's initial disapproval. Suppers with her family, the food like lumps of coal under her father's glaring eyes and biting questions about how could a bank teller expect to support a wife and family. Her mother constantly mentioned other young men's interest in the most beautiful girl for a hundred miles. Mr. Montgomery's attitude had softened slightly when Terrence proved he could ride and train horses with the best of the ranch hands.

Priscilla came to town alone more often, and they'd have quiet dinners or suppers at the Randolph House. At church, as their arms touched, he thought the hymns were just for him. Buggy rides on Sunday afternoons and picnics by a stream ended far too soon. Knowing one of her three brothers or a ranch hand sat within view kept everything prim and proper until a weeping willow shielded their first kiss from prying eyes.

A promotion and supper with his girl and her family. Maybe now that he was advancing in business, a marriage proposal would be favorably received. How soon could they get married?

Yep. Going to be an exciting day.

He skipped around a corner and collided with Emily Peyton.

She cut off his apology. "Terrence, the way we literally keep running into each other, I swear you have an ulterior motive."

Her light tone and smiling eyes teased him. What beautiful eyes. Almond-shaped, light blue, delicate lashes. He shook his head. Priscilla's eyes are …? *Green. That's it. Green. Definitely green.*

Heat rushed up his cheeks, and sounds stammered from his lips. Eventually, words formed. "Em … Emily, I am so sorry. Are you hurt?"

"I'm fine. You might need to start wearing a bell, so people know you're coming." A laugh bubbled under the surface.

"Perhaps I should."

They walked together, chatting like comfortable friends about his promotion, her father, the practice. "You're so comfortable to be with," he said, and immediately wished he hadn't.

Emily cocked her head, her gaze measuring him.

"I apologize, Emily. That was too forward. Please forgive me." His neck burned with embarrassment.

"No apology necessary. I know what you meant. I enjoy being with you too." She pushed a stray strand of blond hair behind her ear. How soft that hair must be to touch. His hand started to move.

Emily's voice brought him back to reality. "It's nice to have someone who isn't scared off when I walk by."

"You mean because you're a lawyer?"

She nodded. "I've dreamed of being a lawyer like my father since I first learned to read. Now people treat me like I'm something from a circus side show."

He grinned. "Well, female lawyers are unusual, but I know you're good at what you do." They walked in silence. "How much does it bother you?"

She sighed. "It hurts." She told him about Delbert Ford looking for the real lawyer.

Emily had never revealed this much of herself. Under the confident, competent exterior walked a vulnerable young woman who risked ridicule every day. How much more would she face now that she bore the burden of the practice? Plenty, but she wouldn't break. Emily Louise Peyton was too tough-minded for that.

He offered his arm as they crossed a side street. "Please let me know if there is ever anything I can do to help."

Once on the next boardwalk, she left her arm looped with his, the touch of her hand light and comfortable. Friendly. They reached her office. He tipped his hat as she stepped inside. "Have a wonderful day, Emily. Don't forget. Let me know if I can help with anything."

She leaned against the doorframe, her smile warm, her slim fingers gracefully resting on the door. "Thank you, Terrence. You're a good friend."

Chapter 12

Terrence grinned at Harry Bannister's low whistle.

The guard cleared his throat. "I don't think I've ever seen that much money in one place in all my life."

After placing the last of the currency on the table, Terrence added a number to his ledger. The small counting room seemed to press in as if to inhale the aroma of the greenbacks and the metallic tang of the gold.

Harry adjusted his gun belt. What held the wide strip of leather on the man's bony hips? Terrence imagined the guard sneezing and the gun and holster ending up around his ankles. He disguised his chuckle with a cough.

"It's sure nice havin' Deputy Quick hangin' around outside on days like t'day."

"Think we need more guards?" Terrence said.

Harry nodded. "Somethin' to consider with all the land deals and railroad business that's been goin' on."

"I'll talk to Mr. Warner."

A knock on the door interrupted their conversation. Terrence picked up his Colt from the table and opened the door a crack. Outside, Micah Jenkins, stood, wringing his hands. "Sorry to interrupt, Mr. McCarthy, but there's a rough-looking gentleman out front with a bank draft from the railroad company."

"Rough-looking gentleman?" Terrence resisted smiling at the man's nervousness.

Jenkins nodded. "I think he's one of those land speculators that have been around." He wrinkled his nose. "Hasn't been near hot water or soap in a while."

Terrence smiled, remembering Jenkins' sensitive disposition, especially around dirt and unpleasant odors. "Thanks, Micah. Tell him I'll be right with him."

Leaving Harry at the door, Terrence walked into the lobby. A man, tall and stocky, stood at the railing separating the foyer from the desks. He held a leather glove between his teeth by the middle finger while he studied a notebook, pencil in hand, skimming the page.

"Good morning. I'm Terrence McCarthy, the head teller. May I help you?" He extended his hand.

The man looked at Terrence's hand like he'd never seen one before. He took the glove from his mouth and shuffled it, the pencil, and the notebook into his left hand. The two shook hands. "Phillips. Mac Phillips. I just sold a passel of land to the railroad." He pulled a slim sheet of paper from the notebook. "Got this here bank draft I need to cash in."

Terrence looked at the amount and cast a raised eyebrow at Phillips.

The paper rattled in front of Terrence. "Can ya cash it or not? Feller at the railroad said you could."

Terrence cleared his throat and opened the small gate in the railing. "Come in, have a seat." He pointed toward his desk.

Phillips sauntered through, his gait rolling on his bowed legs. His spurs jangled, and dust swirled from his boots and pants as he passed. Jenkins sneezed.

"Coffee?" Terrence offered.

"Naw." Phillips shook his head.

"Excuse me for saying this, but you don't look like the usual land dealers we get coming in here."

"Cuz I ain't. Up here from Dallas to sell my brother's land. He died a few months back and his widow wants to go back to her family in Kansas City." The man frowned. "Is that a problem?"

"No, sir. You must be Carl Phillips' brother."

Phillips nodded. "That's me. The oldest and the last of seven brothers." A wave of sadness washed over his face. "Never thought I'd outlive all my kinfolk."

"I'm sorry to hear that."

"Ain't no never mind." He waved the check at Terrence. "At least his wife will be taken care of."

Terrence had him sign the draft. "I'll be right back."

He motioned for Jenkins to join him in the counting room while Harry waited outside. "Double count me, then I want you and Harry to put the rest of the money in the safe."

Fifteen minutes later, Terrence returned to his desk and stacked the money in front of Phillips. "Count it, please."

Phillips did, slowly. Lost his place and had to start over. "Yep— all there." He packed the money into two pair of saddlebags he'd brought and secured the flaps.

"Do you want our guard to accompany you? Or do you want me to ask the marshal to have a deputy go with you?"

"Naw, Just goin' to the hotel. I'll be fine."

After Phillips left, Terrence recorded the transaction in his ledger. Time for dinner. As he stood to leave, a flurry of gunshots followed by screams echoed in the street.

Phillips.

Terrence pulled the Peacemaker from his desk and ran out the door with Harry behind him, gun drawn. At the end of the boardwalk to his right, a large bay horse stood in the middle of the street, reins dangling. On the ground lay Mac Phillips, a pool of blood soaking the dirt around him.

A man stood over Phillips, face white and tight, gun drawn, smoke rising from the barrel in a lazy tendril. His other hand gripped one of Phillips' saddlebags.

Terrence's heart dropped to his toes.

Tiny Waters.

Chapter 13

Marshal John Dobbins stepped into the street, pistol in his hand, waist high, pointed at Tiny.

"Drop the gun, Waters." The marshal's voice was soft in the eerie silence. "Slow and easy."

Terrence discovered the Peacemaker trembling in his hand. He lowered his arm.

Tiny looked at the marshal, then at Terrence, his eyes wide. He moved his mouth, but no words came.

The marshal cocked his pistol, the sound booming in the hushed street. "Now, Tiny. Put down the gun."

Tiny nodded as if coming out of a trance and let his gun fall to the ground.

Dobbins nodded at his deputy. Quick tucked the gun in the waist of his pants and took the saddlebag from Tiny almost tenderly, as if removing a prickly pear pad. He held Tiny's elbow.

After releasing the hammer on his pistol, the marshal holstered his weapon, sighed, and pushed his hat off his forehead. He knelt to examine Mac and closed the dead man's eyes. Over his shoulder he said, "Anybody know this man?"

"His name's Mac Phillips," Terrence said. "He's from Dallas, up to sell his brother's land. He cashed a check for the sale a few minutes ago."

Squatting next to the body, the marshal let his hands dangle between his knees. "Harry Bannister. Go fetch Simon Watkins. Tell him we need his services."

Harry trotted up the street, one hand holding his gun belt.

Dobbins straightened, eyes narrow under shaggy brows. "What happened here, Tiny?"

"I was comin' from the livery." Tiny's voice creaked. He took a deep breath, released it. "I saw two men pointing their guns at this feller." He nodded at the body. "He was backing away, reaching for his gun, and they shot 'im. I went for my gun and managed to grab one of the saddlebags, but they ran off down the alley. I fired a couple of shots at 'em but missed."

The marshal surveyed the people standing in a loose semi-circle. "Anybody else see what happened?"

Most shook their heads. Bill Jaspers stepped forward. "I came out of the store when I heard the shots. All I saw was Tiny standing there, gun out, holding the saddlebag."

Images swirled in Terrence's mind. Just a few minutes ago, Mac Phillips was in the bank, alive, talking about taking care of his brother's family. Now he lay in the street, his blood turning the dirt a dark maroon. And Tiny Waters stood there, head hanging.

The marshal's voice penetrated Terrence's fog. "What'd these two men look like?"

Tiny shrugged. "Like cowboys. They had bandanas on their faces."

"You didn't recognize them?"

Tiny shook his head.

"Did they say anything? Call each other by name?"

"Not that I heard."

"They went down that alley?" Dobbins pointed.

"Yes, sir." Tiny's voice quavered.

Lord, help him.

"Matthew, go see what you can find."

"Yes, sir." Quick released Tiny and jogged into the alley.

"What about me?" Tiny's voice had a plaintive whine. "Can I go?"

"No." Dobbins glared at Tiny, his mouth tight. "You're coming with me. I'm going to hold you while we look for these two men you claim to have seen."

Terrence stepped forward. "Marshal, is that fair? Tiny told you what happened. You can't hold him responsible if the murderers got away."

Dobbins' eyes froze Terrence. "If there were two other men."

Fumbling for words, Terrence gestured with his hands as if speaking sign language. "You don't think Tiny did this?"

"I'm not thinking anythin'. I'm only looking at what I can see. Right now, I just want him where I can get my hands on him while we check out his story."

Terrence opened his hands, palms up. "Marshal, Phillips had two saddlebags. There's only one here. Doesn't that prove Tiny's telling the truth?"

"Maybe. It might also mean he had somebody helping him. He got away and Tiny didn't." The marshal grabbed Tiny's arm. "Come along, son."

A clatter of hooves and creaking harness marked the arrival of Simon Watkins and his hearse. Harry Bannister sat next to him, white knuckles gripping the seat back. The wagon was painted a high-gloss ebony with Watkins Undertaking scrolled in gold on the sides. With practiced efficiency and Harry's help, Watkins slid a coffin onto the ground next to the body.

Watkins, a short, heavy-set man, wiped his sweaty face with a scented handkerchief. The strong lilac aroma startled Terrence, and he sneezed. At the undertaker's request, two men stepped into the street and helped lift Phillips into the coffin, then the coffin into the wagon. Watkins opened a black notebook. "Who's the next of kin?"

Terrence and the marshal exchanged glances. "Carl Phillips' widow, Annamae Phillips," Terrence said. "Carl's widow."

Watkins pursed his lips and shook his head as he made a notation. "Can't add more sorrow to Miss Annamae." He closed the notebook and slid it into his inside coat pocket. "The town may have to pay for this one, Marshal."

Dobbins shrugged. "You know what to do."

"Terrence." Tiny's voice quaked, his face the expression of a dog who lost his master. "Tell Charlotte what happened. Tell her I didn't do it."

"I will." He watched his friend shuffle down the street, head bowed, feet kicking up a small cloud of dust which quickly resettled in the windless day.

Chapter 14

Terrence turned and bumped into Joseph Warner. "My apologies, sir. I didn't see you standing there."

"Perfectly understandable on such an upsetting day." Warner fiddled with his pipe. "You say the dead man cashed a draft earlier?"

"Yes, sir."

"Tragic." Warner sighed. "A man dies because of one man's greed."

Terrence pushed the irritation out of his voice. "I don't think Tiny did it, sir."

"Right. I heard what he told the sheriff." Warner looked down the street. "Still ..."

"Sir, if you can excuse me for a while, I'd like to tell Tiny's fiancée and also talk to George Peyton."

"George Peyton?"

"Yes, sir. I think Tiny's going to need a lawyer to help prove his innocence."

Warner placed his warm, firm hand on Terrence's shoulder. "One of the things I've long admired about you, Terrence, is your loyalty. To this bank, the church. Your friends." He paused, eyes riveted on Terrence's. "I just hope you haven't misplaced that loyalty this time." He pointed up the street and took Terrence's pistol. "Now go. Be back after dinner. We have those accounts to go over."

Dutton's Saloon and George Peyton's office lay in opposite directions, in more ways than one. Dutton's was near the railroad station, a run-down part of Abilene that catered to the drinking, gambling, and whore-mongering population. Places Terrence avoided. His money and his reputation were too valuable to risk on such dangerous pleasures.

Peyton's office stood across from the brick-faced courthouse, representing the town's growth and ambitions to be a major player in the commerce of the prairie. The part of town Terrence wanted to be a part of. Build a home. Start a family. Priscilla's face floated before him, slightly out-of-focus, as it did every time he thought of their future together. He pushed the distraction aside and jogged to Dutton's.

The doors were closed. Terrence twisted the knob. Unlocked. Sunlight dimmed by dirty windows gave the main room the gloom of a cavern. Terrence half-expected bats to swoop from the dark ceiling. He left the door open. A man lay stretched on the floor in front of the ornately carved bar, arm across his eyes, snores rivaling an angry buffalo.

"We're closed." The smoke- and whiskey-scarred voice came from his right. A man sat at a round table, coffee mug and plate of flapjacks in front of him. "Come back this afternoon."

"I need to see Charlotte Taylor."

The man forked some flapjack into his mouth and chewed slowly. "She ain't entertainin' now. Come back later."

Terrence clenched his fists, resisting the urge to pick up the man by his shirt and rattle him. "I'm not looking for that. I need to give her a message."

"I can give her the message when she wakes up. What is it?" He picked at his teeth with a gnawed, dirty fingernail.

Terrence lowered his voice, trying to sound menacing. "I have to give her the message in person."

The man rolled up a flapjack, dunked it in his coffee, and bit off half of it. "You're starting to bore me, mister. I don't like being bored." He slid a pistol onto the table. "You can't see her." He jerked his thumb toward the door.

Terrence took a deep breath and bellowed Charlotte's name.

The man jumped to his feet, picked up his gun and advanced toward Terrence. "You don't hear so good." He cocked his pistol as he took another step.

"That's close enough," Terrence said, pulled back his right arm and drove his fist into the man's face, where it first met the soft tissue of the nose and then harder cartilage. The man plopped to the floor, wiped his nose, studied the blood on his hand. He squinted at Terrence, and then his eyes rolled upward. He wobbled and his upper body fell the rest of the way. His head bounced with a hollow thump.

Terrence bellowed again. A door on the upper level of the building opened, and Charlotte stepped onto the balcony overlooking the bar. She brushed sleep-tousled hair from her face and wrapped a lace shawl around her bare shoulders. Stifling a yawn, she said, "Terrence, what are you yelling about?" Her eyes widened when she saw the man spread-eagled on the floor. "Did you do that?"

Terrence looked at the man, scratched the back of his head. "I guess I did. Listen, Tiny's in trouble."

Her hand went to her mouth as she made her way to the stairs. "What happened? What did he do? Is he hurt bad?"

Terrence met her and took her hand as she walked down the last couple of steps. "I think he tried to stop a robbery, but the marshal thinks he robbed and killed a man."

She gasped and sank against him. He helped her into a chair and squatted next to her, holding her hand. She held her other hand to her eyes, her breathing shallow. Tears welled, and she sniffled. "Do you think he did it?" A childlike softness flavored her voice.

He squeezed her hand. "No, I don't."

Charlotte straightened and inhaled deeply. "What can we do to help him?" Her blue eyes drilled into him.

"Tiny needs a lawyer. I'm going to see George Peyton."

Charlotte nodded. "Will you take me to him? I need to see Tiny."

"Of course."

Terrence waited while Charlotte went to dress. The man on the floor groaned. Terrence picked up the gun and emptied the bullets into his hand. The man sat up, touched his face. "You boke by dose."

"Probably. Doc Everett can fix it for you."

"Ya' didn't hab to bit me so hard."

"You were pointing a pistol at me. My mother would have been very disappointed if I let you shoot me."

"She deach you do punch like dat?"

"No. My sister."

Charlotte descended the stairs in a blue-checked dress that clung to her slender figure. Her black hair glistened from brushing. *Easy to see why Tiny fell for you.*

She stared at the man on the floor, lightly kicked his foot. "I'm going out with this gentleman. I'll be back when my business is finished."

"Dutton won't like dat. Ya know he dants ya here in the afternoon, 'specially with all da railroad people coming to town."

"I expect he won't like it, but I don't care."

"Can I hab my dun back?"

Terrence handed it to him. The man examined it, checking the cylinder. "Hey, where's da bullets?"

"Right here." Terrence walked to the bar and let the bullets drop one-by-one into a cuspidor. He offered Charlotte his arm. "Shall we?"

Chapter 15

Emily's head snapped up as the sound of gun shots bounced off the buildings, the thick law book on the table forgotten. Outside on the boardwalk, she saw Marshal Dobbins run up the street, Deputy Quick next to him. Farther along the street, near the bank, people gathered. A man lay in the dirt. Standing over him was a vaguely familiar figure. She shaded her eyes with her hand. Terrence's friend, Tiny.

The thoughts of guns and death chilled her. She rubbed her arms as she walked to the scene then stood slightly behind Erlene Crenshaw at the edge of the crowd, listening, finding Tiny's explanation hard to believe. When Simon Watkins pulled up in his wagon, she headed back to the office. *At least I'll have some news for Father when I go home for dinner.*

Back in the office, she frowned as she struggled to focus on her research. She nibbled the end of her pencil. A murder trial. That would be interesting. Maybe not this one though. Seems cut and dried unless Deputy Quick turns up some evidence to support Tiny's story.

Emily pushed the scene from her mind and refocused on the law book. She yawned and shook her head. *Contracts can be so boring sometimes.*

Sometime later, a light knock on the door interrupted her and Terrence entered. "Good morning, Emily. Am I interrupting anything?"

Emily scanned the nearly blank sheet of paper at her elbow. Her few notes looked like hen scratches. "Not really. How can I help you?" She gestured toward a chair on the other side of her desk.

Terrence sat and swept his longish hair off his forehead. Hands clasped on the edge of her desk, his hazel eyes pled with her. "I'm here on behalf of Tiny. I'm pretty sure he's going to need a lawyer. Is your father close to resuming his practice?"

Emily clenched her fist under the desk. *You, too, Terrence?* "Don't you think I can help him?"

Shock widened Terrence's eyes. "It ... it's not that. It's ... Well, your father's had more experience." He hesitated, then his eyes softened. "I know what you've faced, I know how people have talked about you—about you being a lawyer. I don't know if the town is ready to have a woman lawyer in the court room."

She sighed and gazed out the office window, the anger draining away. "My father and I have had the same conversation. We've been waiting for the right case."

"Is a murder trial the right case?"

"I don't think that's what we had in mind, but his accident may change our plans. Doc says it may be another month, at least, before he can come back to the office. Doc hasn't said anything about him being in the court room." She started to say more and checked herself. The fewer people who knew about her father's communication problem the better. It would come out soon enough.

She folded her hands on the law book. "Let me ask you this. Do you think Tiny's innocent?"

"Yes, I do. I know he has a hot temper, but I can't see him killing someone, no matter what they did."

Emily nodded. "I'll talk with my father at dinner. If he says it's all right, I'll talk with Tiny this afternoon."

Terrence's grin was so wide it threatened to disappear behind his ears. He stood and extended his hand. "Thanks, Emily. I appreciate it. Can you let me know what you decide?"

She shook his hand. Why did the warmth of his hand stir her so? "Yes, I'll stop by the bank later today."

Chapter 16

Even nearly four weeks after her father's accident, the dining room table still looked strange to Emily. Place settings for two replaced the usual clutter of books and papers only George understood. A platter of ham, bowls of potatoes and carrots, and a basket of sliced sourdough bread restored the dark oak furniture to its intended purpose. Before the accident, the table had served as the home office while Emily and her father took their meals at a small table in the kitchen.

Mrs. Dobbins declared their eating habits unacceptable the first day she came to help take care of George. She cleared the lawyer paraphernalia into neat stacks in the living room, opened the curtains and windows to let sunshine and fresh air drive out the sweet, musty smell of old books. By the end of her first day, the windows were washed, the heavy drapes replaced with linen curtains billowing in the breeze. The oak table, chairs, hutch, and sideboard gleamed with fresh polish, and the hardwood floor sparkled. Of course, George Peyton groused he couldn't find anything but didn't appear to be looking too hard.

He pounced like a fox on a chicken as soon as Emily walked in the door. "Well, what was all that—that—"

He slapped his hand on the arm of his wheelchair—"commotion?" The word came out in a breathy explosion as if forced from his brain by a strong wind. "Things happen and nobody thinks to come—" he twisted his head from side to side—"tell me."

"You don't need any more excitement in your life." She bent and kissed him on the cheek.

"Ahhh." He waved his good hand. "That's just what I need to break the boredom."

"Good. You were able to say a whole sentence without any problem. Doc's right. Time and rest will bring you back to normal." *So how do I talk about Tiny needing a lawyer?*

George drummed his fingers on the table while Emily cut his food. "Feel—baby, people cutting—food."

"You want to eat oatmeal all the time?"

He shuddered.

"Then enjoy people waiting on you. It won't last much longer."

"Lasted—too long."

Emily served herself, using the task to keep her face averted, hiding her concern. Sometimes, the littlest word stumped him. Other times, long sentences left him clenching a fist. If only there was a pattern, maybe Doc could figure something out, some treatment to get his brain working normally again. She blinked back tears before they could seep out.

He tapped his fork on the edge of his plate. At least control of his hand was almost back to normal. "Commotion?"

She sighed and told him about the shooting and robbery, and her conversation with Terrence. He pushed a piece of meat around his plate, lips thin, brow furrowed.

"Too soon."

"What do you mean?"

"You. Trial. Too soon."

"You don't think I can do it?"

He shook his head. "Not yet."

Her fingers tightened on her knife. She cut a bite of meat with such force, the knife slid, knocking food onto the table. She placed her utensils precisely next to her plate. She spoke through clenched teeth. "When?"

He reached for her, and she pulled away. He leaned back. "Not a murder trial."

"Why?"

George pivoted his wheelchair from the table and guided it quickly into his bedroom. Emily clamped her mouth shut, keeping the word "coward" from leaving her lips.

A few minutes later, George reappeared, a leather journal in his lap. He handed it to her, pointing at a marker ribbon that dangled from the bottom. She opened the journal. After half a page, she stopped reading.

"This was your first criminal trial?"

He nodded and pointed at the page.

Her eyes scanned the precise handwriting, drinking in each word of her father's early life, a life she knew little about. The entry ended in mid-sentence. She turned the page. A different entry began on the next page. She frowned at her father. "What happened?"

"I ... He was hung."

"Was he guilty?"

"Didn't matter. Didn't have—chance." He sipped his coffee. "Didn't go—court—six months." He stopped, face contorted as he fought for words. "No—criminal—three years."

"And you don't want me to experience losing?"

"Not when a man—die." He reached again. This time she let his hand rest on hers. "Too much guilt. Could—destroy you—confidence."

Emily stood, walked to the window, arms folded across her chest. In the side yard was her father's rose garden, one of his escapes from the office and the clients. *And me?* Would he be able to tend it this year? She faced him. His head down, he pushed the same piece of meat around his plate.

"You don't think I can handle it?"

He closed his eyes and let the fork clatter to the plate. His fingers crushed his napkin in his fist. "Don't want—have to."

"You can't protect me forever." Anger pounded behind her eyes, her neck muscles tensed. "I'm not perfect. I'm going to make mistakes. Why won't you let me?"

"Not—man could die."

She bit her lower lip and turned back to the window. Minutes passed. Her heart and her brain needed to slow down before she dared speak. "Don't let your emotions rule when you're in an argument," this man she loved said many times. "You'll lose every time."

"Em—?"

Her shoulders tightened. He called again. She turned. Eyes yearning, he gestured to her chair. "Please."

She plopped in her chair, arms still folded.

"You don't—pout well."

She waited while he struggled for words.

"Look like—rabbit caught in—fence."

A smile tugged at her lips, broke through her efforts to stop it.

He rested his chin in his hand. "Dilemma. Ti—Tiny needs a lawyer. We might be it."

She didn't dare open her mouth.

"I want you to talk to Ma—marshal—Tiny. Get all—infor—mation you can. Maybe we can ask Wy—Stoddard to come down from Dodge." He held up his palm when she opened her mouth. "To help. If we de—take case."

"You mean represent Tiny in court?"

George glowered, hazel eyes bright and piercing. "I mean to help." He pointed at his head. "We—can't do it alone."

This time, she let the smile out. "All right. I'll go talk to the marshal now." She hugged her father. "I told Terrence I'd let him know what we decided. What do you want me to tell him?"

"Nothing. See what you find out."

Chapter 17

The town seemed off kilter as Emily walked to the jail. People gathered on the dusty streets or boardwalks in groups of two or three, never more than four, discussing the morning's events. Gone was the usual traffic in and out of stores or along the street. Her gaze was drawn to the dark splotch in the dirt where the dead man had lain. She closed her eyes. Such a waste.

"Miss Emily, I expected we'd see you sometime today." The marshal greeted her with a smile as he arranged a chair at his desk. "Coffee?"

"No, thank you. My father and I have been asked to look into representing Mr. Waters. That is, if you're going to charge him."

Dobbins nodded. "Already have. Murder and robbery. Quick's sending a telegraph to the circuit judge to see how soon he can get here."

"May I ask the basis for the charges?"

The marshal smirked as he ticked off his points on his fingers. "He was standing over the body. His gun was smoking. He was holding a saddlebag with the money. Twern't no sign of the fellers he mentioned." He held up his thumb last. "And he's been spouting off for weeks about how desperate he is for money to buy a ranch and marry that … saloon girl."

A memory niggled in the back of her mind, something she overheard Terrence say. "Weren't there two saddlebags?"

"Yep. I figure Tiny had a partner who ran off with the other bag."

"I see. Did Deputy Quick find any sign of him?"

"Nope. Varmint got clean away."

"Would it be possible to talk with Tiny?" *Father and I may need to think a little more before taking this on.*

Dim light filtering through the barred windows cast shadows across the cells. Emily's nose crinkled at the aroma of human sweat and chamber pots layered under applications of lye soap. Marshal Dobbins followed Emily into the area carrying a hardwood chair for her to use.

She gestured toward a lantern hanging from a beam in the ceiling. "Can you light that for me, please?"

Before Dobbins could answer, Deputy Quick scampered back to the office. "I'll get it fer ya, Miss Emily. Let me get a lucifer."

After lighting the lantern, Quick held the chair while Emily sat. "There ya go, Miss Emily."

"Thank you, Deputy." Emily hid a smile at the grin of the eager young man whose ears stuck out like paddle wheels on a riverboat.

Quick reached to tip the hat he wasn't wearing, and touched a sprig of his unruly, light brown hair. "Anythin' for you, Miss Emily."

Tiny Waters sat on his cot, elbows on the knees of his long, gangly legs. His thin, tanned hands dangled. He frowned at her.

Emily sensed a presence behind her. Marshal Dobbins leaned against the door frame, rolling a cigarette. His stocky build had softened over the years, and his paunch indicated too much time behind the desk.

"Marshal, I'd like to talk to my client in private."

"Client?" Tiny's head jerked up. "Who says? I don't want no—"

"Quiet, Waters." Dobbins snapped like a dog protecting his meal.

Tiny's eyes narrowed at the marshal's clipped words.

Dobbins finished building his cigarette. "It don't feel right, Miss. Leavin' you alone back here with a killer."

"He's not a killer until a jury says so." Emily scooted the chair against the brick wall opposite the cell. "Is this far enough away?"

The marshal scratched a match on the door frame and cupped it in his hand as he lit his cigarette. He spoke through a cloud of pungent smoke. "Still don't seem right, the two of you back here alone."

Emily stroked her forehead. "Nothing will happen, Marshal. Or are you afraid I'll slip a weapon to Mr. Waters? Give him a chance to escape? Do you want to search me? Or, perhaps have your wife come in and give me a really close inspection?" She enjoyed the blush that reddened his cheeks and tinged his ears. "I am an officer of the court, Marshal, and I must be allowed to see my client in private so we can prepare his defense."

Dobbins dark eyes stared at her, his brows knit in a frown. She lifted her chin. *I will not flinch.* With a sigh and a shrug, the Marshal surrendered. "All right, miss. I'll be right outside, and I'll hold you responsible if anything untoward happens."

"I understand." She waited for the Marshal to close the door behind him and turned to her client. "Now, Mr. Waters."

Tiny was at the cell door in one stride. "What are you doin' here? Where's your Pa? I don't want no female lawyer. It ain't fittin'."

Another one. Emily drew her lips together and studied the man. Tall and lean, shaggy black hair, bushy mustache which he now stroked like a cat that needed soothing.

"My father is only partially recovered from a recent accident and is unable to take on full responsibility. However, he will assist me every step of the way."

Waters' chin drooped to his chest, and he shook his head.

Emily sat up straighter, interlaced her fingers in her lap. "Mr. Waters ... Tiny. You need to know I'm here as a favor to Terrence. He asked me to talk with you. Frankly, my father and I have not decided whether we will take your case. I'm here to talk with you, to hear your side. Then my father and I will discuss it and make a decision."

"And what if I don't want you anyways?"

"There are other attorneys in town. You can even try to get someone from Dodge City or Topeka."

He pushed his hand through his hair. "How much is this going to cost me?"

"How much is your life worth?" She waited as Tiny seemed to chew on her words, his eyes darting.

He rubbed his chin. "Well, when you put it that way ..."

"My father will discuss our fee once the decision about representation is made."

Tiny plopped onto his cot. "Terrence speaks right highly of you. And your Pa. I reckon it won't hurt none to talk a bit. What do you want to know?"

"Tell me what happened."

He puffed out an explosion of air and crossed his arms. "I was takin' a short cut from the livery and turned up the alley beside the bank. Just before the alley meets the street, these two cowboys had their guns on that feller, askin' for his saddlebags. He refused and went for his gun. They shot him, grabbed the bags, and ran down the alley toward me."

He gazed out the window as if seeking answers to unasked questions in the pale sunlight. "The first one barreled right inta me, and we both went down. The other one jumped over us like a mustang over a fence and kept runnin'. I grabbed the saddlebags, and we kept pullin' back and forth. He shoved me, but I held tight, yankin' the bags from him. He made like he was gonna shoot me, but I knocked his arm away. The other one came back with their horses and they both rode off. I got off a shot but missed." He shook his head. "Don't know how that happened. Then I went to see how that other feller was doing, and the marshal came, and here I am."

Emily nodded. "Did you recognize either of the cowboys?"

Tiny seemed to relax and rested his eyes on her. "Nah. They had bandanas over their faces."

"When the marshal got there, was Mr. Phillips still alive?"

"I don't think so. He took a bullet in the stomach and one in the chest. Twern't breathing that I could see."

"So, you didn't hear him say anything?"

"Nope. I was too busy looking at the big Colt the marshal was pointin' at me and not wantin' to give him any reason to use it. His finger's gotten a might shaky the last couple a years."

"Did you see anyone else? Any of the townspeople? Other cowboys?"

"No, ma'am. 'Course I was kinda busy."

Emily liked his smile, the way his face softened and his dark eyes glittered.

"You told the marshal about the other two men?"

Tiny nodded.

"What did he do?"

He gestured with his chin. "He sent the deputy down the alley to look. Quick came back and said he didn't see anyone, and the ground was too chewed up to pick out any tracks."

"How long was he gone?"

Tiny frowned. "Uhm ... two minutes maybe. No more than three."

Emily studied a cloud drifting by the window. *What else? Am I missing anything? Oh, Father, if only you were here.* Eyes still on the small patch of sky, she said, "Anything else?"

"Not that I can think of."

She stood, smoothed her dress. "All right, Tiny. I'll speak with my father."

"You gonna take my case?"

"I don't know. Do you want me to?"

He scuffed his boot on the floor. "Rather have a man. But if there ain't one available, I guess you'll do."

"Thanks for the vote of confidence."

Chapter 18

On the boardwalk, humidity pressed down on Emily, and sweat beaded on her forehead. Dark gray clouds churned and roiled in the western sky, much as her mind and heart did now. Only the cell bars had prevented her from slapping Waters. His life's on the line, and he's worried about a woman attorney. *Maybe I'll just tell Father to forget it. Don't see how we can win anyway.*

Three strides past the bank doors, she remembered she'd told Terrence she'd see him after she met with Tiny. Terrence approached from his desk as soon as she set foot in the bank, his smile warm, his eyes asking questions.

"Emily." He held the swinging gate open. "Come in. Thank you for coming by."

He held the chair for her then walked to his side of the desk and settled into his own chair. "How did it go with Tiny?"

Emily touched two fingers to her forehead. "Not well. He doesn't like female lawyers."

"Oh. You'll be presenting his case?"

Anger flashed at the memory of Tiny's attitude and quickly subsided under Terrence's smile. "Yes. Father can't do court room work yet, so it'll be me. If we take the case."

"If? Why wouldn't you take the case?"

She leveled her gaze at him. "Representing someone who doesn't think I'm qualified, simply because I'm a woman, is difficult." She cleared her throat, surprised at the sharp anger in her words. "Besides, I still need to discuss the case with my father. He may decide not to take it anyway."

Terrence shook his head. "Tiny's like a brother to me, but he can be the stubbornest man on earth sometimes. And not too diplomatic, shall we say, about expressing himself."

"May I ask you some questions about him?"

"Sure. Would you like some coffee?"

"That would be very nice."

Coffee served, Terrence settled back in his chair, hands clasped at his waist.

Emily sipped the dark brew. "Tell me about Tiny."

Terrence stroked his chin, staring at some spot over Emily's left shoulder. "He's a good man. Works hard. Doesn't go to church as much as he should, but he's God-fearing. Dotes on Charlotte something awful."

"Have they set a date?"

"Not yet. Tiny wants to buy a ranch so they'll have their own place."

Emily nodded. "How close is he?"

Terrence shook his head. "Not as close as he wants to be. Figures on at least another year. He doesn't want to wait that long. Hates Charlotte working in the saloon. Wants to get her out of there as soon as he can."

"Does the marshal know this?"

"Anybody who's around Tiny more than ten minutes knows it."

Emily squashed the cuss words on the edge of her brain, not wanting to shock Terrence. Her mind blanked. *Why should I care what Terrence thinks? I don't need to impress him. He's courtin' Miss Precious Prissy Priscilla.* She shook her head. *Focus.*

"Anything else?"

"Yeah, he's the best pitcher on the town ball team."

Emily smiled and then frowned as a thought niggled. "Didn't he get in a fight with one of the players from the Wichita team a few weeks back?"

Terrence nodded. "That he did. He thought the pitcher threw a little too close to his head, and Tiny took exception to it."

"Does he get into a lot of fights?"

Terrence shrugged. "His share, especially if you provoke him, and sometimes, it doesn't take much to rile him."

Wonderful. Wait until father hears all this.

Lightning crackled, white light shattering into the room, forcing Emily's eyes shut. Her lungs stopped bringing in air as her muscles knotted. Thunder exploded over their heads. She touched her forehead and forced herself to breathe. She opened her eyes to find Terrence stretching his hand across his desk toward her. She smiled and folded her hands in her lap.

Joseph Warner burst from his office, face pale, hands quivering. He grasped the edge of Terrence's desk, knuckles white against the dark wood. "Who fired a cannon?"

Terrence placed his hand on Warner's arm. "No one, sir. It's just thunder."

Warner shook himself erect, adjusted his custom-fitted suit and grinned, although there was no humor in it. He wiped his face with a silk handkerchief. "Felt like we were at Gettysburg again."

Turning to go to his office, he stopped, bowed slightly. "Miss Peyton. It's a pleasure to see you. Still helping your father keep his paperwork in order?"

Emily smiled as, behind his employer's back, Terrence winced. "I'll tell him you were asking for him, Mr. Warner."

"Yes. Yes. Do that. Tell him we miss him at our weekly poker games."

"I will, sir."

When the office door closed, Terrence exhaled. "I thought you were going to punch him."

"I wanted to until I saw your face." Emily touched Terrence's hand and withdrew immediately. *What do you think you're doing, Emily?* "I'll let you know tomorrow about my father's decision about Tiny."

"Do you have any say in it?"

"I'd say no if it was up to me. There's too much evidence against him. Besides, he needs to respect his lawyer."

Chapter 19

George Peyton hunkered over his stew, letting the steamy aroma float into his nostrils while he savored the tender beef and vegetables. Caroline Everett's culinary skills might lead a man to consider wooing her from her husband. *Can't do that to my best friend. But still ...*

A flash of lightning and crack of thunder jolted him as the wind-driven rain pounded the windows, rattling like stones in a metal pail. The fire sizzled as raindrops plopped onto the burning logs in the dining room fireplace. Across from him, Emily's face pinched in a deep frown, and her eyes darted to the ceiling.

"Still don't like—" *Where's the word?*—"thunderstorms?"

Her head swiveled from one window to the next as if assessing the strength of the glass. "They bring tornadoes."

"At least you don't go—diving under the bed or—or—scream like a banshee—anymore." The last word exploded out of his mouth as the word finally made it from his brain to his lips.

She chuckled. "Haven't done that since ..."

The words hung unspoken between them, a cloud darker than any storm, hovering over the table, over their hearts, over their lives. He toyed with his spoon, stirring his stew. Emily tore a slice of bread in half and dunked a chunk in her bowl, holding it there as broth seeped up the dough toward her fingers.

He coughed and sipped coffee. "So, finish—telling me about—Wa—Waters."

When she finished, he shook his head. "Guilty?"

"I think so. At least a lot of the evidence points that way, especially him wanting money fast."

He nodded and waved his hand, a circular motion as if trying to pull the words from his mouth. "Rights," was all he could say.

Emily rubbed her forehead with the tips of two of her fingers. "What about Mac Phillips' right to live and Annamae's right to her money?"

George clenched his fist. He'd loved these debates with Emily, the back and forth, watching her eyes as new information clicked. He enjoyed the same sensation when she showed him something new. Now, he couldn't say a sentence without struggling. Words that were crystal clear in his mind, wandered into oblivion on their way to his mouth. Now a man's life depended on his lawyer saying the right words.

"Do you think he's innocent?" Her pale blue eyes, so like her mother's, sparked a surge of still-sharp hurt.

He took a steadying breath and, fist still clenched, spoke slowly, letting each word form. "Doesn't matter what ... think. Jury decides." Another breath. "... Deserves our best."

Emily pouted her deep-thinking pout, the one telling him she was digesting his words. Only now she had to read into them the words he hadn't been able to say.

Wind slapped rain against the windows and scooted down the chimney and into the room. A chill danced down his spine and stung his legs. He slurped stew. Cold. Touched his coffee cup. Cold as well. Emily refilled their cups and spooned sugar into hers. She stirred so long, he'd thought she'd wear through the bottom. He tapped his spoon on the table.

She jumped, smiled. "You think we should represent him?"

"Offer." Breath. Wait. "His choice."

One side of her mouth ticked up in the impish grin that always won his heart when she was little. "You think I can represent him?"

He hesitated. *Is she ready for court? For a murder trial? I want her to have more time. I want her to watch me.*

Her eyes narrowed and flashed, her chin lifted. "I guess that answers that question. Will I ever be ready in your eyes?" She made as if to stand.

"Wait."

She settled back in her chair, arms crossed, eyes sharp and penetrating. "Well?"

"With help."

Her eyes widened. "Why do you think I need help?"

"Woman. Town not ready for it." His heart ached. He could have, should have, said it better.

"Who'll give me this help?" Sarcasm dripped like candle wax. "You?"

He shook his head. "No. Wyatt St-Stoddard. To assist. Guide."

"Will he do it?"

"No an-answer yet."

Chapter 20

Terrence hummed one of his mother's tunes from the Old Country as he left Crenshaw's Boarding House, stomach filled with oatmeal and bacon. His mind enjoyed the memory of a pleasant evening with Priscilla that even the rain couldn't dampen.

The warm sun and blue sky contrasted with the multi-hued morass churned in the streets by the previous evening's storms, worsened by the steady horse and wagon traffic. Fortunately, he'd only have to cross side streets on his way to the bank, not the main thoroughfare. A loud slurp and wet plop resounded as a horse pulled its leg out of ankle-deep muck. Man could lose a boot in that slop.

He checked his pocket watch as he approached the marshal's office. Enough time for a few minutes with Tiny.

"Good morning, Deputy."

Matthew Quick turned from setting a battered coffee pot on the Franklin stove in the corner. "Morning, Terrence."

Terrence nodded toward the cell area. "Can I see my friend?"

"Sure. In fact, while yer visitin', I'll run over t' the Randolph House and fetch his breakfast."

The cell keys hung on a peg next to the rifle rack. Very trusting of the deputy.

Tiny lay on his back, an arm across his eyes. "'Bout time you got here with my breakfast."

"Sorry to disappoint you, friend. No food. Quick's gone to fetch it."

Tiny came to the bars, and the two shook hands. An uneven beard stubbled Tiny's face, like a buffalo shedding in patches. Large, dark gray pouches sagged under his eyes. His jaw hung slack, and he needed a bath.

"Heard you had a visitor yesterday."

Tiny frowned. "Oh, yeah." He snorted. "That woman lawyer."

"She and her father are thinking about taking your case."

"Don't want her. Don't want no woman representin' me in court. She'll just mess it up and get me hung. D'you talk to those other lawyers?"

Terrence leaned against the bars, not sure how his friend would take the news. "Yeah. They turned you down."

"What? Why?"

"One said he had too much work. The other said he was going out of town. Both said they didn't think you could or would pay them, especially after you're convicted."

Tiny pressed his forehead into the bars. "So, they think I'm guilty too?"

"Yep. Looks like Emily Peyton is your only hope."

"What about them lawyers from Dodge or Wichita?"

"I think you'll get the same questions. Can you pay them? Are you guilty? Plus, they'll cost a whole lot more. I'll telegraph them if you want."

Tiny picked at the dirt under his thumbnail. Sighed. "Looks like I'm in for it this time."

Terrence heard the catch in his friend's voice and looked down. *How can I help him?* "Give Emily a chance. I'm sure her father's going to help her all he can."

"He's a cripple now, ain't he? How much help can he be?"

Terrence bit the inside of his cheek to keep from describing the extent of George's injuries. The man quit a chess game after three moves, confusion evident on his face. "I'm sure he'll do all he can."

As he pressed harder against the bars, Tiny's voice cracked, tears barely controlled. "What am I gonna do, Terrence? How do I get out of this?"

"Look, let Emily and her father represent you. I'll do all I can to help them."

"Will Warner let you?"

"If not, I'll quit and help them on my own time."

Tiny smiled although his eyes remained as dull as his voice. "Thanks, Terrence. I appreciate it. Sure don't feel very hopeful, though. What's gonna happen to Charlotte if I don't get outta this? She'll be in that saloon the rest of her life."

Terrence shot a quick prayer to heaven. It felt like it didn't dent the ceiling.

Chapter 21

Emily dabbed at the perspiration on her forehead when she entered the house. The warm sun was a welcome relief from the rain, but as moisture evaporated, humidity wrapped around her. *Feels as if I'm walking upstream fully clothed in water up to my neck.*

Her father wheeled in from the parlor, newspaper on his lap. She kissed his cheek and jumped back when Terrence came up behind him.

"Terrence stopped by, and I asked him to join us for dinner."

They exchanged greetings and moved into the dining room. Terrence held her chair, and lightly brushed her shoulder as she scooted in. The touch pleased her, and the pleasing puzzled her. Why these feelings of what seemed like something more than friendship? Besides, he and Priscilla belong together. She sipped the tea Mrs. Marcand had prepared and pushed the unwanted emotions to the side.

"Emily, Terrence has news."

She focused on Terrence's left ear. She didn't want to see the look in his eyes, didn't want to see what he might, or might not, be trying to tell her beyond his words. Plus, she didn't know what her own eyes might reveal. *Stop it,*

Emily Louise Peyton. You're a grown woman. You don't have time for this. Neither does Terrence. Besides, you don't even know how to flirt.

Terrence cleared his throat. "I spoke with Tiny this morning, and he's asked if you and your father will represent him."

Emily glanced at her father, who smiled and nodded.

Mrs. Marcand came from the kitchen and served platters of cold chicken and vegetables. "I thought a cool dinner was fittin' considerin' how humid it is." She sliced George's food.

"Tiny doesn't mind having a female lawyer?" Emily asked.

Terrence blushed. "His words were, 'better than having no lawyer at all.'"

She poked at her food. "That's heartwarming."

"Emily." Her father's eyes spoke even more sternly than his voice sounded.

"I apologize. Saving his neck will be hard when he thinks you're only one step above a rock."

George shook his head. "Like—doesn't come—into it. On either—side."

"I know. I know." She puffed an exasperated sigh.

"Terrence is—go—going to help us."

A catch in George's breath brought her to his side. Sweat sheened his forehead. "You need Doc?"

"Water." George's voice scratched in his throat, a faint shadow of his baritone. Terrence bolted for the kitchen and returned with water, Mrs. Marcand came right behind him, wringing her hands in a towel.

George sipped the water and coughed. Emily felt his pulse. Racing.

"All right, Father. You need to go to bed and rest. You're trying to do too much."

George shook his head.

"Don't argue. I'm going to have Doc look at you."

"Finish this." His finger tapped the table. He drained the water and slammed the glass down. "Need to—talk—about Tiny."

"Now?" Emily planted her hands on her hips. "Can't it wait? What's there to talk about, anyway?"

He motioned the two of them back to their chairs. "No defense."

"What does that mean?" Terrence asked.

Emily folded her hands on the table. "He means Tiny doesn't have anything to support his story. No witnesses. No sign of the robbers he says he saw. So—his word against the marshal's."

George motioned with his hand, a circular motion for her to tell more.

"Tiny's motive is all over town. Everyone knows he's desperate for money to buy a ranch and marry Charlotte. The marshal will make sure the jury knows it. There's also Tiny's reputation for being quick-tempered."

Terrence slumped in the chair his hands splayed on the table. "What can we do?"

He looked from George to Emily and back again. His pleading eyes tore at her. She wanted to cuddle him. *Where did that come from? Be sensible, girl.*

George held up one finger. "Find witnesses." He held up a second finger. "Find real killers."

Chapter 22

The next evening, chandeliers overhead cast a muted glow over the wainscoted walls and pale blue flowered wallpaper of the Randolph House dining room. Terrence enjoyed the ambience of the white linens, fine china, and attentive staff—a long way from the hovel his mother described as her home in Ireland or from three families crammed into the sixth floor Boston tenement before his parents moved west to homestead on the prairie in the 1850s.

A vision sat across from him, a vision he never expected in his life, a vision he thanked God for every day. Priscilla Montgomery buttered a slice of bread, each movement precise and delicate, a dance of slender fingers and blade. The minuscule bite she took left the bread almost unmarked. Did she chew or did it dissolve in her mouth?

"You're staring, Terrence." Her green eyes smiled under gently arched brows. He admired her small mouth and full lips, her straight nose. All perfectly proportioned in her oval face framed by thick auburn hair that tumbled in gentle curls.

"Yes, I am. My eyes feel like singing when they look at you."

She lowered her eyelids, raised them like the sun rising. "You're very kind, but I think that Irish gift of the blarney runs away with you sometimes."

"'Tis true, lassie. 'Tis true." He tried to mimic his Uncle Jack's brogue. "There's always a wee bit o' truth in the blarney. Otherwise, why tell it?"

She laughed, fingers covering her mouth. She sliced a small piece of chicken and slipped it into her mouth. Meals with Priscilla could be endurance contests at times, although she often didn't finish, stopping when he had cleaned his plate. Courting her taught him to slow down and enjoy the act and art of eating as more than some routine activity to get food into his stomach.

She laid her utensils on the table, laced her fingers together and used them as a platform for her chin. "So, tell me about your day. What's new at the bank?"

"Nothing, really." He shrugged. "Getting ready for more land sales as the railroad expands. Mr. Warner's hired another guard."

"After what happened to that poor man who was killed, well he should. Imagine, killing someone just so you can get money to marry some cheap saloon girl."

Terrence clenched his teeth, willed himself to relax, keep his voice calm. "Tiny hasn't been convicted."

Her eyes widened as she reached across the table to cover his hand with hers. The soft warmth eased his anger as he remembered the even softer warmth of her lips. "I'm sorry. I forgot for a moment Tiny is your friend."

He squeezed her fingers lightly before she slid her hand back, glancing around the room.

"That's all right," he said. "I'm grateful he has a lawyer to help him now."

"Who?"

"Emily Peyton and her father."

A deep frown crowded Priscilla's face, and she pursed her lips.

"Something wrong?"

Her eyes were hard now. "Doesn't seem right, her being a lawyer. Shouldn't she be getting married and raising a family? Lawyering is man's work."

Terrence's mind went blank, and he fumbled for something to say. He finally blurted, "Shouldn't she be able to do whatever she wants?" The flash in Priscilla's eyes and the red tint on her cheeks made him wish he hadn't spoken.

"That's fine if she wants to be a teacher or a dressmaker, something women are supposed to do. But not a lawyer." She attacked her chicken as if it were alive and going for her throat. "I suppose you're going to help her."

"Tiny's my friend, and I promised to help him so, yes, I'll help her if she needs help."

"Oh, I'm sure she'll need it. I'm sure she'll be asking you for all kinds of help."

He clenched his fists under the table, trying to squash the sudden flare surging in his heart. "She's not that kind of person."

"Oh, you've been around her enough to know what kind of person she is? She doesn't even go to church." Priscilla's face grew redder, her voice louder. Heads turned toward them. She lifted her hand to shield her face. "See what you're doing? You're embarrassing me."

Terrence's head seem to spin around at least once before settling back to its proper place. Thoughts bounced around his brain, and he couldn't pull them into coherent words. He clamped his mouth tight. *I'm embarrassing her? Will I ever understand women?*

Priscilla, one hand over her heart, took a deep breath. "If you really care about me, you won't have anything to do with that Emily Peyton."

His hands flopped on the table. "I don't understand. She's—"

"She's trouble. Trust me. That's all you need to know. Now, please take me home."

The buggy ride to the Montgomery ranch began in silence. Terrence welcomed the distraction of the reins in his hands while his mind battled to make sense of what happened, to find words to bridge the strain. They were halfway to her home when he spoke. "I'm sorry for upsetting you at dinner."

"I forgive you." She slipped her arm under his, rested her head on his shoulder.

Still not sure what I did but best let that sleeping dog lie. "Tiny is my friend, my best friend, and I still want to help him. I *must* help him. He'd do the same for me."

"But he killed that man."

"I don't think he did. Tiny's not a killer."

She straightened, leaving their arms entwined. "I know you need to help him. I think you're on a fool's errand, and you'll be hurt in the end. But be careful around Emily Peyton. She'll use you—she'll use any man—to get what she wants."

Not going down that road again.

As they turned in at the entrance of her ranch, Priscilla straightened and said, "I almost forgot. Daddy wants to know if you know of anybody looking for work. He has to replace Tiny."

"Tell him I'll keep a lookout."

"Just don't send the two who Mr. Benton fired for stealing his cattle. Daddy won't want anything to do with them."

"Mr. Benton fired two cowboys? I didn't hear anything about that."

She arched her eyebrow. "Probably because you've been spending all your time with Emily Peyton."

Nope, the bridge is out on that road. "When did he fire them?"

She sighed as if already bored with the subject. "A couple of days before Tiny shot that man, I think." She yawned and nestled closer, head on his shoulder.

At her door, Priscilla's lips on his, the warmth of her pressing against him, the tight urgency of her embrace drove thoughts of Tiny and lawyers and cowhands far from his mind.

Chapter 23

"Ouch!" The nick of the razor stung, and bright red blood beaded on Terrence's cheek. "Pay attention before you slice your ear off," he scolded himself and pressed a towel against his skin, then pressed it tighter. He scowled in the dresser mirror, annoyed at letting himself be distracted. Even now, his mind drifted from thoughts of Tiny to visions of Priscilla. Emily appeared, so real he thought he saw her reflection in the looking glass, her impish smile, and blue eyes full of the mischief he saw the first time he met her at the Fourth of July dance two years ago.

She'd welcomed him as a stranger in town, and he enjoyed the cups of punch and slices of cake they shared. At that first meeting, he marveled at her intelligence and her determination to succeed as a lawyer. He had no doubt she'd do it. She declined his request for a dance, but a bond formed.

The friendship cemented over the next few months as he spent time in her office discussing bank business and their shared enjoyment of baseball—of all things. Priscilla thought the game was silly and beneath a gentleman. Emily attended the Sunday afternoon baseball games in the field behind the church, cheering loudly and berating the umpire without mercy. She joined in the victory celebrations and commiserated with the team after every defeat.

He smiled at the memory of her picking up a wayward ball and throwing with a force and accuracy that more than matched several of the players. He had wanted to see what she could do with a bat, but Tiny stopped him with a whispered, "What if she hits better than us too? Then she'll want to play."

Yes, a friend. A good friend. Comfortable to be with. A mind that grasped the complexities of banking and investing as easily as it assessed the quality of a horse.

Now, she faced the toughest challenge of her life. Proving herself as a lawyer while defending a murder charge with her father's limited availability to help. *Oh, yes, I'll help her because of Tiny, but also because I value her friendship. Besides, I admire her spunk.*

Priscilla's words about Emily replayed. The bleeding staunched, he shook his head and resumed shaving. He could think of nothing to spark Priscilla's harsh words. Maybe she's jealous. Nothing to worry about there. Emily was attractive, yes, but not as attractive as Priscilla, not as soft or feminine in demeanor. Besides, she'd clearly indicated she had no inclination for a romantic relationship with anyone. From talk at the ball field and over a beer after work, most of the men in town wanted nothing to do with her. *None of them are in your class, Emily. God will bring the right man to you at the right time.*

Shave done, he cleaned and dried his razor, folding the blade into the bone handle. He laid it in its designated place, aligned with his hairbrush on the small towel next to the wash basin.

His pocket watch, Uncle Jack's gift when Terrence graduated from college, told him he had a few minutes before Mrs. Crenshaw bellowed for breakfast. He sat in the faded leather chair his landlady had provided and opened his Bible. The book fell open to the seventh chapter of Matthew. He skimmed the chapter a couple of times, letting the words slide into his mind and his spirit. Then his eyes riveted on verse eight.

"For everyone that asketh, receiveth; and he that seeketh, findeth; and to him that knocketh it shall be opened."

"Lord," he prayed into the empty room. "I'm asking you to show us the next steps, show what we can't see now, to help Tiny."

He waited with the anticipation of a colt ready to be released into a pasture. No revelation, but peace came, and he knew it was time to trust God. If only he could get Emily to see that. Why did she reject God with such finality? "Lord, help me to help her."

"Come and get it." Mrs. Crenshaw's voice boomed up the stairwell, echoing off the walls. Terrence glanced at the ceiling, expecting to see plaster shake loose and drift like snowflakes onto the furniture.

Soon the clomping boots of the other boarders passed his door, descending the stairs as if gold nuggets awaited them in the dining room. In a way they did, in the form of the landlady's culinary skills that kept her house full. He licked his lips in anticipation and slipped on his suit coat before leaving to join the others, the Scripture in his thoughts. *So, Lord, I pray we receive and find open doors soon.*

Chapter 24

Terrence turned up his collar as the cooler-than-normal breeze scudded clouds across slim patches of blue sky. Would spring ever actually stay more than a day or two? The familiar itch to grasp a baseball and squeeze a bat tingled. Maybe the weather would warm for a game on Sunday.

Mr. Warner stood in his office doorway, impeccable in his pearl-gray suit and black-and-white checkered vest. His hair glistened with pomade. He looked every inch the president of a bank, a wise investor, a town-builder. *Someday, that will be me.*

Warner hooked two fingers in a come here motion. In his office, the president sat behind his desk and gestured for Terrence to sit in one of the studded leather chairs facing him. Tapping a thick envelope on the desk, Warner said, "Terrence, I have an assignment for you."

"Yes, sir."

He held the envelope like a winning poker hand. "I need to get these documents to Walter Grant as soon as possible. They're valuable, so I don't want to trust them to just anybody, and there won't be a stage out that way until late tomorrow or the morning after. This can't wait."

"I see, sir." *Why not send Harry Bannister?*

As if reading his mind, Warner said, "Normally, I'd send Harry, but you're the best rider I know."

"Thank you, Mr. Warner." Harry on horseback was an adventure. He'd seen the man grab the saddle horn with both hands with his face as white as new snow if his horse went any faster than a walk. "I'll leave right away."

Thirty minutes later, Terrence returned to the bank, clad in denim, an open-necked shirt, boots, Stetson, and a wool-lined leather jacket to ward off the chill. His horse, a short, muscular paint named Spot, stood at the rail, flicking his tail as if impatient. He would cover the thirty-five miles to Walter Grant's ranch with a sure-footed instinct to avoid holes and ruts that might trip up another mount.

Warner's Meerschaum puffed a blue cloud toward the ceiling as he handed Terrence the envelope. "Be very careful."

Terrence resisted the urge to salute. "I will, sir."

"No sidearm?"

"Didn't think it was necessary."

"I'd feel a lot more comfortable if you had one." He took a holstered Colt from his desk. "Take mine."

Will it fit? You've got a lot more waist than I do. It fit, but it meant using the last available hole for the buckle. Even then it hung lower than Terrence liked. Warner took a Winchester from the gun rack built into the wall. "This too."

What's in this envelope? "Should I anticipate trouble, sir?"

Warner's eyes shifted to a spot to the right of Terrence's head. "No. I don't expect any, but you can never be too sure."

By mid-afternoon, Terrence berated himself for not thinking to ask Mrs. Crenshaw to pack some food. Spot continued his easy lope under gray skies. Occasional shafts of sunlight pierced the clouds like a lighthouse beam, sparkling on the greening grass and first wildflowers as the prairie gave a feeble welcome to spring.

His thoughts turned to Priscilla, and hunger for food surrendered to desire for her. The question he'd wrestled with for the last several weeks swirled. When should he ask Mr. Montgomery for his daughter's hand? He had no doubts Priscilla loved him and wanted to marry him. She'd all but said so with her words and lips, and her melding into his embrace.

After Tiny's trial. Let things calm down. Hesitation lurched, and Emily's face popped into view. How can I think of proposing marriage when my best friend may be hanged?

Spot leapt a tiny brook, catching him off guard. Didn't see that coming. Too much woolgathering. Buildings loomed ahead, a two-story frame house, a barn with a forge and anvil in front and a large corral to one side. The paint increased his speed to not quite a full gallop.

"Must be smelling water and oats." The horse went faster. Terrence's own hunger surged. "Come on, boy. Let's get some dinner."

A few minutes later, Terrence reined the horse to a gentle walk as they approached the stagecoach way station. Horses in the corral crowded against the fence, eyeing Spot, nostrils flaring, ears back. A few neighed. Spot ignored them and walked to the hitching post in front of the house.

"Howdy." The man in the doorway was bigger than Tiny, his arms straining the sleeves of his shirt. Thick black hair and beard left only a small patch of flesh for his face. Eyes, glittering like a cat's at night, peered from caves deep under thick brows.

Terrence dismounted and extended his hand. "Name's McCarthy. Terrence McCarthy."

The man's firm grip promised a bone-crushing strength. "Linus Abbott. Manager of this here station along with my missus, Eloise."

"Abbot? You any kin to Jed Abbott?"

Linus's grin broke through his beard as it parted like the Red Sea, and his eyes crinkled to slits. "Jed's my cousin. Ain't seen him since Christmas a year ago. How is the old dog? Any new grandkids?"

They chatted for several minutes about Jed and his family and Terrence's contact with him through the bank. A voice sang out from inside the house. "Linus Abbott. Are you gonna keep that poor man standing on the porch all day? Fetch him in here and let's get some food into him. And tend to his horse too."

The voice reminded Terrence of a skylark's song and belonged to a woman about half Linus's height and width, even with the protruding belly signifying a child would soon be here. Flaming red hair crowned a freckled face—she had laughing eyes and a smile that beat back the gloomy day. She pointed to a table situated in front of the fireplace. "Sit while I fetch you some venison and potatoes and cornbread."

Linus came in from supplying Spot with oats and water. Before he could sit, Eloise said, "Linus, offer the man something to drink. Honestly, where are your manners today?"

Terrence basked in the humor of their love, their tender eyes, their light and frequent touches. *Will Priscilla and I have a love like this?* An image flitted on the edge of his mind. He reached for it and lost it like a leaf blown by the wind.

Terrence declined the whiskey Linus offered and gratefully sipped coffee while Eloise placed a platter of food in front of him. Fork-tender venison and potatoes flavored with rosemary and butter. As he chewed, Linus parked himself across the table, his own cup disappearing in his large hands.

"What's new in Abilene, other than my cousin doing that good deed for the lawyer feller?"

Terrence told him about the murder of Mac Phillips and Tiny's upcoming trial.

Linus combed his beard with his thick fingers. "Yeah, a couple of cowpokes rode through and told us about the killin'. It's a shame, a real shame." He clasped his hands around his mug of coffee. "This Tiny a friend of yours?"

Terrence nodded around a mouthful of meat.

"Makes it kind of hard if they hang him?"

Terrence shook his head, swallowed coffee. "They won't hang him. He's innocent, and he's got a good lawyer."

"Oh, yeah? Who's that?"

"Emily Peyton."

Linus's eyes shone wide with a hint of laughter ready to break forth. "If that don't beat all. A female lawyer." He turned toward his wife. "D'ya ever hear a such a thing, Eloise? A female lawyer."

Eloise filled their cups with fresh coffee. "'Bout time, if ya ask me." She playfully backhanded her husband on the arm. "What have you got against a female lawyer?"

"Ain't natural, is it? The Good Book says a wife's supposed to take care of the house and be obedient to her husband."

"I oughta pour this coffee in your lap." She set the pot on the table and faced her husband, hands on hips. Terrence turned his head to hide the grin wanting to burst out on his face.

Eloise pointed toward the bedroom, her freckles dancing as her face grew redder. "You go fetch that Good Book, Linus. And you read 'bout Queen Esther. Then come talk to me 'bout a woman's place."

She picked up the coffee pot and wiped an imaginary crumb off the table with the edge of her apron. "Would you care for some apple pie, Mr. McCarthy?" Her skylark voice was back, sweet and melodious.

"No, thank you, ma'am. I should be getting back on the trail."

"I'd like some, Eloise." Linus's voice was soft, pleading.

"Fetch it yerself, Mr. Abbott. And maybe you can fetch your own supper later too." She walked toward the kitchen area. "A woman's place indeed."

Terrence and Linus burst into laughter. Eloise turned, her face lit up by a smile that could tame a rattlesnake.

Terrence wiped his mouth and chin with his napkin. "Those cowpokes who rode through. Did you get their names?"

Linus's frown deepened. "Les see. They didn't stay long. Watered their horses. One had whiskey. The other coffee." He snapped his fingers. "They called each other Ed and Paul. No last name though. You know them?"

Ed and Paul? The Whitney brothers? Here? And they knew about the murder?

"No, but I'd like to. D'you notice which way they went?"

"South."

Chapter 25

Terrence spurred Spot, and the horse responded with a burst of speed that gobbled the miles to the Grant ranch.

Lord, hold off the rain until I can get back to town.

Emily and George needed to know the Whitney brothers were still in the area the day of the robbery. Why had the marshal said they'd left the day before? Was he confused about the dates? In the time he'd been in Abilene, Terrence had never noticed the marshal to be one who missed details.

He leaned over the horse's neck, mane flicking his face. Another hour to Grant's. Hopefully, no more than an hour there. Should be back in Abilene very early in the morning, ready to see Emily and George at dawn.

Lightning flashed near the horizon. Several seconds later, a faint rumble of thunder rolled past. He pressed his knees against Spot's sides. The animal surged forward, hooves pounding. After a few miles, Terrence eased the reins back, slowing the horse. *What am I doing?* He stroked the horse's sweaty neck. "Forgive me, boy. Not going to break you down."

After a few more miles, an arch of slim logs, weathered gray, rose on his right. An emblem of overlapping Gs hung from the center of the cross piece. The dirt road from the gate to the house cut the prairie like a string stretched straight and taut. Cattle dotted both sides, black and reddish lumps grazing, tails swatting. A bull stepped toward the road, swung his head in a looping circle and resumed grazing.

The one-story, stone structure sprawled in a wide V, with the main door at the juncture of the two wings. Gray smoke spiraled from a central chimney until the wind shredded it. A large barn, corrals, and several smaller buildings were scattered around the house.

Four cowboys stood in front of the house their attention fixed on a tall man standing on the porch. The man stopped talking as Terrence approached, and the cowboys turned. Two stepped away from the others, hands on their pistols.

What is going on? Terrence slackened the reins, keeping his hands on the saddle horn, while Spot ambled toward the house.

"Kin I help you, mister?" The man on the porch stepped to the ground. He had the swagger of a man comfortable in exercising authority. As tall as Terrence, he carried more pounds on his stocky frame. Blond hair and a mustache contrasted his deeply tanned face and dark blue eyes.

Terrence dismounted. "Mr. Grant? Walter Grant?"

"Yep."

Terrence extended his hand. "I'm Terrence McCarthy from the Abilene bank."

Grant looked at the hand being offered as if it were covered in cow droppings. He shifted his gaze to Terrence's face, eyes boring into him. "What's the name of the president of the bank?"

"Joseph Warner."

Grant nodded, worked a plug of tobacco from one cheek to the other. "What's the guard's name?"

"Harry Bannister." Spot shuffled next to him and bumped his arm. "Is there a problem here? Mr. Warner asked me to bring some papers to Mr. Grant. Just a simple delivery."

The rancher poked his hat off his forehead. "Ain't nothin' simple around here these days." He held out his hand, waggled his fingers. "Gimme the papers."

Terrence held up his hand. "Wait. How do I know you're Walter Grant?"

Grant looked like he'd been slapped. "What do you mean? Of course, I'm Wal—" He grinned. Terrence didn't.

"Come inside." He pointed at one of the cowboys. "Perkins, you come too."

Terrence followed Grant into the house. A short, wiry man—one of the cowboys who'd reached for his pistol—followed behind.

In the main room, a leather sofa and two wing chairs in the same material semicircled the fireplace. The other end of the room held a cherry dining table and chairs. The walls were whitewashed, the wood floor clean. A buffalo's head hung above the fireplace and a twelve-point deer's head from the wall over the table. A braided carpet under the table and red and blue wildflowers in a vase were the only feminine touches.

The man who claimed to be Grant rummaged in the drawers of a desk against the wall. Perkins stood behind the couch, hands at his gun belt buckle, gaze not leaving Terrence.

Grant handed Terrence a photograph and a newspaper clipping. The picture was of a Confederate officer, a colonel, if Terrence remembered the insignias from his Uncle Jack's memorabilia. Although leaner, the man in the photo had the same eyes, slender nose and determined chin as the man before him. The handwritten caption read, "Col. Walter Grant, 6th Virginia, March 1, 1865." The clipping was from the *Richmond Dispatch* and contained a story about the Battle of the Crater on July 30, 1864. The clipping related the exploits of Colonel Grant leading his troops in a "gallant repulse" of the Union attack. A woodcut of the colonel illustrated the article. Again, the resemblance left no doubt in Terrence's mind.

He returned the items and resisted the urge to salute. "Colonel Grant. I'm Terrence McCarthy from the Abilene Bank and Trust Company."

The two shook hands.

"I'm just Walter. Titles and rank don't mean anything. That's all in the past. Isn't that right, Perkins?"

Perkins nodded.

Grant held out his hand. "You have some papers for me?"

Terrence slipped the envelope from his coat pocket. Grant ripped it open and yanked the papers out, folding the creases back. He flipped through, giving each a cursory glance before going back to the first one and reading it.

He slapped his leg and waved the page at Perkins. "Good, the bank draft's approved. Fifteen thousand in credit."

He flicked to the next page and read slowly. He continued for several pages. "Good contract." He looked at Perkins again. "We own the water rights. Always have. This gives us clear title." He squinted at the bottom of the last page. "Who's this Emily Peyton?"

"She's a lawyer in town. She must have done the research and drawn up the document," Terrence said.

Grant scratched his beard and frowned. "A female lawyer?" He waved the papers at Terrence. "Are you sure this is legal? A judge isn't going to throw this out because some female wrote it?"

The memory of Emily's face when she talked about the hurt of not being accepted snapped into Terrence's mind.

He waited, fighting the urge to grab the man by his shirt and shake him until both eyes were on the same side of his nose. "Em—Miss Peyton is a licensed attorney, sir. Approved by the State of Kansas." He nodded at the documents in Grant's hand. "A judge isn't going to throw anything out."

Doubt clouded Grant's face. "You'd better be right. Otherwise, if this ends up with men getting shot or me losing land because some female messed it up, I'm holding you and your bank personally responsible."

"Mr. Grant, with all due respect, I have no idea what you're talking about."

Grant cocked his head and studied Terrence. "Warner didn't tell you?"

"No, sir. He just told me to bring the papers to you."

"We're trying to prevent a range war over water rights. These papers will help us settle the matter without any shooting. That's why it's important they be able to withstand any legal challenge."

That explains why Mr. Warner made sure I came armed. "Do you need me to take a message back to Mr. Warner?"

Grant flipped through the pages once more. "No, I don't think so."

"Then I'll take my leave now. I'm anxious to get back to town." Emily and George needed to hear about the Whitney brothers. He turned to go.

Grant clapped a hand on his shoulder. "Can't persuade you to stay for supper?"

"Thank you, sir. No."

The two walked to the door, Perkins trailing. The thunder that had grumbled throughout their conversation roared like a cannon. Lightning blinded him, the bolt touching halfway to the barn. Spot reared from the hitching post, but the reins held him in place. Frightened neighs pierced the air as the horses in the corral milled, pushing against the fence. The rain fell. A solid, wet curtain reduced the barn to a vague, shadowy box, blurred by the pouring torrents.

"You're not going anywhere in this frog-strangler, Mr. McCarthy," Grant said. "You'd drown before you got off the property. Best plan on spending the night." He spoke over his shoulder. "Perkins, bed Mr. McCarthy's paint in the main barn. Make sure he's fed and watered."

Perkins touched the brim of his hat and sprinted through the door, untied Spot from the hitching post and led him at a brisk pace to the barn. Terrence glanced skyward. Clouds rolled and darkened, titans battling. Thunder rattled and lightning casting eerie shadows followed by deepening gloom.

Emily and Tiny would have to wait a few more hours. The news about the Whitney brothers churned. The first ray of hope, the first indication that Tiny told the truth. Could they find them in time? How to even begin searching for them? South meant the Indian Territory and Texas. And that's if the brothers kept going that way. He clenched his fists.

How quickly could he get to town tomorrow? Midafternoon, if he left at dawn. Spot would be exhausted. By dusk, if he paced the mount the way he should. And if the rain stopped. *Lord, you made the sun stand still for Joshua. Please hold back the rain for Tiny. I have to get through.*

Dinner was melt-in-the-mouth steak, beans sweetened with molasses, cornbread with kernels visible, and butter-tender carrots. Terrence ate by rote and didn't appreciate any of it.

He apologized to Grant and his wife, a slim, shy Oriental woman named Lee, for not being better company. "My best friend's in big trouble, and I found some information that may help him."

Grant nodded. "Well, I hope this rain stops tonight. If it don't, there's gonna be floods between here and the stage station. Road'll get washed out." He sipped his coffee. "If that happens, it'll be two, maybe three, days before you can get out."

Chapter 26

After shaking rainwater from her umbrella, Emily leaned it against the wall near the stove in the marshal's office. "Good afternoon, Marshal. I'd like to see my client."

Dobbins' feet rested on his desk, a mug of coffee in his hand. He plunked his feet to the floor, boots sounding like bass drums. "Right this way, Miss Peyton. Can't keep a guilty man from his lawyer now, can we? 'Specially a pretty one like yerself."

Emily resolved to ignore the taunt but noticed a scowl flick across Deputy Quick's face before he bent back to cleaning a shotgun.

As usual, Dobbins brought a chair from in front of his desk to the cell area, setting it against the wall across from Tiny's cell. The marshal leaned against the door frame, arms folded. Emily kept her expression blank and looked at him. He stared back for a moment, then raised one hand in surrender. "Of course. You must have your privacy." He backed into the office and closed the door behind him.

"How are you today, Tiny?"

She inhaled through her mouth to avoid the damp, musty aroma of chamber pots and unchanged blankets. The gray rain enhanced the gloom that permeated the cells. Even if the sun shone every day, there weren't enough windows for the exposure to do any good.

Tiny shrugged and sighed. "Same as every other day in this hole." He nodded at the paper on the bed. "Deputy Quick's tryin' to help me with my readin'." Her client sat on the edge of his narrow bunk, newspaper on the bed beside him. A Bible rested near the pillow.

His eyes, red and puffed, fixed on her. Gaunt face, pale pallor, and a slight tremor in his hands showed a man not used to small spaces. Emily's breath caught. Guilty or not, this man already suffered.

He picked up the Bible and riffled the pages. "Pastor Dalton brought me this Bible and visits every morning to pray with me and teach me from the Good Book."

I'll have to remember not to come when the pastor visits. "That's good. And I know Charlotte comes often."

"Every day." He scowled and clenched his fists. "Wish the marshal tweren't so mean to her."

"What do you mean?"

"Says he has to search her every time, make sure she's not smugglin' somethin' in. Then he stands in the doorway the whole time she's here. And the way he looks at her—" Tiny twisted his hands. "I want to strangle him."

Emily rubbed her forehead with her fingertips. She clasped her hands in her lap, fought to control her breathing. "I know it's hard, Tiny, but you must keep your temper under control. We—you—can't give the marshal any more information to use against you."

Anguish twisted Tiny's face. His mouth drooped on one side as his nostrils flared. "I know, Miss Emily. I'm trying. Really hard." He clenched his fists. "But it's tearing me up inside. It's bad enough she gets treated that way at Dutton's but here too. And by a lawman."

"Let me see what I can do." There must be something. Doc's on the town council. Maybe he'll have an idea.

She took a notebook from her case, opened it to a blank page. "I want to talk with you about character witnesses."

Tiny tilted his head, the look of a small boy struggling with a math problem crossing his face. "Character witnesses?"

She waggled her pencil in the air. "People who know you. People who can tell the jury what a good person you are. I'm thinking of Terrence, but I'd like to have at least three. Can you think of any others?"

"Gee, I don't know." He rubbed the back of his neck as a sheepish grin spread. "Never thought about it."

Emily sketched a horse's head in her notebook and then a cat. She hadn't thought of her cat in ten years. She glanced at Tiny. He stared at the floor as if he had forgotten the question and her.

"What about Mr. Montgomery?" she prodded.

He startled. "My ... my boss?"

"Yes. How long've you worked for him? Three or four years?"

"Near on to five."

"Then he must think a lot of you to keep you that long. Mind if I talk to him?"

Tiny shook his head. "He's been a good man to work for. D'ya think he'd help?"

"Only one way to find out." She jotted Montgomery's name, then Terrence's. "Anyone else?"

"Maybe Pastor Dalton. Been goin' to his church for three years, since that revival they had."

Emily bit her lip. The revival. The last time she'd talked to the pastor. She wrote the name. Maybe Father can talk to Thomas Dalton. She wouldn't. "All right. My father and

I will talk to these two. I'll let you know. You think on it some more and let me know if you come up with any other names."

She tucked her notebook away and stood.

"Miss Emily? Do you think these character witnesses will help?"

They may keep you from getting hung. She took a step toward the cell and lowered her voice. "Some, but we need to find those two men you saw. Keep thinking on them, see what you can remember."

They both turned at the sounds of a commotion in the outer office. Charlotte's tear-choked voice rose, the words indistinguishable. Emily opened the door.

Dobbins held Charlotte by her wrists, the girl twisting unsuccessfully to break his grip. Quick hovered near the two, confusion scouring his face.

"I need to see Tiny." Charlotte's hoarse voice scratched the air.

"You can't go in there. He's with his lawyer." The last word dripped with sarcasm.

"We're done, Marshal. She can see him." She noticed Charlotte's face, her left cheek starting to bruise, a streak of red cutting across the mark. "Charlotte, what happened?" She spun on the marshal. "Did you do that?"

"I ain't laid a finger on her. Jes holding her wrists so she don't claw my eyes out."

Emily looked at Quick who nodded vigorously. "'S true, Miss. She came in real upset—cryin' 'n squawlin'—and went at the Marshal when he wouldn't let her see Tiny."

"Well, she can see him now. But first, Charlotte, tell us who did this to you."

Charlotte gasped short, desperate breaths. "Dutton. He hit me 'cuz I wouldn't go upstairs with one of the customers. Told him I wasn't gonna do that. So, he hit me."

She put her arm around Charlotte's waist and her other hand on the girl's arm. "Come on. Let's see Tiny. Then I'm taking you to Doc's." The girl sagged against her.

Emily glared at Dobbins as they passed him. "And then you and I are going to have a talk."

He shrugged and picked at his teeth with a fingernail.

Charlotte and Tiny embraced and kissed as best they could through the bars. Tiny saw the mark on her face, touched it with the tips of his fingers and jerked his hand away when she winced. "What happened?"

Charlotte lifted her shoulders and looked down, pressing her injured cheek against her shoulder. Emily stood behind her, hand on her back.

"Who did this to you?" Tiny's voice dropped, low, menacing. "The marshal?"

She shook her head.

"Dutton?"

She started to shake her head again, stopped, then nodded.

Tiny banged his head against the bars. "Arrgh." The roar echoed off the brick walls.

The office door opened. Deputy Quick stood in the doorway. "Everythin' all right in here?"

"Yes, Deputy," Emily said. "Everything's under control."

Quick smiled a toothy grin at her. "Okay, Miss Emily. You holler if y'all need help with anythin'."

Emily stood in the doorway, trying to give Charlotte and Tiny as much privacy as possible. The marshal's chair was empty, his hat gone from the peg by the door. "Where's the marshal?"

Quick snapped the last piece of another shotgun into place. "Said he was goin' to talk to Dutton."

After several minutes, Tiny calmed enough for Emily to take Charlotte to Doc's. As they left, Tiny said, "You tell that Dutton, if I ever git my hands on 'im, he'll wish he'd never be—"

Emily stepped up to the bars and pointed her finger in his face. "Keep quiet. Don't say a word. Talk like that is only gonna give the marshal more evidence that you aren't above killing people. Do you understand me?"

Tiny's head fell to his chest. "Yes, ma'am."

"And don't call me ma'am."

"She can't go back to Dutton's. Where's she going to stay?"

"Either with me or the Everett's. We'll take care of her."

As she left with Charlotte, it appeared Quick hadn't heard Tiny's outburst. But it was hard to tell with the deputy. Sometimes, he wasn't the driest piece of kindling in the wood box.

Chapter 27

George's fingers drummed the table as Emily cut his chicken and vegetables. At least, Mrs. Marcand had prepared mashed potatoes. Flexing the fingers of his left hand, he bit back a wave of bitter helplessness. Soon the cast would be off.

Not soon enough.

Across the table, Doc flashed the knowing look, the same look the old geezer used at poker games to determine whether George was bluffing. Doc leaned back in his chair. "I'd think you'd be enjoying all this attention—these beautiful women fussing over you. Milking it for all you could."

George dismissed him with a wave of his hand and scooped a forkful of potatoes.

"Aren't we going to bless the food?" Charlotte Taylor spoke from her seat across from Doc.

George shot a look toward Emily. Her fork froze halfway to her mouth, and a frown pinched her face. George spoke before she could. "—not a habit—we've developed, Miss Taylor."

She giggled. "No one's ever called me 'Miss Taylor' before." Her expression sobered, her eyes wistful. "Feels kinda nice."

Doc cleared his throat. "I guess I could venture a prayer over our food."

"Thank you, Doc." George watched his daughter as Doc spoke a few words. Hands on either side of her plate, body still. Jaw tense, staring straight ahead. When Doc finished, she shook her head as if to dispel the words he'd spoken and resumed eating.

"Miss Caroline." Charlotte's voice trembled. Her eyes looked ready to pour rivers. "I can't thank you enough for all your help today, especially for letting me stay with you and Doc." She paused. "You too, Miss Emily, for helping me get in to see Tiny."

Emily swallowed and sipped her coffee. "Doc, you're on the town council. Can you do anything to stop the marshal from manhandling Charlotte and any other woman who wants to visit someone in his jail?"

Doc steepled his hands over his plate. "I can talk to the council, but there's some who'll think he has to do it so she can't slip something to the prisoner."

Emily started to cuss. "From what Charlotte told me, he goes much farther than he needs to. He humiliates and embarrasses her."

George motioned with his hand to calm his daughter. She glared at him, her light blue eyes turning icy.

"What? You think it's right for him to do that?"

George shook his head. "Not time—for this—fight."

Emily clenched her jaw. Grinding her teeth again. "Then when?"

He shrugged. "Don't know."

Dinner over, Emily, Caroline, Mrs. Marcand, and Charlotte cleaned up in the kitchen while Doc and George started a game of chess.

Emily, washing dishes, jumped when Caroline touched her arm. Caroline took the plate from her hand. "Your mind is somewhere else."

"Before he left, Terrence told Father about making the ride to the Grant place. I was hoping Terrence would get home tonight."

"Terrence? You're worrying about a man?"

Emily dried her hands on her apron. "I'm not worried about him. Going to Grant's place is a long ride for anyone to make alone." She nodded at the rain pelting the window. "Especially in this weather. Besides, he's a friend. Don't you get concerned about your friends sometimes?"

Caroline smiled, touched Emily's arm. "I do. I'm pleased to see you doing the same. Especially a good, young man."

"His being a man has nothing to do it with it." Emily picked up a stack of dishes and returned them to their place in the cupboard. Hands on the plates, she bowed her head. *Stay calm.* She stifled the urge to tell Caroline to stop playing matchmaker. *Terrence is practically engaged.*

The clank of the coffee pot on the stove broke Emily's tension. "The coffee's ready," Mrs. Marcand said.

"You think the two gentlemen are ready for coffee and pie?" Charlotte asked.

Smoothing her dress, Emily said, "I'm sure they're ready for an interruption. Knowing Doc, especially for apple pie. Why don't you take the coffee, and I'll take the pie?"

Prepared to follow Charlotte into the dining area, Emily stopped when Caroline's hand covered one of hers. "I apologize. I was trying to tease, but my words came out wrong." Caroline's reached out to her. "Deep down, I want to see you married—"

"I keep running the men off."

Caroline turned serious. "I think the men don't know what to do with you. Except for Terrence."

"He accepts me as a friend." She picked up the tray. "Which is all I need."

"Really?"

Emily held back the urge to slam the tray onto the table when she faced Caroline. The anger drained away as the older woman's gaze warmed, searched hers. The look that meant a mother's love, comforting, challenging, always offering a place of security and caring.

She touched her forehead. "M—Caroline." They embraced, Emily relaxed into Caroline's arm, enjoying her hand stroking her back. Emily straightened, chuckled. "You're right. As always. At times, Terrence feels like more than a friend, but that's all he ever can be. He and Priscilla'll be married soon. She can give him more than I ever can."

Emily followed Caroline into the dining area.

"'Bout time you got here," Doc grumped. "Thought you were keepin' it all for yourselves."

"Hush, you old coot." Caroline swatted her husband's arm. "When did I ever hold back pie from you?"

Doc stroked his chin, gaze lost in thought. "Well, there was that one time—"

"Quiet, old man. Not in front of the young ones."

Emily and Charlotte laughed.

"Young ones?" Emily said. "Who're you talking about? I don't see any young ones here. Do you, Charlotte?"

"I ain't been young since I was nine."

Quiet settled over the table as they dug into the pie Caroline baked. Emily watched George savor each bite, holding it on his tongue before chewing. Pie making defeated her. As did cake making and any cooking beyond steak, chicken, and potatoes.

The sound of a fork tapping on a plate snapped her back to the room. George pointed at Charlotte. "—Sad?"

Charlotte half-closed her eyes and nodded. "Been a long time since I had a nice meal with such good folks."

"How did you ever—" Emily's question was interrupted by a sharp rap of George's fork on his plate.

He waggled the fork at her. "Don't pry—none of—business."

Heat flushed Emily's neck, chagrined at his rebuke.

Caroline reached her hand across and covered Charlotte's just as she had done with Emily so many times. Love and acceptance. Encouragement and support. So much in such a simple gesture. Emily covered her own hand in the same way, remembering.

Doc slid another piece of pie onto his plate. "What's next, Charlotte?"

The girl's shoulders sagged as she toyed with the pie in front of her. "Don't know. Need to find work. But who'd hire me in this town? And I can't leave Tiny."

"Wait." Caroline straightened, eyes bright. "I think I have the solution."

All eyes turned to her.

"Why don't you move in here and help take care of George?"

George dropped his fork, the pie spilling to the table. "Do—n't need more help." He scooped his pie from the table. "Too much now."

"That's what I mean. If Charlotte moves in, Mrs. Marcand can finally get some rest. You know her daughter in Wichita isn't feeling well. Having someone here all the time will help. And it will take a load off Mrs. Dobbins as well. I'll stop in every couple of days to see how things are and to give Charlotte some time off." She winked at Emily.

"She'll need it too, taking care of a cantankerous reprobate like yourself."

"What do you think, Charlotte?" Emily said.

"Wait—minute. Don't I have—say?"

"Be quiet, Father," Emily said. "You'll scare the girl off before she even gets started."

Charlotte blinked back tears. "Used to help Ma take care of Granny and a passel of young 'uns."

A hand slamming on the table rattled the cups and plates and halted the conversation. Face red, George pointed at Charlotte. "Too—young." He worked his mouth as if forcing the words that wouldn't flow. "Too—pretty." Jaw set, he glowered at Emily. "Hurt her—reputation."

A deep-throated laugh burst from Charlotte. "Mr. Peyton, you can't hurt what I don't have. Dutton and others like him have took care of that already."

"May I say something?" Doc raised his hand like a student in school.

"What?" George's face, still red, was set like a brick wall.

"I think it would be good for someone young to take care of you. You're wearing Mrs. Marcand to the nub. Mrs. Dobbins ain't far behind either. As long as Emily's here at night, there won't be any damage to anyone's reputation." He scratched at his temple and grinned. "Might actually help yours."

George spluttered. Emily covered her mouth to stifle the laugh bubbling in her throat.

Caroline planted an elbow in her husband's ribs. "James Everett. There are ladies present."

Chapter 28

Spot jangled his bridle and tossed his mane. He sauntered into his stall. The stable was warm, the pungent aromas of straw and manure magnified by the intense humidity.

"Easy, boy." Terrence stroked his horse's neck before he undid the saddle cinch. "Let me get this off, and then you can dig into those oats."

The animal bobbed his head and snorted.

Eager to get to Emily's, Terrence brushed Spot's coat with quick strokes, while fighting the fatigue sucking his energy, draining his muscles. He closed his eyes, the heavy, burning sensation behind his lids calling for sleep.

Shaking his head, he finished the chore and patted Spot's rump as the horse dug into a bin of oats. "Enjoy it, boy. You earned all you can eat."

Spot snuffed into his food as if acknowledging the compliment.

Outside the livery, Terrence stretched in the last vestiges of the spring sun as it continued its descent over the endless prairie. A bath, a hot meal, and his soft bed beckoned with the allure of Delilah calling Samson.

Duty called.

At the bank, Joseph Warner greeted him. "Any trouble?"

Terrence brushed trail dust from his shirt before handing his employer the documents signed by Walter Grant. "No, sir. Mr. Grant said to thank you for all the help you've been."

"It's just good business to help him protect what he has." Warner tamped tobacco into his pipe and flared a match to life with his fingernail. Satisfied with the draw, he waved the match like a magician's wand to extinguish it. "My wife and I would like you to join us for supper tonight."

A wave of fatigue buckled Terrence's knees. His bed called. He needed to see Emily. About Tiny. "Could we do it another evening? I wouldn't want to fall asleep in the soup."

Warner grinned and clapped his hand on Terrence's shoulder. "Sure. Let's make it tomorrow. My niece from Cleveland will be with us a few more days."

Niece from Cleveland? "Um ..."

Warner held up his hand. "I know. You and Priscilla Montgomery will be getting married soon. My wife can't resist the urge to play matchmaker. Last night, Harold joined us. Didn't go well. My niece thought he was a used-up scarecrow. My wife has her eye on you, Watkins the undertaker's son, and even Deputy Quick."

"Wow. That's some competition. Don't think I could beat either of those two."

Terrence jumped when Charlotte Taylor answered the front door to the Peyton home. "Charlotte, I didn't expect to see you here."

She gestured for him to enter as her dark blue eyes smiled the smile that turned Tiny into a meek calf. "I'm gonna be stayin' here to help take care of Mr. P." Her simple blue dress contrasted sharply with the saloon get-ups she usually wore. She looked five years younger and more childlike, more vulnerable. And happy. Happier than he had ever seen her.

"Being here seems to agree with you."

"This is only my first day, but Mr. P is very sweet."

Terrence coughed to keep a grin hidden. George Peyton? Sweet? *Never thought I'd hear those words in the same sentence.*

Charlotte led him to the parlor. "Terrence is here, Mr. Peyton, Miss Emily." Terrence was surprised she didn't curtsey.

George and Emily sat next to each other at a long table, papers spread across the surface, law books open before them. Emily's blond hair swooped to her shoulders. Her smile warmed him although the heaviness shrouding her eyes spoke of long nights and hard work. *She needs sleep as much as I do.*

"Welcome back." Her voice serenaded him. Soft and welcoming. Something stirred. Something he shouldn't be feeling. His breath caught, and he willed himself to think of Priscilla.

"Good to be back." Something beyond fatigue weakened his voice.

"Have you—supper?" George's baritone was back, but his face scrunched as he struggled to get words out.

Terrence's stomach told him not to turn down an invitation from good friends. He looked at Emily, a quick glance. She smiled. Just friends. That's all. He focused on George. "No, sir."

"—Join us."

"My pleasure." *In more ways than one. Stop it.*

George nodded at Charlotte.

"'Nother plate on the table, Mr. P. Plenty of stew and sourdough." She darted away. The clatter of another place being set at the table drifted from the dining room.

Terrence tried to keep the surprise out of his voice. "I didn't know she could cook."

Emily shrugged. "We're about to find out."

Their gazes met, held for a long moment. Emily turned to one of the law books, a tinge of pink flushing her cheeks.

Quiet reigned as they dug into the food.

"Charlotte, this stew is delicious." Terrence hoped the sincerity of the compliment came across.

"Thank you." Charlotte ducked her head. "I used my Granny's recipe."

Emily's movements drew him. Her delicate manipulation of her spoon, the way she broke off small pieces of her biscuit. So feminine. Yet she was brighter than most men, quicker with her mouth than many. Complicated, smart, and vulnerable. He sighed and brought himself back to reality, to Priscilla.

"I have some news." He told them what he had learned about the Whitney brothers' travels.

Emily's eyes narrowed. "Why did Marshal Dobbins tell us something different?"

George tapped the table then pointed at his temple. "—his mind. Minor detail to him."

"Maybe," Emily said. "The marshal's usually pretty sharp—not like him to forget something like that."

Her father shrugged. "Hap—sometimes."

Terrence tried to read the look Emily gave her father. A pursing of her lips and a steady gaze. She swept her hair behind her ear. "I'd like to think so."

A scowl flashed across George's face. "Course it is—No reason to lie."

"That we know of." Emily's voice was soft, barely discernible.

George seemed not to have heard her. Or, at least, pretended he didn't. George and John Dobbins' friendship went back a long way. Terrence knew they'd served in the war together, chasing Quantrill's raiders through Kansas and Missouri.

He turned to Terrence. "Direction?"

Confusion warped through Terrence's mind. "Oh, the Whitneys. Station manager said they headed south."

"Indian territory." Charlotte said, her voice flat.

"Easy to get lost there." Terrence said.

Emily tapped the table. "Texas."

Terrence nodded. "Even easier to get lost there."

"Mex—ico." George waited, eyes closed. "If still—south."

"We'll never find 'em." Sobs choked Charlotte's words. She fanned her face with her hand. "I'm sorry."

Emily placed her hand on Charlotte's arm.

"Maybe we can ask the marshal to contact the towns south of here to be on the lookout for them." Terrence looked from George to Emily.

Emily spoke first, sarcasm underlying her words, eyes on her father. "He probably won't have time if he has a lot on his mind.

George focused on lifting a spoonful of stew to his mouth.

She stared into her coffee cup before taking a sip. "Besides, he already thinks he has the right man, and we haven't been able to convince him otherwise."

"Maybe we can find them." All eyes turned to Charlotte. She fiddled with her spoon. "I mean, if the marshal can't look for them, maybe we can."

George shook his head. "Can't—all need to be here."

Tears sparkled in Charlotte's eyes. Her voice rose to the edge of hysteria. "We have to do something. This might be Tiny's only hope."

George plopped his spoon in his bowl. "Slim—very slim."

"Father, right now, slim is all we have." Emily reached across the table to hold Charlotte's hand.

George gestured as if trying to pull words out of the air. "Ideas?"

"I'll go." The words escaped before Terrence realized it. Charlotte smiled at him as she wiped tears from her eyes.

Emily's scrutiny froze him. Her face softened as her eyes turned tender. "You are a brave man, Terrence McCarthy. Brave but insane. You're not a lawman."

George nodded. "'Sides—Joseph won't let you go. Needs you—at bank." George's finger looked like the barrel of a gun pointed at him. "You'll—get—self killed."

Emily waved her hands. "So, what do we do?"

"Hire somebody." He motioned for paper and pencil.

[begin handwritten note]
Telegraph Wyatt Stoddard for names of bounty hunters.
[end handwritten note]

"Who's Wyatt Stoddard?" Terrence asked.

"Friend of Father's. A lawyer in Dodge City."

"Bounty hunters?" Charlotte said.

Emily shrugged, looked at her father. "We'll pay someone to find the Whitneys."

Charlotte whimpered. "Tiny can't afford to pay someone."

George pointed to himself. "I'll pay." His face contorted. "—Pay me in—cattle—later."

Charlotte kissed George on his cheek as he half-heartedly pushed her away.

Chapter 29

Terrence hummed the "Battle Hymn of the Republic" as he entered the bank. Jenkins greeted him with a brief nod and a jerk of his head toward Warner's office. Terrence frowned, unable to interpret the man's sign language. As he asked Jenkins to use English, Warner's door opened.

"Ah, Terrence. There you are. A word, if you please."

Terrence followed his employer's glance to the clock on the wall. Twenty minutes late. Had it taken that long to send the telegraph to Dodge City? Not that he had to be there. Emily didn't need his help. He couldn't let Tiny down though. He wanted to help, had to be involved. Tiny would do the same for him. Besides, what better way to start the day than a few minutes with Emily Peyton.

He winced inwardly. Priscilla. Not Emily. Priscilla. Emily was a friend. A good friend. But only a friend. If Emily loved anything, it was the law. Sometimes, the law seemed to be the only thing she loved. The law and her father. Maybe Caroline Everett. Did Emily have room in her heart for a man? Not likely. Even if she did, it wouldn't be him. Priscilla had his heart.

"Mr. Warner, I apologize for being late. I lost track of the time. It won't happen again."

Warner stood at the fireplace in his office, studying the empty hearth as if trying to conjure a fire out of the air. He gestured to a chair in front of his desk. "Sit down, Terrence."

Butterflies wiggled in his stomach as he settled into the chair. He'd never seen Warner this stern and somber. Something must be wrong. Not the accounts. Everything was in order when he left two days ago.

He twisted in his chair to face Warner. "Is everything all right, sir? Is there anything wrong with the accounts?"

Warner started. "Ye—Yes. Everything's fine. The accounts are in good order. I just need to talk with you for a few minutes."

He walked behind his desk, tugging on the hem of his satin vest as he sat. He picked up his Meerschaum but didn't move for his tobacco. Just sat turning the pipe in his hands, eyes looking over Terrence's right shoulder.

"We—I'm concerned, Terrence, about the amount of time you're spending on this ..." He fumbled for words. "... matter concerning Tiny Waters."

"What do you mean, sir?"

Warner's shoulders heaved as he released a long sigh. "I mean you seem to be giving this an inordinate amount of your attention. I think it's affecting your work." He stared at his pocket watch. "Today, you were over twenty minutes late. I wager it had something to do with your friend." He arched his eyebrows.

Terrence nodded. "Yes, sir. I was at the telegraph office helping Em—Miss Peyton send a telegraph."

Warner set his pipe in its holder on his desk, leaned back in his chair, and intertwined his fingers over his paunch. A thin sheen of perspiration formed on his upper lip. "It takes two people to send a telegraph now?"

Heat spread across Terrence's face. "No, sir. I just—"

"It doesn't matter what you just. You should have been here, working." He cleared his throat. "It doesn't look good for an important employee of the bank to be consorting with the man who murdered and robbed one of our customers shortly after he cashed a large check."

Terrence gripped the arms of his chair and leaned forward. "Mr. Warner, Tiny hasn't been found guilty. Are you saying I'm somehow involved in the murder and robbery of Mac Phillips?"

Warner glanced to his desktop, his thumbs tapping each other. "No, I'm not. But some people in the town—important people—have raised that possibility."

Heat rose into Terrence's neck, into his face. His muscles corded. One more squeeze, and he'd snap the arms of the chair into kindling.

Warner picked up his pipe, reached for his tobacco, let his hand drop to the desk. Looked at the pile of papers in front of him, at the landscape painting over the fireplace, but not at Terrence. Wouldn't look him in the eye.

"Who?" Terrence bit the word like it was a sour apple.

Warner flapped his hand. "Who they are isn't important. What's important is that they're thinking and talking about it." His eyes met Terrence's. "Consorting with a known ...

Terrence shook his head.

... an accused murderer doesn't reflect well on the bank." He quickly filled his pipe, tobacco spilling on the leather desktop.

Blood drained from Terrence's face as his stomach did a queasy flip. The words stumbled from his mouth. "D ... Do you want me to resign?"

Warner looked like he'd just stepped into a mountain stream in February. Barefoot. He sputtered. "No ... Not at all. That's the last thing I want." He inhaled, tamped his tobacco, and took his time to strike a match. After several puffs, he focused his now-calm brown eyes on Terrence. The brandy-scented smoke drifted across the desk. "You're too valuable to me to let you resign."

He aimed the stem of his Meerschaum like a pistol. "I told you before not to misplace your loyalties. Sometimes, loyalty to our friends can lead us down the wrong path. With terrible consequences."

Be quiet. Don't make it worse.

Pipe between his teeth, Warner neatened the already neat stack of papers on his desk. Putting the pipe in a glass bowl near his tobacco, he leaned over his folded arms, eyes intense. "Terrence, you have the skills and talents for banking. You have a gift for working with people and a head for numbers. You will replace me someday." A pen lay near the documents. He rolled it between his thumb and forefinger on the desktop. "I don't want to see you lose that opportunity. I also don't want to see you lose that beautiful young woman you're courting."

Terrence's heart beat faster, straining in his chest. He brought his breath under control, clasped his hands at his waist. "I don't understand. What does Priscilla have to do with this?"

Their gaze met briefly before Warner looked away. "Abe Montgomery is a very rich and powerful man. Also proud. He might not look too kindly on his daughter being associated with someone close to a murderer."

"Did he tell you that?"

Warner shrugged. "The subject came up in passing."

Terrence shot to his feet before he realized he had stood. His mind whirled in a discordant pattern of images. Priscilla, auburn hair loose and falling to her shoulders, her dancing green eyes. Her father behind her, arms crossed, defiant scowl. Tiny, shrunken within himself, staring at the floor of his cell, the shadow of a noose on the wall behind him. Emily, chin set, light blue eyes afire with determination.

He paced to avoid standing in front of the desk, needing physical distance. He stopped behind his chair, white-knuckled grip on the back. "Mr. Warner, if you ask for my resignation, I will give it to you. But I can't—I won't—abandon my friend. Outside of his lawyer and his fiancée, I am the only person who believes him."

He inhaled to slow his heart, gripped the chair tighter to hide his trembling. "The Bible calls for us to help the least of our brothers and those in prison. I've never been completely alone, sir, not like Tiny is right now. I will help him as much as I can. Be assured, though, I will not let my activities affect my work at the bank. I will be here every day. I will be as loyal to you and the customers as I am to Tiny every moment I am here. If that's not good enough, if it doesn't satisfy the important people in town, you can fire me."

Chapter 30

Fading daylight forced Terrence to light the oil lamp on his desk. Motes floated in the last beams of sunlight filtering through the windows as Harry Bannister locked the door after the last customer. Terrence blinked and rubbed his eyes to erase the fatigue before he jotted figures in the ledger on his desk.

The knot between his shoulders had tightened all day and crept into his neck. Pain at the back of his head stabbed into his eyes. He stretched his arms as if trying to touch the high ceiling and twisted his torso. His neck cracked as he bent his head from shoulder to shoulder.

For the rest of the morning, he'd waited for another summons to his employer's office, but Warner stayed behind his dark cherry door. At dinner time, he came out, black homburg squarely on his head, pipe set in his mouth, gold-knobbed walking stick firmly under his arm. He'd nodded at Terrence. "I'll be back later this afternoon."

He never returned.

Jenkins placed a stack of receipts at the corner of his desk. "That's it, Terrence. Do you want me to do the count while you finish the ledger?"

Jenkins offering to help? Terrence scrutinized the man. No apparent guile. "I know you like to get home to your family as soon as you can every night. Why the offer to stay?"

Jenkins' Adam's apple bobbed as the man cleared his throat, fingertips brushing the edge of Terrence's desk. "I heard you mention to Harry that you're meeting Miss Montgomery at the Randolph House. With your traveling, I thought you might be anxious to see her."

Terrence rubbed his chin, searching Jenkins' face. Why so suspicious? The man's doing you a favor. Best thing that's happened today.

Except for seeing Emily at the telegraph office.

Don't go there.

"Thank you, Jenkins. That's very generous. Harry, Jenkins will do the count tonight."

Harry's eyes widened as he looked between the two men. "Real—Well, that's very generous of you, Micah. Let's get started."

A short time later, ledger finished, Terrence poked his head into the small counting room near the safe. Jenkins counted, and Harry noted the numbers in a small notebook. "Everything under control?"

Jenkins startled, fumbling with the bills in his hands.

Harry nodded. "'Bout half done with the first count."

Outside the bank, Terrence surveyed both sides of the street as he locked the door. The back of his neck tingled. Seemed strange to leave the safe open. Like only wearing one sock. He shook his head. This meant he'd have more time with Priscilla.

He passed Emily's office. How easy it had become to refer to the office as her's, not her father's. Disappointment touched his heart to see the office closed, the windows dark. She must have left for home already. Maybe he'd get the opportunity tomorrow to talk with her about Tiny's case, to see if Wyatt Stoddard had answered her telegram.

Terrence hesitated just inside the door to the Randolph House dining room, eyes riveted on the figure across the room. He dared not move, dared not break the spell holding him. Priscilla sat at their favorite table in an alcove tucked near the entry to the hotel proper. Away from the brightness of the chandeliers, soft candlelight played off the strands of auburn hair carefully arranged along the sides of her face. Her satiny green dress matched the hue of her eyes, the dim light giving them a haunting allure. His pulsed raced as his heart crept up his throat. Not for the first time, the thought flashed across his mind, *I am so blessed.*

He glided across the room, the radiance of her smile drawing him like a lighthouse guiding a ship through fog.

His palm and fingers tingled as he kissed the back of her hand. She lowered her eyelids and slid her hands to her lap as he took his seat.

As he studied the menu, she sipped a goblet of red wine, her long fingers and perfect nails cradling the glass. Grace and beauty in every movement. Such a distraction. He sighed and placed the menu on the table. Couldn't concentrate. Fortunately, the offerings seldom changed, and he ordered his usual steak. She opted for some chicken dish smothered in wine and mushrooms.

Like most of their meals, neither spoke at first. Gazing at her was more than enough to wash away the day and Mr. Warner's words. Tiny's problem receded slightly, never out of mind, but supplanted by this woman who held his heart, to do with as she wished.

"I've missed you. How was your trip to see Walter Grant?" Her soft voice was deeper than one would expect from someone so beautiful.

Priscilla broke off small pieces of a roll and nibbled as he told her of his journey. She frowned and pushed the roll away when he told her about finding a clue about the Whitney brothers.

"I don't want to talk about that." Her harsh tone stopped his words.

"I apologize. I didn't mean to upset you." He reached across the table, but she pulled her hand back and placed it in her lap.

She gazed out over the restaurant, mouth grim. "Murder is too horrible to think about." She faced him, a slight smile. "Why concern yourself with such things?"

Her words stung like sleet in a winter storm. He clenched his jaw, fighting back the first words that formed. He inhaled, slowly. "Because Tiny's my friend. I want to help him."

She waved her hand. "People like him are nobody's friend. He'll just drag you down with him." She grew serious, leaned forward. "If that happens, what will become of us?"

"What do you mean?"

"Do you think my father will give his permission for me to marry the best friend of a known murderer?"

He swallowed the anger bubbling below the surface. His words came out in a measured cadence. "He's not a murderer. He couldn't kill anyone."

Her eyes narrowed. "Marshal Dobbins thinks he had good reason. Steal the money to buy a ranch so he could marry that trollop of his."

Terrence pinched the bridge of his nose. The pain in the back of his head inched forward, encircling his skull. Blood pounded in his ears. Now, the steak looked like a dried-up piece of boot leather left in the sun too long.

She covered his hand with hers. "I'm sorry, Terrence. Now, I've upset you. I know how you feel about Tiny." She paused, her gaze holding him. "I'm only thinking about you—how this could hurt your reputation."

Her eyes, and her hand warm on his, seemed to drain the tension. He sank into her words like he would a featherbed, relaxing in their comfort. The muscles in his neck loosened, and the pain in his head eased.

"Thank you. But I have to do all I can to help Tiny."

Furrowing her brow, she narrowed her eyes, pinched her lips together. "Just think about what this dedication to your friend may do to us. To my reputation."

His head felt like a weathervane in a sudden wind change. "Your reputation? This doesn't concern you."

She pushed her plate away, the meal hardly touched, the mushroom sauce congealing into something that could seal windows. "People talk about you, and it reflects on me. About how close you are to Tiny and about how much time you spend with that Emily Peyton." She spoke the name like she had a mouthful of dirt. "People saw you with her at the telegraph office this morning. They talk about how much time you spend at her house. At night."

"I'm never alone with her. Her father's always there. And Charlotte Taylor is there now." Annoyance danced in his heart. *Why do I have to defend myself?* "We're talking about Tiny's case or I'm playing chess with Mr. Peyton. Emily and I have—" He clamped his mouth. Enough. We're not doing anything wrong.

"Emily and you. That's what I'm talking about—makes me look like a fool." She gathered her shawl around her shoulders. "I seem to have lost my appetite."

She stood, looked at him, and opened her mouth. She closed it, and walked out of the restaurant. His stomach dropped to his knees. *Is there any way I can start this day over?*

He gulped the rest of her wine, remembering why he didn't like wine as it stung his throat and roiled in his empty stomach. The glass fit smoothly in his hand—the curve reminding him of a baseball. He forced himself to place the glass gently on the table and not smash it to the floor.

Did she just walk out of my life?

The now-closed door seemed like an insurmountable barrier, an unscalable mountain, exiling him from his dream.

Chapter 31

Emily tapped her pencil on the dining room table and licked her lips as the aroma of lamb roast drifted from the kitchen. Her stomach reminded her of another missed dinner and of the need to make better coffee.

Her father sat across the table, chin in hand, reviewing a list of questions she planned to ask Marshal Dobbins and Deputy Quick at the trial. He handed the paper back to her, his hazel eyes crinkling in a smile. "Good questions." He frowned and tapped his temple. "—ready to follow up."

Was his speech improving, or was she getting better at filling in the blanks? She hoped for the former but feared the latter. "I know. Be ready to pursue their answers." She waved the paper. "Don't lock myself into just these questions."

"Smart girl."

She came around the table and kissed the top of his head. "Good teacher."

Charlotte poked her head around the swinging door to the kitchen. "Are y'all 'bout ready to eat?"

Emily's gaze darted around the room as if she'd misplaced something important. "Terrence isn't here yet."

"Well, he'd better not burn my roast." Her hands fluttered as she smiled.

"You made sure he got the invitation to supper?"

Charlotte's head bobbed. "Yes, miss. Gave him your note right after you wrote it. He was sittin' right at his desk in the bank." She placed her hand at her throat and bowed. "Said he'd be honored to join us for dinner."

George tapped the table and eyed his daughter. "Good manners. Good man."

Emily stopped her eyes from rolling. "Father, stop playing matchmaker. He and Priscilla are all but engaged. I expect they'll be getting married in June."

George touched the side of his nose. "—'S said anything?"

"No."

"Not definite." His jaw worked. "Too good for her."

"Father, stop." Heat rose in her neck. She touched her forehead. "Terrence and I are friends. That's all. Don't make anything more out of it"

A knock on the door interrupted George's response. Charlotte admitted Terrence.

Emily scooped up the papers and deposited them in a stack on the sideboard. Tucking a stray hair behind her ear, she smiled. "Glad you can join us."

"I apologize for being late. Mr. Warner had a question on one of the accounts."

Charlotte headed for the kitchen. "I think I can still save the roast."

For the next few minutes, Charlotte bustled about setting the table and serving the roast with mashed potatoes and corn. She declined Emily's offer to help, and Emily realized, once again, Charlotte could do more alone than with her awkward assistance. *Maybe she can give me kitchen lessons.* Years of living with her father and focusing on the law had left her woefully deprived in the areas of cooking and maintaining a home. Another good reason for not having a man calling.

Once again, Emily realized how grateful she was for Mrs. Marcand's years of service, even though the widow disapproved of Emily's choice of occupation. George's lack of response to romantic hints occasionally resulted in overcooked food. But the woman had held the household together.

When all was ready, Charlotte bowed her head and Terrence joined her in a brief grace over the food. If Charlotte had to pray, at least she was quick about it.

Emily sliced her father's meat, aware of him flexing the fingers on his left hand. An ache grabbed her heart at her father's frustration. For both, the recovery was taking far too long, yet Doc counseled patience, something George had never stockpiled. Emily admitted she saw the virtue in herself only in fleeting passages through her day.

Terrence cleared his throat. "Did you hear from your friend in Dodge?"

George pointed at Emily, who picked up a small stack of telegrams from the sideboard. "Yes. Stoddard gave us the names of three bounty hunters. One turned us down. The second one is in jail in Arizona, and the third one is coming tomorrow."

She held the last slip of paper for a moment. "Stoddard can't help us because he has a trial starting tomorrow." She smiled at Terrence. "So, I guess it's just me." She tuned to her father. "With you beside me."

Her father looked down, poked a piece of meat around his plate. "Not much—help."

"Just having you there will help. You can jab me when I'm missing something or going in the wrong direction."

Terrence sipped his water. "Have we heard when the judge is coming?"

Emily sawed at her meat, much harder than she had to. "Tomorrow. Wants to start the trial the next day so he can catch the late afternoon train to Wichita."

Chapter 32

If I go over these notes anymore, I'll have them memorized.
Emily turned one more page. Nothing. No new ideas, no new strategies. The trial would begin tomorrow. Fingers to her forehead, she flipped another page. Weak. *We're too weak.* Three character witnesses against the marshal's theory, against the evidence of Tiny standing over Mac Phillips, gun smoking.

Sip of tepid coffee. Forkful of cold eggs. Almost time to leave for the office. Maybe working on wills and land transactions would take her mind off Tiny. And Charlotte. The memory of the hope in their eyes stabbed her anew. Realistic as she had been, they still looked to her and her father as their champions. Emily shuddered. Champions who are about to be trampled.

They still prayed—and Terrence with them. Can't they see God doesn't care? Just like he didn't care about my mother leaving or Father's accident.

"Doesn't—look—good?" George peered at her over the rims of his glasses. The Saint Louis newspaper spread before him, the Kansas City paper next to him, awaiting his attention. His morning routine. Coffee, eggs, bacon, biscuit, newspapers. In two days, Charlotte mastered preparing his breakfast to his exacting specifications.

Somehow, on those mornings when Mrs. Marcand wasn't available, Emily managed to get some piece of the meal not quite right.

She shook her head. "No, it doesn't. We don't have one shred of evidence to refute the marshal."

George nodded. "—Make jury doubt—all you can do."

She ran her fingers through her hair, pulling it into a tight clump which she held behind her head. "I know. I know. I don't know if planting doubt will be good enough."

Her father arched an eyebrow. "You—think—innocent?—When?"

"I don't really know. The more I talk to him, the more convinced I am he's innocent. Having Charlotte around confirms my thought. Still, I can't give you a specific reason."

Nodding, George sipped his coffee. "Good. You'll—fight—harder."

"Still don't think it will be good enough."

"Probably." His eyes became hard, his gaze steady. "Give him—best. All you—do."

Three sharp knocks drew their attention to the front door. George glanced to the kitchen.

"Charlotte's visiting Tiny. I'll get it." She turned her notes face down and smoothed her dress.

She gasped when she opened the door. A stranger stood on the porch, taller than Terrence but thinner. Wheat colored hair framed a long, narrow face, beaked nose, eyes the color of a cloudy sky, full mouth half-hidden by a mustache. Saddlebag hung over his right shoulder. The largest rifle she'd ever seen rested in his left hand like a toothpick. A low-slung two-gun rig circled his hips.

He removed a slate gray Stetson and held it against his chest. "Pardon, ma'am. I sure didn't mean to startle you."

He nodded at the house. "Feller at the hotel said this would be the Peyton residence."

Emily's hand gripped the inner knob, ready to slam the door. "And you are?"

He grinned, and his face glowed like a blacksmith's forge. "There I go agin. Forgettin' my manners. Name is Stevens, Frank Stevens. Wyatt Stoddard wired me. Said you might have need of my services."

"Mr. Stevens. Yes." Emily hesitated. The man radiated violence and menace—and knowledge of the skills in how to use both to get what he wanted. "Mr. Stoddard wired us about you."

"Yes, ma'am. I delivered a prisoner to Topeka yesterday. Didn't have no new prospects. Figured I might's well head here."

She opened the door wide. Stoddard was her father's oldest friend. They should be able to trust his recommendations. "Won't you come in?"

He deposited his saddlebags and rifle in the hallway and followed her into the dining room. He pumped George's arm as if drawing water from a well. Afterward, George flexed his fingers and glanced at his daughter. Stevens sat at the head of the table and slurped the coffee Emily brought.

She sat, taking care to arrange her dress just so, placing a blank sheet of paper and pencil in front of her, a small stack of documents at her left hand.

Stevens faced George. "So, what kin I do for you, Mr. Peyton? Wyatt said you had some missing witnesses or somethin'."

Emily straightened in her chair, drawing herself to her fullest height, if not more. "I'll answer your questions, Mr. Stevens, and explain what we're looking for."

Stevens looked from one to the other, eyes narrowed. He pointed at George. "I thought you was the lawyer."

Emily waited until Stevens' eyes were on her. "We're both lawyers. Partners in this matter." George's nod brought her a brief flash of lightheadedness. She hid her smile.

After a moment, Stevens shrugged. "A female lawyer? I heard a few of you women folk was practicing law. Guess you can't do any worse than the men. Might do a durn sight better." He barked a laugh that died in the air. He coughed. "All right. However you want to do this is fine with me."

"Let's get started." Emily folded her hands on the table. "Almost two weeks ago, someone murdered a man and robbed him of the proceeds of a land sale. We believe the man arrested is innocent." She sipped her coffee. "Two other men were around town the day of the crime. We think they have knowledge of who did the shooting. They have disappeared."

Stevens held up his hand. "They could've been killed for knowin' too much."

Emily shook her head. "Unlikely. They were seen afterward not far from here, riding south. We want you to find them."

"South covers a lot of territory."

"We know. Time is crucial. The trial starts tomorrow."

"Impossible." Stevens leaned back and spread his arms wide. "There's no way on God's green earth anybody kin find 'em and bring 'em back in time."

Emily smoothed the blank sheet in front of her. "We're aware of that. If we can find the men and bring them back, we may get the judge to reopen the trial."

"That's a lot of ifs and maybes."

George drummed his fingers on the table.

Stevens held up his hands. "I ain't sayin' it can't be done. I don't miss gittin' my man. It's gonna take a while to find these men. That's all I'm sayin'." He drained his coffee. "And money."

She looked at her father, who held up five fingers. "Five hundred dollars."

Stevens pursed his lips in a silent whistle. "Plus expenses."

George lifted his hand. Emily smiled. "Within reason. Up to two dollars a day. You will provide receipts."

"Receipts?" He looked at George.

Emily waited until she had his full attention. "Receipts. No receipts, no expenses."

She caught George's wink out of the corner of her eye. She picked up the top two sheets from the stack beside her, made some notations on each, and passed them to Stevens. "This is a contract for what we just discussed. You have three weeks to find these men. If you find them within two weeks, there will be a two-hundred-fifty-dollar bonus. If you need more time, we will renegotiate."

Stevens pulled a pair of glasses from his vest. They slid to the end of his nose, so he read the contract with his head tilted back. "Ain't never signed no contract before. It says you're gonna give me descriptions of these ... let's see here ... these Whitney brothers."

Emily picked up two more pages, descriptions Saul Benson had given her. "Right here."

Stevens scanned them, nodded. "Better than most I have to work on." He folded the sheets and tucked them inside his vest along with his glasses.

"Mr. Stevens, you did note in the contract that you will telegraph progress reports at least twice a week? Any problem with that?"

"Only if I ain't near a telegraph office."

"We understand, but we expect those reports nevertheless."

"Yes, ma'am."

"Very good. Please sign both copies of the contract."

After they'd all signed, Emily escorted Stevens to the door. He adjusted the saddlebag on his shoulder and hefted his rifle, and he leaned toward her. Emily froze, ready to back up and slam the door.

He smiled, a lopsided grin that gave him an almost boyish expression. "How about you 'n me stepping out for a bite to eat before I get started?"

"Good day, Mr. Stevens. I expect your first report in three days."

She closed the door and, through the glass panel, watched him shrug and turn away. She rubbed her arms to still the shiver running through her.

Chapter 33

"Careful. Be careful. Please." Emily's hand grasped air as she reached for her father's wheelchair. Terrence and Deputy Quick maneuvered him up the courthouse steps backward. Each jolt over a riser threatened to send the chair and George careening into the dusty street.

She glanced at the sky. Churning clouds mottled the sky gray and thunder rumbled. "Hurry before the rain starts."

Quick huffed. "Doin' our best, Miss Emily. Ain't never worked with one of these contraptions before."

Terrence pulled from behind while the deputy lifted from the front. George swayed like a toy boat swept down a swift-flowing stream. They paused, and the deputy wiped his face with his handkerchief.

George sat, hands clasped at his waist, face red, mouth working.

Whatever you do, Father, don't cuss.

Terrence, hands at the base of his spine, arched his back. "Maybe later this morning, Mr. Jaspers can bring some boards from his lumberyard to make a ramp."

"Good idea," Quick said. "I'll mention that to the marshal."

"Oh, just do it, Matthew. Show some gumption." Emily bit her lip to stop any sharper words. "I apologize, Deputy. I shouldn't have spoken to you like that."

Quick whipped his hat off and held it at his waist with both hands. "Aw, that's all right, Miss Emily. You gotta lot on yer mind without havin' to fret 'bout two lugheads spillin' yer Pa on the steps."

Emily smiled as her father shook his head and rolled his eyes. He rapped his hand on the arm of his chair and jerked his thumb at the door behind him.

Quick plunked his hat on his head and bent to the front wheels. "Yessir, Mr. Peyton. We'll have you up these steps in two shakes. You jes rest easy. Ready, Mr. Terrence?"

"Let's go, Deputy. Only four steps left."

Emily's heart settled back into place when they reached the top step, and Terrence pivoted the chair to wheel George into the courtroom.

She stopped in the doorway, frozen on the threshold. She placed her hand on her chest to slow her racing heart. She scanned the rectangular chamber as if she'd been transported to Camelot and stood at the entrance to enter King Arthur's throne room for the first time.

Tall arched windows marched down the right-hand wall. Outside, trees swayed, and dust swirled in mini tornadoes. The windows rattled as the howling wind pitched tiny pieces of grit against them.

The other three walls were paneled up to the wainscoting and then whitewashed to the ceiling that rose like a small cathedral. As if seen through the wrong end of a telescope, a two-level platform rose against the opposite wall. The upper level held a desk and leather chair. One step below the desk, a plain, yet highly polished, armchair faced the room.

Immediately before her, a center aisle divided three rows of plain chairs. People jostled by her to get to the few remaining unoccupied seats or to stand along the wall. A murder trial right here in their town was an occasion not to be missed.

Emily swallowed, still unable to move. The short aisle ended at a low-railed banister with a swinging gate in the center. Beyond it, two tables stood to either side of the gate. Marshal Dobbins sat to the left with a tall, light-haired man sitting at his side. His table seemed to stretch to Colorado. To the right stood the smallest table she'd ever seen. There was hardly room for a coffee cup, let alone all the material she carried in her case. Her father, Terrence, Tiny, and Charlotte squeezed around it like it was a two-stick fire on a winter night.

She closed her eyes and rubbed her forehead. She exhaled and slowly parted her eyelids, ready to slam them shut. Relief washed through her as her heart returned to normal rhythm. The room was its regular size, distortions gone.

Her father scowled as she joined them at their table. "You—all right? Act never been in court before?"

Hand on his arm, she smiled. "Never in the lead."

His eyes misted, then cleared as he blinked rapidly. "Do fine."

Emily's stomach flipped, and nausea rolled. She squeezed her eyes to drive the queasy lightheadedness away. "I hope so."

She turned to Tiny. Her greeting stopped when she saw the cuffs around his hands and the manacles shackling his legs. She patted her client on his shoulder. "I'll be right back."

At Dobbins' table, she took a calming breath and clasped her hands at her waist. "Marshal?"

Dobbins turned from one of the town councilmen he'd been laughing with. "Miss Peyton. How are you this morning? Your father seems to look much better." He pointed to the man on his right. "Do you know our county prosecutor, William Langdon?"

Langdon stood and extended his hand. "Miss Peyton. It's a pleasure to see you again."

Emily shook his hand briefly. "Mr. Langdon." She turned to the marshal. "Marshal Dobbins, why is Tiny Waters in cuffs and manacles?"

Langdon put out his arms, palms showing. "There's no need to get excited, Miss—"

"I'm not excited, Mt. Langdon. I simply want to know why my client is bound in chains hand and foot."

Dobbins glanced at Tiny. "I wouldn't call it bound, Miss. He's under ... restraint."

"Why?"

"So he won't escape." Dobbins said.

"Miss Peyton," the prosecutor said, "it's not unusual to keep dangerous criminals cuffed in the courtroom." Langdon's voice had the practiced smoothness of years in the law. His smugness irritated her like a broken stay in a corset.

She bit her lower lip to stifle the sarcastic bubble of laughter. "Look around this room. How could he possibly escape? Even if he wanted to, he wouldn't get more than three feet before ten men would be on top of him."

The marshal shrugged. "I don't know about that, miss. Some of these hardened criminals can be pretty resourceful."

"Har—hardened?" She grasped for words. "He's no more a hardened criminal than—" Her gaze fell on Deputy Quick, then scanned the room. "than Bill Jaspers." She pointed at the store owner sitting behind her father.

Finger aimed at her head, Dobbins said, "Don't forget. His partner is still out there somewhere. Probably not too far away. Jes waitin' for the opportunity to break him loose."

Emily clenched her fists, using the nails in her palms to keep her mouth closed. "I'm going to see the judge."

On his feet before she finished turning away, Dobbins said, "We're going with you."

She rapped on the door behind the platform as Langdon and the marshal came up behind her.

"Come in."

The small room was dim in the gray light filtering through a window behind the desk. Judge Josiah Pierce sat at the desk, a law book open before him, a glass of amber-colored liquid near his left hand. An open bottle of whiskey stood a short distance away. He looked up, a frown furrowing his brow. The fine red lines on his cheek seemed to glow. Similar lines spread across the wide nose above the walrus mustache. "Yes?"

"Your honor, Marshal Dobbins insists on keeping my client shackled hand and foot in the courtroom."

The jowly face relaxed, the frown dissolving. "Ah, you must be the Miss Emily Peyton I've heard so much about. Sorry to hear about your father. Ready for your first case?" His voice was smooth, almost gentle.

"Yes, your honor. About my client?"

Pierce looked at the marshal and the county attorney, eyebrows raised.

Langdon cleared his throat. "Escape risk, sir."

"Your honor, please. My client is about as high an escape risk as you are. Keeping him bound in open court gives the appearance he's guilty. It interferes with his right to a fair trial."

"He is guilty, your honor." Dobbins said.

Pierce held up his hand, cutting off Emily's response.

"Now, Marshal Dobbins, you know that's up to the jury to determine." He locked his gaze on Emily. "Miss Peyton, I know seeing a man in restraints can be unsettling to people like yourself who are unfamiliar with what happens in a criminal trial of this nature, and may have, shall we say, delicate dispositions."

"Your honor, with all due respect, my disposition has—"

Pierce raised his hand, palm facing her. "I understand. However, I've had experiences where a defendant tried to escape from the courtroom. The results were not pretty. One time in Wichita, two innocent people were killed before the marshal shot the criminals. The restraints stay."

"You honor, I will personally guarantee Tiny Waters will not attempt to escape. He has ties to the community and plans to stay here a long time."

The judge rubbed his chin. "The jury will decide if he stays here. As for your personal guarantee, Missy, I'm afraid it's not worth anything. How do you think a young woman like yourself can stop a man who's determined to get away?"

"But your—"

Pierce held up his hand. "Enough. The restraints stay." He pulled a gold watch from his vest. "We'll start in ten minutes."

As Emily reached the door, the judge's voice stabbed her ear. "Miss Peyton?"

She turned. Pierce clasped his hands on the desk. His dark brown eyes glowered under salt-and-pepper brows that matched his carefully waved hair. "I dislike being challenged after I've made a decision. Not in chambers. And definitely not in the courtroom. I gave you some slack in here in deference to your inexperience and your ... shall we say, more fragile emotions. But I will not tolerate it in my court." He waved his hand in dismissal. "I'll see you in ten minutes. Make sure you're ready."

In the courtroom, Emily yanked the door toward her but kept her hand on the knob to keep it from slamming. Her face burned, and her knees threatened to buckle as she made her way to the table.

She sat between her father and Terrence, face in her hands, striving to control the ragged breaths that didn't give her enough air. Hands touched her shoulders, gentle, comforting. Charlotte's voice whispered in her ear. "It's all right, Miss Em. Thank you for tryin'."

Someone stepped to the table. Deputy Quick spoke, soft, gentle. "Miss Taylor, y'all have ta stay on the other side of the rail now. Court's 'bout to begin."

Charlotte's fingers trailed away.

A pencil scratched. Her father touched her arm and nodded at the paper between them. His handwriting much clearer now.

STAY IN CONTROL.

She nodded, wiped her cheeks with her fingers. Good. No tears leaked out.

Chapter 34

The door behind the platform opened, and the rumble of noise in the room stilled.

"All rise!" Deputy Quick's voice boomed in the quiet.

Josiah Pierce stepped behind the desk, tall and powerful in his black suit, crisp white shirt, and black tie. He carefully placed a coffee mug to the right side of the desk and a leather portfolio to the left.

He surveyed the room, eyes lingering on Tiny before they rested on Emily. Doubt and pity seemed to pour from them. Something else. Something dark. Ominous. *Stop imagining things.*

The judge nodded at Quick.

"Be seated." Emily suppressed a smile at the deputy's solemnity. "Court is now in session. The Honorable Josiah Pierce presidin'."

Pierce settled into his chair, pulled some papers from his case, stacked them in front of him. He arranged an ink bottle and pen toward the front of the desk and moved his coffee cup further to the right after almost nudging it with his elbow. He fitted a pair of prince-nez glasses on his nose, the ribbon trailing into his vest. Finally, he placed his open pocket watch next to his papers.

"Are you ready, Mr. Langdon?"

The attorney stood, slight paunch pushing against his vest. "Yes, sir."

"Ready for the defense?"

Emily stood, breathed deeply. "Yes, your honor."

Pierce hesitated, eyes on George. "It's good to see you, George. I heard about your accident, and I'm glad to see you seem to be recovering." He pointed his pen at Emily. "If your daughter is half as good as you, we should have an interesting trial."

A chuckled rippled through the people behind her.

The judge looked at twelve men seated to his right. "Good morning, gentlemen of the jury." The members nodded at him.

The judge rapped his pen on the desk. "Call your first witness, Mr. Langdon."

Langdon grasped the lapels of his suit coat. "The prosecution calls Marshal John Dobbins." His voice boomed off the hard walls, drowning out the rain drumming against the windows.

Deputy Quick administered the oath, and Dobbins took the chair before the judge.

Langdon asked the marshal to describe the shooting of Mac Phillips. In a well-rehearsed statement, the marshal took only a few brief minutes to relay the events of the day of the murder and the arrest of Tiny.

The judge scratched notes while he spoke, as did Terrence. Emily leaned forward, elbows on the table, staring at the marshal, listening, hoping for some inconsistency. Nope. He had made up his mind and stuck to the theory he developed on the first day as if it were written in the Bible.

When Dobbins fell silent, the judge said, "Thank you, marshal. Do you have any other witnesses, Mr. Langdon?"

"Your honor." Emily was on her feet, on her toes, she'd risen so quickly.

"Miss Peyton?"

"Doesn't the defense get the opportunity to question this witness?" Out of the corner of her eye, her father clenched his fist and then scribbled a note. Two words: *Temper. Careful.* She shook him off with a quick wiggle of one finger.

The judge ran his hand over his forehead and through his hair. "If you think it will help your client." He studied his watch. "But be quick about it."

Emily smoothed her dress. *My client's more important than your train.* She picked up the list of questions she and her father had prepared. Terrence poised over sheets of blank paper, ready to take notes. Even though she'd memorized every word, she read each question to herself to control her breathing, her heart pounding in her ears.

Terrence on one side, her father on the other, hemmed her in, constrained her, took up too much air. She wanted to pace, but she'd never seen her father pace in a courtroom. She stepped back and shoved her chair under the table and rested one hand on its back.

The judge sighed, loud and long. "Anytime you're ready, Miss Peyton."

Biting back her first words, she smiled. "Thank you, your honor." She looked at the marshal.

"Marshal Dobbins, I believe Mr. Waters told you on the day of the shooting that he saw two men attacking Mr. Phillips and that he intervened to help."

Dobbins snorted. "Yeah, that's what he said, but there weren't any other men 'cept for his missing partner."

"Did you look for these two men he mentioned?"

"Well, yeah. 'Course I did. I sent Deputy Quick to look for them."

"How long did he look?"

"Huh?"

"How much time did Deputy Quick take to look for these two men?"

Dobbins rubbed his chin. "Don't rightly know. Must a been a while, though. Deputy's a pretty thorough man."

"Yes, I'm sure he is." Movement to her left told her Quick was squirming at the other table. *I'll apologize later.* She picked up another paper, glanced at it and laid it back down. She looked at the marshal until he met her eyes.

She kept her eyes locked on his. "Marshal, I have several sworn statements from townspeople that on the day of the shooting, Deputy Quick took no more than ten minutes to search for those two men. I am prepared to have these townspeople testify if necessary. Do you think ten minutes is long enough to do a thorough search for two armed and dangerous men? Remember, Deputy Quick was on foot."

Dobbins shifted in his seat as if a prickly pear grew in his chair. "It don't take too long to look for men who don't exist."

"How do you know they don't exist?"

"'Cuz we couldn't find them."

"Does President Cleveland exist?"

Confusion clouded Dobbins' face. "Well ... yeah."

"How do you know? Have you ever seen him? Do you know where to find him right now?"

The judge's voice boomed before Dobbins could answer. "Miss Peyton. I've given you some leeway because you're new at this and probably aren't all that familiar with how to behave in a courtroom. But you will not argue with the witness or browbeat him."

Her father patted the table.

I am calm. For now.

"Yes, your honor." She glanced at her notes. "Marshal Dobbins, did you look for Mr. Waters' alleged partner?"

"Huh?"

"The man you claim helped Mr. Waters murder and rob Mac Phillips. The man you're concerned may try to help Mr. Waters escape. The man who is as culpable for this crime as Mr. Waters. Did you look for him?"

"Uhh. No." Dobbins hung his head.

"Did you have Deputy Quick do one of his thorough searches for this man?"

The sharp rap of Pierce's pen stilled a ripple of laughter. She sensed the judge's eyes glaring at her. She ignored him.

"No, ma'am."

"Did you notify other marshals and sheriffs that you were looking for such a man?"

"No, ma'am." His voice was barely audible.

"Speak up, Marshal. I don't think the jury heard you."

He raised his head. "No, ma'am."

Emily handed her notes to Terrence and placed her hands on her hips. "Why not?"

Dobbins stared at her.

"Maybe it was because he existed only in your imagination."

Langdon was on his feet. "Your honor—"

"Miss Peyton." The judge shouted. He was out of his chair, leaning over the desk. "I just warned you about this kind of behavior. My tolerance only goes so far, and you are at the limit."

Pierce's face was almost purple.

Emily chewed her lower lip to keep a smile from spreading. Sanctimonious old coot.

"Yes, your honor."

The judge settled in his chair, adjusted his tie, and took a long sip from his cup. "Now, I assume you're done with the marshal."

Emily took her paper back from Terrence. "Actually, your honor, I have one or two more questions for the witness."

Pierce looked at his watch.

"That's all right, your honor. I'm sure I'll finish in time for you to catch your train." She made a show of running her fingers down the list of questions. "Well, pretty sure."

Her father covered his face with his hand. Terrence coughed and turned his head. Peripherally, she saw Langdon bend his head as his shoulders shook.

"Marshal Dobbins, do the names Ed and Paul Whitney mean anything to you?"

Dobbins scratched behind his ear. "They're two local cowboys—used to be anyway, near as I can recall."

"Used to be? Do you mean they're not cowboys anymore or not local anymore?"

"Not local. Don't know if they're cowboyin' somewhere else."

Langdon leaned back in his chair. "Your honor. Relevance?"

Pierce's voice cut like an ax splitting seasoned wood. "Yes, Miss Peyton. How is this relevant to the case before us?"

Emily's mind went blank. She stared at the wall behind the judge, willing her brain to work, her mouth to speak. "Well, your honor." She closed her mouth over her quavering voice. Be confident. She cleared her throat, took a sip of tepid water from the glass in front of her.

"Your honor, the Whitney brothers are shady characters, known cattle thieves, who may have had knowledge of the murder. I intend to ask the marshal what efforts were made to find them."

Pierce frowned. The people in the courtroom stirred as he continued to stare at Emily. He glanced at Langdon and sighed. "Very well. But be quick about it."

"Thank you, your honor." Her father slid a hastily scratched note in front of her.

GOOD. ONE FOR US.

"Marshal, when did you last see the Whitneys?"

He stared at the ceiling and rubbed his chin. "I reckon it was a couple of days before the shootin'."

"Why did you see them on that day?"

Dobbins squirmed in his chair, crossed his legs, clasped his hands at his waist. "Mr. Benson found they'd been stealing cattle from him. He agreed not to press charges if they returned the cattle and left town. I was there to reinforce what he said. Told 'em if they ever came back to town, I'd arrest them for rustlin'."

"So, these were two, shall we say, unsavory characters? Outlaws, really, who received mercy from their employer, Mr. Benson, and you?"

"Yeah. That's right."

"So, when Mac Phillips was murdered, why didn't you suspect them, look for them?"

"I told ya', they left town before it happened."

"Are you sure about that?"

He hesitated, looked at Langdon, then at those seated behind the railing. "Y...Yes, I am. Saw them ride out of town myself."

Emily resisted the urge to see who he might have been looking at behind her. She looked at her list of questions, let it drift to the table.

"Marshal, I have a sworn statement, and I am ready to present testimony the Whitney brothers were seen later on the day of the shooting close to here, and they knew the shooting had taken place."

"News travels fast."

"Not that fast."

The judge rapped his pen. "Miss Peyton, I caution you again about arguing with the witness."

"Your hon—" She pressed her fingernails into her palm. "Yes, your honor." She faced the witness. "Marshal Dobbins, was this information brought to your attention six days ago?"

Dobbins looked at Terrence, who kept his head down, writing on the paper in front of him. "Yes."

"What did you do with this information?"

"Nothing," he mumbled.

"Excuse me?"

"I didn't do anythin' with the information."

"Why not?"

Dobbins hunched forward and rested his elbows on the arms of the chair. He appeared to study some spot on the floor in front of Emily's table.

Emily counted to twenty, stole a glance at the judge who was drinking from his cup again. "Do you need me to repeat the question?"

The marshal picked his head up, something close to defiance in his eyes. "I didn't need to do anythin' with it." He pointed at Tiny. "Already had the killer."

His words stung like a slap, spoken with the tone of last judgment. Emily rubbed her forehead, took a deep breath. "Your Honor. Will you please remind the witness that guilt or innocence is for the jury to decide? Not him."

The judge looked over his glasses as if Emily was something he found floating upside down in his soup. He sighed and turned to Dobbins. "Marshal, she's right.

Please keep your opinions about the defendant's guilt to yourself."

"Thank you, your Honor." She focused on Dobbins, waiting until he made eye contact. "So, you didn't follow up on locating two possible witnesses to the shooting?"

"No."

"And that means you didn't follow up on the two men who might actually have done the shooting because you were convinced you had the killer. Even though you only recovered half the money." She let her voice rise. "And even though you made absolutely no effort to find the partner you alleged he had."

Langdon rose slowly. "Your Honor, I must object—"

Pierce held up his palm at the prosecutor, eyes riveted on Emily. "Miss Peyton, you will not yell at the witness." The judge stood with his fists planted on his desk, leaning forward as if he might leap to the floor. "You have exhausted my patience. I will not accept one more outburst like that in my courtroom. Control your emotions, or you'll be spending time in a cell."

George pushed back and tried to maneuver his wheelchair from behind the table.

Pierce pointed at him. "Not a word from you, George. If you can't control your daughter, maybe you should have brought in a man with more experience and self-control."

George's ears went from pink to red, his knuckles white on the arm of his chair, mouth trying to speak.

Still pointing, the judge said, "Be quiet, George."

Terrence scrambled behind Emily and wheeled George back behind the table.

Pierce stood erect, buttoned his coat, picked up his cup and drained it. He examined the inside as if puzzled by the disappearance of the contents. "The court will take a fifteen-minute recess so counsel for the defendant can calm herself."

He slammed the door behind him.

Chapter 35

Knees wobbly, Emily slumped into her chair. Blood drained from her head and went she knew not where. Her hands trembled, and she pressed them to her stomach where breakfast rumbled as if about to erupt.

Terrence placed a glass of water in front of her. She studied it, wondering how to get it to her mouth. She knew she had done it in the past, but now the mechanics escaped her.

Someone touched her left arm. She turned. Her father smiled at her, and she hugged him, enjoying the warmth and support of his good arm around her back.

Don't cry. No tears.

She straightened in her chair, sipped the water.

Facing her father again, she noted, for the first time, the traces of white—a touch at the temples—in his thick brown hair. The natural curl still sparked her envy. She searched his eyes, the brown and green flecks catching the light. The heaviness in her heart lifted slightly at the warmth in his smile.

"Didn't do so good, did I?"

He shrugged. "Not good—idea—to annoy the judge."

"He shouldn't drink on the bench."

George's jaw worked, and he frowned. "Doesn't excuse making him angry."

She nodded. "I'm sorry. Maybe I am too emotional for this."

His hand slapped the table. He shook his head violently. "No. Need—passion. Tiny's life—stake. You did right."

Emily glanced over her father's shoulder. Several members of the jury watched her, some smiled, some shook their heads, some did both. She nodded toward them. "Did I help Tiny with the jury?"

"Don't know. Made—Dobbins—look bad. Planted—doubt. See if it grows." He squeezed her hand. "Talk to Tiny."

Tiny held Charlotte's hands over the banister separating them. Terrence stood behind them, listening to Joseph Warner.

Tiny grinned as she approached. "Thank you, ma'am. I think you did a great job showing the marshal didn't do all he could."

Emily touched her forehead. "I hope so. I hope the jury listened and believe there is somebody else out there who could have done it."

Charlotte touched her arm. "How couldn't they? You showed how the Whitneys was around. I know they're the ones."

Movement at the back of the courtroom distracted Emily. Abraham Montgomery chatted with Bill Jaspers. Next to her father, Priscilla Montgomery stared at Emily. Lips pressed together, nose flaring, venomous anger seemed to arc from her green eyes. She held Emily's eyes a moment longer, then turned and, with a smile, chatted with Mrs. Jaspers.

Emily shuddered and turned back to find Charlotte smiling. "Miss Em, don't go frettin' 'bout Miss Prissy Montgomery. She's upset 'cuz a all the time Terrence spends helpin' Tiny. She thinks you're tryin' to steal him."

"I don't want him." A blush crept up her neck as Terrence turned her way. "Wait. I didn't mean that the way it sounded. Terrence, you're a good friend and a big help, but I have no intention of getting between you and your fiancée."

Terrence smiled, but it didn't seem to reach his eyes.

"All rise!" Deputy Quick's voice silenced the room, and everyone turned their attention to the judge. Pierce grabbed the back of the chair as he leaned to place his cup on the desk. He sat as if unsure the chair would support him and pulled a blank sheet of paper from his case.

"Be seated. Court is in session." Quick slipped into his seat next to Dobbins.

It took a moment for the judge's eyes to lock on the county attorney. "Do you have anything else, Mr. Langdon?"

Langdon rose half out of his seat. "No, your honor."

"Very good." Pierce glanced at his watch before facing Emily. "Do you have anything, Miss Peyton?"

Emily stood, smoothed the front of her dress. "Yes, sir. I have several witnesses."

The judge frowned, looked at Dobbins. "I thought there were no witnesses to the shooting."

Dobbins spread his arms. "There weren't, your honor. I don't know what she has in mind."

"I have witnesses to corroborate the information I raised in my examination of the marshal. In addition, I plan to present witnesses to testify to Mr. Waters' character and contribution to the community."

A voice rang out from the back. "You mean like his being the best dang pitcher on the baseball team."

"Quiet!" The judge tried to rap his pen on the desk, but it slid from his grasp and rolled to the floor. A juror dashed forward, picked it up and handed it to him.

Pierce wound his watch. "Miss Peyton, I think you did an admirable job of getting your information in already. I don't think we need to take more of the jury's time hearing what you've covered so well, if dramatically, in your examination of the marshal."

"But, your Hon—"

He raised his hand, palm outward. "You said you have sworn statements, correct?"

"Yes, sir." *Stay calm. Don't make him more angry.*

"We'll share those with the jury, and if they have any questions during their deliberations, then we'll have your witnesses testify."

Emily sighed. "Yes, sir."

"Good. Now as to these character witnesses. It's been my experience that character witnesses basically say the same thing. I don't see any need to bore the jury with several versions of what an upstanding citizen the defendant is. One witness should do it. I'll let you decide which one."

Next to her, George shrugged and scribbled a note.

BEST WE'RE GOING TO GET FROM HIM TODAY.

Emily's body wanted to sag to the floor and curl up under the table. She hadn't done enough to help Tiny. But the judge wouldn't let her do more. And her father agreed with him.

She looked at the three names. Terrence, Pastor Dalton, Abraham Montgomery. Which one? The best friend? The pastor? His employer? Her father pointed at Terrence's name. She shook her head. A good man, respected, but young and primarily a friend.

"Your honor, the defense calls Abraham Montgomery." The room stirred as the rancher made his way through the railing and swore the oath with Deputy Quick.

Emily led Montgomery through her questions, establishing that Tiny had worked for him for nearly five years. Tiny came across as dedicated, loyal, devoted to Charlotte and their dream of owning their own ranch.

A few of the jury members nodded as Montgomery described Tiny. If she could put Terrence and Pastor Dalton on the stand, she might persuade the others that Tiny was not a killer. A glance at the judge told her he was barely tolerating Montgomery's testimony.

When Montgomery finished, she sat and read a note from her father.

DID ALL YOU COULD.

She shook her head and scribbled a response.

No. Did all I would let me do. Not enough.

Pierce said, "Mr. Langdon, do you have any questions for this witness?"

Langdon and Dobbins huddled close, the attorney scribbling notes as the marshal whispered. After laying his pencil carefully on the table, Landon stood, tugging at the cuffs of his coat. "Just a couple, your honor." He glanced at Emily. "Won't take too long." He rubbed his chin. "Mr. Montgomery, would you say Mr. Waters has been very eager to buy his ranch?"

Montgomery grinned. "Oh, yes. Constantly asking if there's any extra work or if he could lend himself out to other ranches. Always looking for a way to make more money."

"Would you say he was desperate to get this money?"

Montgomery hesitated, studied his hands. "I know he was very anxious to get married, to get his fiancée out of working in Dutton's saloon."

Langdon turned to look at Tiny. "So anxious, so desperate, he looked to get the money the quickest way possible. To steal it and to kill for it, if he had to."

"Your honor." Emily heard the screech in her voice as she leapt to her feet, her chair banging against the railing. "That is improper."

"You know she's right, Mr. Langdon." A wry smile twisted the judge's mouth. "You should know better than that."

Langdon looked at the floor. "Yes, your honor."

"Now do you have any more questions of the witness?"

"Uh, no, sir. I'm done."

"Are you finished now, Miss Peyton?" The judge drummed his fingers on the desk.

"Yes, your honor. With all you'll allow me to present."

He scowled. "Young lady, it is only out of respect for your father I'm allowing you to remain in my courtroom."

George again pushed his wheelchair from the table.

"Not now, George. You don't want to push me over the edge."

George wrote on his paper, then scratched it out. Emily could make out some of the words.

SO DRU ... WOULDN'T FEE L... THING ... LANDED.

Pierce held his inkwell with one hand and squinted while he guided the pen into it. He scratched on his paper and returned the pen to its holder. "Well, now we're finally able to turn this matter over to the jury."

Folding his hands on the desk, for the next five minutes he gave the jury their instructions for deliberating the case.

As he summarized the evidence, Emily fumed when he made no mention of the Whitney brothers or the marshal's feeble efforts to verify any of Tiny's story.

George covered her hand, stroked the back with his thumb.

Deputy Quick led the jury through a side door. In a few minutes, he reappeared, closed the door, and positioned himself in front of it. The judge motioned for Dobbins and Langdon to approach the desk, and the three held a whispered conversation.

Chapter 36

Emily scooted her chair close to Tiny and Charlotte.

Tiny chewed his lip. "What do you think, ma'am?"

"I don't know, Tiny." She put her hand on his arm briefly. "The verdict could go either way. I think some jurors may doubt the marshal's theory."

Charlotte covered Emily's hand. "Tiny and me appreciate all you did."

Emily nodded and wished the lump in her stomach would go away. Movement behind Tiny caught her attention. Terrence and Priscilla stood at the railing, close together, trying to whisper, but their voices were rising.

"Now that this is over." She gestured at Tiny. "I expect you'll come back to your senses."

Pink crept up Terrence's neck. "I don't think I ever left my senses, Priscilla. I was helping a friend." He touched her elbow. "Isn't that what Pastor Dalton tells us Jesus would do?"

Her eyes narrowed, grew cold. "I think Jesus would be more selective about who he associated with in the helping."

"Come on, darling. Be reasonable. Even your father helped."

Her finger jabbed his chest. "Yes, but he didn't spend hours at somebody's house. Hours he could have spent with me."

Emily opened her mouth, but Priscilla poked her chin in the air, spun on her heel, and walked away.

Terrence looked like he'd just swung and missed for the last out in a losing game. His hands gripped the railing, and he shook his head.

Emily reached to touch his arm, pulled her hand back, smoothed her dress. "I'm sorry, Terrence. I seem to have come between you and Priscilla. I didn't mean to. When this is over, I'll talk to her."

He faced her, his attempt at a smile barely curving his lips. "You didn't do anything. She'll calm down in a few days. I'll see if Mrs. Crenshaw will make some of those fluffy pastries she likes, and I'll bring her some flowers and apologize."

"As long as she understands I'm not trying to steal her man. That's the farthest thing from my mind."

He looked at the floor. "I know."

A rustle of noise swept from behind her like a prairie blizzard. She turned to see Deputy Quick holding the door open as the jury filed in and took their seats. As she settled next to her father, she whispered, "That didn't take long."

George glanced at his watch open on the table. "Seven minutes."

She gulped air, pushing it past the lump in her throat. Under the table, she stroked her stomach.

Judge Pierce dipped his pen and held it over a sheet of paper.

"Mr. Foreman, have you reached a verdict?"

Simon Watkins stood. "We have, your honor."

"Well, that was a most efficient and judicious use of time. I congratulate you."

He turned to Tiny. "The defendant will stand."

Tiny stood, Emily with him. Her fingers touched the table, ready to grab for support as her knees had all the strength of an over-cooked carrot.

"Mr. Foreman, please read the verdict."

Watkins cleared his throat and held the small, shaking piece of paper close to his face. "We find the defendant, Tiny Waters, guilty of the murder and robbery of Mac Phillips."

The room whirlpooled. Emily grasped the table. Her father clenched his fist and banged it hard. She turned toward Tiny. He stood like he had an iron rod up his back. He stared straight ahead, a single tear trailing down his cheek. Behind him, Charlotte curled over, face covered by her hands, body heaving.

The repeated rapping of the judge's gavel gradually silenced the room except for Charlotte's muffled sobs. From the corner of her eye, Emily saw Caroline Everett move next to Charlotte, wrap her arms around the young woman, and rock her. Just like she had done for Emily when her mother left. The lump in her throat threatened to move higher.

"Thank you, members of the jury, for your service. You are dismissed." The judge made a notation on his paper. Still holding the pen, he adjusted his tie and looked at Tiny.

"Tiny Waters." Tiny didn't move. "You have been found guilty of murder and robbery. Under the law of the State of Kansas, I hereby sentence you to death by hanging."

Emily braced her hands on the table and leaned forward, not wanting to hear more, unable to plug her ears.

"You will be transported to the state penitentiary, where you will be hanged on a date to be determined." He paused. "May God have mercy on your soul."

Emily stared at the table, her notes and papers a blur. A tear plopped, smearing the ink. She swiped her eye. *Don't cry.*

Dobbins led Tiny away, Charlotte and Caroline trailing behind. Terrence gathered the papers on the table, slowly, tenderly stacking them before sliding them into her case.

Behind her, she heard the courtroom empty, murmured conversations fading through the doors.

Judge Pierce spoke. "You know, George, crippled as you are, you should have presented this case. Women are too emotional, too fragile for the courtroom."

"Enough." George's baritone was in full force. "You pompous old goat." He wheeled around the table. "You drunken excuse for a judge." George's face burned like a smithy's forge. "You mishandled this trial from the beginning because you had to get to Wichita to see your mistress."

Pierce gulped from his cup. "George, I'm warning you—"

"Be quiet. I'm reporting this disgrace of a trial to the bar—"

George grabbed at his chest, gasping for air, his face suddenly gray.

"Father. No." Emily screamed and scrambled around the table, knocking her chair on its back. Her father slumped in his chair, eyes closed, right arm limp and dangling.

She wrapped her arms around him, tears flowing. "No—No—No."

Doc Everett appeared beside her. "Emily, let me see him."

Gentle hands took her shoulders, helped her stand. She turned.

Judge Pierce stared at her, his face pale, eyes narrowed to slits.

"You—" Emily froze, unable to utter the curses roiling in her. "Look what you've done to my father. You're a sorry excuse for judge, for a human being—"

Pierce pointed his gavel as if it were a sword. "One more word from you, young lady, and I'll hold you in contempt."

"You can't. You already adjourned the court." Emily shook her head. "Even a first year lawyer knows that. You make me sick."

She turned, heart tripping like a telegraph key, breath rasping in her throat.

Terrence was there. Terrence. Sweet, gentle Terrence. She let his arms encircle her, and she cried into his chest.

Chapter 37

Emily sat on the edge of the bed, stroking her father's hair, her own heart pounding at the sight of his ashen face. George lay on his bed, unconscious, covered to his neck by a crisp white sheet. Dark gray bags hung under his eyes, his blue lips hung slack. For the first time, she noticed thin red veins lacing his eyelids. Did his shallow breathing take in enough air?

On the other side of the bed, Doc listened to her father's heart, held his limp wrist, lips moving in a silent count. Doc's own pale face glistened with sweat in the lamplight. Next to him, Caroline stood, hands at her waist, waiting for any instructions Doc might have.

Doc sighed, focused on Emily. "His heart is very bad. He needs rest." He rubbed his face. "I'm not sure how much good that will do." He paced to the window and crossed his arms. "Shouldn't have let him go to court."

"Not your fault, Doc." Emily's voice sounded weak, faraway in her own ears. "I wanted him there." She clenched her fists, then relented and allowed the tears to flow.

An arm wrapped around her shoulder. Caroline pulled her into a tight embrace, smoothed her hair, rocked her. Eight years old again, snuggled in the warmth of a mother's love. But not her mother, who never hugged. But a woman who had no children, a woman who calmed, soothed, encouraged Emily as her own child. Emily wrapped her arms around Caroline and cried.

Caroline murmured. Emily realized the woman was praying. The soft rhythm of the voice relaxed her even as she reminded herself the words themselves did no good.

Another presence hovered in the doorway. Terrence. Hands in his pockets, blond hair hanging damp from the rain, eyes closed. The memory of his embrace in the court room warmed her. Embarrassed her too. She hadn't meant to enjoy it as much as she did. Didn't realize it would be so hard to break away when Doc said they needed to get her father home. Terrence left her then to help Doc and several others take her father home, carrying the wheelchair across muddy streets, while Caroline and Charlotte held someone's coat over him to shelter him from the rain.

Terrence, so tender with her, so gentle. No wonder Priscilla was so protective, so determined to fight for him. *I sure would if I were her.*

Charlotte poked her head around Terrence. "I've made some tea and coffee, heated up some stew."

Charlotte's sallow face drooped from the bags under her eyes to the downturn of her mouth. Her chin quivered. Another lance of guilt stabbed Emily.

"You need to rest too, Charlotte," Caroline said.

The young woman shook her head. "No. It's better if I keep busy—if I don't let my mind—" She buried her face in her apron as Caroline rushed to embrace her.

Doc turned from the window. "Terrence, let's you and I get the food on the table. We all need to eat. Especially you, Emily, after the day you've had. And then I want you to rest."

She placed her hand on her father's shoulder. "But—"

"Don't sass me, young lady." Love permeated his soft tone. "Between court and this," he gestured at George, "you've had to bear too much. I don't want two invalids in the same house."

Caroline, one arm around Charlotte, turned Emily from the bed. Emily stopped and kissed her father's forehead, touched his cheek. "Don't you dare die on me. I'll never forgive you."

With a gentleness that swelled her heart, Terrence served her and Charlotte bowls of stew and poured tea.

She bowed her head as Doc prayed a blessing and took a tentative sip of the stew, convinced it would never get down her throat. The meaty taste on her tongue woke hunger. She had two bowls as well as a large slice of sourdough bread and three cups of tea.

"It's good to see you eat, darlin'," Caroline said. "I believe you were living on coffee and pencils the last few days."

Doc lit his cigar. "Now, I want you and Charlotte to go to bed. Caroline will help you both. Tomorrow, we'll talk about Caroline and Mrs. Marcand taking care of your father until Charlotte feels ready to do more."

"What about me?" Emily's throat burned. "I need to help take care of him too."

He shook his head, held up one finger. "You need to take care of you. And you need to take care of the practice. You're it right now."

"I think this morning proved I'm not that good at practicing law."

"Nonsense." Doc's sharp tone jolted her head upright. "You proved yourself an excellent lawyer this morning. You showed the marshal's theory was full of holes. With a different judge, and more time, you would've won."

She patted his hand. "Thank you, Doc. But a good lawyer would have made better use of what the judge did allow." Exhaustion crept from her ankles to her eyes. Her neck struggled to keep her head upright. Muscles pulled at her, begging her to lie down. Her fingers felt like ten-pound weights were attached to each one as she touched her forehead.

Before Doc could respond, Caroline was at her side, helping her to her feet. "Come, young lady. Bed for you and then a long hot bath and more bed. Doctor's—well, nurse's orders."

Terrence touched her arm. "Emily. I think you were excellent today. I know you did all you could."

She took his hand, smiled, wanted to protest his compliment, could only mutter, "Thank you," as Caroline led her to her room. Her last glance was of Terrence and his warm, cocked-eyed smile.

In her room, she changed into a nightdress, every movement slow and deliberate as she had to coax each muscle to function.

Caroline pulled the covers to her chin as she settled into the bed. She kissed Emily's cheek. "Sleep, child. Sleep."

"Umm. Tell Terrence thank you. Couldn't have done it without him." Soft, pleasant darkness engulfed her. Emily drifted, resting on what seemed a thick cloud. Her last thought *wouldn't have wanted to do it without him ... need him...*

Chapter 38

Awkwardness flowed over Terrence like a too-tight suit. He ducked his head and half-closed his eyes, jingled the coins in his pocket. He wanted to step into the outer office, to give Charlotte and Tiny some privacy in the dank cell area. But if he did, the marshal would step in. Right now, he hovered just outside the door. A compromise to give the couple some time together without Dobbins' leers.

At least the man settled for keeping Charlotte's reticule on his desk and not searching her. Terrence cringed at the memory of the marshal's hands patting his legs and arms, running over his back and front, probing each pocket. Quick had done the same with Charlotte but with a shyness and gentleness that were almost childlike.

The couple stood at the bars in an awkward embrace, the silence heavy, as ominous as the stillness of the air before a storm broke. Tiny rubbed Charlotte's fingers, his eyes riveted to her face. His walnut-colored hair hung over his ears, his face pale and drawn. Sadness filled his eyes, the ponderous bags under them stretched his thin face. Terrence wondered when the man last slept for more than a few minutes.

Charlotte's blue eyes glittered with unshed tears, her black hair hanging long to her shoulders, her bonnet dangling down her back.

Somehow, they were able to kiss between the bars.

He searched for words to give comfort and hope. None came. He closed his eyes and slumped against the wall.

"Terrence." Charlotte's voice snapped him alert. "Come pray with us."

He crossed the distance in one stride. At first, neither spoke. Then Charlotte began, her voice soft, quavering. "Lord God, please give Tiny the strength and courage he needs to bear this burden. We know he's innocent. Show this to others, show us who the real killers are." Her voice broke and she gulped. "Let him know my love will never leave him."

Tiny rested his forehead against the bars. "I'm so sorry, darlin'. Here I thought I was doin' something good helping that man, and nobody believes me." A tear trickled down his cheek, he swiped it away.

"We believe you." Terrence's voice cracked. "Me and Charlotte. Emily and Mr. Peyton too."

"And Miss Caroline and Doc Everett." Charlotte stroked Tiny's cheek. "And God knows you're innocent."

Tiny snorted. "That doesn't seem to help much around here. Even Pastor Dalton was tellin' me to confess, to 'ease my burden' he said, so I can get into heaven."

Terrence bit his lip.

Charlotte said it for him. "Pastor means well, but he can be as dumb as horse manure sometimes."

Tink. Tink. Tink.

The sound of silverware tapping crystal brought Terrence back to the reality of the Randolph House dining room.

"I'm here, you know." The glare in Priscilla's green eyes betrayed her light tone and slight smile. "Your mind keeps going someplace else."

"Sorry. Still thinking about Tiny."

She sipped her wine and smoothed the thick linen tablecloth. "Well, I'm just grateful that's behind us. Now the town—and we—can get back to normal."

"I wonder if we'll ever get back to normal after what happened."

"Well, not if you keep brooding over it." She covered his hand. "You must put it behind you, Terrence. You did all you could—more than you needed to, if you ask me. The man is guilty. You need to accept that."

He nodded, fiddled with his fork.

"And that Emily. Making a spectacle of herself like that."

"She was doing all she could for her client." He didn't realize how sharply he'd spoken until Priscilla pulled back, hand at her slender, elegant throat, fingering the emerald necklace resting there.

"I think Father is right. The courtroom is no place for a woman. We're just too emotional and impatient. I'm glad you won't be spending any more time with her."

Their food arrived, and the waiter refilled Priscilla's glass. Knife and fork poised over his steak, he glanced at her, at the way twin curls of her auburn hair framed her face and accented her eyes. Eyes of deep emerald. So different from Emily's light blue. "Did you ever have a dream of doing something others said you couldn't because you're a woman?"

A frown creased the smooth ski between her eyes, skin darker than Emily's, as she chewed slowly. She shook her head. "No. Father always lets me do anything I want, and Mother makes sure I know how to behave like a lady."

She smiled and leaned forward, the bodice of her scooped-neck, burgundy dress straining. "The only dream I have is to marry someone who'll love me and help me give grandchildren to Mother and Father."

Her eyes bore into him, reminding him he longed to be that man. Did he? Why the question? Emily flashed across his mind. Her laugh, the set of her jaw in the courtroom, her tenderness with her father, her vulnerability.

Enough.

Emily didn't need, or appear to want, a man. At least not one who couldn't accept her and her dream. Could he?

Where did that come from? He drove the question from his head. Priscilla held his heart. Emily and he shared a common cause—Tiny's innocence. With Priscilla, he shared a dream—marriage and a family.

Terrence gazed at Priscilla as she chatted about her upcoming trip to Saint Louis with her mother for clothes. The words rippled like a brook but didn't really penetrate. Her eyes held him, the graceful maneuvers with her knife and fork, the way she snuggled her wine glass in her hand hypnotized him. Not for the first time, he knew the spell of her beauty held him in a grip he never wanted to loosen.

A shadow approached the table. "Miss Priscilla, how delightful to see you." A man lifted her hand to his lips and kissed it, a gesture too personal, too familiar.

Terrence looked at the intruder. As tall as him, dark hair and mustache, small scar on his left cheek. Maybe a couple of years older and ten pounds heavier.

"Lionel." Priscilla's voice dripped like spun honey. "What a surprise. I didn't know you were in town."

Terrence stood.

"Oh, where are my manners?" Priscilla giggled. "Lionel, this is Terrence McCarthy. He holds an important position at the bank, working for Mr. Warner. Terrence, this is Lionel Hutchins, an old friend of the family. His father owns one of the largest riverboat companies on the Mississippi. Lionel is vice president."

They shook hands. Firm grip. Steady blue-gray eyes. His military bearing caused Terrence to straighten his own back.

Priscilla placed her hand on Lionel's arm. "Would you care to join us, Lionel?" Her hand lingered, her eyes bright. Terrence clenched his fist, held his breath.

Hutchins smoothed his mustache. "No, I don't want to interrupt your meal. Plus, I've had an exhausting day. I just stopped in to have a meal sent to my room, and when I saw your glowing presence, I had to come over and say hello."

Priscilla blushed. Fists clenched even tighter, Terrence resisted the urge to punch Hutchins in his patrician nose.

"A pleasure meeting you, Mr. McCarthy."

"Same here." Terrence didn't care how rude he sounded. Hutchins didn't seem to notice and turned his attention to Priscilla once again.

"Will you be attending my father's ball on Saturday, Priscilla?"

"Yes, Mother and I will both be there," Priscilla said. "She's talked of nothing else for the last week."

Lionel bowed slightly. "Please save at least one dance for me."

"Of course." Priscilla's smile would have melted the Missouri in the dead of winter.

With a final nod, Hutchins performed a precise military turn and walked away.

Seated once again, Terrence gulped his water, his meal as appetizing as day-old oatmeal.

Priscilla slipped a dainty bite of chicken between her lips and sipped her wine. "What a pleasant surprise. He's such a sweet man."

"You certainly seemed charmed by him."

She touched her high-swept hair. "Oh, Terrence. He's just an old friend of the family."

"Seemed like it was a little more than that to me."

Her hand covered his. "Terrence, I do believe you're jealous."

Am I? Is that why I feel like punching the wall?

Wine glass to her lips, her eyes smiled, and a warmth washed over him.

"I guess maybe I am. You mean the world to me, Priscilla. And he acted like he was courting you."

"I think it's just his old Southern charm. His grandfather owned a plantation in Mississippi until the war. Lionel graduated from the Citadel. Southern gentility is in his blood."

Terrence nodded, aware of the tender ache slowly dissolving under her smile and touch. He took a small bite of his steak. "You didn't mention anything about a ball in Saint Louis. I thought you and your mother were just going shopping."

"I didn't?" Another sip of wine. Her gazed drifted toward the door Hutchins left through. "Must have slipped my mind."

Chapter 39

Warm sun reminded Terrence summer would soon be here. He bid a good evening to Harry Bannister and turned toward the Peyton house. The previous evening's dinner with Priscilla and encounter with Lionel Hutchins niggled at him, as it had all day. He admitted he was jealous—threatened—by Hutchins. The man offered Priscilla more than he ever could and opened a door to a world Terrence could never enter. A world Priscilla seemed interested in exploring.

Guilt pricked a sharp finger. What about his feelings for Emily? He liked her. Always had. Her confidence and courage were so unusual, so different from any other woman he'd ever met, especially Priscilla. Working with Emily on Tiny's defense opened a door he hadn't expected. Her dedication and vulnerability sparked a tenderness that grew to more than friendship. He suspected Priscilla sensed it. She sure showed signs of jealousy, not knowing Emily would never admit to needing a man.

He passed a feed store, and the sound of heavy sacks thudding to the floor sparked an image of Tiny dropping through the gallows trap door. One hand on his lurching stomach, Terrence wiped away the clammy sweat beading his brow. What more could they do? No witnesses, no evidence to confirm his friend's story. Yet, no one saw him do it either.

As each day passed, Terrence watched Tiny sink deeper into a quiet, somber mood. Hopelessness draped its yoke, and Tiny withdrew more and more. Only Charlotte sparked a smile, a smile too quickly replaced by tear-filled eyes and arms that held his fiancée as close and tight as the bars allowed.

Lord, if there's a way to help Tiny, a way we haven't seen, please show us.

Emily opened the door at his knock. Her slumped shoulders gave the appearance of an old woman humped over by age. Heavy eyes and a pale, drawn face added to the illusion. He wanted to take her in his arms, stroke her hair, and let her rest in him.

He took her hand briefly as she stepped back to let him enter. A smile touched the corners of her mouth then flitted away, a leaf carried by the wind.

"How is he?" he asked as Emily led him to the parlor.

"Resting." Her fingers went to her forehead and her voice quavered. "Sometimes, he's so still, I have to lean over to make sure he's still breathing." She twisted her hands at her waist. He reached for them, and she dropped them to her side.

He shoved his own hands in his pockets. "What does Doc say?"

Emily backed up a couple steps and glanced behind her before perching on the edge of the sofa. Terrence sat an arm's length away. Arms crossed at her stomach, she grasped her elbows and stared at the floor. "He said Father's heart gave out from the strain of the accident and the excitement of the trial." She scuffed her toe across the pale blue carpet.

"Said it didn't help the way the judge provoked him at the end."

Terrence nodded. "Is your father going to make it?"

Emily sighed and leaned forward, as if she wanted to rock herself. "Yes, but he's going to be very weak for a long time, maybe the rest of his life."

She faced him, eyes brimming. "Terrence, I don't know what I'm going to do."

He closed the distance between them. His arms were around her as she snuggled against him, arms around his waist. She quieted, her breathing shuddery and shallow, her back and shoulders tight under his arms.

Hesitantly, he lifted his right hand to her hair, the strands soft to the touch. He stroked it, gentle, easy caresses as his left hand traced small circles on her back. She sighed. Her breathing became more regular. She relaxed into his arms.

His eyes darted to the windows. Can anyone see in? He didn't care. Emily needed someone to do this, and he was the one right now.

The door to George Peyton's bedroom opened, and Caroline Everett entered the parlor. Terrence wanted to jump up as heat crept up his cheeks.

Caroline cocked her head and smiled at Emily. "She's asleep. Good." She touched Terrence on the shoulder. "Thank you for being a friend for her."

He glanced at the window again.

She patted his shoulder. "Don't fret what people will think. They don't matter. What's important is you gave her the right help at the right time." She drew the curtains and the room dimmed to a golden glow.

Caroline left the room and came back with a blanket and small pillow. Very slowly, Terrence shifted his position so he could lay Emily on the couch. As he lowered her head to the pillow, he turned to stop his lips from reaching to brush her cheek.

Caroline spread the blanket over Emily who took the edge in her fist and tucked it under her chin.

"Just like when she was little."

Terrence again shoved his hands in his pockets and wondered at the roiling of his emotions as images of Priscilla competed with visions of his lips on Emily's.

Chapter 40

Voices, soft and murmuring, roused Emily. Through half-opened eyes, she saw the parlor lay empty, the light a dusky gray of the setting sun. She sighed and pulled the blanket closer under her chin and snuggled into the pillow, closing her eyes, seeking the dreamless slumber she'd awakened from.

Wait. Blanket? Pillow? In the parlor?

She sat up, fingers to forehead, memories rushing—almost overwhelming—like the creek in spring rains.

Tiny. Guilty.

Father. Unconscious, lips blue, face ghostly white.

The chaos in his room when they'd brought him home. Doc, the marshal, and the deputy laying him on the bed. Caroline next to her, arm around her. Everything through a blur of tears. Doc tending to her father, stethoscope to his chest, fingers holding her father's wrist or lifting his red-veined eyelid.

She'd unlaced and removed her father's half-boots and socks. She'd massaged his cold, blue-tinted feet, wishing her hands would spread warmth through his whole body.

Shoulders slumped, Doc had sat on the edge of the bed, pinching the bridge of his nose. "There's nothing more I can do right now." Fatigue laced his voice, and something else was there as well. Sadness and a trace of anger too. "Let him rest. And pray."

Emily's fists clamped tight, muscles knotted all the way to her shoulders. Pray? For what? For God to undo what he's already done?

Then Terrence knocked on the front door. His voice so tender, his arms so welcoming, releasing the tension lancing through her muscles, winding them tighter and tighter. His hand on her hair so gentle. She didn't want him to let go. Ever.

She scooped up the blanket and lumped it into the corner of the couch. Smoothing her dress, she walked toward the voices in the kitchen, knees buckling.

Terrence sat with Doc and Caroline at the table where Emily and her father took most of their meals. A cloud of pale blue hung over the table from Doc's cigar. The tobacco aroma mingled with fresh coffee. Emily covered her stomach to quiet the hunger pangs rumbling.

Terrence stood and held her chair, his hand light under her elbow. She wanted to take that hand, hold it to her cheek, stroke it with her fingers. Instead, she smiled. "Thank you."

He nodded and resumed his seat.

Caroline poured a mug of coffee and placed it before her.

Emily inhaled, pulling the scent of the brew deep into her lungs, savoring it with closed eyes. She sipped and welcomed the warmth slide down her throat.

Mug just below her lips, she looked at Doc. "Well?"

Doc took a long drag on his cigar and rubbed his chin. "Your father has the strongest will to live I've ever seen."

If she'd been standing, she would have fallen as the relief of his words flooded her, turning her muscles into wet rope. Terrence reached toward her, then pulled his hand back.

Doc tapped his cigar ash into a dish on the table. "But it will be a long, long time before I let him back in the court room." He drank a long pull from his coffee. "If ever."

Emily's mug clunked against the table. "That may well kill him."

Doc shook his head. "Oh, he'll gripe and complain. Probably yell and cuss too. But kill him? No. George Peyton is too stubborn." He laughed. "He'll want to do everything to make my life miserable. That'll help keep him alive, too."

Emily touched her forehead. "You're not going to be the one living with him."

Doc clamped his cigar between his teeth. "Had enough of that after the accident."

Emily closed her eyes. *He's going to live.* He would be a constant challenge. It'd be like amputating both his legs. But her hero, her mentor, would still be with her, still there to teach and guide her. "We can make it work."

Caroline covered Emily's hand. "Charlotte will be here to help."

Charlotte. And Tiny.

She looked at Terrence.

His eyes filled with a tender sadness. "They're doing the best they can. Charlotte's at the jail every chance she gets. Dobbin's leaving them alone."

"They must hate me."

Terrence eyebrows arched. "Why would they do that?"

She couldn't keep the tremble out of her voice. "Because I lost the trial, and Tiny's going to hang."

Caroline's voice scolded like when she was little. "Emily Louise Peyton, don't you talk like that. You did everything you could for Tiny. That—that—that poor excuse for a judge stole it from you."

Doc patted his wife's arm. "She's right, Em. You had John Dobbins squirming like a worm in the sun because

213

you showed how he didn't do enough. The judge helped Langdon try the case."

The words sounded good, but guilt covered her like snow on a pine tree after a heavy blizzard. "Maybe I should take up teaching. That seems to be one of the places they'll let a woman work."

Terrence's soft voice caressed her ears. "That'd be a waste. You are a good attorney, Emily. God has given you gifts and talents for practicing law. Don't walk away from it. Not now."

God gave me a gift? She shook her head. As much as she liked Terrence, this religious stuff would always keep them from being more than friends.

Three sets of eyes studied her. She nodded. "All right. When Father's strong enough, I'll talk it over with him."

"He is so proud of you," Caroline said. "You know he'll want you to keep going."

"That's right," Doc added. "When he's back to his old self, he'll go over every step of the trial. He'll show you that you have nothing to be ashamed of."

Emily shook her head. "I don't know that will make any difference. I'll still be a woman. And Tiny is still going to hang."

Chapter 41

Emily closed her eyes at the sound of metal clanking. The brittle tones bounced off the brick walls like gunshots. Tiny Waters lifted his manacled hands. They stopped at his chest, jerked short by the chain linking them to the cuffs around his ankles. His red-rimmed eyes sought Emily's. His face hung long and thin in sadness. A puppy beaten one too many times.

"Are those really necessary?" She glared at the marshal.

Dobbins puffed a cloud of smoke toward Tiny's face. "Yes, Miss Peyton. This is a convicted murderer. Regulations mandate all necessary precautions be taken to ensure the safety of the guards and the citizens."

"You recited that very well, Marshal. Judge Pierce help you memorize it?"

One of the prison guards snickered and checked the chain around Tiny's waist.

Dobbins glowered under his bushy eyebrows. "Still need a lesson on showing respect to legal authority, Miss Peyton?"

"I have the utmost respect for the law, Marshal."

He held her gaze for several seconds before he puffed on his cigarette and turned to the guards. "You almost ready?"

The one who snickered nodded. "Yep. All set. You and your deputy ready to escort us to the train?"

"Let's go. Can't wait to get this vermin out of my jail."

Tiny shuffled from the cell to the outer office, chains clanking and dragging on the wood floor.

Charlotte gasped and embraced Tiny, arms twined around his neck, sobs rocking her body. Tears ran down Tiny's cheeks. Emily swallowed the guilt rising in her throat.

Dobbins grabbed Charlotte's arm and wrapped his other arm around her waist. "There'll be none of that."

"Let go of her." Terrence stood in the doorway, leaning forward, fists clenched.

"Or what, banker-boy?" Dobbins held the squirming Charlotte close to his side.

Terrence stepped closer. "Or I'll put you on the floor."

Dobbins looked from Terrence to Emily and laughed. "Someone else who needs a lesson on respecting the law." He released Charlotte who took Tiny in her arms. "Unfortunately, I don't have the time for a lesson today. But show disrespect again, McCarthy, and I'll give you a good one. And I'll have a talk with Mr. Warner and Mr. Montgomery about how unsuitable you are for the bank and Miss Priscilla."

Terrence dropped his fists to his side and exhaled. "Go ahead. If it makes a difference to either one of them, then they're not the men I thought they were, and I'm best shook of them."

Dobbins turned to the gun rack on the wall behind his desk and took down two shotguns. After loading them, he handed one to Deputy Quick and the two proceeded to the boardwalk.

A small crowd arched around a wagon. Their murmurs fell silent at the sight of Dobbins, shotgun braced against his hip, and Quick, who cradled his in his arms.

Emily stood near Terrence as Tiny and Charlotte exited the marshal's office, a prison guard before and behind. Charlotte held Tiny's arms, her back straight, chin up. Emily fought back the tears. She longed to close the distance between herself and Terrence, to feel his arm around her shoulder, holding her close.

Tiny looked straight ahead, struggling with the chains. His jaw quivered as he maneuvered down the two steps to the street. At the back of the wagon, Charlotte again embraced him, kissed him.

Terrence stepped into the street. Emily followed. The four stood in a close circle.

The guards took a step back. Behind them, Emily heard Dobbins' exaggerated sigh and the tapping of his boot. She ignored him.

The marshal ensured Tiny was secured to an iron ring mounted on the side of the wagon. Deputy Quick and one of the prison guards sat with Tiny while Dobbins and the other guard rode on the seat.

Emily, Terrence, and Charlotte followed, a small procession behind the wagon. Each of Charlotte's sobs added to the heaviness of Emily's heart. A twinge of envy stung at the thought of Terrence's arm holding Charlotte's, supporting her. *She needs it more than I do.*

At the station, Charlotte wrapped her arms around Tiny's neck. "I'll write to you every day," Charlotte whispered, her voice catching. Tiny nodded, biting his lower lip, jaw twitching.

Emily put her hand on his arm. "And I'll make sure she gets out to visit you as often as she can."

He nodded again, took her hands. "Thank you, Miss Emily for all you done for me." He exhaled, his shoulders sagging further. "Thank you for believing in me."

Emily didn't dare speak. She nodded and kissed his cheek.

Tiny turned to Terrence, extended his hands. Terrence shook one, jaw working, eyes misting.

"Thanks for all you did, friend." Tiny's voice croaked.

Terrence nodded, gripped Tiny's shoulder.

"Two more favors?"

Terrence nodded.

"Take care of Charlotte."

"Yes."

Tiny's eyes pleaded. "Find whoever did this." His voice cracked.

"We will." Terrence's voice barely registered in Emily's ears, but she sensed the determination and the loyalty in those two words.

Yes, we will.

Chapter 42

"I—feed myself, Daughter." George took the spoon and bowl from Emily. He frowned, pointed at the bowl. "—this?"

Emily smiled. "Broth Caroline made to help you get stronger." She cocked her head. "Good to see your crankiness is back. I was afraid the attack had scared it out of you."

Her father sat propped against a stack of pillows, face no longer gray. Pale still, but no longer blue around his lips or his fingertips. His hazel eyes shone clear and alert. The new strands of gray at his temples added a distinguished cast to his handsome face.

He shoved the bowl at her. "Need eggs—bacon. Biscuits."

Emily placed the bowl on the table next to his bed, folded her hands in her lap. "I'll be happy to cook some breakfast for you."

Eyes wide, George said, "You cook?" He shook his head. "Have Rand—olph House send some."

Standing, Emily placed her hands on her hips. "You're lucky I share your opinion of my cooking. I'll ask Charlotte to fix you something."

"Good." He closed his eyes.

When he didn't open them after a couple of minutes, Emily turned to leave the room.

"Wait." George's voice stopped her. "Talk later."

She kissed his cheek. "After you've had breakfast, if you're feeling up to it."

His hand on her wrist, the grip strong, caused her to face him. "Coffee."

She laughed, relief flowing like warm, spring rain. Father was back. The last five days had rocked her. Tears one moment, Caroline holding her like so many years ago. Heart clutched in fear as her father lay there the first two days, not moving, shallow breaths, grayer than the pre-dawn sky. On the third day, he opened his eyes. Confused and disoriented. She stayed by his side, stroking his hand or his cheek. Then he noticed her and smiled.

When Doc complained about how much of his time George took, Emily knew the worst had passed. Now began the trying period of keeping her father quiet and resting. He would push and test the limits to get back to work despite Doc's orders of no legal work. At all. Emily would handle the practice and not convey a word of any of it to her father.

She remembered Doc's look of consternation when she laughed. Then he hung his head, shrugged his shoulders, and laughed with her. His hand on her shoulder comforted and encouraged. "Well, do the best you can. If he gets too agitated, I'll slip laudanum in his coffee."

"No, you won't," her father had said, eyes closed.

In the kitchen, Charlotte sat at the table, pencil furiously scratching. Emily added wood to the stove and set the frying pan on the top.

"You want something, Miss Emily?"

"Father wants some eggs and bacon."

Charlotte stood. "I'll fix it, ma'am."

"Finish your letter. I'll get this started."

Charlotte stared at the paper, chin quivering. She rubbed her eyes with the corner of her apron. "It can wait a bit." Her voice warbled. "Tiny isn't goin' anyheres."

Renewed guilt staggered Emily. Not yet. The day of his execution had yet to be announced, but the prospect hovered over Charlotte, a mountain of pain she carried herself. Emily wanted to take that burden and add it to her own. My fault.

Charlotte moved to the stove, dropped some bacon in the pan and poked it with a fork to coat the bottom of the pan with a thin layer of fat. She cracked eggs one-handed into the pan. Focused on the eggs, she blindly took a plate from a stack on a shelf over the stove. She slid the cooked food onto the plate, added a biscuit from a covered bowl at the rear of the stove, and handed it to Emily.

"Wait, he'll want coffee too." Charlotte poured coffee into George's favorite mug.

Emily placed the plate and coffee on a tray. "Thank you."

Charlotte nodded, eyes on the table, hands twisting her apron. Emily reached for her, to touch her, embrace her, but Charlotte pulled back. Not a step but a withdrawing inward, shoulders hunching, chin dropping toward her chest.

Emily picked up the tray and headed to her father's room. She looked back from the doorway. Charlotte sat the table, pencil scurrying, her other hand wiping her eyes.

Chapter 43

Emily stole another glance at the grandfather clock. All day the hands crept as if pulling a freight train uphill. The telegraph office would close in thirty minutes and still no message from Frank Stevens.

Caroline's hands covered hers, stopping her movement with the rolling pin. "Take it easy, Emily. You roll that pie crust out anymore, we'll be able to see through it."

"Guess I'm a bit distracted."

The eyes of her substitute mother caressed her with a gentle understanding. "I know. Why don't you go see how James is doing with your father? Charlotte and I can handle the rest of supper."

Charlotte looked up from the carrots she was slicing. Her smile barely lifted her lips. "Go ahead, Miss Emily."

Grateful for the reprieve, Emily hung her apron on a peg near the pantry. Whatever made her think preparing food would keep her from worrying about the report due today?

In her father's bedroom, Doc Everett lifted and turned George's left arm, running it through a variety of positions. Her father's stoic expression followed his arm as if it was somehow detached from his body.

"Well?" George said when Emily entered the room.

She shook her head. "Nothing yet."

George blustered a blast of air. "What—taking—fool so long?"

"Maybe he's not near a telegraph office," Doc offered, grasping George's elbow, and pushing his hand back toward his shoulder.

"Horse—won't get paid."

Doc slid the arm into the sling.

George flexed his fingers. "Feels good."

"Use the sling for another week." He took a baseball from his bag and wrapped George's fingers around it. "Squeeze this as hard as you can for five minutes every couple of hours."

George frowned. "Quack. Not—going to pitch."

"Humor me." Doc lit a cigar and puffed a ring toward the ceiling.

A knock on the front door sent Emily scurrying. Caroline and Charlotte stood in the kitchen doorway, Charlotte's hands twisting a towel.

Emily snatched open the door. Terrence stood there, his business suit looking like he'd just put it on, black hair combed neatly except for the lock that wanted to dip over his forehead.

"Oh, it's you." She craned to look over and around him. Nobody with him, nobody coming up the street.

Terrence smiled. "Good evening to you too, Miss Peyton." He offered her a thin envelope. "I persuaded Willoughby at the telegraph office to let me bring these to you."

She accepted the papers and placed her hand on her chest. "Thank you." She heard the giddiness in her voice. Finally.

She clasped the envelope in her fist as she skittered to her father's room. Caroline, Charlotte, and Terrence followed.

She stopped at the foot of the bed as the others gathered around. Anticipation lit her father's eyes. Charlotte's breath came in short gasps. Doc and Caroline joined hands. Terrence stood next to her, his presence strengthening her.

She tore open the envelope and smoothed the piece of paper she extracted.

FOUND BROTHERS IN FORT WORTH.

FOLLOWED THEM TO SAN ANTONIO.

ARRIVED TOO LATE.

BOTH KILLED BEFORE I GOT HERE.

NO SIGN OF MONEY.

NO EVIDENCE THEY KILLED PHILLIPS.

SEND REST OF FEE.

The page went blank, and her heart dropped to her stomach.

Charlotte moaned, and Terrence and Doc helped her into a chair. She hugged herself, bent over, rocking. Caroline stroked her hair.

George cussed and stared straight ahead, knuckles of his left hand white around the baseball.

Terrence took the wafer-thin paper from Emily's hand as if it were her dead kitten. She clasped his other hand and resisted the urge to step closer, into his embrace.

This can't be it. It can't be over.

She ran. She didn't care where. She ran.

Out the back door.

Through the creek.

Until her sides ached and her heart pounded against her ribs.

Until she couldn't breathe.

Until she collapsed, sank to ground.

Until darkness engulfed her.

"Emily?"

Terrence's voice sounded like she had a pillow over her ears. Such a pleasant voice. But why did he sound so worried?

She opened her eyes. Full dusk with shades of gray to the west, and stars peeking faintly in the black night overhead. A warm breeze from the west brushed her cheeks with gentle strokes.

An arm around her shoulders held her snug. Comfortable. Her eyes drifted closed, and she welcomed her body's settling into sleep.

Someone was patting her hand.

"Emily. Are you all right?" Caroline's voice.

Of course, I'm all right. Let me sleep. Wait. Why am I sitting on the ground? At night? Why is my dress wet?

Her mind cleared like morning fog burned off in the sun. She looked around her again. She could see the lines of the top of the house in the moonlight. Had she run that far?

Caroline squatted next to her, hazel eyes pinched in a frown, stroking Emily's hand. Charlotte stood behind Caroline, hand to her mouth.

Who's holding me? She turned slightly to her right, her cheek brushing against cloth. Terrence. The strength of his hand on her shoulder, his arm around her, steadied her. She started to snuggle against his shoulder. *No. Can't go there*.

She sat up straight, fingers to her forehead. Terrence kept his arm around her. Stevens's telegram flashed in her mind. No evidence. She shuddered.

Caroline's voice soothed as gently as her fingers on Emily's cheek. "You gave us quite a fright, child. Are you all right?"

Emily nodded. "I think so. Embarrassed for causing such a ruckus. I don't know what came over me."

She extended her arms toward Caroline. "Help me up." Caroline took one arm, Charlotte the other, but Terrence's hands on her back and waist, lifting and pushing, warmed her. When he took them away, a chill marked where his fingers had been.

"Can you make it back to the house?" he asked, his voice husky.

She nodded and hooked her arm through Caroline's.

Back in the house, her father's half-closed eyes shot open when she walked into his bedroom. He scanned her from head to toe and back again.

"I'm all right," she said before he could speak. "Feeling embarrassed and foolish for getting worked up like that."

Doc checked her pulse and touched her forehead while Charlotte wrapped a shawl around her. Caroline still held one of her hands as if she were a small child at the county fair. Where's Terrence? In the doorway, leaning against the frame, arms folded. His gaze held hers for a moment before he looked away.

"No—thing to be a—shamed off," George said. "Terrible news."

She nodded and bit her lower lip. She faced Charlotte and took the woman's hands. "Charlotte, I am so sorry."

Charlotte's lower lip quivered, and her eyes filled. She nodded. "I know, Miss Em. You did all you could." She shuddered and lifted her chin. "Everything's in God's hands now."

Look at all the help he's been.

Before Emily could speak, Caroline wrapped her arm around Charlotte's waist. "Let's go get you some tea."

As they left the bedroom, Caroline gave Emily the look that warned her to keep her mouth closed.

Silence filled the bedroom like snow drifts. Doc and Terrence took seats near the windows overlooking the yard. Emily lowered herself into a chair next to the bed. Fatigue burned her eyes and every muscle cried out for sleep. But her mind raced like sheet lightning across the prairie sky.

It can't end like this.

Doc puffed on a cigar, chin in his hand, gazing at the darkness. Terrence's head was bowed, and his lips moved silently. *Praying? How can anyone believe that really works?*

Her father's eyes were half-closed, his breathing shallow.

She picked up the telegraph from the foot of the bed and studied each word as if looking for a secret code. She read the message over and over. The words never changed. Nor did they stimulate any new thoughts. She closed her eyes, the paper clutched in her fist. *Think, Emily. Think.*

The rattle of cups on a tray brought Emily out of her trance. Caroline set the tray on the bed and handed cups to Terrence, Doc, and George.

George sniffed the brew. "Wh—this?"

"Tea," Caroline said.

"—Not—English." He handed the cup back to her. "Coffee."

"No coffee." Doc's voice was sharp and commanding. "Nothing stronger than tea until you're stronger."

"Quack." George took the cup, sipped, and grimaced. "How they—ever get—empire?"

"They didn't have you telling them what to do." Doc raised his cup, little finger extended, and gulped.

George frowned and pointed his finger at his friend.

Doc waved his hand at George. "Yeah. I know. As soon as you're out of that bed, you're gonna punch me in the nose."

George nodded. "Right."

"That'll be the day I quit doctorin' and take up lawyerin'."

Charlotte held her cup in shaking hands and didn't drink. Her lower lip trembled, and her breathing seemed to be barely under control. Her eyes met Emily's, pleading and hopeless.

Emily turned to the message in her hand. "We have to do something."

Her voice quieted the room and every eye turned to her.

"Like what?" Her father wasn't arguing with her. "Can't think—anything?"

"Me either," Doc said.

"What can we do?" Terrence's voice caught. "We've tried everything we can think of."

Emily paced the small room, tapping the paper against her palm. Her mind churned, but she couldn't settle it down, couldn't form a coherent thought.

She stopped in the doorway, gazed across the parlor, at the stack of law books on the floor of the dining room. *What can we do?*

The paper in her hand seemed to call her. She spread it open.

She scanned the others, eyes resting on Charlotte at the last. She held up the message.

"Something's not right. I'm going to San Antonio."

Chapter 44

Silence.

Even breathing seemed to have stopped.

Emily squirmed under the scrutiny of five pairs of eyes. Terrence's half-opened mouth seemed frozen in mid-speech. Charlotte's fingers covered her lips, and her eyes brimmed with fresh tears.

Caroline smiled the indulgent smile Emily saw when, at seven years old, she told Caroline she would be a lawyer when she grew up, just like her father. Doc folded his arms and lowered his chin, studying her from under brows drawn together.

Father smiled—his eyes proud. Then he shook his head. "'Too—danger—" The words stopped.

"Your father's right," Doc said. "Going to San Antonio is too dangerous."

"How?" She rattled the paper. "The Whitneys are dead, according to this. I need to see for myself."

"What if they're not?" Terrence's soft, low voice carried an ominous tone. "If they've killed already, they won't hesitate to kill you." His eyes bore into her. "You're too important to ... to the people in this town." He tugged his ear and looked away.

Emily rattled the message. "This is Tiny's last hope. He will hang if we can't prove someone else shot Mac Phillips. I don't want that on my conscience."

She touched her forehead and inhaled. The whine of a spoiled child creeping into her voice wouldn't convince them. Emily sipped her tea. Father was right. Coffee was much better. Another deep breath, and her heart steadied. Calmness flowed.

"There's nothing we can do here." She looked at the telegram. "And Stevens isn't going to help us anymore. Maybe I can find something Stevens missed, something—anything—that will help Tiny."

"Go—alone?" George shook his head.

"Who is there to go with me? You?" She surveyed the group. "Doc and Caroline need to take care of their patients. Terrence can't leave the bank. Warner is already upset at all the time he spent helping me—us on this."

Her eyes landed on Charlotte, who looked at her hopefully. "Charlotte, I know you're willing, but I think you need to stay here to be with people who can help you be strong for Tiny."

"I want to help anyway I can." Hands linked at her chest, her wide azure eyes pled.

Emily's heart lurched in a heavy grip. Could she ever love anyone like Charlotte loved Tiny? Could she ever have the courage to stand up for him?

Putting her hand on Charlotte's arm, Emily said, "I know you do, but I don't want to have to explain to Tiny if you get hurt. He needs you close by." She looked at George. "And my father needs you. You're the only one he seems to listen to."

George snorted.

Emily smiled. "I think he's smitten. You bring a feminine touch to the house I never could."

"Smit—I never heard—foolishness."

"Not romantically." Emily laughed. "Admit it. You enjoy the way she takes care of you. I think she's helping you get better quicker."

George harrumphed and looked out the window.

"Emily's right, George," Doc said. "Charlotte has more stamina and patience than Mrs. Marcand and Mrs. Dobbins put together. Even my sainted wife has wanted to take a frying pan to the side of your head."

Emily took both of Charlotte's hands in hers. "You understand, don't you?"

Charlotte dropped her chin and nodded. "I'll do whatever you say if it will help you help Tiny."

Emily wanted to embrace her, but Charlotte held herself stiff.

"I'll leave first thing in the morning. I'd better go pack." She turned for the doorway.

"Wait." Her father boomed the one word.

Emily faced him, fighting to keep the irritation from her voice. "What?"

"Alone?"

She sighed. *What have we just been talking about?* "Yes. Alone."

He held her gaze, mouth working, right hand twitching. She waited. After a moment, he seemed to arrive at a decision. He nodded. "Take pistol."

Relief swept over her. Relief and surprise at his quick surrender. She kissed his cheek.

He frowned and waggled his finger at her. "Not happy— No—alternative." He paused. "Don't get hurt."

Emily restrained herself from dancing, and hugged her father instead. His one-armed embrace threatened to squeeze the last of her breath from her lungs.

Charlotte came forward and embraced her. "Thank you for doing all you've done for Tiny."

Doc shook his head and lit a cigar. Caroline, hands clasped tight at her waist, said, "Be careful."

Terrence focused over her shoulder, face somber and serious. "We'll be praying for you. We want you back safe and sound. There's still a lot for you to do around here."

He shifted his shoulders, briefly met her gaze. "I'll be back in the morning to take you to the station." He was gone as quickly as if she blinked, and he disappeared.

Chapter 45

Emily tugged the white linen gloves over her fingers, flexing her hand to get the material to nestle. Silly things. Why do women have to wear traveling gloves, anyway? Caroline's voice echoed. "Because proper young women carry themselves with dignity and respect."

Do proper young women going traipsing off hundreds of miles looking for murderers?

She touched her forehead and breathed deeply. With great reluctance, she positioned her hat as a proper young woman would.

In the parlor, her father waited in his wheelchair, blanket across his lap and legs.

"What are you doing out of bed?"

He jerked his thumb at Doc Everett.

Doc sent a stream of smoke toward the ceiling. "He didn't want to say goodbye that way." Hands on his hips, Doc spoke around the cigar jutting from his lips. "Never saw such stubbornness and pride in one person."

Emily kissed her father's cheek, stroked it with her hand. "Let Charlotte help you shave today. You can smooth wood with that stubble."

George grasped her hand, running his thumb over the back. His eyes pleaded. "—Sure?"

The lump rose in her throat, the words suddenly hard to form. She nodded. "I'm sure. We have to know what happened. No one else can go."

He squeezed harder and her knuckles ground together. "—Careful." His eyes sparked now with their usual glimmer of command.

Caroline's arms cocooned her. No words. The tight embrace, the soft kiss at her temple, told Emily here was love that would never run away.

Charlotte approached, a cloth-wrapped package in her hands. "Here's a couple of sandwiches." Charlotte's fingers lingered on hers as Emily took the package.

A knock on the door broke Charlotte's gaze. Caroline admitted Terrence, who greeted everyone, shaking hands with George and Doc, nodding at Charlotte and Caroline. Finally, turning his hat in his hands, his eyes met Emily's.

She flushed under the intensity of that gaze. Those eyes probed deep, past her mind, into her heart. Unfamiliar, unwanted emotions stirred. It can never be. He belongs to Priscilla. He belongs with Priscilla.

"Are you ready?" he asked.

For what? His warm voice carried the hint of an invitation. Or did she imagine it?

He nodded at her traveling bags by the door.

Heat rushed up her neck. Her smile had no force behind it. She cleared her throat. "Yes, I am. Thanks for doing this for me."

He bowed, a dip of his head, a leaning forward of his shoulders. "I only wish it were a different journey." He paused. "One not so dangerous."

With a brief nod, Emily said, "I'm sure the journey will be uneventful. Just a quick trip to make sure Stevens didn't miss anything."

Terrence rubbed his chin. "We'll all be praying for you just to be sure."

I doubt God cares.

She hugged her father and kissed his cheek. "Now you make sure you do what Doc says. And be kind to Charlotte. Don't be so bullheaded you drive her around the bend."

"Not—bullheaded."

"Right, and church bells don't ring on Sunday."

She embraced Doc and Caroline, then turned to Charlotte. "Thank you for taking care of my father. If he gives you any problems, lock him in his room or wallop him with the frying pan."

Charlotte drew in a shaky breath and fiddled with the bow to her apron. "Can I go to the train station with you?"

Emily glanced at Terrence, who nodded. "Uh ... Sure."

The buggy rolled smoothly on well-greased axles during the half-mile ride to the train station. Terrence's skill with horses showed in the easy manner he directed the animal pulling them.

Emily sat between Terrence and Charlotte on the bench built for only two—grateful they were all fairly slender. Charlotte's lilac perfume helped dissipate the dusky aroma of the horse. Emily's heart smiled at the touch of Terrence's arm against hers. She resisted looping her own through his and started at the thought of resting her head on his shoulder. *What are you thinking, Emily Louise Peyton? You don't have time for such notions. And Terrence is the last man to think about like that.*

Emily touched her forehead and released a deep sigh when they pulled up to the station, and Terrence leaped out to gather her bags from the back. Charlotte touched her wrist, probing, questioning with her eyes.

Emily shook her head. "I'm all right. Should've had more breakfast."

Terrence helped them down from the carriage. His hand seemed charged with warm power as he guided her to the platform. The interior of the station loomed dimly after the bright morning sun. Motes floated in the air like a gathering of birds that couldn't get organized to fly south.

Emily's heart beat faster as the screech of the whistle announced her train. Traveling didn't bother her. What she would find in San Antonio plagued her. Would it help Tiny? Was she just wasting her time? What else could she do? Tiny's last hope lay in that faraway city.

Terrence stowed her bags then took her hand. "God bless you, Emily." His eyes and the tightness of his grip told her he wanted to say more. The lump in her chest told her she wanted to feel his arms around her, she wanted the reassurance of his strength. Her hand covered her heart. Just nerves about the trip. That's all.

Charlotte's hands replaced Terrence's. Her blue eyes shimmered darkly with moisture. She swallowed. "Thank you, Miss Emily. Thank you for doing this for Tiny." She tightened her grip. "I know it will mean a lot to him that you haven't given up." Her embrace pushed the air from Emily's lungs.

"Let's hope I get lucky and find something we can use."

Charlotte nodded. "Oh, Terrence and me and the whole church will be prayin'."

Emily bit back the words that bubbled against her lips and nodded.

She boarded the train and took her seat. The car jolted and lurched when the engine's momentum reached it and the station slid behind her. Terrence and Charlotte waved from the platform. Emily raised her hand and smiled, fighting the loneliness of the task before her and the heaviness in her heart at the memory of Terrence's last smile.

Chapter 46

Emily rested her head against the window and dozed. The rhythm of the train and the monotony of the flat landscape lulled her. She rested her eyes, the lids gently closing. The slowing of the train stirred her.

"Guthrie," the conductor announced. *Not quite halfway. But making good time.*

She studied the platform as passengers and porters bustled about, boarding and leaving, loading and unloading. Families welcomed new arrivals and hugs and handshakes marked departures. So normal. So innocent. Would Tiny and Charlotte ever experience it?

An older pain renewed its stab in her heart. Father. Would he recover all his faculties? Would his heart let him resume the practice? The oldest pain gripped her, a vise that wouldn't let go—that seemed to strengthen each year. Mother. Walking out the door and into the arms of the Army major, into his carriage, and out of her life. Forever.

She bit her lip and swiped at her eyes.

A thump distracted her. A man plopped into the seat opposite. His loud sigh spread the sour aroma of onions and beer. He smiled, but his eyes appraised, evaluated.

Where had she seen him before? Large body. Square head that seemed to sit directly on his shoulders. Eyes dark and small in his broad face. She knew him from somewhere and the memory, while vague, wasn't pleasant.

"Have we met?" His voice graveled. "You look mighty familiar, missy."

She clenched her hands in her lap, regretting the pistol was in the bag over her head. She steeled her voice. "No, sir, I don't think we have."

He shook his head, jowls quivering. "I'm usually good with faces, and I know I've seen yours before." He tapped his pudgy fingers on his chin as if giving the matter deep thought. "Now, where have I seen you before? Ahh. It'll come to me." He leaned forward, extending his hand. "Name's Ford. Delbert Ford."

She held her fingers in her lap, the image of her broken pen flashing through her mind.

He dragged his hand back, a pout making him look like a fish. "And you are?"

Emily pretended to be distracted by something out the window. "Just a traveler, sir."

Peripherally, she caught him cock his head and tap his temple, eyes boring into her. He snapped his fingers, a sound like a wet shirt slapping against a washstand. "Abilene. You're that girl who fancies herself a lawyer. I've had a few laughs over that one."

No weapons close by. A kick to the shin or groin would probably take too long to penetrate. No way would she let her hand come in contact with his face. She glanced up the aisle. No sign of the conductor. Could she pretend to get off at the next stop?

He shifted and leaned forward. "Maybe at the next stop we can have dinner together. Just the two of us. You can tell me all about what it's like to be a *female* lawyer."

Nausea roiled. She touched her forehead. "Mr. Ford, you are the last person in the world I would have dinner with." She scanned him from head to foot. "I'm sure there are pigs who eat neater than you. If you don't move to another car on this train—and I mean now—I will tell the conductor you physically assaulted me."

"I haven't even touched you." He waved his hands, eyes wide.

"You don't have to. Your odor is offensive enough to assault three rows of seats."

He sputtered before finding words. "You sure are an uppity young thing. Somebody should've taken a switch to you when you was younger."

"Would you like to try?" She paused, watching his face purple. "I am out of patience, Mr. Ford. I suggest you leave. Now. You never know what an uppity female lawyer might do."

He waggled his fingers at her. "You've got no respect for your elders, young lady."

She shrugged. "I respect them when they deserve it."

He shuffled and levered his body out of the seat. "You keep treating people like this and you'll regret it one day. Mark my words."

Emily watched him waddle to the other end of the car. At the door, he turned and pointed at her. "Mark my words." He squeezed through the door slamming it behind him.

A warm flush crept up her neck as everyone in the car seemed to stare at her. Some men gave her narrowed-eyed looks. Several of the women smiled and nodded. Emily bowed her head in acknowledgment and returned to letting her gaze drift sightlessly over the landscape.

A shadowed hovered over her. The conductor touched the brim of his black cap. "Is everything all right, Miss?"

She glanced down the aisle. No sign of Ford. "Yes, sir. Why? Is there some sort of trouble?"

"N-No, ma'am. One of the other passengers came up to me and said it looked like a gentleman was bothering you."

She smiled. "'Gentleman' isn't the word I would use. Let's just say he was persistent in his attentions. After a few words, he took the hint and decided to sit in another car."

"Well, that's good. I'm sorry for not getting here sooner. If he bothers you again, let me know, and I'll have him thrown off the train."

Might make better time.

"Thank you. I doubt very much he'll bother me any further." She pointed her chin at the next car. "But he may approach some other woman traveling alone."

"I'll watch for him. Big fella, right?"

"Yes. And shaggy. Sniff for onions and beer. That'll be your man."

The conductor left after a last touch of finger to cap brim.

Emily turned to the window, catching a small smile in her reflection. She sighed and closed her eyes, letting the rocking and rhythmic clatter of the train lull her into a light doze.

She snapped awake. Sat up, back rigid. Looked around. Where was she? Where was Terrence? On the train. Why would Terrence be here?

Her hand tingled at the sensation of his fingers holding hers. She leaned against her seat, clasped her hands together, one thumb rubbing the other hand as she imagined Terrence doing. Soft and gentle. A tender caress. She shook her head.

Chapter 47

The last rays of the setting sun glared off the sparkling white of the Randolph House. Terrence squinted as he approached the building, wiping his sweaty palms on his jacket. His knees wobbled like seedlings in a prairie thunderstorm. At the entrance, he released a deep breath, hoping it would drain the nervous tension away. It didn't.

He entered the dining room. No Priscilla. He compared his pocket watch to the grandfather clock that flanked the fireplace. Not late. Where is she?

Fifteen minutes later, he wondered if she would come at all. Did he have any right to expect her? He thought he did. After church on Sunday, she'd touched his arm, her soft gentle touch that seemed so light, yet promised so much. "Will I see you at the Randolph House as usual this week?" Her voice soft, husky, her green eyes gazing up at him from under lowered brows. The slight pout on her lips offering ... what? Hope for reconciliation?

He stared at the landscape painting hanging in the small foyer of the restaurant. The thought of not reconciling weighed his heart, yet the vision of her with Lionel Hutchins stirred hot embers.

The door swept open as though blown by the wind. Priscilla's chandelier of a laugh preceded her into the foyer.

"You tell the funniest stories, Deputy. You really ought to write them in a book. You'd rival Mr. Twain."

When she saw Terrence, she froze, mouth agape. She snatched her hand from Quick's arm. "Terrence." Pink seeped up her cheeks. "I am late, aren't I? I'm sorry, darling. I met Deputy Quick at the post office, and we got to talking, and I lost track of the time."

Her fingers warmed his arm, her eyes softened, yet seemed to smolder underneath. "You will forgive me, won't you?"

Terrence lost himself in her smile, the even white teeth, the full lips, the way one corner tipped up. More pressure from her fingers. She stepped closer; her rose perfume slipping into his consciousness. The tip of her tongue brushed her lips. Annoyance melted and trickled away like ice cream on the Fourth of July.

"Of course. These things happen."

"My apologies, Terrence." Quick touched the brim of his hat. "Got to tellin' one of my stories. Don't know when to stop, sometimes."

"No harm done, Deputy. Thank you for escorting Miss Priscilla over here."

"My pleasure, sir." He scanned Priscilla from head to toe. "Miss Montgomery. It was an honor visiting with you."

A few minutes later, Terrence spread his napkin over his thighs as he watched Priscilla sip her wine. Delicate as a hummingbird drawing nectar, her lips barely touched the rim, an infinitesimal amount slipping into her mouth.

Placing her glass on the table, her index finger traced the side from the rim to the base, her eyes never leaving his. They glowed and smiled warmth, an invitation. "I've missed you."

He rested his hand on the table, fidgeting with his knife. "I've missed you too." His throat parched suddenly.

Fine one moment, desert-dry the next. He gulped water, draining half the glass.

She crossed her arms on the table, leaned forward, fabric straining.

Heat radiated from the center of his body. Eyes. Focus on her eyes.

"Do you think we can put our little tiff behind us?" Her voice purred.

He wanted to reach across the table, stroke her cheek, feel her thick hair flow over his fingers, taste her lips on his. He fidgeted with his knife, eyes darting around the room. Too many eyes, too many tongues looking to gossip.

"Yes, we can." *Can we? I want to.* The thought of losing Priscilla blazed across his mind. No way he wanted to visit that barren emptiness again.

Priscilla clapped her hands once. "I knew we could. I told Mother we cared for each other too much for that to stay between us."

Over dinner, Priscilla chattered about new dresses she and her mother had purchased, about the new fashions in Saint Louis, and about the party her parents were planning for the next Sunday. Terrence swayed into the rhythm of her words, light and airy as a songbird.

"What are you daydreaming about, Terrence?"

He jumped, knocking his coffee cup, saving it before liquid spilled on the tablecloth. He wiped his mouth with his napkin. "Listening to your voice reminding me of the songs you sang last Christmas. Will you sing at your parents' party?"

She blushed and lowered her eyes as she looked at him, turning her chin toward her shoulder. She touched her lips with the corner of her napkin, sipped her wine. "We hadn't planned that. Would you like me to?"

He nodded. "Very much. I think you have a beautiful voice."

Maybe Sunday will be the day to seek Mr. Montgomery's permission.

She smiled the smile he would follow across the desert and back. "Then I will." She rolled her eyes. "I almost forgot to tell you. Mother's mare, Marigold, delivered a colt yesterday. Black with a small white star and one white stocking. She's named him Rogue's Blaze after his sire. She wanted me to tell you how grateful she is to you for helping to pick the stallion."

Terrence's cheeks hurt from his grin. Finally, Mrs. Montgomery approved of something he did. He remembered the work he and Tiny put into finding the perfect stallion to meet Mrs. Montgomery's demands, which changed from day-to-day until they introduced her to Rogue.

"I'll have to write Tiny. Maybe it will cheer him up a little."

Priscilla's face clouded like a thunderhead swelling over a mountain. "Him." She made it sound like something a horse left in the street.

"He did help find Rogue and negotiated a good price with the breeder."

She gulped her wine and glared at him, eyes narrowed, nostrils flared. "He's a killer, and I'll be glad when he's hung and out of your life completely."

The coffee cup felt like frail glass in his hand, ready to shatter at the slightest pressure from his fingers. He hesitated, daring not to release the words burning his tongue, the words that might drive Priscilla out of his life forever.

"Don't you agree?"

Stay calm. "Tiny's been my best friend since I came to this town. I don't want to see him leave my life. Especially like this, hanging for a crime he didn't commit."

She plopped her napkin next to her plate. "You're one of the few who think so. You and that Emily Peyton. I think she's got you under a witch's spell, leading you around by the nose so you can't see the truth right in front of you."

His chest tightened. Red flared behind his eyes, like a fire in a forge. He forced his voice to stay low. "Emily's not a witch. And I know Tiny. Better than most folk around here. He couldn't kill anyone."

She huffed. "Seems like everyone disagrees with you."

"Doesn't make them right." He knew he sounded sullen, like a little boy with a pout. And he didn't care.

"This time, I think it does." She leaned forward, eyes glittering in the candlelight. "Let's not argue over this. In a little while, it will all be over, and then, you and I can start planning our future together."

A future with Priscilla. Something he'd dreamed about almost since the day they first met. Now, she offered it to him. A few days ago, he'd have latched onto her words and danced her around the restaurant.

Now it was different. Something had changed, she had changed. Or shown a side of herself he hadn't seen before.

I'm different too. Working with Emily for Tiny showed a new side of life. He saw George's vulnerability and pain, and his determination to do all he could to help his client despite his limitations. Charlotte revealed how deep a love could grow as she supported her man, stifling her fears to be strong for him, comforting him while her own anguish went untended. Tiny displayed a stoic strength, a belief in the truth of his story, and a love for his woman that nothing could erode.

And Emily. Her dedication to Tiny, to proving his innocence, to risking her future for this cowboy. No, she didn't risk it for Tiny. She risked it for justice. Every day he spent with her exhibited her intelligence as she researched and planned her case and her determination to give Tiny the best defense possible. He realized now—the new side he saw, a side many people thought she didn't have. Her love and compassion for her father, her gentle tenderness toward Charlotte, the quiet strength and reassurance she gave Tiny.

He recalled the late nights, seeing her bent over her notes, one pencil behind her ear, another in her mouth as she flipped pages and reference books and articles, as she drew up lists of questions. The grim tightness around her mouth in the courtroom when the judge thwarted her strategy. The tight shoulders and the tears ready to fall at the verdict. The gentle touch on Tiny's arm.

He looked at Priscilla and thought of Emily.

Chapter 48

Emily accepted the conductor's hand as she stepped to the platform. "Right on time, Mr. Briggs. My compliments to you and the whole crew."

The tall, gray-haired man touched the brim of his cap. Red bloomed on his cheeks. "Thank you, Miss. I'll be sure to let them know."

The air, heavy and humid, settled on her skin like fine mist. She inhaled and coughed, the hot aroma of the train joined with the scents of the city to assault her nostrils. She fanned her face. *Just makes me sweat more.*

She passed through the depot, the Spanish-influenced architecture streaming by. Outside, a Hispanic man doffed his straw sombrero, bowed at the waist and, sweeping his arm, pointed his hat at a gleaming black buggy, a white horse slumbering between the traces.

"Señorita, you need ride?" He patted his chest. "Joaquin take you."

"How much?" Emily rubbed the tips of her fingers together.

He clasped his hat to his chest and shrugged. "One dollar. Take you anywhere in San Antonio. Show you beautiful city." His mop of blue-black hair glistened, white teeth gleamed under a thick mustache that circled his mouth like a quarter moon. Without his hat, his head came to her shoulder.

His dark eyes danced as he reached to take her carpet bag.

Hiding a smile, she tightened her grip on the bag. "*Uno momento, por favor.*"

He blinked, dropped his arm to his side. "You speak Spanish?"

"No. Did I do all right?"

"*Sí. Sí.*" He made a follow me motion with his hand. "Come. We go now."

Emily scanned the street. So many people. So much noise. English and Spanish competed for dominance. Aromas of spicy food blended with the odors of horses and sweat in the humid air. Her clothes clung to her body as sweat came from places it never had before.

A shadow, a movement skimmed her peripheral vision. She turned to see Delbert Ford emerge from the train station. His eyes roamed the plaza like an eagle seeking prey. She turned away before making eye contact but sensed him waddling toward her.

She handed Joaquin her bag. "Come, Joaquin. Let's go. Pronto."

"Sí, *Señorita.*" He secured her bag in the buggy's rear and helped her into the seat. He clambered onto the front bench, and, with a snap of the reins, spoke sharply in Spanish. The horse shook its head, jangling the harness, and stepped into an easy canter, bells woven into its mane tinkling.

After about half a block, Emily looked back at the station. Ford stood, fists on hips, watching her.

Shivers skipped up her spine as she turned away. The city blurred as Ford's image filled her mind.

Coolness bathed her skin as she entered the shadowy, high-ceilinged foyer of the Menger Hotel. Sweat evaporated from her brow, but her hair hung damp and heavy on her neck. The skinny desk clerk, Adam's apple protruding, greeted her warmly with a lazy drawl that took several seconds to decipher.

An hour later, Emily lowered herself into the copper bathtub, the tepid water cool against her sweaty body. She leaned back and slid into the water until it brushed against her chin. She sighed, folded her hands across her stomach and allowed her eyes to close.

Her father's image drifted across her mind. Her father before the accident. She smiled at the memories of their discussions and debates over the law and politics and human nature. Would he ever come back to that place? His body was healing, and his mind seemed sharp, but would he ever speak normally again? Tell a story to make her laugh? Argue with Doc about God to provoke his dearest friend into a red-faced, cigar-chomping, sputtering pique? Umpire at the town baseball games until too many beers threw his judgment off, and every pitch was a strike—or a ball, depending on who was batting? She swiped at her eyes and swallowed the lump in her throat.

The door to the tub room swung open and Emily jumped, sloshing water over the side. A young girl, barefoot, and in faded yellow gingham, carried a large bucket of water, steam curling in lazy spirals.

"Sorry, ma'am, din't mean to startle ya'. Fetched some more water to heat up your bath."

More heat? Emily noticed the bath water had cooled. "All right."

She bent her knees and resisted the urge to help as the girl rested the bucket on the edge of the tub and pivoted it so the water flowed smoothly.

"How old are you?"

The girl set the bucket on the floor with a soft clunk and wiped her nose with her finger. "Eight-and-a-half."

Misaligned pigtails gave the impression her head wasn't on quite straight.

"How long have you been fetching water like this?"

"Since I was four. Doin' it by myself since I was six." The girl stood straighter, shoulders back, head high as if trying to add inches to her stature. Her gap-toothed smile revealed her sense of accomplishment.

Emily's heart softened. "Don't you go to school?"

The girl shrugged. "Mama sends me when the hotel ain't too busy."

"What's your name?"

"Mikey."

"Mikey? What kind of name is that?"

"It's good name." Mikey crossed her arms and scowled at Emily. "I'm named after my father and my grandma. Michaela Ann. Everybody calls me Mikey."

"What's your father like?"

Mikey's hands dropped to her side, and her chin sank toward her chest. "Don't know. He died 'fore I was born. Got run over by a train." She patted the sides of her dress. "Mama gave me his railroad watch. Wanna see it? It's back in my room."

"Maybe another time." Emily lifted her hand, but the girl was too far away for Emily to stroke her hair. "You help your mother around the hotel?"

Mikey nodded. "I help with the women's baths, mostly. And cleaning the rooms if Mama needs me to."

Emily stretched out again as the new warmth seeped into her muscles, relaxing them. "Thank you for the fresh water."

Mikey plucked the sides of her dress and dipped a perfect curtsy until she lost her balance. Emily bit her lip to stifle a giggle while Mikey recovered her dignity. The girl slipped out of the room, closing the door behind her.

Emily leaned back and closed her eyes. Terrence. Such a strong friend to Tiny, and to her. She sighed. The lock of hair that forever wanted to slip across his forehead. The eyes full of laughter and smiles one moment and focused and determined the next. The ease with which he scooped her into his arms and carried her across the muddy street the day of her father's accident. The ever-so-slight lingering of his hands on her waist when he set her down.

She snapped awake when she discovered her lips pursing for a kiss. She stood, sloshing water up the sides of the tub.

He'll probably be officially engaged by the time I get back.

Emily rubbed the thick towel vigorously over her body and continued to rub after she was dry.

Chapter 49

A short time later, wearing her coolest dress, Emily emerged into the sunshine of the plaza outside the hotel, the heat and humidity smothering the effects of the bath. From behind a pillar, Mikey tentatively waved, dust cloth in hand. Emily smiled and waved back.

Joaquin scampered to her side, whipped his sombrero to his chest. "*Buenos Dias*, Señorita. Where may I take you today?"

A tug on her skirt. Mikey crooked her index finger for Emily to bend over. The child's soft lips brushed her ear. "Don't go with him. He's a bad man."

Emily straightened. Mikey nodded emphatically—arms folded across her chest.

"Why is he a bad man?"

"People he gives rides to don't always come back."

Joaquin shrugged and flashed a grin that stopped at his nose. "Children. They don't always understand how big world works. You are safe with me." He tapped his chest. "Joaquin best driver in all San Antonio. Fast. Safe."

Emily scanned the plaza. There didn't seem to be any other livery drivers around. She chewed her lip and turned to Mikey. "He's the only driver around, and I need to see the marshal."

Mikey's scowl lifted, and her face softened. She turned to Joaquin. "This lady is my friend. You take her to the marshal and right back here." She wagged her finger at him. "I'll be watchin' for ya. If you don't bring her back, my mama will take care of you." Hands on her hips, she rose to her tiptoes and scowled. "And you don't want that to happen again, do ya?"

Joaquin's smile disappeared, and his face clouded. He pointed to his carriage. "Come, Señorita, I take you to marshal," He glared at Mikey. "And I bring you right back here."

Emily focused on Mikey. The girl's gray eyes cast daggers at Joaquin. Emily lifted her hand to stroke Mikey's hair. The girl resisted with a twist of her shoulders and a step back.

"I'll be waitin' right here for ya, Missy."

"Thank you, Mikey."

Emily turned to follow Joaquin when Mikey's voice stopped her.

"What's yer name, Missy?"

"Emily. Emily Peyton."

"Mama always likes me to know the name of the person I'm praying for. She'll be praying too."

Emily clenched her bag tightly. "I'll see you when I get back, Mikey." *And God will have little to do with it.*

In the carriage, Emily tenderly perched on the edge of the hot leather seat, resting a gloved hand on the seat in front of her. "Why would she say something like that?" The weight of the pistol in her bag reassured her.

Joaquin shrugged and focused on the street ahead. "Six months ago, I think. *Dos* Yankee women disappear. Everyone upset. Blame the drivers."

"At the same time?"

"No, Señorita. About *uno* months apart."

"They never found them?"

He shook his head. "Very sad." He clucked the horse into a faster pace. Emily gripped the seat tighter to keep her balance.

She watched the city pass, the mix of whites and Spanish flickering as she pondered Mikey's warning. Why did the girl warn her about Joaquin? Did she know something? Was he hiding something?

"Joaquin, why were you outside my hotel? Were you waiting for me?"

"No, Señorita Emily. Took man from train station. Waiting to see if someone else needed a ride. You came out."

Had she heard a train whistle? Couldn't remember. Check the train schedule or ask the desk clerk?

She studied his profile as he stared straight ahead. Unreadable. Unusual for her not to be able to read someone. Must ask the marshal.

Why am I even fretting over this? It's not my concern. Stay focused, girl. Stay focused.

Chapter 50

"So, you're an attorney." Marshal Michael Cook shook his jowly head and folded the document Emily had given him. "Never seen a female lawyer before. I'm impressed."

Emily searched his face, his smile, for any hint of derision. None. Even his pale brown eyes crinkled warmly.

He fingered the ends of his handlebar mustache as if ensuring the wax hadn't melted in the heat. Satisfied, he folded his hands on his desk. "How can I help you, Miss Peyton?"

"I'm looking for information on two men who were killed here recently. Ed and Paul Whitney."

Cook inhaled. "That was a nasty piece of business. What's your interest in them?"

Emily sat up straighter, clasped her hands in her lap. "I believe they may have been involved in a murder in Abilene. A murder for which an innocent man will hang."

"Your client?"

"Yes."

Cook nodded. "That would explain why you're here. Why didn't the marshal up there telegraph me?"

"Because he believes my client is the right man, and he can't be bothered to investigate other possibilities." Heat rose from Emily's chest to her neck, the warm flush causing more sweat and a squishy stomach in the confines of the marshal's office.

Cook arched his right eyebrow. "Pretty harsh words. Who's the marshal in Abilene now?"

"John Dobbins."

"I remember John from Dallas. He could be stubborn once he figured he had his man."

Emily shrugged. "Stubborn is one word for it. What can you tell me about the Whitneys?"

Cook walked to the stove at the rear of his office, refilled his coffee cup and offered more to Emily. She accepted. Even in the heat, warm coffee always helped her think better.

He settled back in his seat, the wood creaking under his weight. He spoke to the blotter on his desk at first. "Not much to tell. They'd been in town a couple of days." He raised his head, met Emily's eyes. "Flashed a lot of money. Told people they'd made it on a cattle drive to Kansas and a big poker game in Fort Worth on the way home."

He sipped his coffee. "Funny. They weren't very good poker players here. Must have attracted somebody's attention. Shopkeeper found 'em one morning sitting against the wall of the Alamo. Somebody put a bullet right in the middle of their foreheads."

Emily turned her cup in slow circles, mind churning at the gruesome description given so nonchalantly. "Any ideas who did it?"

"Not a one. Nobody saw or heard anything. Or at least that's what they're sayin'." He wiped his hand over his face. "Bartender said they left the saloon alone. Didn't see nobody follow 'em. Near as I can figure, they went from there to a brothel near the river. Stayed a couple of hours.

Nobody saw anything suspicious when they left." He lifted his shoulders. "Nobody ever does in those places."

"Did you find any of their money?"

He lifted his hands, palms up. "Not a penny. None in their hotel room or their saddlebags. I figure they showed off too much, and whoever took their lives took their money."

Emily bit the inside of her cheek. "No clues as to the killer?"

"Nope."

Silence hung in the air.

"How d'you come to follow them brothers here?"

"We hired a bounty hunter to track them."

"Who?"

"Frank Stevens. One of my father's friends in Dodge City recommended him."

Cook rubbed his chin. "I know him. He knows how to get the job done. Not as crooked as some. Not as honest as others. Not always concerned about bringing men in alive."

"Did you talk to him?"

"Didn't know he was here. 'Course, he had no reason to let me know."

He drained his cup in one swallow. "With Stevens, he could have walked right in the door, and I wouldn't have known him."

Something stirred in Emily, a curiosity. No, something stronger, a yearning to peel back what the marshal was saying. "What do you mean?"

"Ha." Cook's faced beamed. "Stevens used to be one of those actor fellers. Claimed he worked with Booth in his younger days. Anyways, he learned all those tricks to make yourself look different. He was always bragging 'bout how he'd used them disguises to trick the outlaws he was hunting."

Emily stood, defeat weighing on her, leaving her bent and shoulders slumped. She extended her hand. "Thank you, Marshal Cook."

His callused grip was firm, yet warm. "You're welcome, Miss Peyton. Sorry I couldn't have been more help."

Mikey's words flashed through as she reached the door. She stopped. "Marshal, someone at the hotel warned me to be careful around a driver-for-hire named Joaquin. I don't know his last name. Are you aware of anything I need to be concerned about?"

Cook chewed his lower lip. "We've had some problems with young women disappearing. At least two in the last few months. Never found any sign of them. Joaquin is one of the drivers I've got my eye on. Nothin' solid, though. Still, be careful around him. Who warned you?"

Emily smiled, almost embarrassed to reveal her source. "A little girl named Mikey."

He tilted his head back and roared a laugh that brought tears to his eyes. Emily joined in, not sure why. He caught his breath and wiped his eyes with his fingers. "Mikey is a hoot. She's my granddaughter, and she wants to be a lawman when she grows up. Always watching for outlaws." He smiled. "Let me guess, she pointed that bony little finger of hers in Joaquin's chest and told him to treat you right?"

Emily chuckled. "That's exactly what she did."

"And threatened him with her mother, not me?"

Emily nodded. "How did you know?"

"Couple of months back, Joaquin cheated an elderly couple. My daughter caught him, almost drowned him in a water trough." He paused. "Besides, my daughter is the best shot for twenty miles around here. If she had been old enough for the war, things might have turned out different. Joaquin don't want no more trouble from her."

Chapter 51

Emily paced her room. Trying to deal with the heat, she'd removed her dress and draped it over the end of the bed. Even in her undergarments, she sweltered. A warm breeze pushed humid air through the window. The temptation to open the door for cross-ventilation yielded to maintaining proper decorum.

Her fingers twisted the handkerchief she used to dab her brow when sweat threatened to flow into her eyes. Defeat swarmed like the summer heat, suffocating, each breath an effort to draw moist air into her lungs. The thought of leaving tomorrow clenched her heart. What else could she do?

She sat on the edge of her bed, imagining her father and Terrence with her. Their opinions, their wisdom, their encouragement would offer some hope, some ideas as to possible next steps. The thought of Terrence's smile distracted her. *Focus, Emily Louise Peyton, focus.*

Charlotte and Tiny shimmered into clarity. Their kiss between the cell bars. Their hands clasped until the last moment. Their love. Would she ever know a love like that? An enduring, unquestioning love. A love that threatened to tear the two apart in anguish and grief.

Unless I do something.

Exiting the hotel, Emily saw Joaquin escort a couple to his carriage and help the woman into her seat. When he turned to climb into his seat, his eyes locked with Emily's. He looked from the couple to her and shrugged, arms extended, palms out. She smiled and waved him away. From the desk clerk, she'd learned her destinations were within a few blocks. Even in the heat, she preferred to walk over riding with Joaquin—or any other driver. The solid weight of the pistol in her bag added reassurance.

Shadows lengthened along the streets as the sun scorched westward. Shades of gray smudged the buildings, blurring their edges. Emily approached the saloon where Marshal Cook told her the Whitney brothers visited on their last night. What would Caroline say at the sight of Emily entering such a place? What would her father say? Or Terrence?

She saw Tiny sitting on a meager bunk in a narrow cell, head down, hands shackled. Charlotte stood at the bars, eyes red and puffed from never-ceasing tears. On the floor between them, the shadow of a noose.

She shook the image from her mind, squared her shoulders, and peered into the saloon. Almost deserted. Two men playing cards at a round table. The bartender wiping the bar in slow, circular motions that seemed more devoted to using time than anything else.

Deep breath. One step at a time. Emily pushed open the swinging door and entered the world of men, stale smoke, old beer, and cheap whiskey. Her tongue could almost taste the aromas that hung in the room like wet laundry.

The bartender stopped in mid-motion, eyes wide. "Excuse me, miss. Are you sure you're in the right place?"

Emily swallowed, took a calming breath. "This is the Silver Dollar Saloon, isn't it?"

"Um ... Yes, miss."

"Then I'm in the right place."

He scratched his ear. "We're not lookin' to hire any girls right now."

One of the card players spoke up. "Maybe you should, Ed. She's a lot better looking than the batch you got working for you now."

Emily focused on Ed. "I'm not looking for work. I'm looking for information."

Ed cocked his head. "What kind of information?"

"About the Whitney brothers. I understand they were in here the night they were murdered."

Ed held up his hands. "Hold on a minute, missy. They were here, sure, but they left alive and standing—well, staggering anyway. They said they was goin' to some wh— brothel down by the river."

"Did anyone follow them?"

The bartender chuckled. "Miss, that were a Saturday night. I was busier than a one-armed carpenter tryin' to keep glasses filled. There were so many men and so much smoke, I could barely see to that first table, much less the door and who came and went."

He poured himself a half glass of beer and drained it with an audible gulp, wiping his mouth on his sleeve. He leaned forward, thick hands pressing the bar. "Besides, the marshal's been all over this. What business is it of yours?"

Emily shifted her handbag, the pistol reassuring. "The Whitneys are suspected of murder in Abilene, Kansas."

His eyes roved over her. "You don't look like the marshalin' type."

Lifting her chin, she said, "I'm an attorney acting on behalf of my client."

The bartender brayed like a donkey. "An attorney? Ain't no such thing as a female attorney."

Emily's fingers danced over the shape of the pistol. "Maybe not in Texas, but there are in Kansas."

"Sounds like a good reason to stay out of Kansas," he said. "Look, miss. I done told ya all I know about them po' boys that got themselves shot."

Chapter 52

Emily sighed as she approached the brothel's bright red door that contrasted starkly with the gleaming white walls. This was the fourth she had visited. The search for clues about the Whitneys was as fruitless as trying to catch smoke in her hand.

A tall, cadaverous man answered Emily's knock.

"Yeah?" His voice rumbled like distant thunder.

"I'd like to speak with the ma—owner of the house, please."

"Who are you?"

"I'm Emily Peyton. I'm an attorney from Abilene, Kansas."

His eyebrows disappeared under the mop of shaggy black hair covering his forehead. "Wait here." He closed the door leaving her outside.

Emily noticed people watching her as they passed. The women "tsked" and shook their heads, averting their eyes. The men appraised her. She'd seen the same look on Terrence and Tiny when they evaluated a horse.

After several minutes, the door opened with a sudden yank. "Come in."

The hallway was dim and mercifully cool. Elaborately furnished parlors opened off either side. The dominating themes were velvet and more shades of red than Emily ever imagined.

He escorted her to the end of the hall, knocked once and opened the door. "Here she is, Boss." He stood aside.

Emily faced a woman a few years older than herself, maybe an inch taller, with piercing brown eyes, and strawberry blond hair that swirled to her shoulders. The low-cut sky-blue dress clung to her figure and moved like a second skin.

"I'm Nadina." She extended her hand. Emily took it, surprised by the soft skin yet almost manlike grip. Nadina flounced her hair. "Sterlings said you call yourself an attorney, so I'll assume you're not looking to work here." Her voice was smooth and rich, like a fine brandy Emily had once tasted in Saint Louis. Her eyes held what seemed to be wry amusement, as if nothing would ever catch her unprepared.

"Have a seat." Nadina's gesture was smooth and unhurried, practiced to an effortless grace. She pointed to a love seat in a dark blue fabric.

Emily scanned the room. Warm colors of multiple shades of blue. A small desk in one corner, ledgers stacked neatly on shelves above it.

Nadina picked up a glass decanter and slipped the stopper out with a soft pop. "Wine?"

"No, thank you."

"Suit yourself." She filled a glass, sipped it, savored before swallowing. She sat in her desk chair and crossed her legs, revealing a slit in her gown that unveiled her lower leg.

Emily coughed, hoped the blush filling her face wasn't too bright. The portrait above the desk showed Nadina nude. Emily focused on her host's eyes.

"How can I help you, Miss Peyton?"

"I'm looking for information on two brothers named Whitney. They may have visited here before someone murdered them."

Nadina rolled her eyes. "Those two, again." She drained her glass and poured another. "They were here that night. Ended up hurting one of my girls and disturbing the other customers. Sterlings had to remove them. Quite forcefully, I regret to say. The evening never really recovered after they left. Very disappointing."

The woman's coolness stunned Emily like someone threw cold water in her face. "These men were murdered that night."

Nadina sipped her wine. "Yes, I know. And that is a shame. but they weren't murdered *here*. From what the marshal told me, they were killed for a large sum of money they did an extremely poor job of concealing."

Emily shook her head. The woman's uncaring attitude stunned her. "Do you know if anyone followed them?"

"Not from here. Sterlings and I watched them until they bumbled around a corner two blocks away."

Emily chewed her lower lip, mind blank. Frustration raged. All this way and still no answers. Saloons and brothels, a world she didn't know and never expected to enter. Marshal Cook was right. A world where no one saw or heard anything.

"Is there anything else, Miss Peyton?"

"I know there is, Miss Nadina, but I don't think I will find it in San Antonio." Emily stood. "Thank you for your time."

Nadina rose with the silky smoothness of a ballerina. "Why is an attorney from Kansas interested in two buffoons like the Whitneys?"

"They may have been involved in a murder. I was hoping to prove that, so an innocent man doesn't hang."

Nadina tapped her lips with a slender forefinger, a tiny sapphire ring glinting in the candlelight. "I do wish I could have been more helpful."

At the door, Nadina scanned Emily. Twice and slowly. They shook hands. "Well, Miss Peyton, look me up if the law business doesn't work out."

Outside, Emily resisted the urge to race to the hotel and sink into the hottest bathwater Mikey could produce.

Chapter 53

Night had fallen as Emily approached the Alamo. A breeze from the north cooled her brow and cheeks. Thoughts and images about the Whitneys last night on earth blurred. Frustration bubbled like one of Caroline's soups. Nothing. No new information to help Tiny. No new evidence to take to Judge Frasier, the appeals judge, and ask him to review the case, maybe order a new trial. She could prove the Whitneys had money, but no way to prove where it came from. She pounded her thighs with her fists as she walked. *Think. Think, Emily Louise. What am I missing?*

The lights from the street didn't pierce the shadows cast by the Alamo.

The breeze rustled the leaves and stirred the hairs at the back of her neck. Refreshing. The thought of a bath before dinner enticed an opportunity to relax. As the tension subsided, it might free her mind to ramble and come up with new ideas.

A hand covered her mouth and pinched her nose.

Something cold and sharp pressed against her neck.

She swung her arms, connected with something, heard a grunt.

The hand over her mouth squeezed tighter.

She fumbled her bag, grasping for the pistol. The base of the knife handle crashed into her wrist. The bag fell, followed by the sound of a foot sweeping it away.

Her brain burst with white hot light as the pain from her wrist met with her constricted breathing.

The hand around her face tightened. The arm with the knife wrapped around her waist and dragged her backward, deeper into the shadows, farther from the lights and people.

She reached behind her head, nails extended, seeking her attacker's face, clawing at whoever held her, finding only cloth, not flesh.

A sharp blow to her stomach. The knife handle again. Air gushed from her lungs. None could come in. Black dots swirled. She closed her eyes. The dots intensified.

She spun as whoever held her tossed her into a corner. She slipped to the ground. A gloved hand grabbed her chin and lifted her to her feet and then higher. Her feet scrabbled for ground as the hand squeezed her jaw and the knife traced a line from her neck to her stomach. No cuts, but whoever it was gave the message cuts would come.

She opened her eyes. A mask. Two slits with dark eyes surrounded by the whites.

The knife at her cheek, the blade pressing.

"Forget the Whitneys." The mask muffled the voice, but the menace was clear. "Forget the Whitneys, or your beautiful face will disappear." The blade slid down her cheek, down her throat, until the point centered on her chest. The blade slit the fabric of her dress. "After we have some fun." He leaned closer, pressing her against the wall, his breath warm and wet through his mask. "And your father will be dead."

Then it came. Pain, searing pain. Pain that burned her lungs. First, a fist to her stomach. Next, one to her left cheek. Her head snapped to the right, smashing into the stone wall. She slumped into blackness.

Chapter 54

Voices. Soft, indistinct. Like she had a pillow over her head. Emily moved to lift the pillow.

Pain pressed her head from temple to temple, and both cheeks stung. Like a scraped knee with shards of glass ground in. An invisible hand ground still more.

Her stomach seemed to have shrunk to the size of a walnut, surrounded by a shell of soreness with nausea roiling.

A wet cloth settled on her forehead. Coolness. Blessed coolness.

She opened her eyes. No, she didn't. Why wouldn't her left eye open?

"She's waking up." Mikey's voice chirped like a squirrel's excited chatter. A small hand touched her shoulder. "You gave us quite a scare, Miss Emily."

Emily touched her left eye. Pain like a dagger of ice straight to her brain. She yelped and yanked her finger away.

She squinted her good eye. Bright light poured through the windows, gleaming off the dark furniture, blurring the figures gathered in the room. Who are all these people?

Mikey sat on the edge of the bed, wringing out the cloth and placing it on her forehead again. Marshal Cook stood in the corner, one arm across his chest, the other fingering his mustache, brows furrowed. A man and a woman stood to one side. The woman was an older version of Mikey without the cockeyed pigtails. The man, dressed in a black suit with thin white stripes, seemed like a grandfather with a whisper of a mustache, thick snowy hair, and sad blue eyes.

The man stepped to the bed and picked up Emily's right hand. When she winced, he gently laid it back on the bed, and reached across to take her left. He held her wrist, his fingers strong and comforting. After a few seconds, he lowered the wrist as if laying a baby in a cradle.

"Tell me how you're feeling, young lady." He lowered himself to the edge of the bed with a sigh that came from a depth three stories below.

"Sore." Emily licked her lips. "Thirsty."

He nodded and turned to the other woman. "Victoria, will you bring a glass of water, please?"

The man helped Emily to a sitting position and shoved pillows behind her. She reached for the glass with her right hand and dropped it when her wrist shot a lance of fire hot pain up her arm and her fingers refused to work. The man caught the glass before water landed on the bed, but a few drops sloshed out.

He brought the glass to her lips, and she drank in gulps, seeking to slake the thirst that left a dusty road down her throat. Her stomached lurched when the water hit, but quickly settled.

"I wish we had met under better circumstances," he said. "I'm Doctor Williams, Gerald Williams. I understand from Mikey and Marshal Cook, you're quite a remarkable young woman. An attorney and solver of crimes. A character worthy of Poe's detection stories."

She smiled.

"Do you think you can take some broth? I want to get something inside you besides water. With that bruise on your stomach, I don't want you eating solid food yet."

Emily nodded.

Soon, Victoria bustled in, carrying a tray with a steaming bowl of yellowish liquid. She placed the tray over Emily's lap. "This is from today's chicken soup so it's fresh and warm." Her voice had the same lilting twang as her daughter's. "Just the thing to soothe a tender stomach."

The aroma drifted up Emily's nose, softening the sharp edges of her pain. She used her left hand to lift and slurp a spoonful. Her throat snuggled to the warm liquid and her stomach sighed as it received the nourishment.

Marshal Cook moved from the window to a chair by the bed. "Can you tell me what happened, Miss Peyton?"

She told him between spoonsful of broth that kept her throat moist and able to talk.

"You have no idea who might have attacked you?"

Emily hesitated, trying to match what she thought was the size of her attacker with anyone she knew. "Sorry, Marshal. He wore a mask. All I know is his eyes were dark."

"But he told you to forget the Whitneys?"

"Yes." She closed her eyes. The voice shivered through her memory.

He nodded and rubbed his chin, his eyes distant. "Makes me wonder who else knew they were here."

"Besides Frank Stevens?" Emily said.

"I'll see if anyone's seen him."

Mikey scrambled to answer a sharp knock at the door. She held the door partly open, mouth agape, staring up at whoever stood in the entry.

"Michaela, don't be rude," her mother said. "Let them in."

Mikey stood back, pulling the door wide to admit Nadina. Victoria pulled Mikey away and gripped her shoulders. Marshal Cook stood and removed his hat. Doctor Williams smiled and nodded.

She strode to the end of the bed, her plum-colored dress more appropriate in so many ways than the blue gown Emily saw the day before.

Nadina's mouth opened slightly. She gulped. "Oh, my goodness. Who did this to you?"

"Don't know," Emily said.

"Marshal?" Nadina's gaze froze the marshal.

"He wore a mask and attacked from behind."

She pivoted to the doctor.

"Nothing broken. Some nasty bruises. She'll be sore and tender for a few days, but she should be able to get up tomorrow."

Nadina nodded, a sharp bob of her head. "Good. Send me the bill for her care."

"Why?" Emily's voice cracked. She slurped more broth. "You don't have to do that."

"For several reasons." Her large brown eyes bore into Emily. "I don't like for people who come to my ... establishment to get hurt. You were the first ... normal person to come to my house and not condemn me. You even seemed to respect me. And I admire you for pursuing your dream. I know what it's like to have men see you as only good for one thing." She glanced from the Doctor Williams to Cook. "Present company excepted."

Victoria covered Mikey's ears. The girl shrugged her mother's hands off, her eyes still wide as she stared at Nadina.

"Thank you," Emily said, struck by this stranger's generosity, touched by her sensitivity.

"Who found her?" Nadina scanned their faces.

"Who did find me?"

Cook chuckled. "Joaquin. He got out of his carriage to get a beer in the hotel and his horse wandered off, straight to the Alamo. Joaquin found him standing over Miss Peyton. Joaquin carried her to the hotel and fetched me and Doc."

Williams clapped his hands together. "My patient needs to rest. So y'all best clear out of here."

The marshal, Victoria, and Mikey left.

"I'll check on you later this afternoon," Doctor Williams said. "If you feel up to it, maybe you can have something more solid for supper."

Nadina walked to her side and stroked the back of her left hand. "I'll be back later—before supper."

Williams and Nadina walked out together, his arm possessively around her waist.

Emily settled against her pillows, her right eye slowly closing, welcoming the sleep that crept up her body like a heavy blanket on a winter's night.

Has anyone telegraphed her father?

Later.

Chapter 55

Emily's eyes snapped open. Disoriented. The cold, hard voice. The tight grip of the hand. The knife. The knife against her cheek. Icy. Sharp. The words. The threats. The fear, freezing her. Nausea roiled up her throat. She squeezed her eyes tight and shook her head, trying to drive the image from her mind.

No. No. Don't go there.

She willed herself to calm. Breathed deeply. Tension receded like a thick fog giving way to the dawn.

I'm all right. I'm in my room. I'm safe.

The door creaked. Emily froze, listening, fear clutching her stomach, cold sweat beading. No time to hide. No place to run. She laid on her side, facing the wall.

She squinted through the half-closed lids of her good eye. Couldn't see anyone. Were they standing in the doorway? Watching? Making sure she was asleep before slashing her throat?

A shuffle of a footstep, the creak of a floorboard.

A hand touched her shoulder. She yelped and spun onto her back, pain reminding her—too late—not to hurry.

Mikey.

Emily's hand went to her chest as if to slow her heart.

"I'm sorry, Miss Emily. I didn't mean to scare you. I was trying to be extry quiet. Mama wanted me to check if you was all right or needed anythin'."

She stroked the child's cheek. "That's all right. I'm nervous and jumpy."

Mikey nodded. "Grandpa put one of his deputies outside your door. Ain't no varmints gonna get in, I can tell you that for a fact."

Emily's stomach cramped as she tried to scoot into a sitting position. She moved gingerly, using Mikey's shoulder for support.

"How're you feelin'?"

"Sore. My head feels like a horse is stomping on it."

"Want me to fetch you some water or broth or somethin'?"

Emily shook her head. "Mikey, do you know if anyone notified my family in Kansas?"

Mikey frowned and puckered her lips. "I don't think so. Once Doc said you were gonna be fine, Grandpa decided to wait for you to do it. Said it wouldn't be good to hear the news from a total stranger, especially if you was gonna be all right."

"Thank you." At least they wouldn't get into a tizzy and come rushing down. Who could come anyway? Not Father or Doc. Terrence would only get in more trouble with the bank. Charlotte needed to be with Tiny and her father. Maybe Caroline. Nice, but unnecessary.

She'd head home as soon as Doctor Williams said she could travel.

She drifted off again, her dreams filled with thoughts of Terrence riding to her rescue and carrying her back to safety.

The bishop slid along the board. Terrence stared at the piece, his strategy blown by the carved wood statuette hovering near his king and threatening his queen. He rubbed his chin and scratched his ear. George's mind was fully back. If only his speech would follow. He glanced at his opponent. The older man sat with his chin is his hand, a slight grin on his face, his eyes almost laughing.

The rattle of coffee cups and the aroma of warm peach pie interrupted his contemplation. Not that he was getting any great ideas, anyway. George had defeated him. Again. Unless he could salvage a draw. Unlikely. George would have to make a mistake, about as likely as Mr. Warner giving up his pipe.

"Thought you gentlemen might be ready for some refreshment." Charlotte set the tray on the side table. Terrence slid the chessboard out of the way so she could serve them.

George compared his watch with the grandfather clock, glanced at the door.

"No telegraph from Emily today?" Terrence asked.

George shook his head.

Unusual. Emily telegraphed every day. Brief reports on her travels. The last telegraph was yesterday morning when she reported she would visit the saloon and brothel.

George was not happy about her going to either place, and telegraphed back for her to ask the marshal for a deputy to accompany her. There'd been no response.

Terrence understood George's concern and tried to argue she was more than capable of taking care of herself in either place.

Now, over twenty-four hours without hearing from her, his heart battled fear as he prayed for her safety. He wanted to board the next train and ride to her, her knight in shining armor. He smiled at the thought she would ever need a knight. Besides, he doubted Priscilla would let him don armor for anyone but her.

Still ...

"I'll send a telegraph to the hotel and the marshal first thing in the morning."

George nodded and gestured at the game. Terrence reached over and laid his king on its side.

Chapter 56

Emily sat on the side of the bed, her hands white-knuckled around the edge of the mattress. A spout of dizziness swirled, as if her head would tumble from her shoulders like a child dropping a ball. Eyes closed, she inhaled, rubbed her stomach.

She opened her eye. One final swoosh and the table next to her bed settled into position like a bird fitting in its nest. She looked around the room. Nothing moved.

She exhaled, shifted so her feet rested solidly on the floor. Inch by inch, she stood, hands splayed to grab the bed if some part of her body failed to cooperate.

Upright. No swooning. Good.

Hand on the mattress, she shuffled to the end of the bed. Grip tight on the bedpost, she breathed deeply.

I can do this.

She let her hand drop and took a step, arms extended. Then another. By the third step, her arms were at her side, confidence rising.

She walked to the mirror in the corner of the room. Her fingers flew to her mouth as she looked at her reflection. Eye swollen shut, deeply bruised. Right cheek scraped where her face slammed into the wall. Hair wild and matted with sweat. She lifted her nightgown. Another deep, dark purple bruise above her navel. Tender under her fingers.

Releasing the nightgown, she touched the flesh surrounding her eye.

Why did I do that? It hurts enough without touching it.

An unfamiliar sensation. Twinges in her stomach. She waited. Hunger. Her last solid food had been breakfast yesterday. The window's reflection in the mirror told her it was afternoon.

She walked to the door, each step stronger, more sure. Opening the door a crack, she peered into the hallway. Across from her door a man sat, his chair tilted on its back legs against the wall. A silver badge on his vest declared him a deputy. A shot gun lay across his lap, a thick book in his large-knuckled hands.

"Excuse me."

"Yes, ma'am?" The man lowered his chair to the floor and was at her door in a step, gun in hand, a finger on the other hand marking his place in his book.

She clutched the throat of her nightgown and slid more behind the door so only her face showed. He brought his book to his chest. A Bible.

"Do you know if the little girl, Mikey, is around?"

The man smiled, his brown eyes sparking with amusement. "She's been around every five minutes, listening at the door to see if you was awake, peeked in a couple of times but didn't go in. I expect she'll be by any minute now."

"Next time she comes by, tell her to come right in."

He touched the brim of his hat with two fingers. "Yes, ma'am. Marshal Cook's wondering if you feel up to havin' a word with him."

"Yes, I am. Whenever he's ready."

"Yes, ma'am. I'll fetch him soon as Mikey comes by."

A short time later, three rapid knocks preceded the door opening, and Mikey swooshed in like a summer zephyr. She hopped up next to Emily on the bed and kissed her cheek. "Thought you were gonna sleep 'til next Tuesday. We sent Joaquin to fetch Grandpa and Doc Williams."

"So, you trust him now?"

Mikey crossed her arms and jutted her chin. "Nope. Wouldn't even trust him to feed his horse regular. He was just hangin' around, so Mama figured she give him somethin' to do so's he won't annoy the guests, 'specially the pretty ones."

Mikey knelt on the bed and fluffed the pillows behind Emily. Taking a brush from the dresser, she stroked Emily's hair. Slow, gentle movements. Emily closed her eyes and relaxed into the child's ministrations.

"You're very good with a brush."

"Mama likes me to do her hair after her bath, and hers is way longer than yours. Reaches all the way down her back." Mikey's voice seemed filled with awe.

"A bath sounds good. Maybe after I talk with your grandfather and the doctor, I'll take one if you can keep the water warm."

Mikey lifted a handful of hair and pulled the brush through it in an easy stroke. "Sure will. Not too hot or too cold."

Emily's stomach rumbled.

"You hungry?"

"Very. But I better wait until Doctor Williams tells me what I can have."

The rhythm of Mikey's brushing soothed. Emily's mind calmed and a pleasant lethargy permeated her muscles and emotions. Eyes closed, she tilted her head forward so Mikey could reach every strand. Although Mikey had long passed a normal stopping point, she continued as if realizing she was doing more than a simple task. Emily knew the girl was helping her heal physically and emotionally.

She looked at Mikey, searching her face, enjoying the scattered freckles and the warm, open eyes. "You're a very special little girl." She kissed the girl's cheek, enjoying the remnants of baby-like softness that lingered.

Head down, Mikey turned the brush over and over in her hands. She reverently placed it on the bed and faced Emily, eyes brimming. She flung herself into Emily's embrace, arms tight around Emily's neck.

A knock at the door. Mikey jumped from the bed, wiping tears away. Emily swept one away from her own cheek.

Marshal Cook entered, hat in hand, mustache as stiff as a telegraph pole. He pulled a chair next to the bed. Mikey scrambled into his lap.

"Have you remembered anything else about last night?"

"No, Marshal. Everything's still a blur."

He nodded. "I received a telegraph from your father this morning, asking me to check on you. Do you want to let him know what happened?"

"I'd better. I'll tell them I'm coming home. No need in making them worry."

Cook wrapped his arms around Mikey, and she snuggled into his chest. "I found out one interesting piece of news. Frank Stevens may have been in town and been in contact with the Whitneys."

"What? How? I mean, how did you find out?" The words ran from her like a horse on a gallop.

Cook smiled. "I went to the Silver Dollar last night to talk to Ed about your visit yesterday. He was his usual helpful self. Deaf, dumb, and blind." He shook his head. "Especially the dumb part."

He slid Mikey to the floor. "Anyway, one of the gamblers was there. One I hadn't seen when the Whitneys were killed. He remembered them. Bet heavy on bad hands. Told me there was another player who seemed mighty interested in them. Didn't know his name, but his description could fit Stevens. Height and weight anyways."

New hope surged. Stevens may have been here. May have seen the Whitneys. The hope crashed. Why didn't he take them to the marshal? Why did he just play cards and do nothing?

"Of course, the gambler's description coulda fit a dozen other men. Stevens bein' able to disguise himself makes it hard to pinpoint him bein' anywhere."

Fists clenched, Emily fought back the tears. Wouldn't help Tiny any. Now what to do?

She leaned back against the pillows and stared at the ceiling.

How can you let an innocent man hang? How can you let the dreams of two people—two church-going people, two people who pray and believe in you—die like flowers in summer heat? What kind of God are you? And Terrence and Charlotte think I should trust you. Can't trust you anymore than I can trust Joaquin or Priscilla.

She slid from the bed, slipped a robe over her nightgown, and strode to the window. Arms crossed, she glared at the plaza below, at the people bustling about, doing business, chasing their dreams. A curse flew from her lips.

She turned. Mikey stood next to her grandfather, eyes wide, mouth open. Cook's eyes glittered from beneath his scrunched brow. Heat surged up Emily's neck.

"I'm sorry. I was hoping to find the real killers." She extended her arms and let them drop to her side. "Now, I don't know what to do. An innocent man will hang, and I can't do anything to stop it."

The sob broke, and she turned to the window again, letting the tears flow.

The door closed quietly behind her.

A hand touched her arm. A small hand. It caressed her arm and took her hand and held it.

Chapter 57

A knock at the door disturbed Emily's storm-tossed slumber. With an exhausted groan, she leveraged herself off the bed. It'd been an hour since Cook left. She opened the door to Doc Williams. His smile faded as he entered the room.

"Are you doing all right?" he asked. "You look like a stampede stomped your heart."

She nodded. "Heard some bad news." She raised her eyes to his. "Doctor, how do you deal with failure? What do you do when a patient dies, and you did everything you could to save them? And you know they didn't have to die, but you couldn't save them."

Williams guided her to the bed and helped her sit against the pillows. He sat in the chair Cook had abandoned and crossed his legs, hands clasped in his lap, gaze resting on some spot on the wall behind her.

"Miss Peyton, I don't know if I have the answer you're looking for, one that will make you feel better about yourself. If I've done everything in my power, if I've used everything I've learned about medicine and the human body, and my patient dies, it hurts, and I'm angry because they should have lived."

He paused. His time-worn blue eyes held her with tender compassion. She nodded for him to continue. He rubbed his chin. "And then I sit and think. I'm reminded I still have so much to learn, but if I gave everything I had to save that patient, if I used everything I knew at the time, I'm not to blame myself. I study the situation to see what I can learn, to take better care of my next patient, to never stop doing what God has called me to do. And I pray, because I can't do anything without him."

Emily's jaw tightened, and her heart beat fast. "Pray." She splayed her fingers on her lap. More preaching. "I've never known prayer to help with much of anything."

Williams cocked his head. A slight smile rippled across his full lips. "I couldn't live a day without praying, couldn't treat a patient without asking God to guide my hands and my mind."

A lump surged into Emily's throat. "Did you ever ask him to bring your mother back? To heal your father? To explain why these things happened?"

"You did?"

Emily nodded, swiping tears from her cheeks, knuckling her right eye with the corner of the sheet.

"He didn't give you an answer you could hear or understand?"

She frowned. "If he won't talk plain, why bother talking at all?"

The silence lengthened. Emily plucked at the sheet covering her lap while the doctor leaned forward, elbows on knees.

"That's all right, Doctor. I don't expect you to know the answer. I've asked this question for years, and nobody's been able to give me anything beyond pious platitudes."

He moved to the side of the bed and gently probed her swollen eye. "That's doing better." He lifted her bruised wrist, flexed it. "Still sore?"

Her other gripped the sheet as a shard of pain lanced up her arm.

"Your arm isn't broken. Time will heal it." He continued holding her hand until she met his eyes. "Keep asking your questions, Miss Peyton. Keep listening for the answer." He touched his ear. "Not just with these things sticking on our heads." He placed his hand over his heart. "But here as well."

He laid her hand back in her lap. "How's your stomach?"

"Hungry."

His laugh sprinkled like a spring shower. "I think we can take care of that. I'll ask Victoria to bring you a meal. Eat what you can but stop if you get any pain and send for me right away."

"Slow down, Miss Peyton. Doc said to take it slow."

Emily looked up from the bowl of chicken and dumplings, wiped a dribble of gravy from her chin. "I am wolfing this down, aren't I?" She dunked a piece of sourdough bread in the bowl and slurped the dripping gob into her mouth. She let the bread dissolve on her tongue. Sipped coffee.

"This is delicious, Mrs. Franklin."

"Just call me Victoria. That's what everyone else does. Except Pa. He insists on calling me Tori." She shrugged. "Can't stand it. I swear he does it just to annoy me."

Emily smiled. "Our fathers do know exactly the right thing to say to get our goats, don't they?"

Three sharp knocks announced Mikey.

"Michaela, you need to wait to be invited into a room. Don't just barge in."

"Yes, ma'am." Mikey's chin dropped to her chest, hands behind her back. "I'm sorry." She brought her hand out, waving a flimsy slip of paper. "This teleygraph came for Miss Emily."

IS EVERYTHING ALL RIGHT?
NO WORD IN TWO DAYS.
TERRENCE

Technically, it's only been a day-and-a-half, but why quibble when the quibblee is not around. His smile danced across her vision. She sighed. He and Priscilla will be very happy together. They're meant for each other.

"Would you like to take the answer to the telegraph office for me?"

Mikey glanced at her mother, who nodded.

Emily ripped a piece of paper from her journal.

No news.
Coming home tomorrow.
Will tell all.

Why disappoint before she could explain? Telling about her injuries would only upset them. Her father didn't need any more torment. He needed to get well. She hoped he'd kept his promise not to do any legal work until she got back. Unlikely, but Doc was there to keep an eye on him. She'd deal with the rest when she got back.

Mikey opened the door to leave but jumped back two steps. Nadina stood in the doorway. "May I come in?"

"Please," Emily said.

Mikey stepped to one side and then scooted around the full skirt of Nadina's gray dress.

Slipping her gloves off, Nadina nodded at Victoria. "Mrs. Franklin."

Victoria dipped her head slightly, lips drawn tight.

"Miss Peyton. How are you feeling today?"

"I'll leave you two alone." Victoria stood. "I'll fetch your tray later, Miss Peyton."

The door closed firmly.

"Do you ever get used to people not liking you much?" Emily asked.

Nadina arranged herself in the chair Victoria had vacated, folded her slender hands in her lap. "Not really. I've learned to laugh it off, but it still rankles." She glanced at the door. "Especially when you've tried to help in the past."

Emily waited.

Nadina waved her hand. "Old history. Not worth mentioning."

"Still seems to bother Victoria."

"Yes, it does." Her blue eyes pierced Emily. "But, as you lawyers like to say, it's confidential. I won't break a trust."

"What brings you here?"

"I came to see how you're doing. I'm bothered that your visit to my establishment might have contributed to your attack."

"That's something we'll probably never know," Emily said.

Nadina stroked her neck. "I expect so, still it nags." She paused. "Have you decided what you will do next?"

"Go home tomorrow. There's nothing more I can do here." A weight settled on Emily's chest. "There's not much more I can do anywhere." She heard the heaviness in her words.

"It must be hard to admit defeat, especially when your cause is right."

Emily nodded.

Nadina's voice broke the lengthy silence. "You'll be traveling alone, won't you?"

"Yes, I will. Why?"

"I don't like that." She tapped her chin with a tapered fingernail. "One of my girls has family in Fort Worth I know she'd like to visit. I'll send her with you as far as there."

"You don't have to. Marshal Cook is having one of his deputies ride with me as far as Austin."

"Please let me. It will help assuage my guilt over what happened to you. Besides, Becky will be great protection. She's a crack shot and knows how to bring a man to his knees."

Heat rose in Emily's face.

Nadina laughed. "I didn't mean that way. She knows how to twist a man's arm until he begs for mercy. She'll be the perfect protection for you."

"Thank you."

"Are you anxious to get home?"

Emily gazed out the window. *Am I?* "I'm looking forward to getting out of San Antonio. And I'm looking forward to seeing my father and ... my other friends." Her eyes clouded. "But I'm not eager to bring back bad news."

Nadina took her hand, stroked the back of it with her thumb. "I understand. I don't know if I'd be able to do that."

Emily watched Nadina's hand holding hers for a moment, tightened her own grip, and then gently slid her hand away.

George handed Terrence the telegraph from Emily. Terrence eyes darted toward the kitchen and the sounds of Charlotte singing while she made supper. The strains of "Amazing Grace" drifted into the room.

Terrence nodded at the paper. "Doesn't sound very hopeful."

George shook his head.

"What do we tell Charlotte?"

"Nothing. Wait for Emily."

Terrence sighed. Wait for Emily. Why did the thought of seeing her soon intrigue him? He looked forward to her return as he did a Sunday after-church baseball game. He looked forward to seeing Priscilla ...?

Priscilla was different. Comfortable and sure. Emily carried an edge of excitement from her desire to be a lawyer to her doing all she could for her client. For Tiny. Would he feel the same way if it wasn't Tiny? Would never know.

Priscilla's edge of excitement was finding beautiful new clothes and teasing him with soft kisses and unspoken promises of more to come.

Emily teased by besting him in a shooting contest three times out of five. Her gelding was the only horse that could beat Spot. He suspected she could play baseball better than half the men in town.

She hated God. That cloud always hovered on the fringe of his thoughts. Now its thickness settled over him, blocking out the sunshine that was Emily. He knew why she hated God, and nothing turned her cold and closed more than trying to discuss the reason. At least she tolerated blessing the food in her own house as a balm to Charlotte. Progress of a sort.

He had stopped praying for God to give him the words. Each effort drove her further away. Now, he prayed for someone else to reach her, and that he would be there to help her understand.

Chapter 58

Stomach still tender, Emily wore her undergarments loosely. No corset to compress her insides to her spine. The sensation was freeing and salacious. Victoria, when helping her dress earlier, commented that Emily, with her figure, didn't need any such accoutrements.

She examined the room one last time to make sure she'd not forgotten anything.

A triple knock on the door.

"Come in, Mikey."

No pigtails today, Mikey's hair tumbled to her shoulders in gentle curls. The effect softened her face, brightened her gray eyes, gave her a little girl look. Emily's heart climbed to her throat. She resisted the desire to snuggle the child into her lap, to feel her thick hair against her cheek, to cover those small hands with her own. A memory, a shadow flashed as quick as a hummingbird. Her body, her heart ached to be held like that. Caroline Everett had tried, but she couldn't fill the hole. The hole at Emily's center, often forgotten or buried, now surged, insatiable.

Mikey's entrance was tentative, her face somber, hands behind her back.

"Why so sad?" Emily asked, her own sorrow a gray cloak over her heart.

Mikey sniffled, wiped her nose with her finger, rubbed it on her dress. She glanced out the window. "Be ... Because ...." She ran to Emily and wrapped her arms around her waist, squeezing tight.

Ignoring the pressure on her stomach, Emily held the little girl close, stroking her hair, feeling Mikey's shoulders shake. "I know. I know," she whispered. She bit her lip, but the tears welled, and, with a blink, Emily let them flow.

Emily squatted, held Mikey's hands in one of hers, caressed her face, thumb gently brushing her freckles. "I will miss you, Miss Michaela Ann Franklin." *Why won't my heart stay in its place?* She swallowed. "You've been a wonderful friend to me."

Mikey nodded, and one more tear slipped down her cheek. Her head rose two inches to absorb one last sniffle. "Mama sent me to tell you they're waiting downstairs for you."

In the lobby, Marshal Cook stood with Victoria. Mikey ran to stand with her grandfather. A short distance away, Nadina, her arm looped through Doctor Williams's, chatted with a woman who looked about Emily's age, brunette hair arranged stylishly under a pink hat. Nadina wore a pale-yellow outfit that covered her from neck-to-shoe, yet left little to the imagination. Some men risked permanent cricks in their necks as they tried to ogle her and walk at the same time.

The deputy who had guarded Emily's door stood apart from the others, shotgun cradled in his arms.

Marshall Cook introduced her to Deputy Luke Hastings, who would ride with her as far as Austin. Luke, tall and slender, looked like stringing more than three words together would turn his ears bright pink.

Nadina introduced her to Becky. The brunette's green eyes carried a hint of laughter, her small mouth smiled, dimples punctuating her round cheeks.

No sign of Joaquin. A movement, a shadow, behind Nadina. A man entered from the bright sunlight, eyes skimming the room, centering on Nadina. Emily gasped and her stomach clenched as if punched again.

Delbert Ford.

He didn't seem to notice her as he half turned and backed into the bar, eyes never leaving Nadina.

Cook and Nadina followed Emily's gaze.

"You know Bertie?" Nadina asked.

Emily nodded. "He came to our office in Abilene wanting legal advice. Didn't think a girl was qualified. He was on the train when I came down here."

Cook rubbed his chin. "Too many coincidences for me. I'll have a talk with him after you leave. I'll make sure he's late if he plans to be on the same train."

Relief coursed through Emily. "Miss Nadina, how do you know him?"

"He's one of our regulars. Girls call him Two Bit Bertie because he's so cheap."

"That's for sure," Becky said. "Always looking to get something extra but don't want to pay for it. And complains we didn't do enough."

"Let's just say, I'll take his money," Nadina said, "but he doesn't get to pick from the cream of the crop when he visits."

Doctor Williams coughed and nodded at Mikey. "Ladies, there's a little one present."

Nadina blushed and covered her mouth. "I am so sorry."

Victoria's brows relaxed, but her hard glare drilled into Nadina.

The faint sound of a train whistle meandered across the heavy air.

"That would be mine," Emily said.

The goodbyes were quick until Nadina stepped up and embraced her. A long, tight hug full of unspoken emotion. Emily couldn't comprehend the confused feelings filling her heart. She only knew she'd found a friend—a very unlikely friend—a friend she would miss. She only now realized how much. Nadina stepped back, caressed Emily's cheek. "You are someone special, Miss Emily Peyton. Keep in touch."

Emily nodded.

Last came Mikey, eyes red, tears threatening, lips pouting. "You'll come back and see me, won't you?" Her eyes pleaded.

Did I look like that when Mother left? "I'll do my best, sweetheart. I'll do my best."

Mikey's fingers lingered in her hand until the little girl returned to her mother, clinging to her.

The train whistle sounded closer, louder, more shrill. Emily reached for her carpetbag, but Luke Hastings lifted it with a soft, "Allow me."

Becky fell in step beside her, the two following the deputy.

Delbert Ford burst from the bar.

Cook held up his hand. "A moment, sir. I'd like to talk with you."

Ford's eyes darted like a trapped rat, gazing past Emily, then returning before wilting and looking away. "I can't miss my train."

"This shouldn't take very long." Cook put his hand on Ford's arm.

Ford looked at the marshal's hand, at his face, and threw a quick glance at Emily. He tried to shake off the marshal's hand but Cook held firm.

"The quicker I can ask my questions, the sooner you'll be on your train." Cook, with a slight turn, guided him back into the bar. "I could use a beer while we talk."

Ford's shoulders sagged, and his head drooped.

Chapter 59

Home. Soon I'll be home. Never had the word filled Emily with such dread.

No new hope for Tiny or Charlotte. No new strategy or evidence to convince the judge or the governor that the prisoner deserved a reprieve.

She studied her hands, hands that had turned page after page of law books and case law, revealing new insights, new knowledge of the intricacies of the law. Pages she studied until she fell asleep, head cradled in her arms, lamp burning low. Then spending most of the next morning persuading her back to return to its normal position.

Hands that prepared legal documents. Documents to clarify, to explain, to protect. All that knowledge flowing down her arm, through her pen, to the page.

Hands that drew up lists of questions to use in Tiny's trial. Questions to cast doubt on the marshal's theory, questions to show Tiny's goodness, questions to show his innocence.

All for naught. She failed. Tiny would hang because she wasn't good enough.

Whatever made her think she could be a lawyer in the first place? A child's dream fostered by an indulgent father.

What next? Almost twenty-six. Too old to marry. Especially after driving off every possibility with her arrogance and sharp tongue. Terrence belonged in Priscilla's arms. That woman knew how to be a wife, trained for getting married her entire life. *I trained for anything but.* Emily heaved a sigh. She would never inflict on any man what happened to her father. And her.

Deputy Quick's puppy dog eyes every time he came near were both warm and amusing. Yet even he seemed to know a romance between them had all the likelihood of the North and South agreeing on why they fought the war.

Despair flooded her. Clerk for her father the rest of her life? Become the town spinster? The focus of town gossip and derision as the Miss High and Mighty Emily Louise Peyton, the girl too full of herself to associate with regular people. Priscilla would lead the parade.

The prairie rolled past her window, a blur of green and tan.

Move to a new town and start over? Teach school? Lots of towns preferred their female teachers to be beyond the marrying age. That was her, all right.

Move where? Kansas City? Saint Louis? The image of San Antonio rose like the sun driving away storm clouds. Mikey. Victoria. Nadina. More friends than she had in Abilene. But not as dear.

The conductor waddled through the car, grabbing seat backs to keep his balance as the train rocked along. He announced Abilene as the next stop.

Emily sighed and leaned her head against the warm glass of the window. *Should've got off at the last stop.* She straightened her spine, tucked stray hairs under her hat.

Face it. Take the consequences and then, as soon as possible, move on. Literally.

Boots ringing hollow on the planking, Terrence paced the platform. He squinted, looking for the faintest trace of smoke. Hand behind his ear, he listened for the whistle, willing the train to appear now.

"You act like she's been away for a year." Caroline stood under the roof overhang, hands together.

Terrence flashed a sheepish grin, hand rubbing the back of his neck. "It feels longer. I want to know what she found out. Can we save Tiny from hanging? I wish she'd at least told us that much in a telegraph."

"And it has nothing to do with you missing her like someone had taken your horse?"

He stopped in mid-stride. He shook his head. "She's a good friend, and she risked a lot going down there."

"And you miss her. More than you care to admit, I think."

"Wouldn't you miss Doc if he went away for a while?"

"Yes, but we're married. Is that how you miss Emily?"

"Poor example," he said, heat rushing up his neck.

"Really? Might it be closer to the truth than you think?"

"No." He swallowed the irritation. "I'm about to ask Mr. Montgomery for Priscilla's hand. Why would I have such thoughts about Emily?"

Caroline sighed, stared down the track.

The whistle pealed, and a ribbon of black smoke smudged the sky above the trees.

"Here it is." Terrence stepped to the edge of the platform, craning as if he could pull the train into the station by the force of his will.

The train crawled to a stop, billows of steam cascading from the engine. Terrence side-skipped down the platform, hopping to glance in the windows. Where was she?

Two cars up, he heard Caroline's voice, fear and worry in every word. "What happened to you?"

He danced around some passengers as he hurried to the two women. What was Caroline talking about? Emily looked fine. As beautiful as ever.

Then she faced him. His feet wouldn't move. His stomach dropped to his shoes and his heart followed.

Her left eye was a slit surrounded by a purplish-yellow bruise the size of a baseball.

Now, closer, he saw the healing scrapes on her right cheek.

Anger swallowed the wave of nausea. Who did this? Who would ever hurt someone so precious? He wanted to reach out, take her in his arms, protect her.

Caroline beat him to it, enwrapping Emily in an embrace close and tight, stroking the younger woman's hair. After a few moments, they separated. Caroline grasped Emily's hands.

He stepped closer. Emily smiled and took one of his hands. The three stood silently. Terrence grabbed the questions wanting to burst from his mouth and shoved them into a corner of his brain. Emily would explain when she was ready and in her own words.

"Speak, child." Caroline's calm voice had the undertone of a parent losing patience.

"Somebody didn't like that I was asking questions about the Whitneys."

"Who? Why? What did they do to you?" Terrene clamped his lips together to keep more questions from spilling.

Emily shrugged, gripped his hand tighter. "We don't know who. The why is because I must have made them very uncomfortable. The what is they punched me in the face and the stomach, knocked me into a wall."

Emily looked down.

"What else?" Terrence jiggled her hand, urging her to speak.

"They threatened to kill Father if I didn't stop."

"Why didn't you tell us?" Terrence's anger wanted to scorch the platform. "I would've come down to help you."

She dropped his hand. "There wasn't anything you could have done."

He clenched his fists, ready to argue.

"By the time I could get word to you, and you boarded a train, I would have been on my way home. Besides ..." She motioned at her face. "This is kind of hard to explain in a telegraph. I couldn't think of any way to tell Father except in person."

Under his roiling fury, Terrence knew she was correct. Nevertheless, he still wanted to lash out, and the frustration of no immediate target rankled even more.

Caroline's hand touched his arm. He jumped. "Are you all right, Terrence?" she asked. "You look like you're going to explode."

He nodded, teeth tight, fists raised. "I want to punish whoever did this. I want to take them out and shoot them. Kneecaps, ankles, wrists to start."

"My dear Sir Galahad." Emily smiled and reached for his arm. A quick touch, and she pulled her hand back. He wanted her to put it back. Her hand calmed him, especially when coupled with the warm affection in her eye.

"Now, let's take our time going to the house so you both can help me figure out how to tell Father."

Chapter 60

George Peyton flexed the fingers of his left hand and rotated his left shoulder, enjoying the freedom from the sling and splints. Sooner than Doc wanted, but the old coot didn't have to live with the thing, didn't have to live one-handed, looking at a perfectly good hand lying useless.

Another few weeks and the splints would come off his legs. In the meantime, Doc planned to bring some crutches over for him to practice under Charlotte's supervision. *Going to burn this cursed wheelchair soon as I figure out those sticks.*

Sounds of Charlotte bustling in the kitchen reached his ears. No singing, though. She'd become more withdrawn the longer they went without hearing from Emily. He was as frustrated as everyone else at his daughter's lack of communication. She deserved one serious talking to once she got home. Not right to leave her client, her family, and friends uninformed. All she needed to do was send a couple of words, something to give us hope.

He turned toward the kitchen. Maybe there wasn't any hope to give. Was that why Emily had been silent other than to say she'd explain all when she got home? Charlotte undoubtedly came to that conclusion as well. The sad eyes, the lips that didn't smile, the voice that didn't sing. How the girl must be suffering. *And I let her.*

He wheeled to the entrance to the kitchen. Charlotte kneaded dough, mushing her hands into the mixture, lifting it, and dropping it on the table for more shoving and turning.

He coughed. She jumped, floury hands brushing her forehead.

"Need something, Mr. P?"

He'd given up trying to get her to call him George.

"I—noticing quiet you've been—last couple days. No singing. Haven't even teased—about—my vegetables."

Charlotte worked the dough. "Dinner will be ready in about an hour."

"Perfect—if train—on time."

"Corn and chicken soup. It'll keep if she's late."

"I—she'll love it."

Charlotte shaped the dough into loaves.

"Charlotte."

She looked at him, eyes moist.

"—worried what Emily—say?"

She bit her lip, jerked a nod.

He wanted to embrace her, tell everything would be all right. But he couldn't lie. He wouldn't.

"Me too."

The carriage pulled to a stop in front of her home. Emily wanted to ask Terrence to take another turn around the block. Or ten. Anything to give her more time to collect her scattered thoughts. To give her more time to gather the courage to walk through that dark green door and face the next step of her future, a future that lay clear as a mist-shrouded dawn.

Terrence placed her bag on the boardwalk and helped Caroline step down. He extended his hands toward her. She looked at them like they were mushrooms growing where mushrooms shouldn't.

She leaned to put her hands on his shoulders so he could grasp her waist and lift her to the ground. She stopped. She might never let go. She extended one hand to him and awkwardly used the narrow carriage step to reach the boardwalk. A moment, then another passed before she released his hand.

As her footsteps reached the porch, the door flew open, and Doc extended his arms. "Emily, welcome ho—" His mouth hung open, eyes bulging. "Oh, my goodness. What happened to you?"

She pushed gently on his chin until his mouth closed. "I'll explain when we're all together."

He moved back, and her foot refused to take the next step. She wanted to run, to streak across the prairie as far as her lungs would take her and then, run some more. Pound the guilt and the regrets out of her with each solid slap of her feet on the soil. Anything but face the father who nurtured her dreams or the young woman who rested her hopes and her future on Emily.

I failed them both.

She stepped forward, stomach flipping, heart pounding, knees weak.

Linen curtains fluttered in the breeze and sunlight glinted off the polished furniture and wood floors. Charlotte's doing, no doubt.

Her father wheeled himself into the room, Charlotte right behind, drying her hands on a towel.

Emily ran the few steps to her father and wrapped her arms around his neck. She held him. No tears, only her arms conveying her love and her joy at seeing him.

His arms held her. "Welcome home, daughter," he whispered.

She straightened.

Charlotte gasped, holding the towel to her throat while her other hand reached for Emily.

George's face clouded, and his creases deepened. He stared at her, lips a grim line.

Every eye on her, Emily waited. The silence hung ominous, like the sky before a thunderstorm breaks.

"When did the splints come off your arm, Father?"

George shook his head. "Not important. What happened—you? Don't—" He waited, eyes half-closed, "tell—walked into a door."

Caroline bustled forward. "Let's sit in the dining room. Charlotte? Let me help you bring the coffee in."

Charlotte looked from Emily to Caroline, eyes trance-like. Caroline touched her arm. She shook her head. "Yes. Right. It's all made." She stared at Emily as Caroline guided her to the kitchen.

At the table, her father studied her, shifted his attention to the kitchen, then back to her, fingers drumming. Anger flared behind his dark eyes. His mouth twitched with what she knew were questions he'd fire at her like a Winchester repeater.

Charlotte came in carrying a tray with cups and saucers.

"'Bout time," George muttered.

After a sharp glance, Charlotte ignored him while she set the table. Emily smiled inwardly. Looked like the girl had figured out how to handle Father's moods. Caroline followed behind and filled the cups. She placed the pot in the center of the table, brushed her hands on her skirt, and sat next to her husband. Charlotte took the seat across from Emily, hands clasped on the table, eyes apparently eager yet anxious for Emily to speak.

George pointed at her eye. "Begin with that."

Emily sipped her coffee, gently returned the cup to its saucer. "Excellent coffee, Charlotte."

"Emily Louise." Her father's voice was a gunshot.

"I was attacked outside the Alamo." She told the story of visiting the saloon and the brothel, ignoring Caroline's sharp intake of breath, and of the attack as she returned to the hotel.

Silence lay on the group. Her father studied the tabletop. Charlotte held her cup like it was a flower, eyes brimming. Doc contemplated the end of his cigar. Caroline stirred her coffee way beyond what it needed to blend the dollop of sugar she'd added.

Terrence, sitting next to her, focused out the window, fists clenched on the table, knuckles white. The side of his jaw twitched.

"I need to look at that eye later," Doc said. "Make sure it's healing proper. Does it hurt?"

"Only when I touch it."

"Then don't touch it." Doc spoke with the exasperation of years of patients doing dumb things. "How's your stomach?"

She stroked the area. "Still a little tender."

"Any problems eating?"

She shook her head.

"Any signs of bl—"

"James." Caroline broke in. "That's enough. Do your examine later, not in front of all these people."

"—never have—go." George's voice was muted, spoken more to the table than the air. "Should—seen it."

"We're not going over that again. I had to go. I went. It's over now." Emily spoke with a sharpness she didn't intend. "We couldn't foresee something like this happening."

"Anything—happened to you ..." George rubbed his face and folded his hands on the table. His age showed in the sagging bags under his eyes, the loose flesh of his cheeks. His age or his worry?

"You could have been killed," Terrence said, anguish shining in his eyes.

"But I wasn't." She touched his arm, wanting to take his hand and hold it, caress away the tension in his fist. She put her hand in her lap.

"Thank God for that," Caroline said.

Emily lifted her cup and drank.

"So, there's even less hope for Tiny?" Unshed tears soaked Charlotte's words, her voice brittle as spun glass.

Emily and her father exchanged glances. She tried to pierce the sadness hanging in her father's eyes. She wanted to hear him come up with a strategy, a plan, to free Tiny.

George shrugged, reached for Charlotte's hand. "—very little. Whitneys—our best shot." He caressed the back of her hand. "—don't have hard evidence."

Charlotte's lower lip quivered, and she wiped at her eyes with her free hand. She snatched her hand away from George and rose from the table, knocking over her coffee cup. Towel to her mouth, she ran from the room.

Caroline rose. "I'll go with her."

A cloak of guilt enfolded Emily, stronger, more oppressive than what she'd experienced on the train. Her brain floundered. *Can't even offer support to Charlotte. Caroline has to do it. Need to get away. Where? Anywhere.*

Doc dropped a napkin into the puddle of Charlotte's coffee.

The four sat. None spoke.

Terrence cleared his throat. "You didn't tell your father everything the attacker told you."

"It's not important now. There's nothing more we can do. Whoever it was won't bother us again."

"What did—say? Need all—," George said.

Emily wanted to stick Terrence's head in a pail and beat it with a spoon. She exhaled. "He said if I didn't stop asking about the Whitneys, you would be killed."

Her father smiled, a glimmer sparking his eyes. "Not the first time—probably not—last." He jerked his thumb at Doc. "—soon as you let—get back to work."

"Not important," Doc said. "Emily's back."

Who knows for how long?

"—frightened someone." George stroked his chin. "—figure out who."

Emily sipped her now tepid coffee. "I have a theory. It might sound far-fetched, but it's all I can come up with. I think Frank Stevens found the Whitneys. I think he tracked them down and killed them for the money."

"Did anyone see him around San Antonio?" Terrence asked.

"No. But the marshal knows him and said Stevens is a master of disguise."

Terrence's face brightened. "Sounds plausible."

"—theory," George said. "Not—enough—convince judge—or governor."

"We have no idea where Stevens is or what he looks like. I bet he was in disguise the day he came here."

"Would Wyatt Stoddard in Dodge know anything about him?" Terrence asked.

"Can we trust him?" Emily blurted before her father could speak.

George's face darkened. "Hate to think—can't trust—friend." He took a deep breath and turned to Doc. "Can I travel to Dodge?"

"When?"

"Yesterday, you old coot—Tomorrow."

Doc rolled his cigar from one side of his mouth to the other. "Let me check at the station. See if they can handle a wheelchair."

"Thanks. I'll take back—half—bad things—said about you."

"Only half. I'm sure they can accommodate you in a cattle car." Doc relit his cigar and checked George's pulse and relit his cigar. "Tell you what. You give me two days of complete rest, and I'll let you go."

"Two days—too urgent. Sooner?" Emily never saw her father beg, but his eyes entreated Doc.

"Nope. Not gonna risk losing you again."

Charlotte and Caroline rejoined them. Caroline's shoulder was wet, and Charlotte's red-rimmed eyes seemed ready to burst. She mopped up her spilled coffee and sat, shoulders slumped, head bowed.

"Charlotte," Emily said. "When's the next visiting day for Tiny?"

"Two days from now."

"May I come with you?"

Charlotte's head snapped up. "Why?"

"Because I need to be the one to tell him where we stand."

Chapter 61

Clothes waited to be put in their proper places. Emily stood, wrapping and unwrapping a pair of stockings around her hands. The house held a late afternoon hush. Doc and Caroline had patients to see. Terrence went back to the bank. Father rested in his room. Charlotte was writing to Tiny.

This should have been an oasis of peace, a time to reflect as she did the mindless chore of unpacking.

Didn't happen.

The darkness of the Alamo flooded her thoughts. Her assailant pressed his body against hers, too intimate, too intrusive. Her heart raced as it did that night. Helpless. Under the power of a forceful stranger and his knife. Her hand went to her chest where he had sliced her dress like it was warm bread. The nausea of violation swelled as his threat of rape echoed.

A pistol in her bag, and she'd stood helpless. He could have had his way with her right then. Her screams, if she could have made any, would have gone unheeded.

The punches hurt, but she'd punched and been punched in school. The threat of him forcing himself on her froze her. Then and now.

She knelt on the floor, arms wrapped around her middle, face buried in the quilt on her bed. The scream tore from her throat. She bit into the quilt and screamed louder.

No one to protect her. Only her attacker's sadistic teasing, using her body as a threat to make sure she did what he wanted. And no guarantee he wouldn't violate her anyway.

She turned and sat against the side of her bed, knees drawn to her chin. The late afternoon sky so crisp and clean. Why did she feel so dirty? She wasn't, but someone had broken through her wall of confidence, her sense of who she was.

He reduced her to the little girl who watched her mother leave, not understanding why, not able to stop it. To the little girl who couldn't trust anyone, couldn't risk love. The little girl who grew up to love the security of the law, not people.

Terrence locked the door to the bank, flipped the key in the air and caught it behind his back, before slipping it into his vest pocket. Despite Emily's somber return, he looked forward to having supper with her, her father, and Charlotte. Especially Emily.

Her vulnerability earlier touched him. He'd seen glimpses at other times, such as after the verdict came in. The woman under the attorney veneer attracted him. Her tone and behavior showed she recognized she needed protection, even if her pride wouldn't let her admit it.

He prayed God would bring someone into her life that she could let into her heart.

Maybe I already have.

Terrence stopped. Did someone speak to him? The surrounding people showed no sign they wanted to talk. He shook his head.

Maybe I already have.

He twirled. No one behind him. I'm hearing voices now? Tiny would get a laugh out of that.

I have someone in mind for Emily.

The words were inside him, feeling like they beat in his chest. *God? You have someone in mind for Emily? Who? I'll introduce them.*

You'll know when I'm ready.

Somehow, knowing God had someone for Emily freed him. His caring for Emily confused him. He valued her friendship, but the romantic attraction seemed to strengthen throughout the trial. He'd put it down to wanting to help and protect her. But then he thought he'd seen signs from her. Her hand on his arm for longer than usual. Their hands would brush or their shoulders touch when looking at papers, and the spark was beyond friendship. Both always took their time returning to the proper distance.

This ambivalence clouded his relationship with Priscilla. He knew Priscilla saw Emily as a rival, despite his constant assurances otherwise. Maybe Priscilla's mind would be eased once she knew Emily was stepping out with someone else.

He ran the eligible bachelors in town through his mind. None struck a resounding "he's the one." He ran through the not-so-eligible men, the widowers and the older men who'd never married. He could not picture Emily with any of them. A stranger, then.

Movement in front of Jaspers Mercantile brought him to an abrupt stop. Mrs. Montgomery? What was she doing here? Priscilla had told him she and her mother would spend the week in Saint Louis to see the newest fashions and shop for a piano her mother wanted.

He tipped his hat. "Good evening, Mrs. Montgomery." He lifted some packages she balanced in her arms. "Let me help you with these." He placed the items in her carriage and turned to face his future mother-in-law, if his future father-in-law agreed on Sunday.

"How was Saint Louis? You're back early."

Mrs. Montgomery's eyes darted over Terrence's shoulders, up and down the street, anywhere but his face. She tugged at the sleeves of her dress. "Saint Louis? I didn't go—Oh, you mean the trip Priscilla and I had planned. Our cousin in Dodge City came down ill and Priscilla went to take care of her."

"Priscilla didn't tell me. I hope your cousin's all right."

"My cousin—yes. Yes. She's getting better every day. Priscilla should be home in time for church on Sunday."

"Good. I'll look forward to seeing you all there."

"Yes. I'm sure you will." She stepped around him. "Have a pleasant evening, Terrence."

"You, too, Mrs. Montgomery."

As the carriage pulled away, Terrence scratched the back of his head. Odd Priscilla didn't say anything about the change in plans.

The carriage made a turn and Mrs. Montgomery looked back at him, a half-smile and brief wave before she disappeared.

Even odder Priscilla would visit a sick cousin. She hated being around any kind of illness, convinced she would catch the affliction.

Supper, half-eaten, cooled on Emily's plate. She could taste nothing and ate only to put fuel in her body, but soon lost interest. Charlotte's plate looked the same, while Father's and Terrence's were clean, and the two of them attacked Charlotte's wild berry cobbler.

Does she cook so much to keep her mind busy? So she won't think about what awaits Tiny?

Emily wished for such a distraction. Reading legal documents and books only reminded her of her shortcomings. Lying down resurrected the same nightmare of the attack that haunted every attempt at sleep. Sitting across from Charlotte reminded her Tiny would soon die. Outside, the setting sun reminded her life would go on no matter what she did. For one person, life would end far too soon. She couldn't face such a verdict happening to another client.

Supper finally over, she retreated to the kitchen to help Charlotte clean the dishes. Neither spoke. Charlotte's shoulders were tight, her movements brisk. Emily's drying couldn't keep up with her.

Halfway through, Charlotte stopped and pinched the bridge of her nose, soapy water running down her arms and into sleeves pushed up to her elbows. She grasped the edge of the sink, arms stiff, and her shoulders shook.

Emily stared at the damp towel in her hands, twisting it as she had her stockings. She laid it on the counter next to the sink and put her arm around Charlotte's shoulders, stiff and awkward. She remembered Mikey's hugs and Nadina's embrace. Why couldn't she do that now? Why couldn't she give what she had so welcomed from others? Because she hadn't failed them and sent their intended to die.

She squeezed Charlotte's shoulder and turned the young woman to face her. She wrapped both arms around her and pulled her into a close embrace. Holding at first and then, stroking her back. Charlotte yielded, slipped her arms around Emily, buried her face in the crook of her neck, and sobbed.

Emily pulled the pins holding Charlotte's hair in place, so it tumbled down her back. Emily combed it with her fingers, hoping it offered the comfort she'd received from Mikey. The sobbing eased, Charlotte's breathing became more regular, and she seemed content to stay snuggled against Emily.

After a few moments, she stood back, wiped her face with her apron. "Thank you. It's so hard."

"I know." Emily rubbed Charlotte's arms. "You look exhausted. Why don't you try to sleep? I'll finish this up."

Charlotte chuckled. "You? In the kitchen?"

Emily smiled. "I know my way around. I can't cook anything. But I know where things go."

Charlotte's face sobered, accentuating the bags under her tear-stained eyes. "I know. I appreciate you doing this. My mother always said things will look better after a good night's sleep." She kissed Emily's cheek and headed up the stairs to her room.

I don't think this will.

"I'm leaving."

Terrence and her father snapped their heads in her direction, their chess game forgotten.

"What do you mean? Leaving?" George asked.

She huddled her mug of coffee against her chin. "I mean after all this is over." She made a sweeping gesture with her arm. "I'm leaving Abilene. Going to live somewhere else."

"Why?" Terrence croaked the word before George could speak.

"Because there's nothing for me here. I've shown I don't belong in a courtroom. I've embarrassed you and Father and gotten a man hung."

George cursed, his hand slamming the table caused the chess pieces to jump. "Nonsense." He struggled to find words. "—Good attorney."

Terrence nodded, started to speak. She held up her hand.

"I might make a decent clerk, but I don't think I have what it takes to be in a courtroom."

"Of course, you do," Terrence said. "You were brilliant. I was proud of what you did, proud to be part of it. Your father was too."

"My client got convicted." She swallowed the hard lump in her throat. "And he will hang."

George pivoted from the table and wheeled toward, stopping just short of his legs hitting her.

"—Wasn't you. Judge rammed the trial."

Emily nodded. "I wasn't good enough to stop him."

Her calmness surprised her. Once the first words were out, her heart stopped pounding. Her brain cleared. *This is the right thing to do. Yep. Get away from here. Some big city. Teach school. Work in a store. Anything but the law.*

"Big mistake," her father said, voice rumbling.

"I agree," Terrence said. "You've put in too much blood—" he pointed at her eye. "Literally—to pull back now."

"What will you do?" Her father paused, working his mouth. "Too old for marriage."

His eyes widened as if he couldn't believe those words came from his mouth. He reached for her.

She folded her arms across her chest. "Yes, that's something else I gave up for this dream of ours."

The calmness vanished. She wanted to hurt him; she wanted to see shame and guilt course through him. Why? Because she didn't want this to be her failure alone. Her heart clenched. Because she wanted to know why he let her mother go, why he didn't fight for her. The words burned her tongue. She couldn't say them. They would lance his heart, shred it.

She slipped around the wheelchair and went to the window. The first stars popped into the sky. There would be no moon tonight. In the window, she saw the men's reflections. The two looked at each other, at her, and at each other again.

Terrence walked over to her. Her father remained by the sofa, watching.

"Where will you go?" Terrence asked.

"Denver." She didn't know until she said it. "I've always wanted to see the mountains." Mikey's image danced before her, Victoria and Nadina standing behind the child. "Or San Antonio."

"What will you do?"

She shrugged. "Teach school. Work in a store. Maybe write or work in a library."

"No law?"

"No." She shook her head so hard her hair swirled into her face. "Definitely no law. I want to work at something where I won't have to worry about somebody dying because of what I did." She touched her cheek under her swollen eye. "Or getting myself killed."

"Coward." Her father had wheeled up close behind her.

Arms folded, she drummed her fingers on her upper arm and bit her lip. She spoke to the window. "Maybe I am.

Is that another disappointment for you, Father?" She spun and leaned toward his face. "At least I fought for something I believed in as hard as I could."

Her father seemed to deflate and curl into himself. His hands slipped into his lap; his chin drooped to his chest. He raised his head, face gray and drawn, his spirit flickering in tired and hurt eyes. He nodded. "Do what you want—can't stop you. Think—a little more."

He wheeled back to the table. She stood rooted in her spot. What would she have done if he'd reached out to her? Extended his hand? Would she have taken it? Embraced him?

She returned to looking out the window. In the reflection, she watched her father pick up the black king and curl it through his fingers like he did when he was ready to concede defeat. Her heart split.

"What about your father?" Terrence said. "He's still recuperating."

She touched her forehead. "Once he gets on the crutches, he'll be fine. Doc will take care of him, and if Charlotte doesn't stay, Mrs. Marcand will be more than happy to step in and make sure he's fed and what not. He'll have everything he needs."

Terrence acted like he would say one thing but changed his mind. "You know he can't run the practice without you."

"Yes, he can. He can always find some widow or young girl to clerk for him."

"I think your father has a good point. Think about this some more before you make a final decision."

"The decision is final. I'm staying until after the hanging to make sure Charlotte's got someplace to go. By then, Father'll be scampering around like a colt on those crutches and looking to chew up a judge for dinner."

"Will you let me pray with you about it? To make sure you have God's direction."

His eyes were soft, concerned, reaching out to her.

"No."

She spun, and all but ran out the back door, keeping her pace to a rapid walk. Once outside, she ran. Her stomach lurched, the injury tender and painful. She couldn't get a full breath. She slowed to a walk over the familiar ground. After several minutes, she made out the shape of her favorite tree. She was at her father's fishing spot. She sat against the tree, bark digging into her back. She raised her eyes to the sky and cursed.

Chapter 62

The deserted platform basked in the early morning sun. The six gathered in a close group. Emily stood behind her father and brushed his hair across his spreading bald spot. She gave one strand a light tug. "Soon you'll look like one of those monks we read about. We can put you in a monastery where you can contemplate all day."

He slapped at her wrist, missed, and hit himself on the top of the head.

"What do you think, Doc? Think my father could be a monk, live a life of silence?"

"Knowing George, he'd find some way around it and then convince the leaders he was innocent."

"I'm sitting right here." George waved his arm.

"Sorry, George," Doc said. "Didn't recognize you with your mouth closed."

"Horse doctor."

Emily kissed the top of her father's head and kneaded his shoulders. Two days since she announced her decision, and her father acted like the conversation never took place. Yesterday, he had gone over some contracts and wills with her. She made notes, her mind wandering to ponder what Denver was like, what kind of work she would do. He'd decided she was too distracted by recent events. They'd put the work aside until after her visit to Tiny and George's return from Dodge City.

She'd not seen Terrence since turning her back on him and leaving the house. Today, he stood a short distance away, George's carpet bag and crutches in his hand, scanning the silent tracks.

Caroline and Charlotte stood close together, amused at the interchange, but smiles shadowed by sadness.

She and Charlotte would leave first on the train to the penitentiary and return tonight. George's train to Dodge City left later, and he would be gone one or two nights, depending on his meeting with Stoddard. Stoddard needed to be in court today, so George might not see him until tomorrow.

The first train pulled into the station, the ebony locomotive gleaming with fresh paint, passenger cars newly painted red with muted green trim. Emily embraced her father, received a peck on her cheek from Doc and a tight embrace from Caroline. The coolness of Terrence's handshake startled her. Eyes on Charlotte, he kissed her cheek. "Tell Tiny the entire team is still praying. I'll meet you here tonight." He touched the brim of his derby and stood by George.

As the train pulled away, Emily's last glimpse was of Terrence in conversation with Doc, his profile cold.

She rubbed her forehead with two fingers and settled into her seat. He knew she didn't believe in praying. He shouldn't have asked.

Charlotte pulled yarn and needles from the large bag she carried.

The melding of strands of yarn into a sock mesmerized Emily. Charlotte's lips moved in silent time with the needles, as if counting. Or praying? Maybe she could learn to knit, something to replace reading law books and journals, and have a useful product at the end.

The clicking of the needles joined with the rhythm of the train. A soft, pleasant lethargy seeped over Emily and her eyes closed. Multi-hues of green scattered across the trees and crops in the passing fields faded as sleep enveloped her.

She gasped, jumped. Someone touched her. She fumbled for the bag in her lap. No Colt this time. Her heart raced and panic seized her brain. Where was she? How did she get here?

Gradually, the person next to her came into focus. Charlotte. A soft, feminine hand on her arm, not a fist clinching a Bowie knife.

"Are you all right, Emily? You were moaning and squirming like you couldn't get away from something."

The nightmare. The attack relived. The stink of her fear as palpable as the original night. Would it ever go away? Her shaky hand pushed hair behind her ear.

"Bad dream."

"He keeps attacking you when you're asleep, doesn't he?"

Emily nodded.

"I understand."

"You were attacked too?"

Charlotte chewed her lip, eyes seeing something faraway in time. "Not like you. I've only told Tiny." She paused as if weighing Emily. She decided. "It was in Laramie. I got a job in a saloon. I thought it was just to dance with the men and get them to drink and gamble. One night, a cowboy wanted more. And took it."

She gazed out the window. "I told the owner. He told me it was part of the job and to get used to it. I ran away that night. Ended up in Abilene. Dutton hired me to run the roulette wheel. The customers liked me and gambled more. Some wanted, let me call it, extra attention. I told Dutton if he let that go on, he'd start losing money big time. He made them leave me alone. Some still tried until Tiny started courting me. Two broken jaws put an end to that."

She faced Emily. "That first night still wakes me from a sound sleep, sheets all knotted, sweating and biting my tongue to stop the screaming."

Emily touched her arm. "I'm sorry."

Charlotte lifted her shoulders. "I try to keep the horror in the past, but it won't stay." Her eyes filled with tears. "The dream doesn't come as often now, but it still comes." A tear slipped down her cheek. "I used to worry about how to prepare Tiny for it after we were married."

The columns of numbers danced before Terrence's eyes. He squinted. No better. He tossed his pencil on his desk, stood, arched his back. Seated again, he beat a tattoo with his pencil.

Emily at the station. Her eye better, the swelling receding, the color more yellowish. Vulnerable yet distant, seeming to avoid looking at him. He couldn't bring himself to look at her either.

Her "No" to his offer to pray stung like a hornet, and the stinger festered. He knew she was angry at God, but she'd always tolerated his beliefs before. Why so vehement this time? Why so intentional to reject and inflict hurt? To treat his Christianity like a pariah? She hadn't used those words. She didn't need to. Her rejection pierced like a shot from a Peacemaker, her face cold and hard as granite, eyes like ice. The quick turn and departure out the back door. He'd made to follow her but, by the time he got to the door, she was halfway to the creek and drawing farther away.

As they waited for the train that morning, Emily focused everywhere but on him. The set of her jaw, the steel in her eyes, showed him the barrier, and she blamed him for it.

The hurt pulled his heart like a circus strongman stretching a horseshoe.

Was he losing two friends? Could he still help Emily meet the man God intended for her?

He closed his eyes and prayed for her in spite of her resistance.

Chapter 63

The prison loomed over them. Cold gray walls. Men with rifles and shotguns patrolled along the top. Charlotte approached the gate with the calm assurance of a repeat visitor. Emily's insides churned. Another part of the world she never expected to see. Men, violent men, cooped up in cages, forced to work mind-numbing, back-breaking tasks. Men who deserved to be here, who deserved their punishment. She shuddered at the thought of so much violence bottled in one place.

Except for Tiny. Were there other innocents in here too? Not her problem anymore.

Inside, the dim light, moist air, and the stench of unclean bodies and human waste mingled with putrid fear, anger, and hate, clear in both guards and inmates. Waves of nausea swept over her like summer thunderheads building in the west. She gritted her teeth and resolved to see this through without losing her breakfast, grateful she'd decided not to eat on the train.

Two guards escorted them to the visiting area, brushing against her and Charlotte with every step. One put his hand at the base of her spine.

"Do you like having that hand?" She spoke out of the side of her mouth, pouring as much venom into her words as she could.

"Hey, Jerome. We got us a feisty one here. Maybe we need to make sure she's not trying to smuggle in contraband." He ran his hand up her back. Emily shrugged it off and side-stepped away.

Jerome kept walking and spoke over his shoulder. "Stow it, Maxwell. You want to go up in front of the warden again?"

"It'll be her word against mine."

Jerome touched Charlotte's arm to stop her. He faced Maxwell, holding his club in two hands. "And mine." He tapped Maxwell's chest. "I'll take her side. And, after the punishment, you'll be out with the field hands for the summer, and on the north wall for the winter."

Maxwell cussed.

Jerome shrugged. "In fact, walk in front of me, so's I can make sure you hold to the straight and narrow."

The corridor opened to a small dirt courtyard. Four high walls restricted the sun to a small patch of light when directly overhead.

Tables were scattered around. Many empty. Others occupied by small groups centered on an inmate in the gray and black prison uniform.

Jerome directed them to an empty table near the east wall. The morning's heat radiated from the hard stone. Jerome ordered Maxwell to fetch Tiny.

"Why don't you go get 'im? I'll keep a watch on the ladies to make sure they don't try nothin'."

Jerome rapped his club in the palm of his hand and pointed to a door in the west wall.

Maxwell cussed and shuffled toward the door.

Charlotte opened her bag and lay out the meal she'd brought. She glanced around the courtyard and slipped a wrapped package to Jerome, who slid it inside his shirt.

Emily arched her brow. Charlotte whispered, "Jerome likes my chicken sandwiches. Says it gives him the strength to hold off Maxwell and the patience to not kill him."

Emily looked at Jerome, who gave a brief nod and then studied the sky. Emily shook her head and touched her forehead. *Now I'm abetting the bribing of a prison guard. Glad I'm moving on.*

The door in the opposite wall opened with a loud clang as it swung wide and slammed into the wall. A tall, thin, emaciated man shuffled out, manacles on his wrists and feet joined at another around his waist. The chains allowed less than half a normal stride.

The man stumbled when Maxwell gave him a hard shove. Emily's hand went to her mouth when she realized the stranger stutter-stepping toward them was Tiny Waters. Unkempt beard, shaggy hair elongated his already thin face.

Charlotte ran to him, arms extended. She stopped short and took Tiny's hands in hers, Maxwell's club between them. The two lovers stood in the small patch of sunshine, not speaking, just smiling. They walked to the table. Emily stood.

Tiny's faced beamed when he recognized her. "Miss Emily. It's so good to see you. Nearly as good as seein' Charlotte." He frowned. "What happened to your face?"

Her heart split and panic flooded her. She wanted to run, sink into the ground, fly over the wall. Anything not to break his heart and explode his hopes one more time. They were quiet as Charlotte spread out the sandwiches and cake she'd brought. Maxwell's hand reached for a sandwich. A sharp rap on the table from Jerome's club startled them all.

The guard wagged his club at Maxwell like it was a giant, dark finger. "Now, Maxwell, you know it's against regulations to accept gifts from visitors. Cookie'll take care of us."

Emily's hand flew to her mouth to stifle a laugh. Charlotte lowered her head and hugged herself.

Tiny blessed the food and devoured a thick sandwich in two bites, his eyes never leaving Charlotte. After his third sandwich, he turned to Emily. "So, what brings you up here? Did the governor answer your request for a reprieve?"

Emily shook her head. "They denied our request." The letter denying the request came while she was in San Antonio.

Tiny shrugged. "Never put much stock in it anyways."

His gaze intensified, shoulders hunched as he leaned forward, unspoken questions on his face and in his hands that clasped and unclasped in their chains. Charlotte covered his hands with hers.

Maxwell took a step forward, club raised. "Hey—"

"Let it go, Maxwell." Jerome's voice was soft yet filled with authority. "In fact, take another step back. I don't think we need to hear what they're about to say."

Maxwell protested until Jerome glared at him from under his brows. He stepped back. Jerome did the same.

Emily's mouth dried up like bread left out too long. She couldn't get her tongue to form words. She swallowed and licked her lips, looking for moisture. She gulped her water. It seemed to evaporate before it touched her lips.

Charlotte rubbed Tiny's hands while he stared. His eyes narrowed as he seemed to realize why Emily couldn't speak.

"Go ahead, ma'am. Long as Charlotte's here, I can take it."

Emily inhaled and began. "We found the Whitney brothers." She hesitated. "They're dead. Killed in San Antonio."

Tiny's chin dropped to his chest, and his shoulders shuddered.

"They had a lot of money, but it was stolen by whoever killed them. We can't prove where they got it."

Charlotte's thumbs moved faster over his hands. A tear coursed down her cheek.

"Tiny, I'm sorry," Emily said. "The Whitneys can't talk. We can't prove they got their money by killing Phillips. And there are no other clues of who killed them."

"So, we're done? We're finished?" His voice warbled and choked.

Emily looked over his shoulder and nodded.

He pulled his hands from Charlotte and slid them under the table. "You best move on, darlin'. Find someone who can give you that ranch, who can take care of you. Maybe one of the Montgomery boys. Walter's the best of the bunch. I'll write him a letter."

Charlotte half rose from the bench, hand poised to strike. "Don't you dare. I'm not done yet. Neither is Emily or Mr. Peyton. Or Terrence. They're still fighting for you." She sank back to her seat.

"What use is it? Any hope I had is dead and buried in Texas."

"God can still give us a miracle." Charlotte's voice was fragile as a butterfly's wing.

"That's all we have, don't we?"

"Don't you dare stop praying, David Waters. God is our only hope. He has been all along. Don't stop trusting him."

Emily bristled at such naivety. How can grown people think like that? Think God has a magic wand to make all their troubles go away? Especially when he makes them happen, anyway.

The sooner she was out of this, the better.

Chapter 64

Emily and Doc waited as the train carrying her father pulled to a halt.

"Think we'll need this?" she motioned to the wheelchair in front of her.

"Hope not. He should be used to the crutches. If he's really tired, we'll use it."

The passengers filed off in twos or threes, greeting relatives or friends, or totting their luggage and heading for a hotel or saloon. After several minutes, the train stood silent other than the puffing of its engine. A conductor strolled the platform, checking his watch.

Emily's heart tightened. Where was he? Did he miss the train?

On board, a hulking shadow lumbered toward the door of one of the passenger cars. Her father appeared, standing at the top of the steps. He looked down as if he'd never seen steps before.

Emily and Doc hurried to him.

"Need some help?" Doc extended his hand.

George shook his head. Emily smiled at the grim determination in his face. One more challenge he would overcome. Jaw clamped, he maneuvered the crutches, one step at a time. Once he tottered as a crutch nearly skidded off the edge of a step. Fingers to her mouth, she watched him recover, reset the crutch, and make the rest of the way to the platform.

He glared at Doc. "Did you work in the Spanish Inquisition? You come up with more ways to torture people than anyone I ever met. Where did you learn medicine, anyway? Marquis de Sade?"

Doc grinned at Emily. "He's back. Ornery as ever."

"Get me home—put my feet up. Charlotte make lemon cake?"

He looked at Emily. "Hello, daughter."

"Father." She kissed his cheek. She stepped back, keeping still under his scrutiny. His eyes searched hers, unspoken questions probing for unspoken answers.

"Eye looks better." He cocked his head. "Change your mind?"

She shook her head.

"Figured. Come on. Get me home."

George hoisted himself onto the bed of the carriage, crutches beside him.

"Better hang onto those crutches," Doc said. "If you fall off, you'll be able to walk home."

"I hope you drive a buggy better than you practice medicine."

Emily half turned to look at her father. He gripped the edge of the seat, shoulders hunched, head down, waving occasionally to greet someone. Would he ever forgive her? She chewed on a knuckle. *I know I hurt you. But it would hurt even more if I stayed.*

At the house, George settled into the sofa with a long sigh and lifted his feet onto the foot stool Emily arranged to his specification. He wolfed down two pieces of cake and gulped three cups of coffee.

Holding his mug for a refill, he wiped his mouth with his sleeve.

"Father. Use a napkin."

"Don't fret, Daughter. You'll only have to put up with me for a little while longer." He paused. "Where's Terrence?"

Emily looked at the floor. "He hasn't been around in a couple of days. I guess the bank's keeping him busy."

George frowned, pinched his lip. "Get him. Please. Needs to hear this."

Emily and Charlotte exchanged glances, neither moving. Charlotte nodded. "I'll go."

She shrugged off her apron, wrapped a shawl around her shoulders, and tied a bonnet under her chin.

Emily cleared the dishes to avoid her father's scrutiny, taking her time in the kitchen. Why would he expect her to change her mind? He should know she could be as stubborn as him. He taught her. The visit to Tiny only confirmed it. Did Father think he could stare her into changing her mind? That hadn't worked since she was twelve, although he still tried it. Why couldn't he accept it?

George leaned back against the sofa, eyes half-closed. Did he really expect Emily to change her mind? All the way to Dodge and back, he wished she would. He daydreamed of getting off the train and stepping into her warm embrace to hear her say, "I'm staying."

How to heal her heart from the hurt? How to restore her confidence, her belief in herself?

The prospect of life without her spun into a void, dark and empty. Eleven years ago, at fifteen, she'd begun working in his office after school. By sixteen, she was studying law. At twenty, she declared she would pass the bar and intensified her studies. At twenty-three, she passed. In the last four years, they'd formed a bond—become a team. Now they were partners. The trial proved she could do it all. He wouldn't be able to run the practice without her even if he were completely healed, never mind in his current condition.

How could he help her understand that, even though Tiny was convicted, she had been brilliant in the courtroom? Better than he ever was.

He knew she saw what he saw when he lost his first murder trial. A noose. Only she put her career in that noose. How could he show her the loss was not a professional death sentence?

He shook himself out of his reverie. Doc paced the room, cigar chomped between his teeth and glowing. He'd be pacing too if he could. No way would he clomp around the room on these sticks. He pulled his notebook from his coat and reviewed his conversations with Wyatt Stoddard.

A scuffle of footsteps on the porch preceded the opening of the door and the entrance of Terrence and Charlotte. Charlotte went to fetch Emily while Terrence arranged chairs in a semi-circle in front of the sofa.

George swallowed the hurt when Emily sat in one of the dining room chairs rather than next to him. His eyes lingered on her, back straight, knees together, hands folded in her lap. Blond hair cascaded to her shoulders, light blue eyes alert. She looked so much like her mother. And now she was leaving too.

He cleared his throat and ran his finger down the first page of notes.

"Stoddard didn't steer us wrong. Stevens—good bounty hunter. Wyatt didn't know about his shady side. He investigated while I was there."

He flipped a page. So far, so good, speaking all right. Throat dry. He sipped coffee.

"If Stoddard knew about Stevens, he wouldn't recommend him." Too much. Didn't come out right. Wait. Try again. "Stoddard found out more. Cook right. If Stoddard had known, wouldn't recommend." Better.

"Stevens gambles. Enormous debt. In trouble. Needs money fast."

"So, he had motive to kill the Whitneys?" Emily's voice was pensive.

"Yes."

"Any idea where he is?" Terrence asked.

George shook his head, consulted his notes. "Likes Denver, Dallas, Saint Louis, New Orleans, Chicago."

Doc flicked ash from his cigar. "Big places. Easy for a man to get lost. And stay lost."

"Emily, do you think Stevens attacked you?" Terrence leaned forward, elbows on knees.

Emily frowned, concentrating. "Maybe. Whoever attacked me was wider than Stevens, than the Stevens who came here."

"The ability to disguise himself makes it all the harder to say it was him," Doc said.

Terrence stood, shoved his hands in his pockets and rocked on his heels. "George, Emily. Did you ever send him the rest of the money he wanted as his fee?"

George darted a look at Emily, who shook her head. "No," he said. "Forgot."

"Hmm." Terrence rubbed his chin. "Do you think we could smoke him out if you asked him to come here to collect the money?"

"No." Emily's was emphatic, her tone final, flavored by a tinge of sarcasm.

"Why not?" Terrence asked.

Emily inhaled, looked at her father, and counted off points on her fingers. "If he killed the Whitneys, he knows we probably suspect him. He may be a murderer, but he's not stupid. He'll only tell us to send him a bank draft or a wire. You know how those work."

"Could we send it and alert the local sheriff to watch for him?"

"Assuming the local sheriff isn't partners with him," Doc said. "Sorry, Terrence, but I think that's a dead end, especially this long after he asked for it. After all, he hasn't asked for it again."

"He probably doesn't need it now," Emily said.

"And doesn't—want attention." George said.

Charlotte sniffled. "It just seems to get more and more impossible to save Tiny."

"If we're even right in our thinking," Emily said.

Charlotte bowed her head. Terrence placed a hand on her shoulder. "Charlotte, don't give up hope. God can still do a miracle."

Emily walked into the kitchen.

George wished he could join her. Why get Charlotte's hopes up?

The back door closed. Where is she off to now?

A few minutes later, a blur flashed by the window accompanied by the sounds of a horse trotting away. *Good. Maybe the ride will help her calm down.*

Why was she so rude to Terrence? She acted like they'd had a lovers' spat, and they're not even courting. He pinched the bridge of his nose, fatigue rising.

"George." Doc's sharp tone snapped him to the present.

"What?"

"You're gray again. I knew I let you do too much. How am I going to explain it to Caroline if you get sick again?

I don't want to face Emily's wrath either. Go to bed until supper time and stay in bed all day tomorrow too."

George used his crutches and Terrence's arm to lever himself off the sofa.

Maybe if I'm sick, Emily will stay.

Chapter 65

The plains rolled silently by as Emily guided Lincoln out of town. Her gelding seemed to read her mind as he trotted to a line of trees that bordered a creek. He slowed to a walk and followed a meandering trail to a weeping willow.

The drooping branches formed a cathedral aglow with light green as they arched over a plot of ground and the creek. The sweet mixture of grass, summer sun, and clear water filled the air. Emily slid to the ground and looped her reins around the saddle horn. The gelding nibbled on the soft blades as he meandered toward the creek.

Emily ran her fingers through her hair, clearing the wind induce tangles so it fell loose to her shoulders. She rested against the trunk, head back, eyes closed, relishing the gentle breeze wafting across her cheeks. Memories followed the breeze, gentle, wafting …

Caroline had first showed her this spot when Emily was nine—a sad little girl who couldn't understand why her mother left, and her father sat for hours staring into a lantern or fire, a glass of whiskey at hand.

Caroline's tender love opened the world of books to her, stories of beautiful princesses and noble knights, *Gulliver's Travels*, *Robinson Caruso*, *Uncle Tom's Cabin*, *Moby Dick*.

The stories charged her imagination and stimulated her mind to read and keep reading. On several visits, they made up stories for each other about the clouds dancing beyond the branches, about the fish in the creek being under a magician's spell, and about the cardinals and the crows being bitter enemies, battling for control of the willow kingdom. The cardinals always won because their songs were prettier.

They'd have picnics, and Caroline would teach her to write out her stories. Dresses above their knees, they'd dangle their feet in the cold creek and splash each other, giggling and tickling until falling on their backs. Emily caught a frog once and laughed at Caroline's squeals when she shook it at her.

With her dolls, she and Caroline played family, one where the mother never left, and the father always smiled.

So long since her last visit, a distant memory. Why she came here now, she couldn't answer. Except she wanted peace, and this spot called from her hidden places.

She plucked a blade of grass and rubbed it between her fingers and waited.

But the peace wouldn't come.

Instead, the image of a noose around Tiny's neck loomed, Charlotte standing close by. The image of her father's sad face at the news of her leaving weighed on her. Guilt. Leaving him just like mother did. She bowed her head to her knees. But she couldn't stay. She couldn't practice law again, not when she couldn't keep an innocent man from prison.

The image of Terrence popped into her mind. Such a good friend. Why did she have to hurt him? Drive him away? Because of his faith. How could he honor a God that let mothers leave, who caused accidents that nearly took her rock away, who let the innocent hang?

She leaned back, closed her eyes, willing her mind to quiet and peace to come.

Something deeper dug into her, reaching a spot she'd closed off years ago. The spot where love should be. She closed it, except for her father and Doc and Caroline, and kept it shuttered so hurt would not blast her heart to oblivion. Again.

Besides, she had needed to focus on her studies, on fulfilling her dream. Her dream didn't allow for a man or romance. Not if she would be the best attorney in Kansas.

Now her heart told her something she never expected to hear: She cared for Terrence. More than she thought. She wanted more than a friendship with him. She wanted his arms around her, to taste his lips.

He was promised to someone else. Priscilla better never hurt him, or she'd get another punch in her nose.

A dark cloud of doubt covered the horizon of her heart. If Terrence somehow became hers, how did she know she wouldn't run off with another man who promised more than the staid existence of a small-town banker?

That's what her mother did, drawn by a golden-haired man in a sparkling uniform, promising the delights of Washington, DC, never to be heard from again.

Emily couldn't remember what her mother looked like. An image of blonde hair and blue eyes blurred by time and hurt.

Could she leave such an image in Terrence's heart?

Didn't Emily plan to doing the same thing now? To her father. She wasn't doing it for love of another man though.

Could she and Terrence really love each other when they had such different attitudes about God? There was no common ground, no negotiating a compromise. Her heart cringed and her stomach lurched every time he mentioned

God. She was immune now to him and Charlotte praying over the food. But speaking of miracles with the certainty of speaking of the sunrise was foolishness. If God did perform miracles, it was only to take them back at the first opportunity. Offering prayers to someone who didn't listen was a waste of time.

Emily rested her head on her knees.

Could love survive the pressure of such opposites constantly pulling and tearing at each other? Did she dare to find out?

Chapter 66

Terrence walked to the bank, his mind on anything but banking.

"Whoa. Watch out yer durn fool."

The shout startled Terrence into finding himself standing in the middle of a street, a horse two feet away from him, its locked forelegs spewing a cloud of dust. The red-faced driver of the wagon glared at Terrence. "Tryin' to get yerself kilt?"

The driver's eyes widened. "Terrence, is that you? Better get your head out of your sleeve 'fore you run into a horse who ain't as quick to stop as Gilfy here."

Heat surged into Terrence's cheeks. "Sorry, Mr. Clayton. Wasn't paying attention."

Clayton grinned. "'S all right. Wouldn't want to hurt the town's best player before Sunday's game."

Terrence smiled and waved before walking on.

At his desk, his pencil guided his eyes down a column of figures, but where his mind should have seen numbers, he saw Emily. Why did she bother him so? Why did what she thought of him matter so much? And when did that happen?

He replayed the scene at her home. First, his surprise when Charlotte came for him instead of Emily. At the house, she wouldn't look him in the eye. Her jaw went tight, and her eyes narrowed whenever he spoke. When she replied, subtle sarcasm oozed beneath her words. The chill in the room still shivered his heart. And then she walked out without a word to anyone. Right after he'd told Charlotte a miracle could happen. His attempt to give the girl hope, to keep her praying and believing, drove Emily further away.

He wanted her closer. He wanted their friendship back. He did. But suddenly, he was aware his heart wanted something more, more than friendship. But that could never be.

He loved Priscilla. He wanted to marry Priscilla.

Romance with Emily stood outside the realm of possibility. No way would he ever be unequally yoked, as the Bible said.

He would marry Priscilla.

But he missed his friend.

Chapter 67

Thunk. Swing. Thunk. Swing. The rhythmic pattern of the crutches carried George through the parlor to the front porch. Charlotte followed with a cup of coffee for him. Settled in his rocker, coffee within easy reach on a nearby table, he sighed.

"Why don't you join me?" He indicated another rocker.

"I need to make sure the bread doesn't burn," she said, glancing into the house.

"All right. Check your bread. Then fetch yourself a cup of coffee and join me out here for a few minutes. Please."

She slipped into the house.

Please? Did I say please? Why do I not want to be alone?

The sun looked to be half an hour from setting. Where was Emily? Would she be home before dark? He remembered the pig-tailed little girl scampering up the porch steps, her mother threatening a switch for being late for supper. Again. The excuse was usually she, Matthew Quick, and Sally and Nathan Jaspers were off on some adventure, and she didn't realize it was getting dark. *She's a grown woman now, and she still can't get home before dark.*

Charlotte returned. She placed her cup next to his and sat on the edge of the other rocker, back straight, hands clasped at her knees.

"Thank you for sitting a spell with me."

"You're welcome, Mr. P." She lowered her eyelids. "Is there somethin' y'all need to talk about?"

"No." He glanced at the darkening sky. "Didn't want to be alone right now."

Her shoulders sagged, and she sniffled. "I know what that's like." She dabbed at her eyes with a handkerchief.

"I expect you do."

"Must have been hard for you too. What with your wi—" She stood quickly, hands twisting the cloth. "I best check the chicken." She dashed into the house in a swirl of skirts.

The clop of hoofbeats drew George's attention. Emily walked her horse to the fence surrounding the front lawn, hands resting easily on the saddle horn.

He glanced at the blue-black sky and the white dots of the first stars. "Made it home just before full dark. Thought I would have to take a switch to you for being late for supper."

Her soft laugh, though short, tingled in his ear. "In your condition? You'd never catch me."

He waved a crutch at her. "You'd be surprised at how fast I can move on these sticks."

"Let me put Lincoln up, and I'll be right in."

George hobbled inside. Charlotte hummed one of her blasted church hymns as she set the dining room table. Doc said let her do it, it helped comfort her. At least she didn't sing out loud. Except in her bath. No way George would interrupt that.

Several minutes later, Emily came in and helped bring the food to the table. Emily poured coffee while Charlotte bowed her head and prayed a barely audible blessing.

Taut stillness filled the room. The clink of utensils and the clunk of coffee cups on the table sounded brittle and tight. Both women kept their eyes on their food. For once in his life—maybe twice—George could think of nothing to say.

"How was your ride?" he asked at last, desperate to break the ominous hush before it shattered like ice.

Emily shrugged. "Good. Nice to be out in the air. Lincoln needed a good run."

Horse wasn't all that lathered. "Where d'you go?"

"No place. Just out on the prairie for a few miles."

He halted his forkful of chicken in mid-air. Emily's eyes were neutral, distant. She scooped a mouthful of mashed potatoes and returned her attention to her food.

After dinner, George set up the chessboard.

"Doc coming over?" Emily asked.

George snorted. "Doc? Need more challenge. Terrence coming. After dinner with Priscilla."

A knock at the door. Emily froze, eyes wide.

"I'll get it," Charlotte said.

Charlotte and Terrence greeted each other warmly, but Emily acted as if she hardly knew him.

"Miss Emily," Terrence said.

"Terrence." She removed the last plate from the table and turned toward the kitchen. "Y'all enjoy your game. Let Charlotte know when you're ready for coffee and pie."

A flash of hurt crossed Terrence's eyes before he turned and took his seat opposite George.

The first game ended in a draw. As Terrence reset the pieces, George said, "Neither one—sharp. Maybe first—game cleared our heads."

The second game resembled their usual matches. Moves and countermoves. Long pauses as each tried to plan several moves ahead. Even then, George blundered and left his queen exposed to a pawn. Terrence's eyes widened slightly as he took the piece. George conceded.

"That's not like you, George."

"I know. Dumb mistake."

Terrence gestured with his king.

George shook his head. "Enough for one night."

As if waiting for her cue, Charlotte poked her head in from the kitchen. "Ready for coffee and pie?"

She declined George's offer to join them and retreated to her room.

"What do you think of Emily's leaving?" George asked.

Terrence pondered the forkful of pie he held. After lowering his fork to his plate, he crossed his arms on the table. "Big mistake. She's too good to quit. I never thought she'd be one to run away."

"Me neither." George paused. "Feels responsible for Tiny hanging."

"Did you take each case so personally?"

"When I was her age. Felt like running ... too."

A whippoorwill sang.

After Terrence left, George turned down the lamp and sat in the semi-dark, rolling a bishop between his fingers.

Emily strolled in, hair mussed, eyes puffy. She freshened his coffee and stacked the dishes. "You boys had an early night."

"Couldn't concentrate."

She headed toward the kitchen.

"Sit with me a spell," George said. *I'm pleading again. I can't face being alone tonight. Why?*

Emily hesitated, head down. "All right." Her voice was husky and soft.

A few minutes later, she sat across from him, her hair pulled back and tied with a ribbon. He turned the lamp up and studied her. Such a beautiful young woman. A sharp pang. So like her mother.

"Your eye looks a lot better."

She touched the diminished puffiness. "Don't even notice it much anymore. Can see better too."

The ensuing silence grew awkward.

"I don't want you to leave."

She traced a small circle on the table. "I have to. I have to get away. Make a new start."

"You're too good an attorney."

She shook her head and smirked. "Tell that to Tiny."

George closed his eyes and inhaled, forcing the anger, the urge to lash out, down.

"He knows you did your best." He sipped coffee while waiting for words to form. "No one could have done better."

She shrugged, head down, defeat shadowing her. He'd seen that look on too many clients.

He extended his hand toward her. She didn't move.

"I need you," he whispered, afraid to voice it too loud, afraid it would shatter the relationship, drive her further away.

She sat up straight, dropped her hands to her lap. Her light blue eyes flashed. "Charlotte's smart. She learns quick. She can take care of things in the office. And don't forget, Widow Marcand is always willing to do anything for you. And Caroline will take care of any other pampering you need. You'll do fine without me."

George looked at his daughter, his colleague, his best friend, and saw her flying away. An eagle soaring high and out of sight. His heart cracked.

Chapter 68

Two nights later, Terrence sat in Joseph Warner's office inhaling the sweet aroma of his employer's pipe while a cloud of blue smoke wreathed the latter's head. Warner leaned back into his leather chair, laid his pipe in a glass dish to the side of his blotter. He sipped from a glass of whiskey and patted his lips with a handkerchief.

His face came into clearer focus as the cloud drifted toward the ceiling. Hands folded across his stomach, he peered at Terrence. "Excellent report. Clear. Concise. Just what the board is looking for."

"Thank you, sir."

Warner tapped the papers spread across his desk. "I am especially impressed with your idea to help some farmers and ranchers who are having trouble meeting their payments. I think the board will be open to rewriting some of the loans."

Terrence nodded his thanks.

"Yes, I think they'll be most favorable." Warner rubbed the side of his nose with one finger.

He placed both hands on his desk and stood. "Well, I think I've kept you late enough."

Terrence rose, not sure he was officially dismissed. The previous evening, Warner had said and done the same thing and then talked for thirty minutes about how the politicians in Washington were ruining everything.

Tonight, however, he strode from behind his desk and plucked his black homburg from the coat tree near his door. "I hope I haven't made you late for an engagement with Miss Montgomery."

"No, sir. She's out of town. I'll have a quiet night in my room, reading a novel by Mark Twain."

Warner clapped him on the shoulder. "Splendid. I need to have more evenings like that myself. Unfortunately, I have a town council meeting."

The two separated outside the bank and Terrence headed for his boarding house and the cold supper Mrs. Crenshaw promised to save for him.

The soft breeze tickled the hair on his neck as he approached the train depot. A familiar giggle echoed from the recessed door of the telegraph office. He stopped, confused and unsure. He shook his head. It couldn't be. She was supposed to be out of town for at least two more days. But who else sounded like that?

He cocked his head as if it would help him hear better. Voices, soft murmurs, words indistinguishable. One pitched low, the other high.

Part of him wanted to block his ears, turn, and go the other way. He couldn't be hearing what he was hearing and shouldn't be listening to. It must be some other woman and man sparking. It was none of his business.

The other part had to know, had to be sure, it wasn't her. His brain needed to know. His heart told him he didn't—to go the other way, to his cold supper, his room, and his new book. His brain said he wouldn't enjoy one minute of his evening unless he knew for sure. His heart said he might not enjoy one moment of the rest of his life if he did.

He hesitated.

Another giggle slid into a soft, throaty sound he couldn't quite place.

Silence.

Then, "Oh, Lionel," spoken quietly, yet full of passion.

Silence, except for the rustle of clothes.

He stepped to the doorway.

Lionel Hutchins stood in the tiny alcove, his arms around a woman, his mouth pressed to the lips of ...

"Priscilla?"

The couple broke apart, Lionel adjusting his cravat, Priscilla smoothing her dress.

"Terrence," she said. She coughed. "What are you doing here? I didn't expect to see you out this late at night."

I'm sure you didn't.

"I thought you wouldn't be back for another couple of days."

She darted a glance at Lionel, who stood with a small smile that Terrence wanted to punch down his throat.

"Sudden change of plans. Daddy sent me a telegram that Mother was sick and needed my help. Lionel was on the train. We're just on our way to rent a buggy so he can take me home."

Fists clenched, Terrence inhaled. "I'd've thought you'd hurry to get to your mother as quickly as possible and not ..."

Her eyes flared. "Not what? Lionel is just comforting me. Mother's never sick and I'm very distraught. I resent what you're implying."

Terrence folded his arms across his chest, spread his feet. "I'm not implying anything. I'm just observing."

Lionel stepped forward. "Maybe you should take your observing somewhere else." His drawl was molasses.

"This is a conversation between Priscilla and me."

She moved between them, hand on Lionel's chest. "Stop this. You're both acting like schoolboys. I need to get home. Terrence, I will see you at the Randolph House the day after tomorrow. Our usual time." She looped her arm through Lionel's. "Lionel, I need you to take me home. Now."

Terrence watched them go, arms looped, shoulders touching, Priscilla's sway brushing her hip against Lionel's. He remembered that walk, the slight touch that promised so much but only teased. Numbness crept over him like stepping into a January blizzard.

What a fool I've been. Did she ever really love me?

He wanted to hit someone, Lionel's face his first choice. He wanted his bat to crush a baseball. He wanted the satisfaction of his bullet hitting the bull's-eye, the rifle recoil pushing against his shoulder. He wanted a drink. No, I don't. A lot of drinks.

Instead, he stood still and saw his future pass into the shadows of the street.

And wondered where he'd be the evening after tomorrow.

Chapter 69

Terrence sat on the edge of his bed as sunlight gradually filled his window. His Bible lay open beside him, the familiar words and phrases devoid of comfort. He squinted in the brightness and unbuttoned his vest. *Can't wear the same clothes two days in a row, can I?*

He washed his face, enjoying the roughness of the soap against his hands as he worked up a lather. The stubble on his face scratched his fingers and palms. Maybe I should grow a beard. Make a new start. Become a different person. Mr. Warner and the board didn't like beards on their employees. Found them suspicious. Maybe a new job too.

He brushed shaving cream on his face, the faint aroma of roses tickling his nostrils. He stropped his razor and examined the edge of the blade. Could slice a throat like tender ham.

The figure in the mirror over his dresser frowned.

What? You don't think I could do it?

The man in the mirror arched an eyebrow.

You're right. Nice to think about, though.

Shave finished, he dried his face and checked for any stray whiskers. Dark circles around the eyes of the Terrence in the mirror reminded him of the downfalls of neglecting sleep.

Terrence almost dropped his razor as he flicked it closed. Stay awake. Need not to be slicing a finger off.

He dressed with extra care, each movement taking longer to communicate from his brain to his fingers. He shrugged into his suit coat, took one last glance in the mirror, and pushed his forelock to one side.

In the dining room, two other boarders lingered over their coffee, newspapers before them. Two others ate heaping platters of Mrs. Crenshaw's flapjacks, biscuits, ham, and eggs. A murmur of chatter ran underneath the clinking of utensils and rattle of newspaper.

"Mr. McCarthy, you didn't touch that supper I left for you," Mrs. Crenshaw said.

"Wasn't hungry." Terrence poured himself some coffee, stopping in mid-action as a shocked silence fell over the room. Replacing the pot, he stood, hands crossed in front of him. "Please forgive me." He cleared his throat. "No, ma'am, I did not. I wasn't hungry when I arrived home last evening. I apologize for any inconvenience my actions caused you."

She peered at him, eyes roaming his face. "Are you feeling sickly, Mr. McCarthy? You look like my dear, departed Walter after a five-day hunt with no success."

"Just tired, ma'am,"

She waggled a serving spoon at him. "You see you take better care of yourself, Mr. McCarthy. I don't want people thinking Crenshaw's Lodging is bad for their health. Besides, you want to be in your best health when you marry Miss Montgomery."

He felt as if a knife shafted through his heart, and he grabbed the back of his chair. Mrs. Crenshaw raised her chin to target her gaze down her nose. She opened her mouth but apparently decided not to say anything.

He slumped into the chair and gulped his coffee. He served himself a couple of flapjacks and a slice of ham. His stomach threatened to send the first bite back up. Terrence lowered his fork and knife and grabbed his mug as if it were all that kept him from falling down a mineshaft.

A sigh from across the table brought his head up. Mrs. Crenshaw studied him, the light-hearted teasing gone from her eyes, replaced by pinched brows and unasked questions.

He shrugged and smiled a smile that didn't even fool him.

In the bank, he held his forehead in his palm, toting up the figures before him for the third time and getting a third result. Coffee. He dropped his pencil on the desk and reached for his cup as Charlotte entered the bank. Skin pale under her ebony hair, eyes red, she made her way to one of the tellers.

"Good morning, Charlotte."

She jumped at the sound of his voice. He touched her arm. "I apologize. I didn't mean to startle you."

Her tiny smile barely curved her lips. "My mind was off in its own world. Just doing some banking for Mr. Peyton."

Terrence frowned. "Emily couldn't do it? Is she all right?"

"She seems to be." Charlotte bit her lower lip. "Very quiet. Said she wanted to catch up on some paperwork."

"Going to see Tiny?" He nodded at the basket on her arm.

Her eyes lit for a second, then faded. "Yes. Going from here to catch the train. The Everetts will have the Peytons to supper tonight, so I can take the last train home."

"Emily's not going with you?"

Charlotte shook her head, glanced around her, lowered her voice. "She's really distraught. She feels terrible about not being able to help Tiny. She don't say nothing, but I can see it in her eyes, and the way she has a hard time looking at me sometimes."

"I know this has been hard for her." He'd seen the guilt cloud Emily's face, rob her smile. "For you too. But you still believe God can work a miracle to save Tiny?"

She nodded as tears welled. "I want to. I've been praying he will. But it's hard. Especially when Miss Emily seems to have given up hope."

He took her elbow, a quick squeeze and release. "Emily's relying on herself and man to save Tiny. You and I—and all those in the church who believe Tiny's innocent—are depending on a higher authority."

"Thank you, Terrence." She rose on tiptoe and kissed his cheek.

Later, a sharp knock interrupted a meeting between him and Mr. Warner. Harry Banister tucked his long, thin face around the partially opened door. "There's a young woman to see you, sir."

"Well, who is it, Banister?" Warner's annoyance steamed. "You know I don't have time for every minor interruption that raises its head."

"Beggin' your pardon, sir. She's asking for Mr. McCarthy. It's Miss Montgomery."

"Oh well, that's different. Best go tend to her, Terrence." The world went blank, empty.

"Terrence."

Warner's sharp tone brought him back to reality.

"Sir?"

Warner waved his hand dismissively. "Go. Don't keep the daughter of our most important customer waiting. It's not good for business." He smiled. "Or a future wife."

"Yes, sir."

Terrence rose and turned toward the door, wishing he could fly through the window.

Priscilla stood at his desk, beautiful in a maroon dress that clung softly. He approached her as if an anvil was shackled to his feet. She turned, mouth curving in a smile. She kissed his cheek.

"Terrence." She hesitated, glanced around the bank, lowered her voice. "I want to talk to you about last night, and I didn't want to wait until tomorrow evening."

He sipped his coffee. "How's your mother?"

Confusion washed over her. "My moth— Oh, she's much better. Thank you for asking."

He waited.

"Is there someplace we can talk?"

He nodded at his desk. "I'm working. This should be fine."

Hand at her throat. "No, I meant somewhere more private." She put her hand on his arm. "Can we go to the Randolph House?"

He looked at her hand until she let it drop to her waist. "I don't think I'll be going to the Randolph House for a while."

She frowned. "Why?"

"I seem to have lost my taste for it."

"Why are you being so difficult?"

He sipped his coffee again. Shrugged. *Why am I being so difficult? Is she really that dense? No, she's not.* "I'm kind of busy today."

Warner came out of his office and greeted Priscilla enthusiastically. She smiled brightly and cocked her head to one side, eyelashes fluttering.

"Is Terrence taking good care of you?"

"Well, Mr. Warner, I was hoping he could get away to discuss a private matter, but he seems to have a lot of work."

Warner's hand landed on his shoulder in a hearty clap. "Nonsense. Any work he has can wait. Get your coat and hat, Terrence, and help Miss Montgomery here resolve her private matter. Take all the time you need."

Chapter 70

Outside, Priscilla hesitated, scanning left and right and across the street. "Where can we go?"

"Dutton's Saloon should be empty this time of day."

She flushed red. "I should slap you for that."

He shrugged, greeted people walking past. "Go ahead."

She walked toward the Randolph House but stopped about halfway. She pointed across the street. "How about around the courthouse?"

"That's fine."

They strolled among the oaks in the open area around the courthouse. She faced him.

"I need to explain about last night."

"I'm listening." He kept his eyes focused ahead.

"It's not what you think it was."

"How do you know what I think it was?"

She stared at him, mouth open. "Mother's being sick upset me. You know she's never been sick a day in her life."

"No, I don't know that."

Her fingers fluttered. "Well, it's true. I started crying when we got off the train, and Lionel was comforting me."

"He looked to be doing a pretty good job."

"Oooooh!" She raised her hand.

He stared at her. "Do you really want to do that?"

She lowered her hand. "Do you believe me?"

A cardinal landed on a branch, examined the area, and chirped for his mate to join him. That's what a relationship should be like. He faced her, faced those eyes that drew him to pleasure he had never known before, eyes that once promised a future together. "No. I don't."

She paled and sniffed. Pulling a handkerchief from her purse, she wiped her nose. "I really care about you, Terrence. About us."

"Do you love me?"

She closed her eyes and sighed. "I care about you deeply."

He shoved his hands in his pockets, elbows tucked close. "Priscilla?"

She stepped closer, her arm touching his. "Yes?" Her voice had the breathless quality, like after every kiss.

"Do you love anyone besides yourself?"

She stopped—head bowed. "How can you say something so cruel?"

"Did you ever intend to marry me?" He lifted her chin, eyes riveted to hers. "The truth. For once in our relationship, tell me the truth."

She tried to stare him down. He waited. Her chin quivered, and she looked away. "No."

The pain was less than he expected but still stung, a lance through his heart. "Was I just something to fill the time until someone better came along?"

"It wasn't like that. I like you." She lifted her face, hands reaching for him. "I care for you."

"But not enough." He stepped back, and she dropped her hands.

She inhaled, straightened her shoulders. "No, not enough. I'm in love with Lionel. I finally met a man who understands me and my needs."

"The man or his money?"

Her face reddened. "How dare you?"

He sighed, all anger and hurt and energy drained away. She never loved him. Marriage was something she dangled in front of him to keep him in line. She'd played him for a fool, and he happily went along with it.

He stretched his arms wide. "Priscilla, we're done here. I hope you have a very happy marriage with Lionel for however long it lasts."

He turned to walk away. Her voice followed. "Now, I suppose you'll run after Miss High and Mighty Emily Peyton. She's been trying to steal you from me ever since she learned we were courting."

He barked a sharp laugh and faced her. "Emily's not interested in me. Whatever gave you the idea she was?"

Priscilla touched her nose. "I know her kind. She would never let me be happy. The daughter of a trollop will show her true colors."

Terrence sighed the anger down. Emily a trollop? "That's funny, Priscilla. I would never have thought of your mother as a trollop."

Chapter 71

Emily settled into the chair behind her desk, contented as Lincoln in his stall after a long ride. Good to be back in the office. Working at home always felt like she was wearing wet stockings.

The clock on the wall ticked its familiar rhythm. The aroma of fresh coffee, leather furniture and book bindings held the promise of sweetness and new discoveries. Her desk, arranged the way she liked, anchored her to her world.

Her father had wanted her to research some titles, so she'd spent the morning at town hall going over deeds and maps, losing herself in the research and the language of the law. Now, she organized her notes and outlined the requirements of titles and deeds. Seeing it all come together in coherent form pleased her. People's property would be protected, and they could set down their roots and raise their families.

Her gaze roamed the room. The room she'd dreamed of working in for so many years. Is it right to throw it all away?

The pen she'd thrown at Delbert Ford lay on the desk.

She'd failed. An innocent man would hang because of her.

She couldn't face that again.

Moving on was the right thing to do.

Wasn't it?

The door opened and one of the telegraph operators entered. "This message just arrived for you, Miss Peyton."

From Marshal Cook? She read the cryptic jumble of letters.

OUR MAN IS IN KC.

NOT ENOUGH TO ARREST HIM.

MARSHAL KNOWS YOU'RE INTERESTED.

COOK

Heart pounding, hope leaped in her chest. *If he stays there long enough, we can catch him. Must tell Father. And Charlotte.* Glance at the clock. *She's on her way to Tiny. And Terrence.* Her heart clenched at the memory of their last words. *But he needed to know.*

"Is there an answer, ma'am?"

The messenger's voice startled her.

She flustered, patting the papers on her desk as if they held a secret formula. "Yes, there is." She tore a sheet from her notebook and scribbled,

Thank you.
Please write details.
E. Peyton

She fumbled a coin from her bag and sent the operator on his way.

She re-read the message. *I can be in Kansas City this afternoon.* She grabbed her bag and hat, locked the door, and headed home. She kept her pace to just short of running. No tripping on her dress and landing face down in the street.

A figure crossed the street ahead of her, head down, hands in pockets, shoulders slumped.

Terrence.

Why isn't he at the bank?

"Terrence," she called as he stepped onto the boardwalk.

She almost stopped at the sight of the pain and anguish on his face, the hurt that clouded his eyes and caused his mouth to droop.

"What happened?"

He shrugged. "Nothing. Where are you off to in such a hurry?"

She handed him the telegraph. His eyes widened, and a smile almost wiped his hound dog expression from his face.

"You're planning on going there, aren't you?"

"Yes, I am. Stevens holds the answer to who killed Phillips. I have to talk to him."

"You're not going alone."

"Father can't travel like he needs to for something like this. Doc can't leave his patients. The marshal won't spare Matthew Quick."

"I'm going with you."

"You? What about your job? Mr. Warner warned you about taking time to help Tiny."

Terrence glanced to the courthouse. "All that's changed now."

He faced her, jaw set, eyes narrow. "I will *not* let anyone hurt you like they did in San Antonio. I'll be at your side every minute."

Her heart swelled, and she stopped herself from caressing his cheek. Her voice seemed to drop a notch as she spoke around the lump in her throat. "Thank you. I know Father will appreciate knowing you're with me." *In more ways than one.*

"When are you leaving?"

"Today. On the next train."

"Let me tell Mr. Warner and pack a bag. Meet you at your house?"

"All right."

They both turned to go. *Tell him. Don't let another minute pass.* "Terrence?"

He turned, brows raised, waited.

She sighed. "I apologize for being so rude to you lately."

He nodded. "I forgive you."

"It wasn't you. Really. I can't forgive God." She shrugged. "I get angry seeing people like you and Charlotte and Tiny put so much stock in him. Because I know he will only hurt you too."

He reached for her, then stopped. "A conversation for another time. When you're ready."

Terrence hurried to the bank, the pain of Priscilla's betrayal yielding to hope for Tiny. He'd get over Priscilla. God would heal his heart and build him up so he could trust again. In time. But Tiny needed help and hope now. He thanked God for so quickly unearthing Stevens. He knew Stevens held the answer to the mystery. He also knew what Emily risked if she went alone.

He strode past his desk and knocked on Mr. Warner's door. The man hadn't even finished saying "come in," before Terrence entered. Abraham Montgomery sat across from Warner, pipe and cigar smoke a grayish-blue cloud above them. Terrence resisted the urge to open the two windows behind Warner's desk. Warner quickly turned a paper in front of him face down on the desk.

"What is it, Terrence?"

"I need to take a few days off, sir. A friend of mine needs help."

"How many?"

"Three. Maybe more."

Warner's brows rose like flags. He pursed his lips, glanced at Montgomery. "That's a lot of time, son. I don't know if I can spare you that long."

"Micah Jenkins has come a long way, sir. He can handle most of the routine stuff until I get back."

Warner snorted. "He'll probably soil himself with his first angry customer."

"Harry can help him. He knows the routines."

Warner puffed his pipe, clouds rising like a locomotive. "Who needs your help?"

Terrence looked down. "Emily Peyton."

"What does she need help with?" Warner leaned forward, elbows on his desk, rubbing his cheek with the stem of his pipe.

Terrence swallowed. "Tracking down a witness."

Warner's palm slammed his desktop. "Is this about that Tiny Waters?"

Terrence nodded.

"I told you to leave that alone. It's not good for the bank or your reputation to be involved with a convicted murderer."

Montgomery raised his hand. "Joseph is right, Terrence. The bank needs to distance itself from a situation like this. A financial institution must maintain its integrity."

"And I have to help my friend, sir. Especially when I believe he's innocent."

"I think you'll end up stained with the same brush if you insist on this," Montgomery said.

Terrence faced Warner. "Mr. Warner, may I have the time off?"

Warner exchanged glances with Montgomery. "No. It's out of the question."

Terrence nodded, crossed his arms. "Then, I resign. Effective immediately."

Warner's jaw dropped, and color drained from his face. "You resign?"

"Yes, sir."

"Then you're a bigger fool than I thought. You're throwing away a promising career for a cowboy too greedy to work for his money."

"Is there anything else, Mr. Warner?"

Warner sputtered.

"I'll have Jenkins draw my salary, and I'll clean out my desk." Terrence extended his hand. "Thanks for the opportunity to work here and learn from you."

Warner glared at the hand until Terrence brought it back to his side.

Montgomery stood and offered his hand. "Goin' through a lot of changes in one day, son. Hope your heart ain't ruling your head. That's never good."

Terrence shook his hand. "It's not, Mr. Montgomery. I think I'm seeing things more clearly now than I ever have before."

Chapter 72

"Terrence said he'll come with me." Emily strove to control the stridency in her voice. She had not expected her father's vehement opposition to her going to Kansas City.

"Don't care. Too dangerous." Her father hulked over his crutches. "You could have been killed in San Antonio. Your doggedness may finish the job."

Hands on her hips, she leaned over the kitchen table. "I get it from you. You taught me to never give up for a client."

George nodded. "That I did. I never expected your life would be at stake." His voice cracked. "I can't stand the thought of losing you."

She came around the table and stood on her toes to kiss his cheek. "I don't want to lose you, either. You know Terrence is the best shot in town outside of Marshal Dobbins."

"At targets. Has he ever shot a man?"

"He will if he must. Especially for Tiny."

A strange look passed over her father's face, as if he saw something no one else could.

"What is it?"

He shook his head and shoulders as if driving off a chill. "Nothing. I don't think Tiny—only one Terrence will shoot someone for." He paused. "At least, I hope so."

George opened the door to allow Terrence to enter. "So, she's got you—in this—adventure too?"

"No, sir. I offered to go with her."

George gestured with his shoulder. "Coffee's on the stove. She's—packing."

Terrence returned to the parlor in a few minutes, mug in hand, wisps of steam carrying the aroma into the room. He sat opposite George, his carpetbag on the floor next to him.

"Son, can't tell you how much I appreciate you—helping my little girl."

"Don't let her hear you call her that."

George chuckled. "I know. Haven't called her—since—twelve." He sipped his coffee. "How d'you—Warner—give you the time off?"

"I resigned."

"The fool. I'll talk to him."

Terrence shrugged. "I don't think it will make any difference, but I appreciate your help."

"Did you tell Priscilla—running off—her worst enemy?"

"I resigned that too."

"Sorry to hear that."

"It's for the best," Terrence said. "Turns out I wasn't the man for her."

George shook his head. "Women."

"Sir, do you know why Priscilla hates Emily so?"

"She never told you?"

"Just made it clear she didn't like Emily, and especially didn't like me spending so much time with her during the trial."

"Happened in school." George chuckled. "Emily was eight, maybe nine—Priscilla a little younger. Priscilla made—remark—Emily's mother running ..." His face tightened. "With army officer. Emily punched her—nose. One punch. Priscilla wailed—pig in barbed wire."

Footsteps on the stairs brought them both to their feet. Emily put her bag next to Terrence's. "Are we ready?"

"I think so," Terrence said.

"Father, Doc will be over in a little while to take you to supper and keep an eye on things until Charlotte gets back." She handed him an envelope. "This is a letter for Charlotte. I wanted her to know all that's happening."

An awkward silence filled the room, as if they were strangers who didn't know what to say.

George spoke past the lump in his throat. "I don't want you to go."

She put her hand on his chest. "I know. But I have to if Tiny will ever have a chance."

George nodded and blinked.

Emily nodded at Terrence. "I'll be in excellent hands. My knight in shining armor will protect me."

"Telegraph—soon—you get in—then every two hours."

"Is that all? Not every thirty minutes?"

"D—sass me, young lady." Her cheek so soft in his palm. He liked the way she snuggled her face into his hand, the soft smile on her lips so like when she was a child.

Heaviness rose from his chest to his throat, pressing against the tears he fought to hold back. He embraced her with one arm, crushing her to him.

He turned to Terrence. "Take care of her."

"I will."

He stood on the porch as they loaded the carriage and, with one last wave, headed for the station.

"*Dear God, protect them.*"

Chapter 73

Emily studied the somber man sitting across from her. Terrence's usual outgoing confidence seemed muted, blocked behind a curtain. Something had happened, but he sat tight-lipped, staring out the window.

"Is everything all right?" she asked. "You look like Spot died."

His smile touched the corners of his mouth and came nowhere near his eyes. Definitely not the Terrence she knew.

"Not as bad as that." He resumed his vigilance of the passing countryside.

She glanced around the car. No one sat within three rows of them. She ventured one more question, seeking some way to heal her friend's hurt. "Do you want to talk about it?"

A slight shrug. He didn't face her. "Did you ever have someone you trusted betray you?"

"My mother." The words were out before she even thought of what to say.

He looked at her now, eyes warm, compassionate, yet veiled with pain. "Yes. Your mother." He nodded. "Well, the same thing happened to me."

She closed her mouth before any words could get out. *I don't know what to say.* The memory of that day burned afresh, the hurt as real each time she remembered her mother riding off. Time had not ended the pain. Nor had the law. And she'd let no man close enough.

"I'm sorry."

"Thank you." His eyes darted back to the window.

The silence lengthened. They'd never gone this long with so few words. No teasing; no talking baseball, banking, the law. No funny stories about people in town.

The rhythm of the train settled in her eyelids, causing them to grow heavy despite her excitement and concern. They closed.

Terrence's voice startled her, the hurt and anger under his words like darts. "Priscilla played me for a fool."

She waited, unsure she wanted to have this conversation, not knowing what to say.

He extended his legs, crossed his arms, and studied his feet. "She's been seeing other men and has decided to marry one of them." He half-snorted, half-laughed. "Right when I was getting ready to propose myself."

He wiped his face with his hands. "I loved her. Thought she loved me."

Hands clasped tight, Emily restrained the urge to move next to him, to touch his hunched shoulders, to give some physical comfort. In her imagination, she gave into the urge to punch Priscilla in the nose. Again.

"Terrence, I kno—I have no idea what you're feeling. I can't even tell you time will heal your pain. I can't hold you or kiss the pain all better like a mother would a child. I don't have any trite religious sayings to offer." She paused. "I can listen when you want to talk. But I can't tell you how to stop hurting because the pain of loss never does."

The hotel, a modest three-story plain building, stood one block off the main street. Terrence remembered it from a previous trip for the bank. "I think we need to be as invisible as possible until we know where Stevens is," he'd said on the way from the train depot. "I don't want a repeat of San Antonio happening to you."

The desk clerk was several inches shorter than Terrence. His beard needed trimming, but his welcome was warm. He turned the register to face them and handed Terrence a pen.

While Terrence signed, the clerk plucked a key from a peg on the wall behind him and placed it on the counter next to register. "We have a lovely room on the third floor. I think the two of you will enjoy it very much, Mr. and Mrs. ..." He angled his head to read the register. "... McCarthy."

"We're not married," Emily said.

The clerk snatched the key back as if it were the last piece of chicken at a church supper. "You're not?"

"We never said we were," Emily said. Terrence recognized the annoyance that could quickly morph into sarcasm. "We require adjacent rooms near an outside wall. The second floor or higher will do nicely."

The clerk looked from one to the other before turning to the wall and examining the rows of keys. He didn't move for several moments.

"Is there a problem?" Terrence cringed at the irritation and annoyance flooding his voice.

The man rubbed his chin. He took down two keys and placed them on the counter, hand covering them. "You'll both need to register." The clerk seemed unusually taken with Emily's leaning over to sign the register.

"What brings you to Kansas City?"

"Looking for work," Terrence said. "Are any of the banks hiring?"

"Wouldn't know. Don't have much truck with banks." He handed them their keys. "Second floor to the right, last two on the left."

"Much obliged," Terrence said, hoisting both their bags.

As they started up the stairs, Terrence glanced back to see the clerk studying the register and writing on a small piece of paper.

Chapter 74

Emily stood, hands on hips, and surveyed her corner room. She smiled at Terrence standing in the doorway, ensuring he was visible to any passersby. Such gallantry.

Two windows graced the walls. One overlooked the rear of the hotel. The tall, sharp peak of what looked to be a livery rose. The other window overlooked a side street, the side of a mercantile shop about thirty feet away.

"Seems fine," she said, although the creak emanating from the bed when she plopped her bag on it didn't please her. "Hopefully, we won't have to stay here long."

Terrence rubbed his hands together. "Which first? Food? Or the marshal?"

Her stomach reminded her it liked to be fed more than once a day. Something besides coffee. But her heart and her mind raced. Need to find Stevens before he has the chance to get away. "The marshal first."

She locked the door and turned to go when Terrence held his hand up and stepped toward a door at the end of her hall. He opened it to reveal a set of stairs attached to the outside wall running from the street to the top floor of the hotel.

"Must be for guests to use in case of a fire." Emily leaned out and shook the railing. "Kind of rickety. Hope we never have to use it."

Terrence's gaze lingered on the street below. "I pray nobody tries to use it to get in." He placed his hand lightly on her arm. "When you're in your room, make sure you lock the door and wedge a chair under the knob."

Her stomach lurched and her cheek and eye tingled as she remembered the punches in San Antonio. Seeing Terrence in the hall, his eyes intense, reassured her like her father's embrace. "But you're with me now."

"You still need to be careful. Watch for strangers who show too much interest."

"Do you think Stevens knows we're here?"

"After San Antonio, we must assume he at least thinks you'll come here. Or you'll send someone."

Uneasiness crept over her like the house creaking on a quiet, still night.

Emily took a step back, hand to her chest, when Marshal Will Stuebens rose from behind his desk. She'd never seen a man so tall or ominous. His military bearing made her stand straighter. Dressed all in black except for a silver belt buckle, his right cheek scarred from chin to temple. His left hand had only the thumb and index finger. His jaw sat offset to the left from the rest of his face.

He offered them seats and coffee and folded his body back into his chair. He rubbed his scar. "Marshal Cook telegraphed about this Frank Stevens. How can I help you?" A slight lilt of a European accent flavored his speech.

"Did Marshal Cook tell you Mr. Stevens is under suspicion of a double murder in San Antonio?" Emily asked.

"Yes. But he said there's not enough evidence."

"That's true," Emily said. "We think the men he killed also murdered a man in Abilene. He may have information that could save an innocent man due to be executed."

"How well do you know Stevens, Marshal?" Terrence asked.

"Enough not to trust him. But I trust no bounty hunters. They're nothing but scavengers and marauders." He touched his jaw as if it were still painful. "He visits Kansas City occasionally, but I do not let him conduct his business here."

"May I ask why?" Emily said.

Stuebens shrugged. "He brings in too many dead men. I prefer them alive." He looked over Terrence's shoulder. Emily sensed his mind was in some far-off place. "His father and brothers rode with Quantrill. They brought Frank into it when he was barely in his teens." He stopped. "He was worse than any of them. He enjoyed the burning and the killing and …" He glanced at Emily. "… other things."

Emily's heart surged at the anguish on the man's face. "Your wife?"

He shook his head. "My sister. Thirteen years old."

"You couldn't arrest him?" Terrence asked.

The marshal nodded. "Arrest him we did. But no one would testify against him or his family."

"Marshal Stuebens, will you help us find him?" Emily spoke past the lump, making it hard to breathe.

"Yes. But it will be difficult. He wears disguises and doesn't always go to the same places. But we will try."

Chapter 75

Emily touched her fingers to her forehead, wishing the tension would wash away like the suds from her bath. Their third day of searching after two fruitless days spent talking to saloonkeepers, gamblers, brothel madams, storekeepers, and horse traders.

No one would acknowledge seeing Stevens. Those who knew him from his previous visits could not agree on his appearance.

This morning, she and Terrence sat with Marshal Stuebens in a restaurant near his office. Her breakfast sat untouched while the two men scooped food into their mouths like they were feeding a steam engine. She sipped at her fourth cup of coffee and nibbled a slice of bacon.

Stuebens leaned back, balancing his chair on its hind legs, and rubbed his stomach. "That was excellent." He pulled a toothpick from his shirt pocket and began working at his teeth.

What little appetite Emily had went under the table.

"Where do we search today?" she asked.

Stuebens sucked on his toothpick. "We go back to the same places. Someone has seen him. We must keep asking until we find that person."

Someone passing by in the crowded restaurant jostled the table, spilling Emily's coffee. She jumped to her feet, but the liquid landed on her dress, a brown lake spreading toward the floor.

"Oh, dear," she said, blotting with her napkin. "I need to go change. I'll be right back."

Terrence stood. "I'm going with you."

"I'll only be a few minutes. You stay and finish your breakfast." She refrained from commenting the marshal might finish it for him.

"Emily." He stared at her, voice hard. "I'm going with you."

"You do—"

He raised his palm. "San Antonio."

A few minutes later, Terrence accompanied Emily to her room. Early morning gloom was rapidly leaving the hall as the sun rose higher.

At her door, Emily reached for the knob while extending her key toward the lock.

She gasped.

When her hand closed on the knob, the door swung slowly inward. Terrence slipped his Colt from its holster and pointed for Emily to move away from the door.

He'd been with her earlier and seen her lock it. They'd both tested it.

He flattened himself against the wall and pushed the door further open. No one he could see.

He peered through the narrow gap between the door and the frame. No one standing behind it.

He motioned Emily to stay in the hall, and he took a tentative step over the threshold. He froze when the floor creaked. Sweat trickled down his back.

Another step. The room still appeared empty.

One more step and he cleared the door. Gun at the ready, he scanned the room. No sign of anyone.

He peered under the bed. No one. He exhaled with relief.

Standing once again, his heart sank at the realization all was not right with the bed. Emily's dresses lay strewn over the surface, shredded by jagged cuts.

A folded sheet of paper rested against the mirror on the dresser. He picked it up.

Stop looking for Frank Stevens.
The next time you'll be wearing the dress.
And who's protecting your father?

"Can I come in?" Her voice sounded fragile, tremulous.

He couldn't postpone it, couldn't put everything back to normal.

She entered before he could answer, wringing her hands.

"My clothes."

He handed her the note. It fluttered to the floor as both hands went to her mouth.

Holstering his gun, he pulled her into his arms and held her while her stiff body shook.

Chapter 76

Emily handed Stuebens the note. His brows puckered, and he pulled at his lower lip. "We seem to be annoying someone. Making them very nervous."

Up in her room, he examined one of the dresses, turning it over, pulling the cut edges together. "Looks like a Bowie knife. There are probably hundreds within fifty miles." He laid the dress gently on the bed. "You all right, Miss Peyton?"

Emily ignored the weakness that threatened her knees. Her stomach rolled and her head seemed to drift toward the ceiling.

Stuebens put his arm around her waist and guided her toward a straight-backed chair by the small table. "Here. Sit." He held the chair as she braced herself on the table before lowering herself to the seat.

"Thank you."

Terrence placed a tumbler of water in front of her, his hand skimming her shoulder. A light touch. She wanted it to be longer, more firm. She sipped the water. "Guess I should have eaten more breakfast."

"Probably wise you did not," Stuebens said. "With a shock like this, the stomach often rejects the food."

The marshal squatted, peered through the keyhole, twisted both sides of the knob. Using Emily's key, he locked and unlocked the door several times. He disappeared into the hallway. Emily heard the door to the outside stairs open and close three times. He rubbed his chin as he came into the room, hefting the key with his other hand.

"Your door was opened with a key. No one forced it or used a tool." He spoke to Terrence. "Mr. McCarthy, would you be so kind to ask the desk clerk to join us?"

While they waited, Emily drank more water and forced herself to breathe calmly. Her heart slowed its pounding, and the tension in her neck dissipated with rolling her shoulders. However, the images of San Antonio hovered over her, the sense of violation churning her stomach. What if she'd been in the room? Her sense of safety lay shattered like fine crystal dropped on a tile floor. She hugged herself.

A large hand rested lightly on her shoulder. "I know this must be hard." The marshal's soft voice and gentle tone sounded so out of context from his size, she almost laughed. To hear those words come from that torn and disfigured face warmed her heart.

"Thank you, Marshal."

Terrence and the clerk entered the room. The clerk scanned the room and opened his mouth to speak. He stopped at the marshal's upraised hand—the palm seeming as if it could cradle a small child or knock a wall flat with one smack.

"Percival, I have some questions for you," Stuebens said.

The clerk moved toward a chair at the table.

"This won't take long."

Percival stepped back.

The marshal pointed to the door and the bed. "Someone entered Miss Peyton's room this morning and violated her personal belongings."

The clerk stuttered and sweat broke out on his forehead. "S-s-someone must have snuck up the outside stairs and broke in." His hands fluttered like butterflies.

"They used a key."

"Maybe she left the door unlocked. Lots of guests do that."

Stuebens glanced at Emily and Terrence and shook his head. "That did not happen here. I am quite convinced she securely locked the door."

Percival's eyes widened, and his lips quivered. "Marshal, I swear I don't know nothing about it."

"You saw no one enter the hotel and go to the stairs?"

He shook his head.

"Percival, where is the passkey?"

"Passkey?"

Stuebens sighed. "Percival, I dislike these games. Where is the passkey that lets you unlock the doors of all the rooms?"

"It's in the safe where we always keep it."

Stuebens stood. Percival shrunk back.

They all filed downstairs. Emily clung to the banister as her knees wanted to buckle at each step.

Behind the front desk, and out of sight under the counter, a small black safe with ornate gold trim snuggled in a corner. Percival opened the door. "See, it's right he—" He cussed. A small hook in the side wall was empty.

"That is a shame, Percival, that you have lost the key." Stuebens pointed at the safe. "I noticed you did not use the combination."

Emily thought if Percival got any paler, she'd be able to see through him. Terrence stepped closer as if to look into the safe. The brush of his sleeve on hers sent goose bumps coursing up her arm. She welcomed the strength and protection she drew from his nearness.

"That's very irresponsible," Stuebens continued. "This young lady's life was in mortal danger because you left the safe unlocked."

Percival clasped his hands at his waist. "Please don't tell Mr. Owens. He'll fire me." His plaintive whine irritated Emily.

Stuebens may have felt the same. "You deserve to be fired, Percival. Valuables could have been stolen from that safe. None were, which leads me to believe whoever took the key only wanted access to Miss Peyton's room."

The marshal planted his hands on his hips. "Percival, you have put the lives and property of every guest in jeopardy because of your laziness. Who took the key?"

"I don't know," the clerk pleaded. "They must have done it when I was away from the desk."

"I don't believe you. Come with me. You're under arrest."

"But I didn't do anything."

Stuebens took him by the arm. "I know. In your case, that should be a crime." He turned to Emily and Terrence. "Miss Peyton, Mr. McCarthy. Please pack all your belongings and come to my office. We must find a safer place for you."

Chapter 77

Two hours later, Emily stood in a small second-floor room on the outskirts of Kansas City. The marshal's home. Upstairs bedrooms for her and Terrence. Dolls arranged on a shelf above the bed reminded all who entered this was once a child's domain.

A strong breeze blew the floral print curtains almost horizontal to the floor. Tucked under the eave, a metal bed with a quilt matching the curtains offered a soft, cozy place to be pampered. From the window, the city spread before her. Directly below, the largest vegetable garden she'd ever seen promised a bounty from plants in various stages of growth. Won't starve here.

She placed the last of her undergarments in the dresser across from the bed. She'd thrown her slashed dresses away, seeking to banish what they represented but still fighting the violation crawling over her body. *At least, I have an excuse to buy new clothes.*

The mirror mounted on top reflected sunshine throughout the room. Her hair yielded to the brush she ran repeatedly through it, taking on a luster that seemed to sparkle in the sunlight. Rather than twist it into a bun, she worked it into a long, blond braid that lay gracefully over her shoulder and down her chest. She had worn it this way until she was eight. Father couldn't braid like mother. Nor could Caroline.

The face looking back at her held the same sadness Emily saw reflected every day until that day in Father's office when she opened a law book for the first time and found her passion. The passion, a faint flicker now, burned low, fuel exhausted.

I will not cry. Her dream might be over, but she still lived. She could move on to a new life, one where her actions didn't put anyone in danger of losing their lives, one where she did not face the humiliation from people, humiliation that wasn't one-tenth of what she herself felt. Her arrogant pride could still cost Tiny his life. She would not be part of that again.

She gazed out the window, fingering the end of her braid, wondering what she'd find over the next horizon.

She gasped and stepped to the side, peering around the edge of the window frame. A man walked in the backyard, rifle cradled across his chest, his face shadowed by his hat.

The sun glinted off metal on his chest. He raised his eyes to hers and touched the brim of his Stetson.

The deputy Stuebens had assigned to guard the house. She couldn't remember his name.

She waved back, relief battling silliness. Nobody knew they were here.

She wandered downstairs. Mrs. Stuebens was in the parlor, hemming a dress.

"Ah, Miss Emily. I was just going to look for you." She stood, almost as tall and lean as her husband, coal-black hair with wisps of white at the temples, eyes a deep blue that spread humor and compassion. "I've hemmed a couple of my daughter's dresses for you until you can buy some new ones. She's taller than you but your builds are similar."

"Thank you, Mrs. Stuebens." She lifted a striped blue dress from the arm of the sofa and held it against her. Not something she would have chosen but it would do in the situation.

"Tea for you? Yes?" Her accent was stronger than her husband's.

"Do you have coffee?"

"*Ja*. Always. Vill, he must always have his coffee ready." She gestured in that universal way that said, "men, who can understand them?" Caroline showed the same expression with Doc. Had mother ever done that about Father?

The bright sun and white kitchen dazzled Emily until the other objects asserted themselves. Glass-fronted cabinets displayed dishes with an intricate pink pattern. The black stove with gold trim gleamed in front of a brick wall at one side of the room. A light wood table surrounded by matching chairs centered the room, standing on a multi-hued braided rug.

I might even enjoy working in this kitchen.

Mrs. Stuebens took two thick ceramic mugs from a rack on a shelf over the stove. "Vill likes his mug warm, so the coffee stays hot. Tsk. If I had known he would be so fussy, I vould have changed him before we married." She poured the coffee and motioned for Emily to join her at the table. "My mother warned me, but I was too much in love."

Emily sipped the delicious brew with its hint of mint. "Thank you, Mrs. Stuebens."

"Please, you vill call me Gertie. My name is Gertrude." She shuddered as her face split into a grin. "I hate it. Sounds like name for a duck."

Emily laughed, a sound that seemed to lift, even if only for a moment, the heaviness surrounding her.

"You have a beautiful smile, Emily. I saw it when you said goodbye to Mr. McCarthy."

A flush crept up Emily's neck. Terrence and the marshal had left an hour earlier. Stuebens refused to let her come and assigned the deputy to guard her. When she protested, Terrence took her hand and said, "Do it for me, Emily. I don't want to face your father if something should happen to you."

Fear of facing her father wasn't in his eyes when he spoke. Instead, she glimpsed a warmth, a caring, a friend. And something more?

"So, you and Mr. McCarthy, you are courting?"

Emily sputtered into her coffee. "No. We are friends, only friends. And he is good friends with my client, so he's been helping."

Gertie's eyes studied her before the woman nodded and said, "Ahh." She paused. "You are stepping out with someone, then?"

Instead of annoyance at the woman's boldness, sadness crept from Emily's stomach to her heart. "No, I'm not."

"But you are so pretty. Surely the men are chasing you like dogs after a rabbit?"

"No." Emily caressed her cup, drawing the warmth into her palms. "Being a lawyer seems to drive some of them in the other direction." She smirked. "And others don't like that I ride and shoot better than they can."

"Men. Such fools they can be." She rose, poured a third cup of coffee, and carried it to the back door. "Deputy Allen needs coffee too."

From the front of the house, a gong echoed. Gertie glanced at the clock hanging near the stove. "Soon Vill and your Mr. McCarthy will be here for dinner."

"May I help?"

Gertie arched her brow. "You have done cooking?"

"For me and Father sometimes."

"You are smart. You will learn our cooking fast."

In the next hour, Emily learned to cut carrots evenly and how to make sauerkraut. Gertie wielded a knife like a master swordsman, and soon, five thick ham steaks sizzled in the oven, glazed with a thick raisin sauce. With an elaborate flourish of her hands, Gertie waved her away from the counter and the preparations of a strudel filled with canned peaches and wild berries.

Finished, they returned to the table, Gertie with tea and Emily with coffee.

"You learn a lot?"

Emily shook her head. "Everything went by too fast. I didn't even see you make the sauce. And the strudel—"

Gertie waved a finger at her, mouth firm but eyes glinting with humor. "No one touches my strudel. Not even my daughters. The recipe goes to the grave with me."

Emily laughed again.

Gertie reached across the table and covered Emily's hand. "You feel better? You don't look as sad as when Vill brought you home."

"I do. Thank you."

Rubbing the back of Emily's hand, Gertie said, "But there is still sadness around you. The man in prison?"

Emily nodded.

"And your father?" She paused. "And Mr. McCarthy?"

"Yes. Terrence gave up his job to help me, to help Tiny."

Gertie squeezed her hand. "Yes, to help you and protect you is important to him." She rose to check the ham and the strudel.

She took plates down from the cabinet, and Emily helped her set the table.

They worked in silence. The woman's words preyed on Emily's mind. Did she mean Terrence had feelings stronger than friendship for her? Must be because he ended the relationship with Priscilla. Can't encourage him. *I have nothing to offer him, not like Priscilla could.*

She smiled at the memory of seven-year-old Priscilla flopped in the muddy schoolyard, fancy dress all askew, blood seeping from both nostrils, and a wail that would frighten rabid coyotes. That was worth the switching the teacher gave her. Father tried to give her one that night, but after three halfhearted taps, he couldn't stop laughing and sent her to her room.

Priscilla had grown up to be as mean and cruel as she'd been in school. She didn't deserve someone like Terrence. He was well rid of her.

Emily placed a knife by the last plate as heavy thumping sounded from the front porch. Terrence and Stuebens entered the kitchen, filling it with their presence, their essence.

Terrence, eyes beaming, crossed the room in one stride and grasped her hands, squeezing tight. "We found him."

Emily staggered and clutched the back of the chair. Her heart pounded a beat that echoed in her brain. She embraced Terrence, then quickly withdrew.

"Where?" Her voice trembled.

Stuebens sat at the end of the table, snapped his napkin open and tucked it into his shirt. He grabbed a thick slice of bread and buttered it, an even spread that covered every inch of the slice. "A brothel on the north side of town. He hardly ever went there before, but I guess he must be trying to change his stripes to confuse us.

Gertie placed a platter of ham steaks and bowls of carrots and sauerkraut on the table. "Stripes is stripes. Men like him never change." She cocked an eye at Terrence and motioned him to sit.

Emily's legs twitched. She wanted to dash upstairs, get her pistol, and go get him. How can they eat at a time like this? Even Terrence heaped food on his plate. "What are we waiting for? Let's go arrest him."

Stuebens washed ham and sauerkraut down with a gulp of coffee. "Sit, Miss Emily. Eat. He's not there right now. He was there last night. One of the ladies knows him very well from another house she worked at."

"With all his disguises, how did she know it was him?" Emily waved away the bowl of carrots Gertie offered.

Stuebens looked down and blushed, while Terrence grinned. The marshal cleared his throat. "He has certain tastes."

Heat warmed Emily's own cheeks. "How do we know he'll go back there again?"

Stuebens heaped sauerkraut over his ham. He glanced at Gertie. "The lady owes me a favor. She knows how to get word to him that there'll be a big poker game tonight. Stevens likes his gambling as much as his women."

"Does she know where he is right now?"

Stuebens shook his head. "If she does, she is not telling."

Emily drummed her fingers on the table. "How do you know she'll keep her word?"

"Because if she does not, she'll have a very difficult time keeping her house open, and that is more important to her than anything." He smiled. "She has a son studying to be a doctor at a fancy school back east. She needs the money."

Chapter 78

Clouds blurred the moon and dimmed what little light shone. Branches scratched against the house as Emily lay in her bed, hands folded on her stomach. She listened for the clock downstairs. Would ten o'clock never get here?

The marshal planned to meet several deputies at his office, and from there, go to the brothel and surround it. He and two deputies would crash into the room with the poker game and arrest Stevens. The cooperative madam would stand behind Stevens to identify him. Simple plan. Should work.

Emily stood and paced, willing the butterflies in her stomach to settle down, stroking her forehead to force the lightheadedness away without success. Soft rustles from the next room told her Terrence shared her nervousness. She imagined him pacing in his socks so as not to disturb anyone.

A new sound emerged. Something sliding on leather over and over.

He's practicing drawing his pistol.

She picked hers up from the bed, emptied the cartridges and pointed the weapon at the mirror, using a two-handed grip to steady it. Her arms trembled the longer she held the pose.

Could she shoot someone?

She liked to think she could to save someone else.

Could she shoot Stevens?

Absolutely.

Really? She lowered the pistol. She didn't know.

If it would save Tiny? Yes. Maybe.

If Stevens was escaping? She'd have to. She had to stop him, or Tiny would die.

What if Stevens couldn't help Tiny? What if he truly didn't know enough?

She slumped on the edge of the bed. Stared at the floor, the wood grain weaving a confusing whorl that left her dizzy.

Her stomach queased and blood drained from her head.

A gong echoed from the clock downstairs. Finally. She exhaled and stood. The pounding in her chest steadied.

Pistol reloaded, she slipped it in her bag.

She was first to the foot of the stairs. Will came from the kitchen, Gertie behind him. Terrence's footsteps tattooed a quick dance down the stairs.

"Where do you think you are going, Missy?" Will's scowl would warp a horseshoe.

Emily pulled herself as straight as she could. Will still towered over her. She thrust out her chin. "I'm going with you."

"Wha—" Terrence looked like Spot had stomped his toe.

"No, you are not." Will stroked his scar. "Where we go is no place for a woman."

Emily laughed. "There are plenty of women in that place."

"Not for a woman like you."

"Marshal Stuebens." Emily planted her fists on her hips. "Those women are just like me. Trying to make it through this world the best we can. Just using different means."

Jaws clamped, he turned his back on her.

Terrence reached to touch her arm. She yanked it back. "Emily. Don't do this! It's too dangerous. I can't let anything happen to you. I ... I promised your father. I ... I couldn't live with myself if anything happened to you."

Sweet Terrence. How she wanted to caress his cheek, feel his arms around her, taste his lips—*No*.

"Terrence, I've come a long way for this. I want to be part of the end."

"You will be, Missy. When Stevens is in my jail, you can be there when I question him. I want you to ask him the questions that will free your client. But I cannot allow you to be part of arresting him. You will distract my men. They will think they have to protect you first. I don't want my men hurt or see Stevens get away again because they were protecting you."

"He makes sense, Emily," Terrence said.

She knew he did, but anger fumed. She clenched and unclenched her fists. "How come you get to go?"

"I've been deputized." Terrence opened his suit coat to reveal a badge pinned to his vest.

"Of course." She lifted her arms and dropped them to her side. "Why can't you deputize me?"

"Because I will not." Stuebens rubbed the back of his neck. "Miss Peyton, I need you to promise you will stay here until I send for you. I cannot afford to have a man stay here to make sure you do." He leaned forward, eyes drilling into her. "And I have no time to put you in one of my cells. My men are waiting."

Gertie's arm slipped around her shoulder, pulled her close. "Vill, he is right, Emily. Stay with me. We vill pray together."

Emily shook the woman's arm off. "Pray if you want." Emily's heart wrenched at the hurt that flooded Gertie's eyes and caused her face to drop. This woman had shown her nothing but kindness and generosity, even love. "I'm sorry, Gertie. Please forgive me."

Gertie patted her back. "Of course, I do. You have much on your mind and vords come out without thinking."

Emily held the woman, not daring to tell her the truth behind her words. She couldn't hurt one more person. Not someone as sweet as Gertie.

"May I have your answer, Miss Emily?"

Tears welled without warning. Emily said, "I'll stay. But I expect you to send for me soon."

Stuebens adjusted his hat. "As soon as Stevens is at the jail, one of my deputies will come for you."

Chapter 79

The clack of Gertie's knitting needles contrasted with the steady ticking of the clock at the foot of the stairs, whose rhythmic beat filled Emily's ears as she paced the room. Fifteen minutes? Is that all? Why did it seem like hours?

Gertie's eyes seemed closed, but her fingers moved with speed and accuracy. The woman's breathing became steady and deep, but the needles continued sending their message. Can she knit in her sleep?

"Why are you so angry with God, Miss Emily?"

Emily jumped. Gertie's voice. But the woman hadn't stirred. Eyes still half-closed, needles taking a string of yarn and turning it into a sweater or blanket.

"What are you knitting?"

"Vill needs a new sweater for vinter. This is his birthday present." She rolled the garment and stuck the needles in the bundle before laying it gently in a straw basket. "I could rob a bank and hide the money in this basket and Vill would never think to look in it. A woman's world is so strange to that man."

Gertie pushed herself from the sofa. "Time for tea." She shuffled toward the kitchen, the pleasant tiredness of a hard-worked day evident in her ambling gait. "Come, help me fix it."

"Are you my jailer? Keeping me in sight all the time?"

Gertie laughed from deep in her throat and her shoulders shook. "*Meine tochter*, I cannot keep you here. You stay because you promised."

She touched her forehead. "I need to know what's happening. I can't wait like this. Not knowing."

"Talk will help us wait." She set a kettle on the stove and added wood. She folded her hands across her middle. "So, you were going to tell me why you are so angry at God."

I was?

Gertie gestured at the table and Emily sat, fingers crimping the tablecloth.

The tea, warm and sweet with honey, soothed as it slipped down her throat. The piece of strudel tasted soft, the sweet-tart mix of peaches and berries teasing her tongue. "I can see why you will take this recipe to your grave."

The older woman smiled, the glimmer in her eye like the sun peeking from behind a cloud. "I'm not really. But I like to watch my daughters try to get it out of me." She cradled her teacup in her hands. "You are about the same age as my oldest. Twenty-six? Twenty-seven?"

"Twenty-six."

"*Goot*. I vill talk with you like I talk with her. Your anger with God is not healthy. It vill eat you from the inside. Happiness vill never come."

"He took happiness away a long time ago."

"You lost someone. Your mother? You have not mentioned her."

Emily nodded, eyes on her tea.

"She died when you were young?"

Emily's head snapped up. "She ran away with another man when I was eight."

"You are still angry about this. I hear it in your voice. And you blame God." Gertie's voice was gentle as a warm quilt.

"He let it happen."

"Emily, your mother decided to leave. It was her choice. And I'm sure she did not talk to God about it."

"Why didn't he stop her? Didn't he see the hurt she caused?" Tears threatened to spill. She blotted her eyes with her napkin.

"God allows us to make choices. He won't force us to do things."

"Even when it hurts others?" The anger flared anew.

"Because ... I know you don't believe it, Emily. But he does care about you. When your mother left, it hurt him as much as it hurt you."

"Sure has a funny way of showing it."

"He is there to help those who are hurt," Gertie said, eyes soft, voice low and calm. "If they are ready to receive it. He's always there."

"He could have prevented my father's accident."

"Maybe he tried. Sometimes, God will try to tell us things, but we ignore him, thinking ve know better."

Emily fought against Gertie's words. It was so much easier to blame God, to believe he didn't care.

She remembered asking her father to postpone his trip to Jed's to another day, but father said he would be fine. And then the accident happened. Were her words God's attempt to speak to her father? So many questions roiled. Like gathering thunder clouds. "Why is he letting Tiny hang?"

Gertie freshened their cups. "Maybe he isn't. Maybe he arranged for this Stevens to be found."

"Your words are sweet, Gertie. And I'm sure they bring comfort to some people, but I still don't understand why God lets bad things happen. My mother ran away, and I didn't feel his comfort. I felt empty and alone and scared." She stifled the tears that choked her voice. "I didn't hear him tell me to tell my father not to go to Jed's that day. He sure has strange ways of doing things."

"It is hard to understand his ways sometimes." Her voice became softer and husky, grief in every word. "When Vill Junior died of the pox, God helped Vill and me and the other children survive and grow closer to each other."

"But he still let your boy die."

"We don't know why our son died. We only know we could not have gotten through it without God. And you vill only get through all you are facing with him."

Emily shrugged. "I've gotten through it so far without him."

"Have you?"

Chapter 80

An hour later, Emily sat in a rocker on the back porch, wrapped in a shawl against the cool night air. Crickets chirped their rhythmic song. An owl glided across the yard, a mouse wriggling in its talons. Fingers to her forehead, she identified with the mouse. Caught in things she struggled to understand.

Gertie's words described a God she'd never experienced, one she doubted existed until she heard this woman speak of love and pain and triumph and comfort. Is that what Terrence and Charlotte experienced? Is that what they tried to tell her? It slipped from her mind's grasp. Her legal mind needed to know every minute detail, a mind where the unknown had to be understood or otherwise discarded.

Gertie appeared at the back door, Bible close to her chest. "Emily, Deputy Allen has come for you. Vill vants you to come to the jail."

Emily dashed to the front door where the deputy stood, shotgun resting against his shoulder, handmade cigarette dangling from his lips. Gertie grabbed her arm and embraced her and planted a kiss on her cheek.

Impatient to go, Emily's feet danced with the desire to be moving. But Gertie held her hands and gazed into her eyes, searching. No, trying to communicate, to pass not thoughts, but something deeper. Emily waited. This woman had wisdom she did not want to miss.

Gertie squeezed her hands. "More than ever, trust God tonight."

The deputy set the horse and buggy into a quick trot. Emily stopped herself from grabbing the reins and slapping the animal to a full gallop.

At the jail, Stuebens and Terrence and several deputies spread out over the few chairs. Two deputies sat on the small cot in the corner. Two others perched on Stuebens's desk. Conversations, murmuring like a creek in springtime when the deputy opened the door, fell silent when Emily entered the room.

Terrence's face beamed. He was safe, and she wanted to leap the space between them and wrap her arms around his neck.

Stuebens cleared his throat. "Gentlemen, this is the little woman who caused our adventure tonight, Miss Emily Peyton."

Every eye in the room seemed to appraise her like a filly for sale. Heat crept up her neck.

One deputy on the cot spit into a spittoon. "Little woman? She looks like she's got more spunk than any woman I ever seen." He jerked his thumb toward a door. "Sure got that Stevens feller all stirred up."

Emily stamped her foot. "Terrence, will someone tell me what happened, or do I have to stand here all night and listen to this palaver?"

Stuebens bowed to Terrence. "Go ahead and tell her. Just make sure she knows who the real hero is."

Terrence stood. "It went just like we planned. We busted in the door, guns ready. The … Miss Daisy was standing behind this dude with silver hair in a fancy blue suit. She pointed down at him. Stevens didn't know what was going on. People were yelling and scattering all over the room. One gambler dove out the window and broke his leg. I think he forgot he was on the third floor.

"Stevens tried to draw his gun and stand at the same time. Miss Daisy conked him over the head with a whiskey bottle. 'No shootin' in my establishment.'" He pantomimed her actions, including standing on tiptoe. "Then she told us he was staying at a little cabin five miles out of town. The marshal and I went there and found this."

He motioned her closer and opened the saddlebags that were on the desk. Having his arm brush against hers tingled.

From the saddlebags, he took a pocket watch and showed her where it was engraved to Ed Whitney. Next, he withdrew a Colt with Paul Whitney's name crudely carved in the butt.

Her heart surged, and she grabbed Terrence's arm. "He knew the Whitneys. He killed them and stole their belongings."

"Wait until you see this." Terrence turned over the saddlebags and opened the other pocket. From it, he withdrew large bundles of money. He handed one to her. "Read the label."

The bundle seemed to throb with life. She turned it over. She could only stare, and she was sure her mouth hung open. The words she wanted to see. The words that would free Tiny. First Bank of Abilene, Kansas. And below were the handwritten initials TM, and below that was the date. The day Mac Phillips was murdered and robbed.

Tears flowed, dripped on the money. Tiny would be free.

She embraced Terrence, arms tight around his neck. His arms around her were strong and tender, holding her close. She never wanted him to let go. The embrace lingered, she nestled in it, enjoying his closeness, the scent of his leather vest, the scratch of his stubble on her cheek.

Stuebens coughed.

They stepped apart, Emily enjoying the blush that tinged Terrence's ears. Were her ears as bright as his? She handed him the bundle of cash. "I am grateful that you are so thorough."

Terrence smiled.

"Makes him a hero, does it not?" Stuebens asked, stroking his mustache.

Emily smiled at Terrence and turned and arched her eyebrow at Stuebens. "Seems like Miss Daisy was the one who took all the risks. Leave it to a woman to show men how to do a job right."

When the laughter died down, Emily touched Terrence's arm. "You are a hero. In so many ways. Tiny will be proud of all you did for him."

She turned to Stuebens again. "Has Stevens admitted to anything?"

Stuebens shook his head. "Not a word. Says we can't prove anything."

"Can I talk with him?"

"Right this way."

Stuebens and another deputy led Terrence and Emily to the cell area. Stevens lay on a cot, hands behind his head, humming Dixie.

"Stevens," Stuebens said. "Someone here to talk to you."

The four of them stood in a cramped semicircle facing the cell. The deputy was near the cell. Emily stood between Terrence and the marshal.

Stevens sat up and scanned the group. When his eyes met Emily's, he shot to the bars, eyes wide, nostrils flared.

"You—you." He cursed and rattled the bars with his fists. "This is all your fault. You couldn't let it go. Had to follow me to San Antonio. Shoulda killed you rather than try to scare you off. That's what I get for being a gentleman."

His hand flashed. Before Emily grasped the speed of Stevens' movement, the deputy was sprawled on the floor and his gun was pointed at Emily.

The black hole of the barrel mesmerized her. Suddenly, her mouth and throat were dry. Her stomach dropped to her ankles. She begged her legs to move. They wouldn't.

"Emily." Terrence's voice sounded miles away, but his hands on her arm and back sent her reeling as a loud explosion filled the room.

Smoke and the odor of gunpowder burned her eyes.

The sound of metal striking human flesh was followed by Stevens' howl of pain. Through smoke-stained eyes, Emily saw the marshal's pistol crack onto Stevens' forearm, breaking the bone and sending the deputy's gun to the floor.

Smoke drifted toward the ceiling. Steven's head was pressed against the bars as he cradled his arm. The marshal stood, gun at the ready. The deputy slid his weapon into his holster, head slumped as he looked behind where Emily lay.

Where's Terrence?

She looked behind her. He lay on his side, back against the wall. Eyes closed. A bright red stream seeped from his chest, across his shirt, to the floor.

Her screams echoed around the room. She reached for him, stroking his cheek, her tears washing his face.

Chapter 81

Where am I?

Soft light diffused through linen curtains on the window across from Emily.

Where am I?

The aroma of lilacs tickled her nostrils. Her head rested on a pillow.

Where am I?

She bolted to a sitting position. Blue wallpaper with yellow flowers. A dark dresser and mirror. A blue pitcher stood in a washing bowl.

I've never been in this room before.

Why am I still wearing yesterday's dress? This isn't my dress.

A hand touched her shoulder. She leapt from the bed. Her throat tightened, squeezing the air out of her lungs. She couldn't force any in. She spun. Where's the door? Have to get out. Have to find Terrence.

Terrence.

She stopped.

Emily closed her eyes, willing the images to go away. They wouldn't. The push that sent her to the floor. The explosion of the pistol. Terrence against the wall, face ashen, blood seeping.

An arm around her shoulder now. Pulled her close to another body. Comforted. A hand stroked her hair. A foreign language whispered in her ear.

Gertie.

Emily let the embrace soothe her as fresh tears fell.

Terrence. Her heart felt like an anvil was tied to it. Would it ever beat normally again? Would she ever breathe normally again?

She lifted her head from Gertie's shoulder. "Terrence?"

The older woman nodded. "I'll take you to him."

"He's alive?"

Gertie stopped, eyes somber, shoulders slumped. "Barely. The doctor removed the bullet. Terrence still bleeds and has trouble breathing."

Emily grasped the woman's hands. "Will he live?"

Gertie's mouth narrowed and her eyes. "We are praying he vill."

Gertie led her down a short hall, and into a room that was stark white. Morning sunshine poured through windows whose curtains were thrown wide. A rose-scented breeze stirred at the wisps of hair trailing down Emily's cheeks.

Terrence lay on a bed. A sheet covered him from the waist down. A large bandage covered the right side of his chest. A stranger stood by the bed, raising Terrence's eyelids. Emily darted to the other side and clasped Terrence's cool hand. Sweat plastered his hair to his head. The dark stubble of his beard stood out against the gray pallor of his face.

She stroked his hair, kissed his forehead.

"You must be Emily." The man across the table extended his hand. Emily shook it. His grip was firm, a smile graced his small, round face. "Doctor Wagner. Homer Wagner. Most people call me Wags."

"How is he, Doctor?"

Wagner lifted Terrence's eyelid again. Peered under the chest bandage, wiped blood with a white cloth. "Not good." He tugged at his salt-and-pepper goatee. "I saw wounds like this in the war. Very few made it. Most lasted less than twenty-four hours"

He rested his fingers on the bed. Short yet slender, the right pinky missing. "Do you pray, Miss Peyton?"

Emily shook her head as dizziness whirled, and her bones seem to dissolve. She grabbed the edge of the bed, willing herself to stand.

"Now would be a good time to start." He nodded at Terrence. "Only a miracle from God can save this man."

Emily awoke with a start, disoriented until the sight of Terrence lying on the bed brought her back to reality. The reality of losing her friend. She rose from her chair and pushed his hair off his forehead and found her fingers lingering on his cheek.

More than a friend? Her heart pounded. Yes, more than a friend. She picked up his hand and kissed it, pressed her cheek into the palm. More than a friend and too late to let him know.

She touched his wrist. His pulse seemed weaker, faint throbs very far apart. His chest hardly rose and fell.

She loved him. Why had she waited for so long? Why had she denied it, even to herself? She could have fought Priscilla for him. And won. How blind she had been to her own heart. To its thrill when he smiled, when their hands touched, to his grin after getting a hit at a baseball game, to his bantering with Tiny, to that soft, questioning look in his eye when he thought she wasn't watching.

She walked to the window, stared at the gathering dusk. She folded her arms and gazed skyward.

"I know you're up there somewhere. Do you really care about people, like Gertie says? Or, are we just child's toys to you, for you to kick around and throw away when you're done with us? Because that's what it feels like to me. Maybe I deserve it.

"But Terrence doesn't. He's a good man. But I shouldn't have to tell you that. He's done a lot of good for people. For you. He loves you, although I sure can't figure out why.

"I'm not asking for me. I want nothing from you. You've brought enough pain into my life.

"I'm asking for him. If you're this wonderful God people talk about, then do one of your miracles and let him live. You owe him that much."

She spun from the window, choking back sobs. She leaned over Terrence and kissed his cheek.

"I love you."

"You're not eating, Emily," Gertie said. No one had spoken to her like that since Caroline when Emily was ten. "Mr. Terrence is much on your mind."

Emily nodded as she forced a forkful of chicken into her mouth, followed by a gulp of coffee.

"I have been praying for him. All the ladies at our church are praying."

"I know Terrence appreciates it, even if he can't tell you."

"Have you tried to pray for your friend?"

Emily shrugged. *Did I pray? Felt more like I gave God a piece of my mind.* Somehow, she didn't see Gertie and her friends speaking to God like she did. "I tried talking to him, but I'm not sure it did any good. Probably irritated him more than anything. Why would he listen to someone like me?"

Before Gertie could respond, Will Stuebens came in, kissed his wife on the lips and apologized for being late. "Stevens still isn't talking." He poured coffee and scooped half the mashed potatoes his wife served him into his mouth. After swallowing, he pointed his fork at Emily. "I telegraphed Judge Frasier. Told him all the evidence we found." He took a flimsy sheet of paper from his vest. "Thought you might like to see his answer."

Emily smoothed the sheet and squinted to decipher the telegrapher's handwriting.

> WILL ASK GOV TO STOP HANGING
> GET EVIDENCE TO ME QUICK
> NEED TO SEE IT
> TELL E PEYTON GOOD JOB
> FRASIER

Her eyes fixated on the first line. The hanging will be stopped. Tiny will live. She covered her mouth with her hand and let the tears flow, each drop washing away tension and guilt.

Tiny will live.

Chapter 82

It was all Emily could do not to skip to the telegraph office. This was the giddiness she felt on the first day of school. The day the other children dreaded, but she loved because of all the new adventures, all the new worlds that would open.

She addressed the message to Charlotte.

> Whitneys did it
> Judge stopped hanging
> More later
> E

How to tell them what happened to Terrence? She couldn't. Didn't know how. Wouldn't. Not by telegraph. Had to be face-to-face, even if it meant riding with his body

Marshal Stuebens and Gertie met her outside the telegraph office.

"Has Stevens said anything?"

The marshal shook his head. "Says he wants his lawyer. Some guy name Stoddard from Dodge City. I might get around to sending a telegraph tomorrow afternoon. If I can remember."

"I can always represent him," Emily said, batting her eyes. Stuebens's deep, loud laugh caused passersby to stop and stare.

Doctor Wagner's two-story, brick building loomed like a hulking red menace, threatening to crush whoever dared enter. Emily's feet moved slower and slower. *I can't face him, can't see his ashen face, feel his pulse barely register on my fingers, see his chest hardly move.*

Emily shuddered.

She wanted to remember him laughing and running on the ball field, face flushed with excitement. She wanted to treasure their last horse race, Spot and Lincoln pounding across the prairie, Lincoln pulling ahead in the last few feet. If it meant he lived, she wanted to see him walking arm-in-arm with Priscilla down the aisle of the church, husband and wife.

And then I'll punch her in the nose again.

They were at the stairs leading up to the front door. Only three, they seemed like three hundred. The door seemed to float in the sky above where the stairs ended.

I don't want to. Don't make me.

Gertie's arm was around her waist. "Easy, *weibliches*. Do you need to sit? Do you want some water?"

Emily grasped the rail and shook her head. She rubbed her stomach to settle the breakfast that had tasted so good an hour ago and now rumbled like buffalo across the plains. She touched her forehead and her fingers slid on the clammy sweat beading there. "What if he's died during the night? I wasn't even here to say goodbye."

Gertie massaged her back, soft, small circles that somehow calmed her stomach. *This woman must be enchanted. Maybe she's a druid that has lived for centuries. One of the good ones.*

"Come, Emily. God will help you, and you and I vill face this together."

It seemed like in one step she was at the door. The portal, hovering blood-red in the early morning sun, opened as if by some unseen hand. As they entered the shadowy foyer, a shrouded figure changed into a dark-gray garbed Mrs. Wagner, who welcomed them and offered coffee and cake.

Emily shook her head, stomach revolting at the words.

The hallway seemed to stretch to infinity, yet again, Emily was at Terrence's door in an instant. Her head spun at the disorientation swirling like a dust devil.

Mrs. Wagner opened the door and stepped back. "I'll let the doctor know you're here. He's most eager to see you."

Emily grabbed the door frame to keep from falling to the floor. Her heart pounded as it leapt to her throat. Tears spilled.

Terrence's bed was empty, fresh linen taut.

Blurred eyes scanned the room, comprehending nothing.

He was gone.

She was too late.

Died saving her.

Died before she could tell him she loved him.

"Good morning, Emily."

She knuckled tears from her eyes.

Terrence sat in a chair by the open window, a Bible in his lap.

She blinked, shook her head. *Now I'm seeing things. Is this what grief does to you?*

The illusion closed the book and placed it on a table that held a mug.

The figure stood, rising with the smooth grace of the man who rode a horse like he was born to it, a man who could run the bases with the power of a gazelle.

She closed her eyes.

"Emily, it's really me."

She heard the moan that escaped her lips—she felt the arms that caught her before she crashed to the floor. Then everything disappeared.

Her eyelids fluttered. Closed. Fluttered again. A ceiling spread across the space above her.

I'm in a bed. Where? Terror clenched her heart. *I'm in Terrence's bed.* She sat up so quickly her brain rattled like a stone in a tin can. She closed her eyes and squeezed her temples.

"Emily." His voice and a hand on hers, a large hand, a tender hand.

She opened her eyes. It was him, standing by the bed, holding her hand.

"Yo ... yo ... you're ... not dead?"

His smile banished the clouds of darkness and grief and fear. "No, I'm not."

"What happened?"

"Just before sunrise, I heard this voice. Then, all the pain left, and I could breathe with no problem. I sat up." He chuckled. "The doctor was sitting by the bed. I thought he would fall off the chair."

"Darn near did." Dr. Wagner entered the room, carrying a small brown bottle. "You're awake. Guess I won't need this." He handed the bottle to his wife, who came in behind him.

He sat on the edge of the bed, gaze freezing Emily in her place. "You remember me telling you to pray because it would take a miracle to save his life?"

She nodded.

"Will, missy, you must have done some powerful praying because a miracle happened. This boy—" he clapped Terrence on the shoulder— "is completely healed. Open your shirt, boy."

Terrence did, and the doctor pointed to a small indentation on Terrence's chest. The spot where there had been a gaping hole bubbling blood when they carried him into the room. "That's the only sign he's even had an injury there. Never mind a .44 bullet from a Colt at close range. Yes, Miss Emily, your prayer saved him."

"How do you know it was my prayer? I don't even know how to pray. I just gave God a piece of my mind."

"Well, it must have been the right piece." He turned to Terrence. "Tell her what that voice you heard said."

Terrence took her hand in both of his. "He said, 'This is for Emily.'"

Chapter 83

The next day, Terrence basked in the morning sunshine outside the Stuebens's house while Emily finished preparing to leave for Abilene. His breath caught as the vision stepped onto the front porch. Slim and graceful in her brand-new cobalt dress. Blond hair swept up and twisted into a stylish bun under a matching hat with a soft yellow ribbon around the crown. He imagined that hair loose and falling to her shoulders, each strand passing over his fingers, his hands caressing it, inhaling the lilac perfume she favored.

Her light blue eyes smiled for what seemed the first time in weeks. She touched his arm. "Are you ready?"

Ready for anything with you.

Will and Gertie followed her out of the house, Gertie toting a large wicker basket. She handed it to Terrence. "A little something in case you get hungry on the train." The basket jerked his arm. His travel bag was lighter.

We're only going to Abilene.

He helped Emily into the carriage that would take them to the station. Will and Gertie rode in front, Will guiding the twin bays as easily as casting a fishing line.

Emily's closeness made him wish the ride would last forever. Yet, he burned for time to be alone with her, to speak the words churning in his heart. Maybe the train won't be crowded.

"Has Stevens said anything?" Emily asked.

"No. Still waiting on his lawyer," Will said. "Stoddard should be here this afternoon. I hope he gets here before Stevens leaves."

"Leaves?" Terrence and Emily spoke in unison. Emily sat straighter while Terrence gripped the seatback in front of him.

"I'm sorry. In all the excitement yesterday, I forgot to tell you." Will spoke over his shoulder. "Marshal Cook is sending two deputies to escort Mr. Stevens back to San Antonio to stand trial for murdering those two brothers. Deputies should be here about noon."

Emily's smile was an impish grin.

"What?" Terrence asked.

"Texas justice can be a lot swifter than Kansas law. I'd sure hate to see Mr. Stoddard miss his client's trial."

At the station, Emily took both Gertie's hands and gazed into her face. Words wouldn't come. The ache of goodbye pressed in her chest, squeezing her heart. Emily tried to speak again but had to settle for squeezing the woman's hands even tighter.

Deep breath. Finally, words came. Halting. Broken by tears. "You ... You've done so much for me." She glanced at Terrence. "For us."

Gertie brushed tears from Emily's cheek with the back of her fingers, ignoring the ones pooling in her own eyes. "Vill and I, we do vhat ve can. Vhat ve think God vants us to do. To love people. To help them."

She patted Emily's hands. "We are honored to know you and Terrence. Maybe, ve helped you to know God a little better."

Chin quivering, Emily nodded and pulled Gertie to her, holding her tight. Gertie's arms were tender and strong on her back.

Emily pulled back and fingered a tear from her eye. "I'll never forget you."

Gertie framed Emily's face with her palms and glanced at Terrence. "No. You von't forget us. Bring your babies for us to see."

From the corner of her eye, Emily saw Terrence blush and scuff his feet while Will only half-hid his smirk behind his hand. Her stomach flipped. Babies? Her? With Terrence? Why not? She ducked her head to hide her smile.

Chapter 84

So much for having privacy on the train. Terrence and Emily were squished like cattle awaiting the slaughterhouse.

Emily sat, Gertie's basket on her lap, eyes focused out the window, oblivious to the squalling baby across the aisle. She seemed able to ignore the man directly across from her who sprawled across his seat, head against the window, each snore releasing the odor of cheap tobacco and old whiskey.

Frustration chewed at Terrence's patience, his fingers drumming his thigh, words on his tongue, ready to burst forth like a thunderstorm.

He inhaled, and settled for enjoying her being next to him, their shoulders touching. She'd said she loved him. In the haze of pain and medication, he'd heard her. Now, clear-headed and healed, he let those words roll over him again and again.

When Priscilla said, "I love you," she could have been saying it about her new gown as much as describing her feelings for him.

From Emily, those words were the rarest jewels. They opened the door to her heart. A door he wouldn't let her close. A heart he would treasure and honor.

The conductor entered the carriage, announcing their next stop.

Terrence held up his hand. "Sir, how long will the stop be?"

The conductor studied his watch, walrus mustache twitching like something lived in it. "Supposed to be twenty minutes. But we may have to cut it to twelve. We're behind schedule."

Twelve minutes. He'd have to make the most of them. He leaned toward Emily. "Let's get off at the next stop and stretch our legs."

She nodded. "All right." She glanced at the man across from her as he snorted and changed position. "Some fresh air would be nice."

Her smile drove the noise and the stench from the carriage. Terrence basked in it, letting it warm him. She leaned over and whispered, "I'm so glad you're alive. I guess God does care."

Her lips brushed his ears, and he pinched his thighs to stop from turning and kissing her. He studied her eyes, the perfect almond shape, the tiny gold flakes in the light blue. "So am I. So am I."

At the station, he and Emily strolled to the far end of the platform, away from the huffing engine, and the people milling together. He covered her hand where it looped around his arm. He enjoyed the relative quiet. A cow mooed from a field on the other side of the tracks. In a nearby corral, a horse tossed its long mane and stomped its foot.

He faced her and words flew away like a robin fleeing a cat. She lifted her face, eyes soft and caressing.

"I heard what you said the other night."

She frowned, puzzled. "What do you mean?"

"The night before I woke up healed."

"You heard me talking to God?"

He paused. Boy, she was making this hard. Did she really not remember? Had she not said it? Was it only his imagination that had wanted to hear it?

"All right. If I imagined it, please don't make fun of me. I need to know." He inhaled. "I remember—it's the only thing I remember before waking up healed—you kissing my cheeks and saying ..." *Oh, God, don't let me mess this up.* "You said 'I love you.'"

She stepped back, looked down and folded her arms.

Great. I imagined it. What a fool.

She raised her head. "I said it." Her voice was soft and husky, as if coming from someplace deep in her throat.

"Did you mean it?"

Silence.

She looked past him, down the tracks, her eyes faraway.

He lifted her chin, studied her face. So solemn. Her eyes tender, a trace of fear flickering in the corner.

She licked her lips. "Yes, I mean it."

His knees threatened to buckle. She meant it. She means it.

Her lips moved. "I didn't know if you could hear. I didn't know I would say the words until they were out. But I said them, and I mean them with all my heart." She walked to the edge of the platform. He stayed by her side, slipping his arm around her waist.

She looked down the track. "I was afraid to say those words. I was afraid to admit to myself, never mind you, that I was in love with you. Priscilla is so beautiful and offers so much more than I can. All I can offer is a stubborn pride that gets in the way with everybody. I was afraid to say those words. I didn't want to be rejected again."

She faced him. "The other night, I didn't care about any of that anymore. I didn't care if you heard me or believed me or rejected me. I needed to hear myself say I love you. Something opened in my heart that night." She shrugged and shook her head. "I don't know if it was talking to God without cursing him that did it. Gertie said when I talked to God, I opened the door to let him into my heart. And what I'd kept all tied up in knots could be released.

"Terrence, I don't know about any of that. Don't care either. I just know I love you, and I needed to say it."

He didn't know what to do with his hands. He wanted to do something because his mind and his mouth had suddenly stopped working. Finally, he took her by the shoulders.

"Emily Louise Peyton, I love you."

Her lips met his, and the world disappeared.

Chapter 85

Three days later, Emily blinked her eyes against the dust the strong west wind flung around the small group standing at the prison gate. She tucked herself tighter to Terrence and pulled her shawl across her mouth.

Her father stood a few steps away, crutches anchored to the ground, his chin tucked to his shoulder.

Charlotte placed herself a little in the front, eyes riveted on the gate, ignorant of the wind whipping her hair out of its neat bun and plastering her dress against her body.

A sudden quiet filled the area. The wind settled to a soft breeze. The clouds that glowered moments earlier scattered like gray wisps as sunshine poured.

Emily squeezed Terrence's arm. He slipped an arm around her shoulder and pulled her closer.

Charlotte turned to George, her face taut, eyes darting. "What's taking so long? They didn't change their minds, did they?"

George wedged a crutch tighter under his arm and extended one hand toward her. "No. They're just making sure they're releasing the right inmate."

Charlotte smirked. "How many Tiny Waters do they have in there? He's kind of hard to mistake for someone else." She turned back to the gate, hands clasped at her chest. "I wish they had let us inside."

"We'd still have to wait."

A passing cloud focused the sun's rays on a spot just in front of the gate. Emily looked skyward. *Are you showing off again, God?*

The sound of a bolt being thrown came from behind the gate. Charlotte's hands went to her mouth, and she leaned forward.

The gate creaked but didn't move. Another creak, and a small gap appeared between the gate and its frame.

A hand in a blue sleeve appeared on the outside of the gate, pulling it further open. More movement. The wall of a building, gray and windowless, appeared.

A guard pushed the gate all the way open.

Tiny Waters stepped into the sunlight, wearing the same clothes he'd been sent to prison in. Now they hung on his frame.

Charlotte ran and leapt into his arms, smothering his face with kisses.

He held her, buried his face in her hair. His body shook as he clung to her.

After a few moments, they separated, and Tiny and Charlotte walked toward the rest. Tiny shook hands with George and then Terrence.

He came to Emily. He spread his arms wide. "Look, Miss Emily. No shackles. I feel like I can fly."

Emily tried to hold back the tears. Gave it up. She stepped closer and stretched on tiptoe to kiss his cheek. "Welcome home, Tiny."

Tiny's chest heaved, and his voice cracked. "Charlotte told me all you done for me, you and Terrence. How you never gave up. Thank you for believing in me."

The silence grew as Emily and Tiny surveyed the small group.

George cleared his throat. "Come on, folks. We have a train to catch. And Tiny, Mr. Montgomery said he wants to see you at the ranch at noon tomorrow."

Charlotte clung to her man's arm. "You can go right after we see Pastor Dalton to set the wedding date." She stopped his protest with a kiss. A long, hard kiss.

Footsteps pounded behind them. "Miss Peyton."

Emily and Terrence turned. The warden trotted toward them, a paper in his hand. Breathless, he offered it to Emily. "Judge Frasier sent this message. He wanted me to deliver it personally."

She opened the single sheet of telegraph paper.

DON'T QUIT

YOU'RE TOO GOOD

WE NEED YOU

J. FRASER

She passed the message to Terrence, who grinned and embraced her.

Her father stood there, a cockeyed grin on his face.

"Did you have anything to do with this?"

"Who? Me? The judge and I had a lovely dinner while you were in Kansas City, and we discussed many things."

"Including me?"

"Your name did come up in passing."

About the Author

Tagged as "one to watch" by Publishers Weekly, award-winning author **Henry McLaughlin** takes his readers on adventures into the hearts and souls of his characters as they battle inner conflicts while seeking to bring restoration and justice in a dark world. His writing explores these themes of restoration, reconciliation, and redemption.

Besides his writing, Henry treasures working with other writers and helping them on their own writing journeys. He is a member of American Christian Fiction Writers. He regularly teaches at conferences and workshops, leads writing groups, edits, and mentors and coaches.

www.ingramcontent.com/pod-product-compliance
Lightning Source LLC
Chambersburg PA
CBHW070542030726
47505CB00001B/131